T4-AIP-691

THE LUDI VICTOR

THE

LUDI

Coward, McCann & Geoghegan

VICTOR

James Leigh

NEW YORK

 Published on the same day in Canada by Academic Press Canada Limited, Toronto.

Library of Congress Cataloging in Publication Data

Leigh, James, date.
The ludi victor.

I. Title.
PZ4.L5256Lu [PR6062.E445] 823'.914
ISBN 0-698-11038-2 80-13626

Printed in the United States of America

"Of course, no one can 'know' the future in any absolute sense. We can only systematize and deepen our assumptions in an attempt to assign probabilities to them. Even this is difficult. Attempts to forecast the future inevitably alter it. . . .

. . . We can anticipate the formation of sub-cults. . . . We can even see on the horizon the creation of certain leisure cults—tightly organized groups of people who will disrupt the workings of society not for material gain, but for the sheer sport of 'beating the system.'"

—Alvin Toffler, *Future Shock*

THE LUDI VICTOR

From the Journal of Denfert Rochereau, Ludi Victor IV

. . . I lay face-down in the leaf mould of Navarre, feeling more angry than frightened, which was perhaps as well. Under the circumstances, anger was the more useful emotion, for it stimulates rather than diminishes the capacity for decisive action.

Still, I had momentarily to struggle to control my trembling limbs. Why the hell, I asked myself silently, was Alexander the Great trying to kill me with a bow and arrow? It wasn't allowed. Regulations are very clear on the subject. No blades, no firearms. Was the Greek being stupid or dishonorable? Who told him the tines of an arrow needn't count as blades?

A meter in front of me, the dead doe lay on her side among long grass, the arrow that transfixed her reflecting an afternoon sun that dappled down through branches dressed in new, acid-green foliage. Her eyes stared candidly back at me. Large, dark eyes not yet glazed in death. She was fat, and the moment before she died her belly had heaved. She had been pregnant and near her term. Probably her young had put up a tiny, instinctive struggle to be born before their life support system failed. But she was still, now.

I had time for such reflections, because I am used to the kind of situation I describe. I have been in it before. It no longer has the power to startle me with strangeness. I even had time to look up and register the snow-capped mountains beyond the trees.

Everything was still. I listened but heard nothing above the rustle of leaves in a light breeze and a distant tinkling of bells that reminded me of the Jura. A matt of secondary growth hid me on three sides, so Alexander the Great must have shot at a venture, hitting the doe by pure chance. Behind me, a gully shelved steeply down a hillside.

I thought carefully. As yet, I knew nothing of my opponent. What would he do next? I tried to put myself in his place. He could not know the results of his marksmanship, so he would have to investigate. I, however, was not yet armed. Arrogantly, I had decided to see my enemy's choice of weapon before making my own.

I looked around again. The gully rose once more after a few dozen meters and passed through a stand of half-grown oaks. I got to my knees, making sure that I was still completely hidden, and reached out. The arrow was harder to remove than I thought. I had to push it through the doe's body. I squeezed her carcass after piercing the diaphragm with my knife until the blood welled out. I let a small pool of it form on the open ground. Then I shuffled on my knees towards the thicket in front of me, letting fall as many drops as I could on the way.

I stuffed the carcass behind a fallen branch and retreated the way I had come, avoiding the blood. Then I crawled down the gully as fast as I dared. I did not stop until I was inside the stand of oaks. There I found a comfortable bole and rested. There was still no sound.

I breathed more easily. The peaks of the Sierra de Andia glittered in the sunshine. The sloping meadows were bright with early flowers. I should have felt privileged. This was Navarre, the cradle of guerilla warfare, where partisans had given Napoleon more trouble than all the armies of Europe put together. Instead, I felt anger.

I had brought the Greek's arrow with me. I inspected it now. It was a simple length of ash, split at one end to take crosspieces of stiff plastic that acted as flights. The tines were of thin sheet metal set into the other end. I guessed that Alexander the Great had manufactured the thing after arriving in the zone rather than bringing it with him, but the contrivance was still very irregular. I decided to make a long-range weapon for myself in order to equalize the odds. I, though, would not breach regulations.

I worked quickly, using a spare pair of bootlaces from my pocket supplies and a soft piece of leather from what had until then been my left glove. I cut holes in the leather with my knife and tied the laces so that my slingshot had a slightly concave pocket. It was an honourable weapon with a pedigree stretching back to the armies of Imperial Rome and beyond.

There was a bed of pebbles running along the gully. I had selected some smooth, round ones when I heard the cracking of branches. My guess had been correct. Alexander the Great had decided to investigate the results of his shot.

I kept carefully hidden as I watched him step into the clearing where I had lain with the dead doe. His bow was ready, another arrow fitted to the knock. He was a big man with lank, long hair and a badly trimmed moustache. He looked sloppy, out of condition and dull. He also looked very strong. He wore an olive-drab combat jacket like my own and thick-soled plastic boots laced up to his calves. He was a careless mover and seemed unconcerned about noise. I was encouraged by the fact. Perhaps his size made him overconfident. It certainly made him a big target.

He quartered the clearing, stooping sharply when he saw the pool of blood I had left. He followed the trail cautiously towards the undergrowth, his back towards me, and I smiled resignedly. This might be easier than I had expected.

As he leaned forward to part the bushes, I stepped quietly from cover, fitted a stone and whirled the slingshot round my head. A breeze sprang up providentially, masking the whickering sound with the murmur of its passage.

The shot was a fine one. Unfortunately, the Greek straightened up again while my stone was still in the air. Instead of hitting him on the skull, it struck his bull-like neck with a loud smack. He roared with pain and crashed off through the thicket.

I moved after him immediately, unwilling to forgo my advantage. I thought my cunning and woodcraft were probably far superior to his. On the other hand, he still had an advantage in armoury. Whirling my slingshot took up vital seconds, and I could not always rely on a breeze to mask its sound. Besides, I had been impressed with his speed and athleticism. Granted that I had given him good reason to display them, I still made a note to avoid close quarters combat if I could.

I shadowed him for several hours, not taking many risks, while the sun passed its height and the Greek got used to the idea that a slingshot was my only weapon. Once, catching him in the open, I cannoned a stone off the trunk of a tree he was running towards. Later, I messed up a shot taken at speed. My stone flew far wide, and I had to dive fast into cover. I had given him time to use his bow, and a shaft explored the branches softly very close to my head.

The afternoon wore on. The sun would soon disappear behind a high peak, although there was still an hour or two of daylight left. I decided that the time had come to deploy the major stratagem which I had contrived for the Greek's death. I needed only a few minutes to set it up, and I had already noted the perfect place for its execution—a tall patch of timber on a ridge which dropped steeply behind into a fair-sized stream. A few yards down, the stream was dammed by a tree trunk that had fallen across the flow.

I made my way to the place along a track which I hoped would guide my lamb gently towards his slaughter. I arrived at a gap where the path entered the trees and found the branch I wanted. It was horizontal, whippy, and I could just manage it. I untied the thin nylon rope I kept round my waist for climbing purposes and lashed one end to the end of the branch. Then I took a turn round a neighboring trunk with my rope and hauled the branch back as far as I could. I secured the whole thing with a slipknot and adjusted it until I was sure that a small tug would release the branch. Now all I had to do was entice my lamb.

I found him without difficulty. His movements were as discreet as those of a randy bear. I closed in on him. When I was sure he had seen me, I retreated the way I had come, leading him carefully. I had to warn myself against overconfidence. With his bulk and weapons, he was still formidable. He would hardly have progressed so far as Navarre were it not so. It was hard to lead him without inviting a shot. Twice he skimmed arrows uncomfortably close to me. Twice I retaliated for appearance's sake, for I had determined that he should fall to my stratagem. My second attempt, however, was an unintentionally good one. The stone hit him on the shoulder and appeared to enrage him, which was an advantage.

I had one major risk left to take. The last few meters of track leading to the trees lay across open ground. It was essential that the Greek should follow my path precisely, but I did not want an arrow in my back. I maneuvered quietly until I knew he would expect me to appear next some sixty degrees farther away, then I sprinted for the gap in the trees. I was immensely lucky. His arrow hit me just as I arrived. It struck the thick, serge-sheathed canteen I wore at my belt and glanced off.

I dived into cover and fumbled for the slipknot on my rope. There was no scope now for further maneuver. The Greek and I were committed. He was fast, angry, and not entirely a fool. He, too, could see the kind of cover into which I had gone and would understand that neither of us now had a chance to use weapons. The outcome of combat would seem to depend on simple strength and size. He could scarcely be deceived as to which of us held the advantage on that score. He had no choice but to follow me.

He was even faster than I thought. His arrival at the gap in the trees almost took me by surprise. I released the slipknot, however, at exactly the right moment. The branch I had tied whipped forward and smashed into him precisely where I had intended that it should—full in the throat. I know something of medicine, and I think he must have died instantly from paralysis induced by the blow. But he stumbled on, arms flailing, until he fell forward in the stream with a huge splash. The current took him, and he fetched up at the dam caused by the fallen tree trunk. He bobbed there, face down.

I blew out my cheeks with satisfaction and relief and stood up. I climbed down to the water's edge and crawled across the tree trunk to where he lay, a big piece of sodden flotsam. Green, icy water filled my boots. I knew it was impossible that he should be alive, and I could not have hoped for a better outcome.

I reached forward and pulled back the collar of his combat jacket. The key was on its chain round his neck. I pocketed it and threw the chain downstream. To get at his armband, I had to turn him over. I did so with difficulty, and he floated on his back, stream water slopping untidily from his mouth. His eyes were shiny as the flanks of a gudgeon as he stared past me. I removed the strip of yellow material and turned him over again.

Depression hit me as I made my way back to the bank. It always does at such times. Thank God it rarely lasts, though I sometimes wonder whether others feel the same. There is so much I would like to know about the others now. Alexander the Great was dead. He had used what I thought of as an illegal weapon. He had been clumsy and unexpectedly stupid for his rank. Yet he had also been brave and fought hard. Now he was dead.

Back on the bank, I took off my boots and squeezed some of the water from my socks. I was shivering, for the breeze had become a sharp wind cutting through the damp flannel of my shirt. But as I dismantled the simple components of my slingshot, my spirits lifted again. Alexander the Great was dead, but I was alive, able to feel the discomfort of my clothes and see the flushed sun setting enormously over high hills of snow. The air was full of birdsong and I could almost hear emerald grass grow under my feet. I was exalted with a feeling few men are ever privileged to know.

I returned to the ridge, untied my nylon rope from its branch and wound it round my waist again. I dismantled the Greek's makeshift bow and carried the stave some distance away before abandoning it. I think it right to be punctilious in such matters. I also stripped all the arrows I could find, burying the heads and flights deep inside an old badger set. Finally I quartered the whole zone several times, taxing my memory. I found three more arrows and dismantled those as well.

I made my way to my car, changed and drove off in the direction of the French border. At a town some miles short of it, I found a post office open for its evening session. I parked in a narrow, smelly side street between bars, returned on foot and made my telephone call, consulting the scrap of paper in my pocket. While I waited for the connection, I wondered idly what arrangements Alexander the Great had made in the event that I, not he, had ended up bobbing face downwards in a mountain stream. The cop who took my call sounded bored or half asleep.

"*Soy forastero,*" I mumbled earnestly. "*Si . . . de vacaciones. He visto un hombre muerto en las montañas . . . Creo que se haya ahogado.*"

I told a very confused story, making no attempt to hide my bad accent or grammar. Eventually, the cop ordered me to the station from where I could take him to the "accident" I described. He gave careful directions. I agreed and hung up. I went back to my car and drove on towards the border.

I got to Bordeaux in time for a late dinner at a cafe near my apartment block. I was alone in it by the time I had finished my bad couscous. Waiting for the barman to coax coffee from an ancient Gaggia machine, I borrowed some *jetons* and made my call from the other end of the bar where I would not be heard. The owner of the voice I spoke to is unknown to me, of course, but his thick and fleshy accent of the *Midi* is as familiar to me as my own.

"This is Denfert Rochereau," I announced quietly. "I have returned from Spain."

"Good evening, Colonel. You were successful, then?"

"Alexander the Great was unfortunately drowned. It was an accident."

"I congratulate you most heartily. These facts must be verified, of course."

"Naturally. The local police have already been informed of the accident. There was nothing compromising in the Greek's rented Seat Ritmo which he abandoned nearby. You will be in touch?"

"In the usual way and in good time. You have your key and insignia?"

"Yes."

"Then send them to me and prepare for your final step. It will be good to have a Frenchman break the stranglehold of the Germans."

I agreed, hung up, and took my coffee and *marc* to a table by the window. I looked through it into the unattractive street beyond. I wondered how Gustavus Adolphus and Oliver Cromwell had fared in the Ardeche. The man from the *Midi* had presumably not been informed.

A group of boys in denim and leather were revving up their motorbikes outside, deliberately annoying the residents of the *quartier* and attracting the attention of a cop who was strolling towards them, loosening his white-painted truncheon in its holster. They awaited his arrival with scant interest.

I sympathized with them, but my sympathy was more than tinged with contempt. They were trapped, boring children of boring parents, leading boring lives in a boring *quartier* of a very boring town.

I had a sudden recollection of a pair of hawks I had seen raping the thermals high above the sierras of Navarre. I smiled in the empty bar. I wondered how these children would react if they knew how I had spent my day.

The pressure of the headrest on the back of my neck was a soothing massage as McVeigh's maroon Rolls accelerated. It was a pleasing sensation. It was only early afternoon, but I was already tired. Understandable, since I'd been up half the night tearing the scales from a man's eyes, then up again at six o'clock to shoot his vermin.

We were cruising southeast on a stretch of dual carriageway to join the M4 near Swindon. It was a fine, brisk day. I watched a motionless kestrel stand on its tail and flutter briefly to maintain station over a grass verge between carriageways, hoping for a fat vole flushed by the wind of our passage. I thought sententiously of how the forward march of progress always creates new scope for old savageries.

McVeigh was concentrating on his driving, so I dozed. The top of the Rolls was down, but the heater was on. I was sumptuously warm, feeling enough slipstream to ruffle one side of my hair.

I had just finished a short, boring engagement for a short, boring man called Huddiesford. He was a tiny tycoon who earned his daily caviar making rustic garden fencing for a million suburban homes. He had started out with nothing but a simple idea, some borrowed capital, and a load of Dr. Beeching's cast-off railway sleepers. We were passing his place now, a series of low workshops with a prefabricated two-story office building. I could see the company slogan on a big billboard in front of it. FIDELITY IS THE FENCE. The word "the" was heavily underlined and painted in red longhand.

Mine isn't an easy job to define, even though London Provincial Five tax district knows me simply as a business consultant. Huddiesford's brief had been pretty typical. He knew in his bones that he was being ripped off by one of his suppliers. He wanted me to confirm the hunch and show him how it was being done.

Finding answers had been easy. Huddiesford had mobile display centers for his products up and down the country. The suspect supplier sold him booths fitted with tape and slide shows intended to impress potential customers. The design was unique, patented, and overpriced. It turned out that Huddiesford's own marketing manager, a cherubic West Countryman called Bennett, had poached the idea from a naive freelance designer in the Midlands and set up the supplying company himself through front men to make and sell the booths to Fidelity Fencing at an inflated price.

Huddiesford hadn't been willing to accept my findings, and that was normal, too. We'd punished a lot of single malt whiskey while I worked hard to convince him. I knew what the trouble was. Huddiesford had come up the hard way himself and probably had bigger and better skeletons in his own closet. On the other hand, he'd invested a lot of time and profit turning himself into a bucolic country squire with rolling acres and a nineteenth-century mansion that looked as though it had started out as a workhouse and been converted to Catholicism halfway through the building.

He hadn't liked being reminded of the kind of business he was really in, or the kind of man he really was. At first he hadn't relished the idea of wrestling in mud to sort Bennett out. But I had the feeling he'd get used to it. The upshot of our long meeting was that I'd started the day with a pain in my head and Huddiesford's Cogswell & Harrison 12-bore in my hands. He was a bad landowner. According to his gamekeeper, he regularly shot the hell out of every bird on his land, with the predictable result that vermin found nothing in the larder at the end of the season and took to terrorizing local farms instead.

Earlier in the week, I'd been drinking in The Malt Shovel with one of Huddiesford's tenant farmers. He'd told me how a fox had got into his house via a small trap in the door. "Thik bugger did even kill the bleedin' cat," he'd said. "There were blood all up the bloody walls."

So the gamekeeper suggested a vermin shoot before the breeding season got too far ahead, and I'd spent the morning motionless inside a bare, black, freezing covert. All I'd got for my pains were frozen feet, one jay, and a vixen dropped with a load of number four shot in her head.

Eventually we'd gone back to Huddiesford's mansion for lunch. McVeigh had been waiting for me in a small withdrawing room where glycerine-preserved flowers drooped funereally in urns and Mrs. Huddiesford kept a bottle of gin hidden in case of sudden emergencies. McVeigh and I had sipped manzanilla while he explained Sir Bryan Proctor's need for my services. Hadn't explained, rather, except to say that the job would be worth a very large fee, which was explanation enough.

Afterwards, McVeigh and I joined Huddiesford for a morose lunch of watercress soup, King o'Fife pie, treacle tart, and Stilton in a dining room decorated with paneling looted from a monastery in some bygone age. Huddiesford's only contribution to the small talk had been to remind me that I was invited to a football match. He was a director of one of the top London clubs involved. McVeigh and I left soon after, I with a fat and comforting check in my pocket.

I'd been dozing, but I came awake as McVeigh sailed into the M4 with ruthless panache, neatly intercepting the paths of two other cars. The small sports job behind sounded twin battle horns and tried to ram us. The Rover in front gritted its teeth as McVeigh left both of them effortlessly behind. McVeigh slipped a Vivaldi cassette into the stereo player and lit a cigar.

I knew quite a lot about him although I'd only met him a few times. He was a handsome man in his fifties, beautifully suited in some light grey material with a regimental tie. I wasn't sure what the regiment was, but I was sure it was a good one. His hair was sleekly brushed, with just a certain touch of grey at the temples. He probably tied his tie in the high gloss of his Lobb shoes. He was impeccably unsurprising.

His boss, Sir Bryan Proctor, I knew a lot better. In fact, I'd known him before he acquired his "Sir" and a Queen's Award for services to overseas earnings. He was one of the last self-made myths of British commerce like Clore, the Grades, and Freddie Laker. He'd taken control of an insignificant insurance company after the War and turned it into a giant international corporation, specializing at first in the fast-growing car insurance market where his hard nosed selling and cut throat premiums had raised eyebrows in City boardrooms. He'd sailed close to the wind, but he'd used good judgment and avoided the reefs that wrecked lesser competitors. After that, there'd been no stopping him. He'd expanded his life insurance division and got in early on the mutual fund and pension fund boom, making all important investment policy decisions himself.

Now Global Alliance was one of the Big Five in the business, probably the biggest, and Sir Bryan was a household name. He had all the flamboyance the British love in his type, plus a canny talent for public relations. He kept a string of racehorses and backed several wildlife conservation agencies. Since his horses often won, and since various species the British love to get sentimental about were usually on the endangered list, that meant there weren't many days when you didn't come across his name in either the news or the sports pages of the popular press.

McVeigh was a different proposition altogether. He had a reputation as a brilliant and abrasive loner with a lethal actuarial brain. He was feared and disliked both inside and outside the Global empire. Sir Bryan had picked him early in both their careers and set him on his right hand as first lieutenant and general hatchet man. Why they were still in harness, though, was a popular and well-aired mystery, since they were known to dislike each other. At all events, it looked as though the mystery might soon be resolved, since rumor had it that Sir Bryan was preparing to hand over his empire. He was only just in his sixties, but he was said to be ill and tiring. The question was, who would take his place? If McVeigh were being groomed, he would be taking a giant step from unpopular henchman to one of the top jobs in British business. If he were not, the odds were he'd be out on his ear into complete obscurity. Even inside the Global empire he had many admirers but no friends.

I inspected him covertly. He certainly didn't look as if he had many worries. His suave, mordant style was pretty much in evidence. If anything, he had more assurance and assertiveness than I remembered. There was something in him that suggested he was playing a winning streak in a game the rest of us weren't aware of.

He registered my inspection and guessed wrongly at the thought behind it.

"I wonder," he murmured, "how much *you* earn."

"Enough," I said. "I'm not greedy."

McVeigh laughed softly. "Sir Bryan rates you highly. I gather you've worked for him several times before."

I had indeed, but if McVeigh hoped to pump me about past Global problems he was going to be disappointed.

"I met him years ago in a grubby first-floor gaming room over a Soho restaurant," I said, "but I can't remember for the life of me how the hell either of us came to be there. We were playing poker for high stakes. I took about a thousand off him."

McVeigh laughed again. "That would impress him," he agreed. "But the old boy's esteem goes further than that. He rates you very high professionally. We were talking about you before I came down. I was wondering why you'd never gone into business on your own account. Real business, I mean."

I didn't like the condescending reference to "the old boy." Nor did I like the suggestion that my job was unreal.

"What you call real business bores me," I said. "Most of the real businesses I come across are just games played by people who only take them seriously to avoid getting bored themselves."

McVeigh shrugged, still smiling. He had needled me, and he knew it. He'd intended to. He overtook another line of cars and resumed station in his original lane as though he owned it.

"Looked at in that light," he observed, "it is reasonable to ask whether anything in life isn't fundamentally a game. Don't you find your prejudice hampers you in your work?"

"Quite the reverse. Most of my clients overcomplicate their games. They get so close to their complexities that they can't unravel even simple problems close up. Coming from outside, I have an advantage."

"You mean you see things more objectively?" he asked lazily. It wasn't a serious question and he didn't expect an answer. Open countryside was coming to an end. The fields stopped unfolding like fans as we swept by, and I could see a huge plane coming in to land at Heathrow. It looked stationary in the sky.

"I have been studying the files on your last job," McVeigh added after a few minutes. "Do you remember it? It concerned a man called Ezra Harrison."

I remembered, and I wondered why McVeigh had taken the trouble to do his homework.

"I remember," I said. The Harrison saga hadn't been the prettiest one I was ever engaged in. He'd been on the board of a company Sir Bryan wanted to take over, only Harrison hadn't liked the idea of being taken over. He'd been spoiling for the kind of fight that culminates in a very golden handshake.

My job had been to dig up dirt so that he could be got rid of easily and without comeback. I'd succeeded better than expected. Obviously Harrison had dipped his fingers in the till in various ways. More surprisingly, he'd turned out to be a kind of patron saint to the Paedophile Information Exchange. The whole takeover had been dirty like that. Rumor even had it that one of Harrison's fellow directors had been stabbed in the chest by mistake.

"Were you ever aware of the real purpose for which Sir Bryan engaged you?" McVeigh enquired.

"There was a gang of middle managers under Harrison just waiting to see the outcome of battle before putting the boot in themselves," I said. "I imagine Sir Bryan wanted to squash Harrison in order to cow them into submission."

"With your customary acuity, you are right in seeing that an effect upon the gang of middle managers, as you call them, was the real object of the exercise," McVeigh observed tartly. "However, you are wrong in supposing that Sir Bryan's intention was to cow them. A cowed and beaten man is of no use to anybody. Those young men were an important reason for taking Harrison's company over in the first place. I'm afraid the history of the affair is an object lesson in what happens to able and ambitious young men subjected to weak and self-indulgent management. They become *méchant.*"

"Like gun dogs that don't get enough exercise," I suggested mischievously.

"Exactly. Sir Bryan wanted those young men, but they needed a lesson, and both the nature and method of the lesson were important. I'm glad to say the results of your enquiry had the intended effect. The young men found in Sir Bryan a leader whom they could respect. Most of them are still among his most loyal and capable staff."

"Would I be correct in supposing that you wish to point up the moral of the story?" I sighed.

"In the main, it speaks for itself," McVeigh said primly. "The particular point I bring to your attention is that it is a fallacy to suppose that you or anybody else can remain ultimately uninvolved in a business matter in which you are engaged. In your case, the real object of your enquiry was not made clear to you because of your known prejudice."

"You mean I was manipulated?"

"If you insist."

"In my own best interests, of course."

"In those of the Company."

"Thanks for the warning."

McVeigh was heading north from Hammersmith towards the extension of the M4 that arrows into the heart of London. The dying sun was a sliver of fevered brilliance far away to our left. The tower blocks around Shepherd's Bush were lost against the grey sky, only their lit windows forming geometric patterns of soft yellow squares. We wheeled to the north of Paddington. Our side of the road was empty. The other was crammed with cars crawling back to their little grey lives in the west. They got snarled up at every traffic light, and their owners glared as we ghosted by, as though we were breaking some unwritten law of commuterdom.

I dozed again until we passed King's Cross on our way to the tangle of roads that suddenly become streets as they enter the City. I sniffed the air and caught for the first time in weeks the odor of decaying brilliance and dazed apprehension that emanates from all boardrooms and wine bars of the Golden Mile these days. Byzantium, I thought, must have smelled something like it shortly before the Fourth Crusade. We passed under Holborn Viaduct with its heraldic beasts around a shield and the motto *Domine Dirige Nos.* He'd be lucky, I thought. There wasn't a board of directors in London that would have let him have a say in company policy. I was getting more and more curious about why McVeigh himself had travelled all the way to Huddiesford's mansion to collect me. It was a bit like Sir Bryan Proctor slipping out to buy paper clips.

"Can't you give me some idea what this engagement is about?" I asked.

McVeigh thought carefully. "The matter is so important that Sir Bryan insists on briefing you personally."

"So important that he had to send you all that way to find me?"

"Quite." McVeigh, I realized, was deaf to anything remotely resembling sarcasm. He eased the Rolls through the heavier traffic around the Tower of London.

"I, however, will be in day-to-day charge of the investigation he wants you to conduct." He glanced sideways. "The business has been weighing on him, and he is not well. I want to take as much pressure off him as possible. That information, by the way, is confidential.

"You will find him a changed man," he added.

Global House lay deep in the City, not too far from the great crumbling docks and warehouses and not too near the P & O Building than which it was a shade smaller, though older in style. Chronologically, it had been built midway between *Titanic* and Concorde. Its worst enemies would have said it had the drawbacks of both, being uneconomic and doomed, but if such rumors ever got back to Sir Bryan Proctor, Bart., I doubted whether he cared. He'd acquired the place at a time when it dominated the skyline and the Global empire had yet to savage its competitors into second place or nowhere at all in the running. Sir Bryan was a great sniffer of the winds of economic change. He'd long ago diversified abroad. The real power of Global Alliance International S.A. now resided in a more modest but even more prestigious skyscraper outside Brussels, though Sir Bryan himself still operated from London. As he'd once told me, with his sly and ageless grin, the financial world is sentimental. It still expects London to know something about insurance which the rest of the world doesn't.

An evening mist was collecting along the Thames. I could smell its rank richness as the Rolls negotiated the tight concrete bends into the underground car park of Global House. McVeigh got out without switching off. A uniformed attendant who looked like a film extra slid the car in the bay assigned to McVeigh while we crossed to the directors' lift.

We soared upwards in discreetly lit beige silence to the top floor. The well-bred doors sidled efficiently out of our way, and we padded into the deep-piled luxury of Freda Harman's outer office. She was Sir Bryan's personal secretary and looked like a passionless Theda Bara. I winked at her. She smiled uncertainly back. Protocol was the essence of her job. She knew my face but couldn't place me for a moment in the corporate pecking order.

McVeigh raised an elegantly enquiring eyebrow. Miss Harman nodded in reply. He went through the heavy oak doors into the chief executive's sanctum. Left to myself, I inspected the Chagalls and Kokoschkas on the walls. It had been the boss's own idea to fill the building with art treasures back in the heady sixties when there'd been too much investment money chasing too few stocks. Just being in Miss Harman's office told you that you were either in a national art gallery or the headquarters of an insurance conglomerate. Nobody else could have afforded the premiums.

A buzzer sounded on Miss Harman's desk. She attended to it, cooed briefly into a desk console, and smiled at me invitingly. I followed McVeigh into the sanctum. I'd seen it many times before, but I still prepared myself to be jolted with awe.

Like most of the men in his family, Sir Bryan's father had been a career soldier. Sir Bryan himself had spent his childhood in India, although he returned to England long before the old man got himself and Sir Bryan's mother killed in the troubles leading up to independence. The father had blown the remnants of the Proctor fortune on cards and good living. The son had returned to study accountancy and law, determined to rebuild the family fortune any way he could, alone and from scratch. Their dislike had been mutual, though I'd never known whether Sir Bryan's business ambition had been a cause or effect. The young man had despised his father's raffishness as much as the old man had despised his son for going into trade. But, consciously or unconsciously, there was a lot of filial piety in the penthouse suite Sir Bryan had built at Global House.

It was an immense conservatory of tinted glass, occupying almost half the roof area. On one side were panoramic views of the Tower of London, HMS *Belfast* moored upstream, and the West End. On the other side, a tangle of cranes, warehouses, and scummy quays stretched beyond St. Katherine's dock into the Pool of London. Between them, the grey Thames bore a scabrous cargo of split packing cases and debris against a backdrop of the old Courage brewery. The inside of the conservatory was alive with creepers, palms, and concealed lighting. Exotic birds screeched from midair perches and crapped into shallow pools of brightly-colored fish. It was a cantle of the old Raj, assembled from memory by Pinewood set designers. The temperature was a constant and fetid 75°.

Sir Bryan Proctor sat at a desk not more than thirty feet long beneath a green-shaded overhead lamp and a slowly revolving fan. As usual, I looked for, but didn't see, a turbanned flunky with a tray of gin and tonic water. Sir Bryan was fitting the cap back on a pen that might have been made in Benares. He looked up impassively as the door hissed shut behind me. He stood up, walked across and poked me in the solar plexus without registering any expression.

"You're looking fit and well, boy." His voice had always been curiously soft and hoarse. "You're going to need to be. Champagne and orange juice, isn't it?"

He turned on his heel without waiting for an answer and walked to the drinks cabinet, a priceless piece of teak, blackened with age. It was just as well, because I was too surprised by the change in him to give an answer, or even be flattered by the fact that one of the best known men in England remembered what I drank.

When I'd last seen him, he'd been big, deftly groomed, and solid, a man who rolled slightly on the balls of his feet like a high-class sailor. Now he'd shrunk. His shoulders were rounded and the grey at his temples had spread over his head and chin. He needed a shave. But when I analyzed what I'd seen, I realized he had an infection of some kind, like facial dandruff. It must have been painful and made shaving difficult. But he was still a big man, well over six feet, with a gambler's deadpan lack of expression and a computer-like facility for weighing up people and odds with little, if any, emotional involvement.

He glanced with irritated impatience at McVeigh, who stood deferentially beside the cabinet like a court emissary from a smaller but more dapper republic. McVeigh had coughed meaningfully towards the decanter in Sir Bryan's hand. Even the hand had white flakes of skin peeling from the back.

"Shut up, Ted, will you?" he grumbled. "It's the first today."

He stoppered the decanter, handed a delicate Lalique crystal glass to McVeigh, and brought across my drink. He stopped in front of me with a half-hostile, half-calculating grin.

"As you are no doubt aware, I have been instructed by the physicians to take things quietly. The degree of their concern is, of course, in proportion to the liberality of the hand that feeds them."

"I had heard something of the sort," I admitted.

His expression still didn't change, but the temperature around him dropped sharply.

"Had you now? From whom did you hear it?"

"In the West Country, as a matter of fact. Come off it, Sir Bryan. When a man like you gets ill, you can hardly keep it quiet. It's my job to hear things."

There was a pause before he nodded and grinned again.

"Have you been told anything about the matter we are to discuss?" The engagingly hoarse tone was very noticeable.

My drink was cold and good. By golly, it might even do me good.

"Just that it's important," I said. "And that you wish to brief me personally."

"Very well. Sit down. You, too, Ted. I will give you a resumé of the facts, preferably without interruption. Afterwards, I should like your reaction. I shall then leave you to discuss details with Ted."

I sat down obediently in a leather chair so big it ought to have been supplied with a compass and emergency rations. Grinning sardonically, McVeigh perched himself on a corner of Sir Bryan's desk. There was something in the grin I didn't like. It looked like malevolent anticipation.

Sir Bryan walked to the desk and took up a Meissen jar. He filled one hand with grey fishfood pellets and went round distributing them among the fish pools. The fish almost collided in their rush to get at them. He paused before recapping the jar.

"Briefly, the Global Alliance group of companies is being swindled on a massive scale. Has been for the past four years. Not just in England, but throughout the Continent. I should add that murder is a component element in the situation."

I took a big pull at my drink. This looked a much more interesting job than James Huddiesford's domestic comedy of tape and slide booths.

Sir Bryan put a small heap of unused pellets down beside the Meissen jar and sat at his desk. He examined the backs of his hands, rubbing one softly against the other, before taking a first delicate pull at his whiskey. McVeigh removed himself from the corner of the desk and sat in another armchair.

"An insurance fraud is not like theft. With theft, you know your property's gone. The only problem is to discover who's now got it. An insurance fraud is different. You generally know who enjoys the benefit. It's a simple question of *cui bonum.* The problem is evidence. Assuming, that is, you know that fraud has been committed in the first place."

He got up and began to prowl the room, rustling the ice in his glass to make the whiskey last.

"In this case, we do not really claim to know how the swindle works or who is perpetrating it. If it were not for Jake, we probably wouldn't know anything at all—except that Global is losing money and that men are dying."

Jake was a pet name given to the giant IBM computer housed in the basement of Global House beneath the car park. It was the apple of Sir Bryan's eye. I lit a cigarette from the silver presentation box on the low table beside me.

"What size swindle are we talking about? How many murders?"

Sir Bryan rubbed one hand softly across his face, palm uppermost. "We are talking about losses in the region of one and a half million pounds annually in this country alone. Total losses to the Group are in the region of fifty million pounds. Eleven murders have been committed to our knowledge. The actual number is probably higher."

I didn't question the statement. Apart from the public record, Sir Bryan had access to secret and semiofficial sources at the kind of level and scale that would have made a citizens' rights activist blench.

"A swindle that size is big enough to be called taxation," I said flippantly, more to ease the oppressive silence than anything else. The immense penthouse was soundproofed, but you could still hear quiet descend when the commuter trains pulled out of Cannon Street and London Bridge.

McVeigh grinned back at my probably inane grin.

"Insurance is the science of the predictable imposed on facts of the unpredictable," he remarked. "Using statistics and experience, we formulate actuarial tables that enable us to quantify risk with a remarkable degree of reliability. Naturally, we continually assess performance in the light of expectations. Our first unexpected losses on the scale Sir Bryan has mentioned occurred three years ago. We were perturbed, and carried out an immediate investigation. But we discovered nothing. We wrote the matter off as an unfortunate aberration of no significance. What Voltaire would have called a *lusus naturae*."

Sir Bryan had listened in silence, his head bowed. "Cut the pedagoguery, Ted," he said quietly, curtly. "I said I'd like to make this exposition in my way."

"Certainly, Sir Bryan," McVeigh murmured with undisguised irony. "I do apologize."

I suddenly began to get angry. I realized that McVeigh was enjoying Sir Bryan's worry, but my reaction surprised me. I'd worked often for the old man, and I didn't consider myself his greatest fan. He could be ruthless and arrogant. Still, there was a lot to admire. He'd built up Global from scratch with his own sweat and brains. It was his life. Thinking about that, I realized why I was afraid for him. Global was literally his life. He was the kind who had no opinion of himself as mere man, good, bad, or indifferent. He defined himself by what he created.

It made him vulnerable. Or perhaps I just felt that because his creation was under attack and because he looked ill.

Sir Bryan returned to his desk. He seemed to have forgotten the interruption.

"Losses of the same order occurred during the following year," he went on quietly, "and again last year. The matter was taken up at the International Board level, and it was established that similar losses were being experienced in seven other major European countries where Global companies operate. A top secret committee was set up to supervise an enquiry using all available resources. To date, neither it nor our Army of Ferrets has yielded anything of significance.

The Army of Ferrets was another code name, this time for the corps of investigators who examined every dubious claim on Global policies.

"Unexplained coincidence isn't evidence of fraud, surely?" I said as intelligently as I could.

"I haven't finished yet."

This time, I got the quiet brush-off.

"During that second year, we set up an exhaustive computer program based on all holders of the kind of policy in question who had died over the preceding two years throughout Europe. We were looking for correspondences of the kind that might tell us something about what was happening. Jake fed us back a detailed and homogeneous list of them. A list so comprehensive," he placed his glass abruptly on the desk, spilling a few drops, "that there is absolutely no possibility of coincidence."

McVeigh picked up my glass and carried it to the bar. I didn't object. Sir Bryan's story was having an effect on me. Besides, I have a theory that champagne is the best antidote to too much whiskey the night before.

"What correspondences?" I didn't care anymore whether he welcomed interruptions.

Sir Bryan scooped up the remaining fishfood pellets on his desk and opened the Meissen jar. He slipped one pellet inside.

"The type of policy in question was always straight-risk life, the sum assured being exactly fifty thousand pounds—or its equivalent in the currencies of the other countries affected. In every case, the policyholder was a young man, sometimes married but usually not, who had held the policy for less than a year at the time of his death."

I accepted my refilled glass. "Let's get this straight," I said carefully. "You're telling me that every single one of the policyholders in your program died?"

"You catch on remarkably well," Sir Bryan snapped with a touch of his old fire.

"How many policyholders?"

"Between thirty and thirty-five per year in each country. Allowing a small margin for computer error."

"Computer error." My implied question hung in the air.

Sir Bryan shrugged. "No doubt one or two cases crept into the program that shouldn't have been there. Perhaps one or two that should have been there were omitted. The possibility simply highlights the overall consistency of the pattern."

"What happened to them?"

He rubbed the back of his hand across his face again. I might have been wrong, but it seemed to me he was already more tired than when he started.

"As I told you, eleven men are definitely known to have been murdered. But all died violently, apparently from accidents. Drownings, falls from rock faces, that sort of thing. In every case, death took place in a remote country district, usually in summer." He looked up at me expectantly.

I obliged. "Young men have a habit of taking up dangerous pastimes," I said. "Particularly in summer."

He nodded. "That is true. Except that, as you'd expect, the majority of the policyholders lived in towns, though none died in one. An unusually high proportion were of the complete city-dweller kind who wouldn't know the difference between a cow-pat and a pussy willow."

"You've been doing your homework," I commented.

Sir Bryan jumped up. "We've researched these kids till research comes out of our ears." There was a sudden, passionate irritation in him. "Sometimes I think I know more about them than their own mothers. I've had synopses made up of all important matters, just so you don't spend the next month reading paperwork."

"Fine," I said soothingly. "What does your third bit of fishfood stand for?"

He had the Meissen container in his hand. He smiled fractionally, a little self-consciously, and slipped the pellet in the jar.

"At this point," he said quietly, "you might say the plot thickens. Every policyholder specified a beneficiary in his application who was not a member of his family. A young male like himself. A beneficiary who, so far as our researches can determine, he had never met before in his life."

McVeigh chuckled sardonically. Again, I had the feeling he was enjoying the situation. Even Sir Bryan noticed.

"What the hell's so funny?" he snapped, wheeling.

McVeigh looked unconcerned. "I see no point in getting emotionally disturbed," he drawled. "It will hardly help." He smiled at me. "There's an interesting sidelight to the last fact. We checked all the beneficiaries very thoroughly. Remarkably, every one of them had an unimpeachable alibi. They were all definitely somewhere else when the accidents happened. Not only that, I checked for socio-demograhic similarities. Common backgrounds, friends, activities, that sort of thing. There was nothing. Like the policyholders themselves, they were a completely mixed bag."

He drained his glass and laid it carefully on the thick, umber-tiled floor. "Most interestingly, a few of the victims were, inevitably, relatively wealthy. In all those cases, policy had been written under trust so that benefits from it couldn't be lumped with the rest of the estate for tax purposes."

"Fascinating," I remarked. "Only why should someone want to bequeath a fixed sum with no tax strings to someone he'd never met before in his life?"

Sir Bryan was definitely tiring. His face had turned pale and blotchy, and if he noticed McVeigh's second interruption, he didn't react.

"Answer that," he said despondently, "and I expect you'll have earned your fee."

He slipped a final fishfood pellet into the Meissen jar and locked it away in his desk.

"There's another important correspondence that should have helped us but hasn't." He looked at me with a kind of despairing anger. "I've checked carefully. No other insurance company is affected by this syndrome. It is unique to Global companies. From that, I infer not only that a fraudulent and murderous conspiracy is in existence, but that the conspirators, whoever they are, are waging a personal vendetta against me. Against Global. I want to know why."

His intensity made me uneasy. "That's sweeping, isn't it?" I asked. "As you said, a discovery like that should be a giveaway. Why should your conspirators take the chance? If they exist, that is."

"There's no other explanation," Sir Bryan said softly. There were more blotches among the facial dandruff. As I'd thought, there was a condition there, maybe psychosomatic in origin. He controlled himself. "There's no other explanation," he repeated.

He got up slowly. It was an old man's motion. Usually his movements were lithe, for he'd kept himself in shape through squash. Now he placed the flat of his hands on his knees to lever himself upright.

"I've built this place up for forty years," he said with quiet intensity. "It's my life. Someone is trying to destroy it. I don't know why, but I want you to find out, boy. I don't care what it costs. Nobody is going to do this to me."

I could feel his insistence like a trap closing round me. I got up to escape. I walked to the big window. Early evening clouds had cleared to show a bronze sun westering melodramatically over the forward turrets of HMS *Belfast.* McVeigh came forward to take my tankard again and renew it at the bar. I made no objection. If this was happy hour at Global, I was all for it.

I turned. "Your story makes no sense," I said at last. "I'm sorry, Sir Bryan. It's too bizarre. Let's start at the beginning. There's no point in examining the correspondences you say you've found unless you assume that all your case histories are alike in all significant respects. That's got to include the way your policyholders died. So if eleven were murdered, the rest must have been as well. With around thirty-five a year spread over eight countries and four years, I make that getting on for a thousand murders." I accepted my refilled tankard from McVeigh and took a long pull. "That's not fraud, Sir Bryan. That's war. An organization capable of carrying out mayhem on that scale would make the Mafia look like a village rotary club. There's got to be something wrong with Jake's circuitry."

It was my longest speech since making my presentation to Huddiesford, and it reminded me of my hangover. I went back to my armchair and took another long pull at my drink.

Sir Bryan looked up from an inspection of his hands. McVeigh hadn't given him another drink, but I noticed there was a lot left in his glass. He was taking it easy.

"I don't accept that." He put his hands firmly in his pockets. "There's nothing wrong with Jake, and the program's been checked again and again. A small but efficient organization would be perfectly capable of killing that number of men over that period of time."

"Without its existence even being suspected until now?" I asked. I was irritated. The chief executive of Global might be ailing, but he wasn't normally stupid. I should have been warned. He hadn't ever been the type to dodge inconvenient truths before.

"I'm not just thinking about the killers," I said, "assuming they exist. What about the policy beneficiaries? I take it they've been thoroughly investigated?"

"They certainly have." McVeigh was grinning all over his evil face. "Most thoroughly. Not only have we failed to establish any connection between them and the men from whom they benefitted, we have also failed to find any connection among the beneficiaries themselves. They appear to have been total strangers."

I sighed. My head was beginning to hurt. "You said it yourself, Sir Bryan. With an insurance fraud, it's a matter of *cui bonum*—who benefits. The beneficiaries would have to be involved in some way, and there's a thousand of them, too." I got up and began to prowl. "Anyway, what would be the point? There's no motive."

"My companies have lost in the region of fifty million pounds since this business started," Sir Bryan snarled. "What the hell do you mean there's no motive?"

There was no real anger behind his snarl. I began to feel guilty. I saw thoroughly now why he wanted me to investigate. He valued my judgment but hated the obvious conclusions he must have reached for himself. He'd been hoping desperately that I would immediately turn up some simple explanation that would get him off the hook. And here I was, sealing off the exits and redoubling his worries.

"A lot of money," McVeigh agreed humorously, "but spread out in a strange manner, don't you think, Sir Bryan? Straight-risk policies for fifty thousand pounds are very small beer these days, the kind we usually sell for mortgage protection. These were fit young men, presumably well able to look after themselves. Why should an organization that wanted to murder for gain pick on such men, when we've got doddering invalids on our books insured for ten times the amount?"

"It's a lot of money," Sir Bryan repeated defensively. "Plenty of men have murdered for less."

"Indeed they have." There was an edge to McVeigh's voice that I noticed but Sir Bryan didn't.

"O.K., smart arse, so different men have different prices. What would yours be?"

"Are you buying or selling?" There was more than an edge to McVeigh's voice this time. There was viciousness. He made no effort to hide it, and Sir Bryan noticed. He glanced at me uncertainly. Of all the things I had seen that afternoon, that look disquieted me most. Sir Bryan Proctor never brooked backchat from an employee, still less, insolence. I realized then that I was looking at more than a simple case of an old lion weakening and a young lion scenting its chance for power. On some instinctual level, Sir Bryan had already recognized that he was engaged in a fight he could not win. There was no ferocity to his fear, no fight-back. What he saw as an attack on his empire galvanized him temporarily into something like his old fire, but there was no energy and self-belief to sustain it anymore.

"Murder for simple gain appears to be out," I agreed reluctantly. "Apart from anything else, it wouldn't explain why the sum assured was always exactly the same." I turned to McVeigh. "I take it there weren't victims who didn't fit the pattern. Men insured for much larger sums, for example?"

"No. And the value of the policies taken out by the group Jake analyzed corresponded almost exactly to the exceptional losses we have been experiencing," McVeigh said quietly. "The pattern appears to admit of no exceptions."

I got up. Sir Bryan wasn't going to like this. I walked to the window. The sinking sun was now hidden behind the forward turrets of HMS *Belfast.* It looked as though the great battle cruiser were firing a salvo at Westminster. I turned back reluctantly.

"I'm sorry, sir. I don't think there's any way I can help. If you're right and you're up against a criminal conspiracy of the kind you'd have to assume, you'll need a lot more than me to sort it out. You'd need the police forces of Europe. In this country alone, they'd probably call in Special Branch, the SPG and God knows what else to help crack it. As for putting a stop to the deaths right now, there's a simple solution. If Jake can pinpoint unvarying characteristics in past victims, he can use those as a template to identify policyholders at risk in the future. Young men who've held fifty thousand pound straight-risk life insurance policies for less than a year, and so on. You could revoke the policies, or have your Army of Ferrets investigate the holders. If there really is a conspiracy, the conspirators would see the game was up."

Sir Bryan's reaction was too fast. I knew then for certain that he had considered but rejected all the sensible options already.

"You're bloody mad," he shouted. "Do you imagine there's any way I could keep this thing quiet if I did what you suggest? What the hell do you think the brokers, the banks, and the lawyers would say if I started special investigations and quoted special rates, not to mention the bloody press? Insure with Global," he snarled bitterly, "and get killed in God's clean countryside."

He controlled himself with an effort. "Listen, boy," he pleaded, "I know you can help. We've got more than enough information already. It's not more manpower I want. It's an idea. There's a conspiracy. It's big, but it's basically simple. I feel it in my bones." He held my eyes, still pleading. "The bulk of deaths has always taken place in summer. We've got a month or more before they start again. Just have a look at it, will you? There's got to be a simple key, something we've overlooked. We're too close to the problem here. All I'm asking you for is a fresh, objective look at things."

The sardonic, vulpine grin was back on McVeigh's face. He, too, remembered hearing those words recently. I'd had more than enough of

McVeigh and the look decided me. It was my first serious mistake in the business.

"Very well, Sir Bryan, I'll look at it. On two conditions."

"Name them."

"First, as of today I'm three hundred and fifty pounds-a-day's-worth of business consultant. Plus expenses."

"Itemized and with properly receipted bills, I trust?" McVeigh murmured politely. Sir Bryan and I ignored him.

"And the other condition?"

"I'll work on it for a fortnight. If I've got nowhere by then, I'll turn it in."

"Agreed."

There was a corollary to that condition, but I wasn't going to worry Sir Bryan with it yet.

"There's something else. I'll start by going over the basic source material myself. I'll want to interview some of the policyholders' families. I'll also want to check your computer analyses. There's a small firm of private investigators I know. They'll save time on the leg work. They're cheaper than I am, too. I'll also be renting a small, private research facility in Soho. Don't worry, I've worked with them before. They're completely reliable."

Sir Bryan didn't like the idea. "I don't see why you need a research facility," he objected. "There's no more sophisticated machine in the country than Jake, and all the information we have is in his memory banks."

"You said you wanted a completely fresh and objective look," I reminded him. "That means untried computer expertise. Personally, I wouldn't know the difference between an input terminal and an electric toaster."

"Very well." He got up painfully and slowly again. He walked to the door. "I'll hold you personally responsible for security," he warned.

He went out of the room, leaving the door open. I heard him grumbling querulously to Freda Harman about the cleaners leaving birdshit and sand all over the floor. He came back swathed in a thick coat with a fur collar, even though spring was pretty much on schedule.

He looked like an expensively wrapped but dull present. His hefty chauffeur hovered solicitously behind him.

"I'm going home," he informed us. He looked at me. "Ted will give you any more information you need. Just do your best, boy, and report back at intervals of not more than a week." He turned to McVeigh. "Freda says Don's back from South America. Have you seen him yet?"

"Not yet, Sir Bryan."

The old man nodded gloomily. "Find him and see what he's up to, will you? Tell him I'd like to see him if he can spare a piece of his valuable time."

He nodded vaguely and wandered out, attended by the chauffeur. I heard the lift doors whine before McVeigh closed the heavy door again. It was the most depressing moment of the long, depressing afternoon. When I'd last known Sir Bryan Proctor, he'd been a mainstay of half the deadliest and most stylish gaming clubs in London. His household was lucky if it ever saw him between working hours. His stamina had been legendary. Now he was tottering home before the evening had started. Probably to play patience, eat his gruel, and get an early night.

McVeigh walked to the big bronze windows and stood teetering, his hands in his pockets. It was now dark outside.

"What exactly is wrong with Sir Bryan?" I asked.

McVeigh shrugged, his back towards me. "His genes, his history, and his age. In that order. Isn't that usually the case? The men in his family generally die young. He picked up some condition while he was in India. He's also got heart trouble." He took a tubular plastic toothpick from his breast pocket and began to pick his left teeth fastidiously. "And then, of course, he's a diabetic."

I was surprised. I'd never seen the old man ordering special diets or giving himself an insulin fix, but then he'd always have hidden a personal weakness.

"I thought people with diabetes weren't supposed to drink," I said. I hadn't seen him touch tobacco or alcohol before, but there was no doubt he'd started on the whiskey.

"They're not," McVeigh said briefly. "We try to keep him off the stuff, but don't ask me why he's started. Different men look for oblivion in different ways. They don't always throw themselves off the Clifton Suspension Bridge."

He pocketed the toothpick. "Interesting little problem, isn't it?" he said brightly. I knew he'd dropped the boring topic of his boss's life and health.

"You don't seem so worried about it," I said. "If Sir Bryan's right, this little problem could knock Global sideways. It could put you out of a job."

"Really? I hardly think so. It's serious, I agree, but getting passionate isn't going to help." He turned, smiling brilliantly. "Besides, I'm sure Sir Bryan's confidence in you is well placed. I'm sure you'll come up with an answer."

I shrugged. "What have you got for me to go on?"

"I guessed you'd want to look at the grass roots stuff. I've had full biographies and case histories made for last year's victims in this country. It should be enough to get you started. You can tell me what you need after that. The last dossiers are being typed now. I'll get them all to you tomorrow morning by special messenger."

"Anything else?"

"There's a synoptic report on our investigations to date. Not much in it, I'm afraid. There'll also be a print-out of all victims in all countries, listing basic information only. Names, addresses, and ages, where and when they died, that sort of thing. How much nicer London looks at night under all that cosmetic lighting, don't you think?"

He turned away from the window and crossed the wide, umber-tiled floor. A white bird with a curly head screeched at him in passing. He handed me a folder from Sir Bryan's desk. "You can have the synoptic report now. It makes interesting bedtime reading, though I doubt there's enough of it for the job. As Sir Bryan said, you should report back to me on a casual basis. Unless something turns up, of course. I'd like to spare him unnecessary stress."

I'd seen him enjoy needling the old man sadistically, and I wondered what was in his devious brain. The thought reminded me of something I'd been meaning to ask.

"By the way," I said. "How did you know where to find me this morning?"

"I have my methods, my dear fellow. Yours is not the only intelligence service in London."

I was sure it wasn't, but I didn't like the idea of being so easily traceable. He looked at me with concern.

"I'll drive you to your flat if you like."

"Thanks. I left my bag in your car anyway."

"It's no trouble. It's on my way."

I didn't believe him, but then he probably didn't expect me to.

The duty attendant drove McVeigh's maroon Rolls round to the main doors while McVeigh and I took one of the six staff lifts to the ground floor. After hours, Global House looked like a documentary film set. It was empty except for office cleaners and a few miles of electric vacuum cleaner lead.

McVeigh was quiet as he drove along the Thames-side fast road towards the Mermaid Theatre and Ludgate Circus. I didn't say much myself. I was too busy wondering what I'd let myself in for and how to get a toe-hold on Sir Bryan's problems. McVeigh turned off the Strand at Aldwych and crawled up Drury Lane where the pavements were packed with theatre-goers. He got stopped outside the Theatre Royal by two drunks from the nearby doss-house who were having a spot of bother in the middle of the road. One of them, an old man in a ragged coat, tried to land a haymaker on a scrawny Scot who probably got stranded the last time Scotland played England at Wembley. The Scot dodged, and the old man staggered round, spraying drops of blood from his nose. A crowd of theatre-goers watched the unequal contest.

McVeigh waited for a gap, then eased the Rolls between them. Neither noticed until they almost collided with his taillights. They made a truce to bawl obscene insults after us.

McVeigh lit another expensive cigar. "It's remarkable," he mused. "None of those cultured foreigners would dream of watching a title fight on TV, but they'll happily miss the first act of whatever they're waiting for in order to see two drunks beating the shit out of each other in the street."

There was no answer to that, and McVeigh was silent again until he pulled up outside my flat in Henrietta Street.

"Will you be attending the opening of Don's exhibition?" he enquired politely.

"Don who?"

McVeigh grimaced. "Sir Bryan has a son of that name. You must have heard Sir Bryan mention that he's just returned from a professional tour of South America. He's a trendy photographer. His first one-man show opens on the eleventh at the gallery in the building where you live."

"I didn't know you were a patron of the arts," I said.

"I'm not. As you presumably also gathered, Sir Bryan does not get on well with his son, but he worries about him. He likes me to keep an eye on him. Also on his investment."

"What investment?"

"Sir Bryan financed Don's career as a photographer. He doesn't think much of it as an occupation for a grown man, but it beats some of the shady businesses Don was in before. I shall be bringing Charles Omphrey, by the way."

So that was it. I knew McVeigh had brought me home for a reason. I also knew Charles Omphrey, though not well. He was a Harley Street quack with an interest in psychology. He'd read almost everyone from Freud to Tomas Szász without, so far as I could tell, taking in much more than the coffee table jargon. He was also Sir Bryan's personal physician. I wondered what McVeigh wanted me to meet him for.

"Is Omphrey supposed to be keeping an eye on Sir Bryan's investment, too?" I asked.

McVeigh eased a cylinder of fat ash the colour of a patriarch's locks into the tray. The conditioning was on, but the air was fouling.

"Like a number of elderly gentlemen whose health is failing, Sir Bryan is convinced that every misfortune he suffers must be the result of his imperfect understanding of life. I expect him to start a course of transcendental meditation shortly. Sir Bryan admires Omphrey. He has seconded him to the committee investigating the business you are now employed on."

I was riled again by the contempt in McVeigh's voice, but I tried not to let it show. I took my bad temper out on Omphrey instead.

"Omphrey's a quack. Most of his general medicine's out of date, and what he really knows about clinical psychology you could stuff up Ronnie Laing's bottom without causing noticeable discomfort."

"Very possibly, though I gather Omphrey isn't much interested in the clinical aspect of his study. He's into some rather personal amalgam of psychology, philosophy, and sociology. The point is, the old man has faith in him. Under the circumstances, you ought at least to meet him. I know the day after tomorrow doesn't give you much time, but you may have formulated some views by then. Just come along and have a talk, there's a good chap."

I got out of the Rolls, hitching my bag off the back seat.

"What time?" I asked.

"The exhibition opens officially at six-thirty. Don't bother to dress. I believe they've forgotten how to in Covent Garden."

He didn't say good-bye. I watched him drive off, calling him an imposing variety of bad names in a low voice. I had definitely decided that I didn't like McVeigh. I climbed three sets of stairs to my flat, the latest in a long line of residences. I wasted three minutes trying to open the door with the wrong key before I managed to let myself in. The air smelled like a ghost's fart.

I switched on all the lights and opened most of the windows. It had turned into a mild, springlike evening, so I sat on my tiny terrace which was really the roof of the flat below. I thought I might tile it with Spanish *azulejos* one day and surround it with tinted glass like Sir Bryan's penthouse. It gave me a good, angled view of a church by Inigo Jones that looked like a sacred brick factory.

After a while I got cold, so I went out to dinner at a restaurant near the old flower market and thought about Sir Bryan's problems again. I finished dinner with a brace of calvados doubles and some espresso.

I was still asleep when McVeigh phoned me in the morning. I swore as I knocked over a bowl of purpling, shrivelled tangerines while reaching for the receiver. I switched on the light. It was eight-thirty.

"Sorry to disturb you." McVeigh had heard the bowl hit the floor. "I have a meeting at nine o'clock. I'm sending the documents I promised round to you now. I don't have to remind you to keep the whole business under wraps, do I? A word out of place could cause us a great deal of trouble."

"If you don't have to remind me, why remind me?" I snarled.

"Splendid," McVeigh murmured soothingly. "I'd get some breakfast and an Alka-Seltzer if I were you."

"More to the point, McVeigh, I'd like several sets of Global Alliance credentials. You don't mind me using the familiar mode of address, do you?"

"Dear me, Sir Bryan warned that you could be difficult. He blames your nocturnal habits as well as your upbringing. I'll get them to you with the other documents."

He hung up, and I swore again. The bastard was right. Wine and calvados hadn't sat well with Huddiesford's whiskey and Sir Bryan's champagne. I got out of bed and put a cassette of a four-part Mass by Byrd on the machine while I took a shower. The music seemed to rationalize my intimations of mortality.

Afterwards I dressed and looked for breakfast in the refrigerator. There was nothing, of course, so I telephoned Harry the janitor who did odd jobs around the place for a consideration. He was a small man with a permanent, knowing expression of irony. He'd lost an arm in an industrial accident years ago and wore the empty sleeve pinned across his jacket as though he had a stomachache as well.

I gave him a ten-pound note and a fiver. "Ask Mrs. Harry to get some shopping in," I said. "I need milk, bread, and the usual refrigerator stuff. I'd also like her to clean the place up and get some cut flowers." Harry took the notes wordlessly. I assumed the fiver would never see the inside of his wife's purse.

I walked to The Italian Joint for breakfast. It was a fine morning, and I could pick up a morning paper en route. The restaurant had suffered when they closed down the old market, but business was picking up again fast. The trendies who are always looking for a new place to have a trend in had seen to that. The bar was long and narrow in the Mediterranean fashion. It had clear plastic containers stacked with salami rolls and more chromium piping than the engine room of a cross-channel ferry. The capuccino was a hell of a lot better, though.

Opposite the bar was a narrow counter and a row of stools. There was almost no room between bar and counter, which made me nervous in the evenings, when the place was full of Italian waiters who sounded on the brink of civil violence even when they were discussing their ulcers. Above the bar was a long row of *sirop* bottles and a giant, retouched poster of Rocky Marciano with his record printed underneath. When challenged, I can usually recite a full list of his victories, TKOs and all, with my eyes shut.

I ate at the back, underneath the big color TV. By the time I had read my *Mirror* and eaten an enamelled bowl of scrambled eggs, the Disprins I had taken earlier were beginning to have an effect. I was in a better mood when I walked home.

Harry's wife was doing the cleaning. The flat door was open, and my groceries were in a bag in the hall. I took an orange from the top and walked through to the main room where I did most of my work. It had several comfortable chairs, a desk with a built-in filing cabinet and a small piano that sounded better than it looked. McVeigh's documents were blowing around on the floor because of the open door and the balcony windows. So much for security. I closed the windows, reminding myself to bring in the pots of dead geraniums sometime. They'd been a tribute from a girl who wanted to turn my flat into something beautiful and shared. Our friendship hadn't lasted.

I collected the documents, sat down, and peeled an orange. There were thirty-two Digby Portfolio files and a large brown envelope. I opened the envelope first. Inside was a long sheet of print-out paper and another folder containing McVeigh's summary of events to date. Paper-clipped to the print-out were two typed letters stating that the bearer was an accredited representative of Global Alliance Assurance Ltd.

I flipped through the summary folder and glanced at the print-out. Then I turned to the Digby folders. Each one was packed with A4 sheets densely typed. The top sheet was a photostat copy of an original insurance proposal. The rest contained detailed biographical information covering everything down to whether the subject picked his nose with his right or left hand. There were also copies of reports from outside and inside the Global organization and a long, thoughtful summary.

I ate my orange, taking care not to get juice on the pages, and read the top folder through to get the hang of things. Then I flipped through the other folders, paying attention only to the coroner's report and postmortem findings. Looking at the files as a whole, I could see the scale of Sir Bryan's problem. Most of the verdicts were death by misadventure, but there were just too many falling branches, rock falls, and treacherous rivers in the peaceful shires of England for my liking.

I paid particular attention to the eleven cases where the verdict had been murder by person or persons unknown. The most blatant case concerned a kid who had been garrotted with a badger snare. The noose had been found miles away by a farmer's terrier and identified by forensic analysis. On the whole, though, I was struck by the absence of injuries inflicted with obvious weapons. I made a note of the fact and stuck it on the cork wall I use as a memorandum pad.

I closed the last folder and walked into the kitchen. Harry's wife was lighting a tiny high-tar cigarette. I borrowed one. She looked mousier than ever. She always did. I thanked her for buying the groceries. There was a cellotape-sealed packet of freshly ground coffee on top. Its smell reminded me of tiny corner shops when I was a boy, where perforated copper cylinders half-filled with beans rotated slowly over gas flames. I'm not really that old, though. I just happen to come from a backward village. I told Mrs. Harry she had done well on seven pounds.

"Eight," she smiled weakly, handing me change from the ten. I gave her another five anyway and told her to buy something for herself and not to let Harry know. I always get generous when I scent a fat fee on its way.

When Mrs. Harry had finished and gone, I telephoned Starkey Brothers in Holborn. I asked for Eric Starkey, who was one half of the team that ran it. Eric was an idealist, one of nature's Quixotes, with a childlike sense of adventure. Most of his work involved unfaithful partners and delinquent children, but Eric didn't care. He was an eternal, ebullient romantic with an unexpected passion for collecting stamps. His favourite dreams were of finding a penny black and rescuing some golden girl from the clutches of an international vice ring. The jobs I gave him were usually cleaner but not necessarily more interesting than his usual ones.

As always, he came over the line with the sober restraint of a nightclub disco. I waited for a gap in the torrent of joviality to ask after Marian and the kids.

"They're fine," he bawled. "Terrific." He told me his eldest son, young Jase, whom I remembered from his skateboarding days, had just been awarded a place at Bristol University. Eric's pride was boundless.

"Hold it," I said, when I could get another word in. "Are you free to do a job? It's an important one, and it could take a while."

"Of course I'm free," he shouted. "I'm on my way." I could hear him snapping the brim of an imaginary fedora.

I told him to make it faster, hung up, and called another number.

"I'd like to speak to Rose Panayioutou," I said.

"This is she speaking." The voice was that of a bored archangel. "What the hell do you want?"

Rose was a market analyst and researcher. She had also trained in computer technology. She was absurdly beautiful. Her eyes were actually violet, and her skin had just the right touch of Mediterranean translucence. Like a lot of other beautiful women, she had a good but unexpectedly prosaic mind.

"I need you, Rose," I said truthfully. "I want you here right now."

"No way. I'm doing a study on cakes and cookies. I can send Denise, or I can come myself the day after tomorrow."

"Damn Mother Hubbard's Krummy Kookies," I said. "Put Denise onto them. My job's more interesting and a lot more important. You could help save lives. I mean it."

It was unfair, but it was true. I also knew it would work. Rose was conscientious, but she had her priorities ruthlessly right. She was in love with humanity and justice and got passionate about them. Only two things puzzled me. One was why she bothered to work in market research when she really belonged at the side of a gallant partisan. The other was why I had never got round to putting her humanitarian passion to more practical use.

She hesitated only a moment. "O.K., tiger. Will one o'clock do?"

"Half an hour, Rose," I repeated before putting the phone down. I knew she'd be there.

Eric breezed in while I was peeling another orange. He was a big man with a dirty coil of blond hair that fell into his eyes. As always, he was dressed in the style of an off-the-peg tailor whose stock had suffered flood damage. He had a heart as big as his body, so I let him pump my arm for a few minutes.

"Eric," I warned him. "Rose will be here soon. We'll wait till she is before I give you the story. But get this straight. It's a sensitive job. I don't want a word whispered to anyone about it. Not even to Olly." Olly was Eric's brother, the other half of the Starkey partnership.

Eric's face widened in a grin of boyish enthusiasm. He was already on his way to defeating The Panther in single combat and restoring the heroine to her rightful inheritance.

"Big job, is it?" he asked in a huge whisper.

"Very."

He sat down, rubbing his hands. He was wearing too much deodorant as usual. His bulk flooded fragrantly over the edges of the chair. It was an over-small, over-smart chair that I'd inherited along with the flat. I kept meaning to replace it sometime.

"Do you want a drink?" I asked.

He brightened. "So long as it isn't any of that gassy lager stuff. It gives me wind."

I got two Guinness cans from the six-pack Harry's wife had thoughtfully placed in the refrigerator. Eric unzipped his and drank from the top. We talked about old times for a while. He showed me Polaroid shots of the conservatory he'd built onto his big, rambling house in Nightingale Lane between Clapham and Stockwell. He was mad about his tiny Maltese wife, his kids, and their chaotic life together. I hadn't met them all in a long time. It wasn't that Eric kept himself to himself. Under his extroverted exterior, he had an unexpectedly prim sense of what was proper. His work was often dirty, so he was at pains to keep his domestic and professional lives separated.

Rose floated in as I was going to the kitchen for another Guinness. She wore a Samsonite briefcase, a thin frock of some expensive silk-like material and almost invisible sandals. She wore no jewelry, make-up, nor, so far as I could see, underwear. She gave the erotic impression of being about three ounces away from total nudity. How she survived an English spring I wouldn't know. I asked her faintly if she'd like a Guinness.

"I have a late luncheon appointment, thank you." She sat down crossing her beautiful ankles. "An unbreakable one. I trust you mean it when you say your business is important. Can we get on with it?"

I tore my eyes away from her ankles and read the same riot act I had read to Eric.

Rose looked bored. "Your clients are always dreadfully shy," she commented. "By the way, how did you know the project I was engaged on was Mother Hubbard's Krummy Kookies?"

My sanity wobbled. "Never mind," I said. I sat down and straightened out the big pile of Digby Portfolio files.

"These are personal case histories of young men who held life policies with one of the big insurance companies. The young men are all dead now. Some of them were murdered. It may be that all of them were. You should also know that these files refer only to holders of policies last year in this country. There are equivalent cases over the last four years in seven other countries where my client operates."

I had their undivided attention. There was a long, stunned silence, and Rose compressed her lips with an expression of sudden pain.

Eric swore uncharacteristically. "Are you having us on?" he demanded.

I shook my head.

Rose uncrossed her ankles. "I assume this is a police matter," she said quietly.

I had to be very careful. Eric was a simple, upright, and stubborn man. Rose, regrettably, was conventionally respectable in almost everything. They both knew me well, but they also knew that my work was sometimes dirty and that I played it by the appropriate rules when necessary, so they didn't altogether trust me. I explained the background to the deaths the way Sir Bryan had explained it to me.

"Somewhere," I said, "there's got to be a connection that accounts for what's going on. I want you to help me find the connection so that we can put a stop to the deaths. The police are not involved because my client has no more actual information at present than the police themselves. The only difference is that he, and now you, are aware of certain statistical correlations. Perhaps the situation will change if you help me."

I reminded them about the predominantly summer pattern of deaths. "A lot of young men may start dying again in a month or so if we don't come up with the answers," I concluded.

Eric's expression had become a worried frown. He thought for another long moment and exchanged quick glances with Rose, who nodded briefly.

"We'd better get started," she said with a bright, wary smile.

I sighed with relief and got up to avoid the temptation to grab her lovely olive knees. I picked up the Digby files.

"Eric and I will start with these," I said. "So far, all we've got is cold data. We want a feel for the thing." I divided the pile into halves and handed one half over to Eric.

"Study these first," I said. "Then get out in your car. These boys had families and friends. Go and talk to them. Ask all the questions you can think of. If anyone wants to see your credentials, show them these."

I handed him one of McVeigh's letters. I would have preferred them not to know who they were working for so soon, but I didn't think it made much difference. They were both reliable.

Eric read his letter and looked impressed. "That lot? They're bigger than the crown jewels." He tucked the letter in his pocket. "What sort of questions do I ask?"

"I want to know about their lives, their work, their families. I want to know about their hobbies and what they did with their spare time, the groups they ran around with, what books they read. Everything. Remember, we're looking for a connection of some kind. If they all parted their hair on the left, I want to know it. If they all drank coffee without sugar, I want to know that, too."

"What can I do?" Rose asked.

She was a kind, determined girl, and I didn't think Mother Hubbard's Krummy Kookies would be getting much of her attention for a while.

I gave her McVeigh's long computer print-out. "This covers all the deaths in every year and in all the countries I was talking about. It's just basic information. I want you to put it through your mincer in every damned way you can think of. Again, we're looking for any kind of pattern or anomaly. Anything that suggests the deaths may not have been completely random."

She took the list and stood up, smoothing her dress over her lovely hips. "I'll get started right away. What happens if I need more information? Can I go to the client direct? It would save time."

I thought for a moment and agreed. I gave her McVeigh's telephone number. "I'll warn him," I said. "Only make sure you speak to Mr. McVeigh personally. Nobody else."

Eric prised himself loose from his chair and stood up. "I'll get started as well," he said. He buttoned his creased jacket and persuaded the wings of his shirt collar to stay under it.

"Fine. We'll meet back here the day after tomorrow. We'll fix a time. Four o'clock, say. If either of you needs more time or wants to get in touch before then, we'll arrange it through your office, Eric."

Eric nodded and took Rose's arm. She surprised us both by kissing him on the cheek and then me as well. I patted her beautiful bottom without thinking.

"Everybody be careful," she said solemnly. "I don't like this. I've got a feeling somebody may get hurt. Don't ask me how I know."

She walked out before I could recover, take advantage, or even say good-bye.

After they'd gone, I cleared away the beer cans and telephoned McVeigh. He wasn't in, so I left a carefully worded message about Rose Panayioutou. I packed a grip with spare clothes, shoved my share of the Digby Portfolio files on top, and locked the flat behind me. I walked round to the garage where I stabled my old Alfa. On the way, I remembered the knocking noise that had developed in the engine. I mentioned it to Sean, the Ulster mechanic who looked after the place.

He scratched his head and listened. "Do you know what it is, then?" he enquired.

"Sean," I sighed, "it could be a rock band stuck in the big end for all I know. That's what I want you to find out."

He started up the engine and listened for a while. "She'll do," he said briefly. "Bring her in when you get back."

I thanked him and threw my grip in the co-driver's seat. The first file on my list concerned a young lad who'd broken his neck falling from the roof of a barn at Woodbridge in Suffolk, not far from an American Air Force base. So far as anybody knew, he'd never been in Suffolk before in his life, and nobody had any suggestions as to what the hell he'd been doing on the roof of a barn.

I headed out of London on the M3 for the Aldershot army complex.

The day was a fine one with a heroic blue sky and a smattering of high cloud draped across it in a herringbone pattern.

I missed the exit from the motorway and got lost twice before I found the officers' married quarters at Aldershot. I finally got directions from a tall chit of a boy wearing the insignia of the Parachute Regiment, a gold bracelet, and blond fuzz on his upper lip. He was the new breed of soldier, and he appalled me. He was courteous, diffident, and he could probably have shot my navel off at a thousand yards with his carbine.

The house Grant Levis had lived in was the usual single-story building with a dwarf patio surrounded by delicately patterned imitation stone blocks and a green sliver of lawn that had to be Astroturf.

Mrs. Levis answered the Avon chimes. She was a tall, bleached-blonde with a wonderful complexion, tapering fingers, and almost no breasts. She let me in without really bothering to listen to my explanations. It probably wouldn't have made any difference to her if I'd been selling encyclopedias or collecting for a mission to the Solomon Islands. I was someone to talk to, a feature of interest in a featureless day.

We talked in a living room understuffed with the kind of furniture that packs easily and conveniently. There was a shortage of the bric-a-brac that people with settled lives collect around them. The Levis taste was sound but conventional.

I brought the conversation round to Grant as soon as I thought I decently could. It turned out to be easier than I thought. Mrs. Levis didn't mind discussing the boy in the least. Even though he'd been an only son and had died less than six months before, she sounded detached, even complacent about his death, as though he'd finally done something remarkable. Listening to her, I got the impression he'd been quiet and secretive by nature, except when with a small group of friends who were fellow members of an amateur free-fall parachute team sponsored by the Army. According to Mrs. Levis, the group thought it no end of a laugh when he died falling twenty feet from the roof of a barn. I gathered she didn't consider them a very polished band of brothers.

I formed impressions as we talked, looking for clues to what had made Grant tick and the kind of life he led. Mrs. Levis wasn't much help. She seemed to have been only peripherally aware of him, and then mainly as a duty to discharge, an expense to meet, and a possible threat to the placid tenor of her days at postings round the world. I guessed at the boy's emotional rootlessness, surrounded by so many upheavals and so many adults engrossed in their own lives. I guessed, too, that it must have been hard for him at the end of his life to believe in the possibility of strong attachments. Even his friends had found only a joke in his death. That grated. I asked Mrs. Levis about them, but she shrugged.

"Really, I've no idea. None of them was the son of anybody in our circle. They were all army boys, of course, and some will have moved anyway to find jobs. There's so little work around here. Would you care to see Grant's room?"

It was an odd invitation. I wondered why she should expect me to want to. Then the answer came. I wondered how many members of Global's Army of Ferrets had been round before me.

"I'd like that," I said.

My impressions were strengthened by the room she took me to. She said it was just as Grant had left it. From inertia, I guessed, rather than sentiment. There was a single bed covered with a cheerful quilt knitted for him, Mrs. Levis told me, by a grandmother he'd never seen. There was a small utility desk, all tubular alloy and inferior-grade ply, a fitted wardrobe with drawers, and a shelf of textbooks. Mrs. Levis said the boy had had good school results but failed to find a university place because of government cutbacks at the wrong time. He'd been undergoing a late engineering apprenticeship at the time of his death. It seemed to me that his talents and inclinations had probably always been along those lines, only his parents had wanted some more prestigious and less greasy occupation for him.

Stacked beside the books and within easier reach of the bed was a pile of *Motorbike News* back numbers. I leafed through the top ones and asked more questions about Grant's hobbies. Again, she wasn't much help.

"The child was always so secretive," she complained. "Young men are sensitive, of course, and one doesn't wish to pry. He never let me or his father know what he was doing." She didn't say whether they'd ever asked.

"Did he tell you why he was going to Woodbridge on the day he died?" I asked.

She shook her head. "We had no idea he'd gone there at all until the police brought the news. But I knew it was somewhere special. I remember he was nervous and excited, like the time I took him up to London as a child to see the Oxford Street lights at Christmas." A flicker of something like maternal fondness passed across her face, though she was probably remembering the little black dress she'd bought in Beauchamp Place.

She was getting restive. The quilted bed was the only thing to sit on in the tiny room, and she wasn't the type to consider sitting on it while there was a strange man in the house. We left and walked back through the corridor to the living room. I remembered to ask her whether Grant had had any letters or telephone calls during the days before he died.

"It would be interesting to know what he was doing," I explained. "Perhaps someone wrote or telephoned an invitation or something."

She shook her head positively. "Grant knew absolutely nobody in that part of the world, and he rarely received telephone calls. Most of the people he knew lived around the camp, and he preferred to visit personally on that dreadful motorbike of his when he had the chance."

I bet he did, I thought.

"How about letters?" I reminded her.

"He received very few for the same reason." She looked at me sharply. "The few I found have already been given to your colleague. There was one that escaped my attention, though. It was a bill, and I had it in my own drawer. I came across it a few weeks ago. One had to check, you see, in case the child had left any debts behind when he died. That sort of thing soon gets around in an enclosed community. One doesn't wish to be embarrassed." Her voice, I suddenly noticed, was a refined and penetrating baritone.

She went to a drawer and laid her hand straight on the letter. I knew very few women who could do that, but I reminded myself that this was a military household.

"The odd thing is that I couldn't locate the sender afterwards," she complained. "I even checked with directory enquiries. Still, it seemed to be a first demand for payment, and no reminder has ever arrived. Perhaps Grant settled it up before *it* happened." She gave it to me. "Would you care for some coffee?"

"That would be nice," I said gratefully. She left the room, and I examined the letter. As she'd said, it was only a bill, a typed sheet with a typed business address in Southampton at the top. It told the receiver that his Ordnance Survey map order was enclosed and that the catalogue numbers of the other items he had enquired after were thirty-four and forty-seven respectively. It was signed with an indecipherable initial.

I folded the note and looked round the room while I waited for Mrs. Levis to return. I was sitting underneath the only conventional ornaments I'd seen in the house. They were a row of framed photographs of her husband, herself and what I supposed were fellow officers and their wives. The settings ranged from Ulster to the Trucial States.

Mrs. Levis returned with coffee. Instant with Coffeemate, of course. She noticed my interest and was more than happy to change the subject. She told me Captain Levis was a bomb disposal expert whose services the Government were lucky to retain, though they weren't likely to do so for much longer if they didn't improve their pay scales. She added that his work was sensitive and went on to tell me almost everything an IRA terror squad would have wanted to know about him, including the fact that he was currently posted to Aldershot as an instructor.

"That's why we're still here, you see. Frank's job is so specialized, it would be very hard to replace him. Normally, we would expect to have been posted away long before this. Actually, I'd like to go to Germany again. We have friends at Minden. Among the natives, I mean. Such a clean country, and such a lesson to us here."

I'd already decided that she was more interested in her husband's career and her own trials among the highly political circle of officers' wives than in anything else, her son's death included. I picked up the folded note from the bookseller.

"Do you mind if I hang on to this?" I asked.

She smiled wintrily and fitted a State Express 555 into a short, mannish cigarette holder.

"It hardly has any sentimental value," she said. The combination of ironic leer and the rictus imposed by gripping the cigarette holder in her teeth suddenly made me think she was going to solicit me.

"There's something funny about this insurance business, isn't there?" she demanded.

I swallowed a big mouthful of hot coffee. "How do you mean?"

"Well, you're not the first chap who's been round asking questions. Personally, I've never understood why Grant took out the policy in the first place. I mean, he was a fit young man, and young people always think they're going to live forever, don't they? He could hardly have known he was going to have a fatal accident. It really is most mysterious."

"You've had time to think about it," I said neutrally. "What explanation have you come up with?"

There was a sudden, bashful distaste in her manner. "Grant was such a *secretive* boy. I mean, when I turned his room out, there weren't even any girlie magazines hidden under piles of underwear, that sort of thing. I mean, young men do, don't they?"

"I wouldn't know, Mrs. Levis," I said, not quite truthfully. I wasn't interested in her vague sociosexual guesswork, but I was beginning to wonder about Captain Levis. "What are you trying to tell me?"

She shivered slightly. "It wasn't the first time Grant had been out on these mysterious trips. There'd been several others that year which he wouldn't explain. And why on earth should he take out an insurance policy naming as beneficiary some awful outsider, some young man his father and I had never heard of?" She hesitated. "Frankly, I wonder whether he was sexually odd."

I didn't know which shocked me more, the casual guesswork or the fact that she cheerfully admitted to having no way of knowing the answer to her own question. It was as though she had read my mind.

"Still, I don't see how he could have been homosexual, really. After all, I'm his mother. I would have known, wouldn't I? Is there some trouble about the claim still?"

I hurried to disappoint her. "No trouble at all, Mrs. Levis," I said. "If Global Alliance hadn't been fully satisfied, they would hardly have paid out."

"I suppose so." She was reluctant to accept the point, but the financial logic couldn't fail to impress her. I followed up my advantage.

"Nobody's querying the claim anyway. I'm just here to carry out a survey on the target market. Young people are getting much more insurance-conscious these days. The sample I've been given is random. It just happens that one or two of my subjects are deceased."

She nodded vaguely, disappointed. "I understand," she said. She probably thought a target market was some kind of end-of-season sale for small-arms instructors. "Would you like some more coffee?"

I declined and said good-bye as soon as I could. I waved from the sliver of green lawn, looking round the slickly uniform collection of buildings on the complex and wondering how many more young men like Grant Levis they were hiding.

The herringbone clouds of the morning had had treason in their hearts. The sky was now overcast, and a stiff wind had blown up. I drove northwest via Hereford, Wolverhampton, and, finally, Birmingham. I checked into the Holiday Inn, where a convention of bronzed travel agents and their secretaries were whooping it up and discussing ways to bring down the cost of package tours.

I was up early next day. I pushed on through the Midlands towards East Anglia, making more calls. I was back in North London by midafternoon. My last call was at St. John's Wood where I talked to a tiny, sorrowing widow called Jacobs. She called the district *Johanniswäldchen* and showed me a picture of her son who had still been a police cadet when they fished his body, face down, from a shallow tributary of the River Medway at Bockingford in Kent.

There was a sharp difference between Mrs. Jacobs and all the other people I had talked to in my grueling two days. I pinned it down as I drove home. Her son had been her only surviving relative, and she had actually loved him. She was still ravaged by grief and loss. I felt very sorry for her.

Two details puzzled me, though. Like Mrs. Levis, Mrs. Jacobs produced a letter from a bookseller who couldn't be traced after her son's death. The second was that I couldn't see why young Jacob Jacobs had written away for an Ordnance Survey map in the first place. Mrs. Jacobs' late husband had run a bookshop in the Charing Cross Road, and Mrs. Jacobs still owned it. Why hadn't the boy bought his map there? Throughout my trip, I had come across young men who had been completely secretive about their last journeys, even when their nearest and dearest had known they were going anywhere at all. I wondered what was so shameful and exciting about young Jacobs' last journey that made it necessary even to conceal from his old mother the fact that he was buying a map.

I left my car at the garage for Sean to look at and called by The Italian Joint for a late pizza lunch. Then I walked back to my flat, unpacked, and peeled an orange from the bowl on the refrigerator. The place smelled musty and depressed again. They should have warned me it was a flat that liked being lived in.

I ate the orange while listening to the messages on my telephone recording machine. There was nothing from Starkey Brothers, so I assumed Rose and Eric would be round later. While I waited, I reviewed the events of the last two days. I wasn't happy. In any business I get called into, there's a period at the beginning when all I can do is sift information, generate hypotheses, and just let the caverns of the subconscious get on with things. The big problem is to maintain a balanced attitude. If things don't go well, there's always a danger of losing conviction and momentum. On the other hand, there's also a danger of latching on to the first half-baked hypothesis that comes to mind and missing the real direction, just so as to keep the momentum going.

I'd expected right from the start to have trouble getting an insight into Sir Bryan Proctor's problem. I reminded myself that all I'd set out to do so far was wander round the territory under investigation. A territory which I knew had already been gone over at least several times by Sir Bryan's own Army of Ferrets. Still, I expected a mood, an impression of some kind, to have been created in my super-fertile brain. But there was nothing. The only impressions I had from the people I had visited were of indifference and resentment. Indifference towards the deaths of young men with most of their lives in front of them, or so it should have been. Resentment towards me because I was a Global Alliance representative, and they were all sure they should have got any insurance policy benefits going. Most of all, assuming I wasn't confronting a case of mass, cunningly concealed suicide, I hadn't picked up the faintest suggestion of why anyone should have wanted to kill a very large number of very ordinary young men.

I was starting another orange when the doorbell rang. I let Rose Panayioutou in. She flashed me a serious smile and walked straight through into the main room, unzipping the giant artwork bag she was never separated from for long. She took out a flat sheaf of transparent acetate sheets covered with chinagraph markings in different colors and began to pin the top one up on my cork memorandum wall.

"Provisional findings only," she said briskly. "I've spoken to your Mr. McVeigh. I don't like the sound of him. He gives me the creeps. I'm afraid there's nothing here that you probably don't know already."

"Rose, shut up for a minute. Would you like a drink?"

"No, thank you. I'm in a hurry."

"You're always in a hurry. Can't you wait till Eric gets here? I don't like repeating myself."

"Yes you do."

She had finished pinning up the acetate sheet. It was a graph with the current year's date over it and the usual range of statistically pointed mountains marching across thousands of tiny squares. Only I wasn't looking at the graph. I was looking at Rose. Today she was dressed in a severe two-piece suit with a raw silk blouse and her hair was piled up in a Grecian knot. For me, she could have launched a thousand super-tankers.

She tapped the chart with her plastic ruler. I shifted my attention and noticed that it was carefully marked. The vertical axis was divided numerically. The horizontal one had twelve divisions corresponding to months of the year.

"This," said Rose, "illustrates the chronological distribution of all deaths throughout Europe last year. Notice that the number starts around zero in the winter months, peaks during the summer and falls off towards the end of the year."

"Rose," I sighed, "it's what we would have expected. These were young men and they died outdoors."

Rose was unperturbed. "I know that, tiger. Suppose you wait before interrupting?" She was pinning up more acetate sheets. They all looked the same to me except that the year printed at the top was different each time.

She tapped the second chart. "Now notice that the same sort of pattern occurs in each of the other years. Yes, I know what you're thinking. I keep reminding myself that you're not numerate. I know you would expect it. But that's not the point."

She turned, frowning slightly. Amazingly, the frown didn't even begin to spoil the perfection of her face. "The point is, the pattern is more complex than you suppose. Let me get that in perspective before I go any further."

She turned back to her charts and used her ruler again. "The interesting thing is that there's a regular acceleration in the number of deaths towards the summer peak and the same sort of deceleration away from it. It's the same every year. The pattern is progressive, if you follow me."

"Explain it, Rose."

She pursed her beautiful lips as though blowing life a kiss. "I'll give you an analogy. If I were plotting similar graphs for the growth in men's salaries or women's pregnancies, say, over a period of years, I would expect to find such progressions."

"You mean men get richer and women more pregnant as the years roll by?"

"Precisely. The point is, the findings in both cases would reflect predictable causes operating on a progressive time-scale."

"Whereas the deaths we're investigating are supposed to be random except for a generally greater incidence during the summer months?"

"That's it. There's no suggestion in the graphs as to what the causes of a progressive time-scale might be in this case, but the pattern suggests there ought to be one."

"Thank you, Rose." I was making notes on my jotting pad. "Anything else?"

"Certainly." She was hauling another sheaf of acetate charts from her art bag and pinning them up one on top of another. This time the charts had outline maps of Great Britain drawn on them. Each map was covered with a different coloured rash of dots in varying degrees of concentration.

"These charts plot the geographical distribution of deaths last year in Britain alone. I've got equivalent ones for the preceding years. I'll make similar ones up for the other seven countries later." She tapped the top acetate sheet through which I could see the different colored dots on all the sheets underneath. "The first thing to notice is the remarkably even distribution of deaths over the country as a whole."

"Why remarkable?"

"Because, even allowing for the fact that all the deaths took place in the country, some parts of the country are more populous than others, so you'd expect a corresponding bias on the charts. There isn't any. As many people got killed in Central Wales last year, for example, as in Kent, Sussex and Hampshire put together."

"Go on."

"In addition, after making up my chronological charts, I decided to run a kind of geographical countercheck. I divided the year into four roughly equal parts and used a different colored chinagraph pencil to mark the location of each death according to the time of year."

"And?"

"The regular distribution remains perfectly regular. It's quite extraordinary." She removed the top sheet which had a mere handful of blue dots over it. "This shows the geographical distribution in the last quarter of last year, for example. The dots are near as damn it equidistant from each other."

"What do you make of it?"

"Nothing. Except that it shouldn't be allowed. Certain minor observations are, of course, possible."

She stopped and began to tap her impossibly white and even teeth with a sound like little tambourines.

"Such as, Rose?" I asked quietly, not wanting to break into her thoughts.

"Well, try this for laughs. These few dots are spread about as widely as possible, and Global's young men came from all parts of the country." She thought again for a moment. "If you were one of your client's policyholders, it seems likely that the later in the year you got killed, the farther you'd probably have to go for it." She nodded decisively. "I think that's a very interesting conclusion. If you don't mind, I'll go back and work out a proper correlation between the time factor and the distance each victim travelled to the place where he was killed."

"Do that." I stood up. "You've done well. Keep in touch and let me know how you get on."

She smiled with pleasure. She had unloaded her geographical charts for the other three years and was zipping up her art bag again.

"How are you getting on yourself?" she asked.

"I'm not. Eric will be here later. Maybe he's got something."

"Don't worry about it, tiger. You'll unravel the mystery. You always do. Look after yourself." She stopped and flushed slightly. The last time she'd said that, she'd kissed me. I knew she remembered it, but she didn't kiss me again. She smiled and let herself out of the flat.

I telephoned Starkey Brothers' offices. Little Miss Malone took my call. She had a voice of Irish camphor and dried rose leaves. She'd been the brothers' office manager for years and should have been pensioned off long ago to run a tea-shoppe on the south coast. She told me Eric wasn't back but had telephoned to say he would be calling by in a couple of hours.

I thanked her, changed and jogged my way to the big glass and ferroconcrete YMCA behind New Oxford Street. The sky was chilly, and fat spots of leaden rain were smacking down onto the pavements. The Easter rush was already under way and Tottenham Court Road was full of tourists, some of them English.

I swam twenty lengths of the club pool until my shoulders creaked, dozed briefly under the pool-side solarium and took a shower. At the end, I hadn't discovered the secret of eternal youth, but I felt better.

Eric was waiting on the stairs when I got back. He looked terrible. There was stubble over his face, and the remaining button was missing from his jacket. I let us both in, and he slumped in a chair while I fetched the Guinness from the refrigerator. Eric tore the tab off his as though he were wringing its neck. He leaned back with a gasp.

"Christ," he groaned. "Don't ever give me a job like that again."

"Bad, was it?" I sat down in the other chair and prepared to listen carefully. Eric had unique talents that all stemmed from the fact that he was a marvelous man. His brain would never win him a fellowship at All Soul's, but his good heart made all sorts and conditions of people open up to him in a way they wouldn't with their own mothers, while his innocent good sense retained impressions with uncanny fidelity.

He drank deeply until he was recovered. His distaste was almost but not quite comic.

"You know," he said, "I get to deal with a lot of unpleasant people in my job. Sometimes I think I'm getting too inured to it all." He shook himself and smiled slightly. "Have you ever met a man who throttled his own wife?"

I admitted I hadn't.

"Well, I have. They tell me most murders happen within the bosom of the family. I can believe it." He crushed his empty Guinness can slowly and threw it on the table. "But choking your old lady to death is at least one way of recognizing the fact that she exists."

"What are you getting at?" I asked patiently.

"I'm getting at the fact that I've just met about the most self-centered and callous lot of people I've ever met in my life," he exploded. "Nothing illegal, no commandments broken, you understand. Some of them even go to church on Sundays, probably with clear consciences. But look for any trace of ordinary human warmth and you can forget it."

Remembering his sprawling and chaotic household as I'd last seen it in Nightingale Lane, I thought I understood his anger. His ménage had its faults, but it made a litter of kittens look aloof in comparison.

He hauled a note pad from a jacket pocket and leafed through it. "Listen to this," he demanded. "A young kid living in Northampton.

His old man works for one of the private security firms. Works all the hours God sends, that is, and earns a fortune. No need for it, though. I mean, I talked to him, and he doesn't even have to do overtime. You want to know the reason? He can't stand his family. He used to be a merchant seaman. He spawned the kid and his three sisters on shore leaves. After the Navy invalided him out with an ulcer, he found he just couldn't take his family except in small doses. Lost the knack, if you know what I mean. So now he spends as much time at work as he can and actually feels noble about it. The wife's bored out of her skull, of course. She spends half her days blowing the old man's money at bingo and the other half getting her leg over with an old-age pensioner down the road. An old-age pensioner, I swear to God. I got that from the neighbors, and it wasn't malice, either. The sisters are always out with their boyfriends and only come home for a bite to eat and a change of knickers. What sort of life did the kid lead, I ask you?"

He leafed through a few more pages. "There's one here whose old man runs an export-import business in Lincolnshire. Exactly the same pattern only a lot richer, so it's not a class thing. He spends all his time in places like Rotterdam and Duesseldorf when he's not in his office or golfing with clients. The wife spends her days chairing W.I. meetings and doing good works. The kid was an only kid, and the Filipino maid, who speaks about six words of English, was the only human face the boy saw around the home from one week's end to the other. Think about it."

I'd never seen Eric so angry. Or perhaps he was just depressed and tired. We'd both covered a lot of ground.

"We're looking for a pattern of some kind, Eric," I reminded him gently. "Something that accounts for why they all died. You're telling me these kids all lived the same sort of life?"

"Lived the same sort of life?" he exploded again. "Didn't get a bloody chance to, you mean." He subsided slowly. "I'd put it different. I'd say their families killed them all in the same way."

"Do you mean that literally?"

"Of course I bloody don't. I mean they were all driven to it in the same way. We've worked together before, boss. You know what it's like when we're trying to build up a picture of someone we've never seen.

We get impressions. Well, I've got impressions I don't like. I feel sorry for these kids."

"I understand."

I tried to steer him like a hand-held camera. His impressions were no good when he thought too hard.

"Did any of the people you talked to actually know where the boys were going on the days they died?"

He shook his head. "Most of them couldn't have cared less and didn't ask."

"How about the others?"

"Some got lied to. Some got told to mind their own business. All those kids were keeping something dark."

Eric was like a medium at a séance. When he was in the right mood you still had to interpret carefully.

"What were they keeping dark, Eric? How do you know they lied?"

He looked surprised. "Even when they said where they were going, their bodies weren't found in the places they mentioned. I checked. It's not something I was told." He thought for a long moment. "They were in a funny sort of mood. It's as though they were going off to rob a bank or join the Foreign Legion, or something." He blinked. "Have you got any more of that Guinness?"

The séance was over, but I'd got as many notes as I had from Rose Panayioutou. I fetched the last can and threw it to him. He drank dexterously.

"Anything else?" I asked.

"Only one detail. It puzzled me, though."

"What is it?"

He wiped froth from his chin. "You gave me all the kids in the North to check over," he said accusingly. "I fitted in a batch of three late last night. They were all the same kind, from the same sort of families. They lived in Liverpool, Huyton and Manchester. I suppose it must be coincidence, but they all had *The Times* on order. There were some others earlier."

"Are you sure?"

"Yes. It's not as if they were secret intellectuals or anything. The *Sun* page three was more their line. Their families used to kid them about it, but they kept taking it."

"Funny choice of paper," I commented.

"That's right. But if it were important, there could have been more."

"How do you mean?"

"Well, as I said, their families ribbed them, and these boys led private sorts of lives. So others of them might not have had the paper actually delivered. They might have picked it up on their way to work, say."

"It's possible." I remembered seeing *The Times* folded over the back of a chair in the Levis household.

"There's another thing. I worked with a bloke in the newspaper business once. He told me the actual circulation of a paper's always bigger than the nominal circulation. Our lads might not even have had their own copies. Maybe they read the boss's at work or dropped into the public library."

"It's worth checking," I agreed.

Eric looked pessimistic, as though he wished he hadn't spoken. "I suppose you want me to do the checking?"

"Please. Take my folders as well as your own. You should be able to do most of the work from your office. There's something else I want you to look into." I told him about the letters from bookshops I'd found and showed them to him.

He turned them over, mystified. "Can't see what you're on about," he grunted. "They look pretty much the same, but they're that sort of letter, aren't they? Doesn't mean much if you can't trace the firms who sent them. Small businesses are always moving or going broke."

"But why go to small businesses in the first place?" I said. I told him how young Jacob Jacobs hadn't even ordered through his own widowed mother's firm.

Eric nodded, comprehending. "I get it. Our lads wanted to keep their final trips secret, so they sent off to small shops where nobody knew them."

"That's right. And for that reason, some of the booksellers may remember the order."

"Why are you interested?"

"Because both letters refer to other books our lads wanted to know about, only they don't give the titles. I don't get the impression our boys were big readers as a rule, do you?"

"I follow you. They had these trips on their minds when they ordered the maps, but we still don't know what the trips were all about. You think the titles of the other books might give us an idea?"

"Right. So you get on to tracing the two addresses we've got and see if you can find any more letters. When you get results, call the shops and ask what books they've got with those reference numbers."

"Gotcha. I'll get onto it right away."

"Let Miss Malone know where you are," I said. "We'll keep in touch through her. Don't forget, I want results as fast as you can get them."

The telephone rang just after Eric had left. Luckily I recognized McVeigh's voice. Like a lot of expensively educated people, he made a point of being rude and never announcing himself.

"I take it you had forgotten about Don's exhibition," he drawled. "I'm leaving for it now with Charles Omphrey."

"Of course I'd forgotten," I lied. "I'll meet you there."

I hung up and changed into an old denim suit.

It isn't the intellectuals' uniform anymore. On the other hand, it took *beaujolais primeur* in its stride. It had had plenty of practice.

I waited half an hour before I left. I smoked in a chair, thinking over the afternoon. I was more cheerful now than when I'd got back from my field trip. It wasn't that the problem was any clearer. I just felt that it was at least taking on some sort of shape that I could understand. Of all the things I'd heard, the most interesting was Eric's insight into the mood of Sir Bryan Proctor's policyholders when they took their last trips. They'd all been keyed up in the same way, he'd said, nervous but excited. It chimed with what I'd felt, only I hadn't realized it at the time. I didn't suppose for a moment that they had any idea they were going to get killed. But I was instinctively certain that they had all left for the same sort of reason. I thought that if I could find what that reason was, I'd be more than halfway to finding out what had happened to them.

I left the flat, pinning all the notes I had taken to the cork wall beside Rose's charts first. I locked the flat up carefully behind me.

I went down the stairs, passing Harry on my way out. With his empty sleeve pinned across his chest as he bent forward to pick up letters, he looked like a flunky executing a courtly bow.

"Why do they bother?" he complained, stacking the letters on the shelf of an alcove by the main door. "This bloke Yeend hasn't lived here for years. I keep telling them. The council's been round to cut him off twice." He smoothed a streak of hair across his balding head. "I tell you what, the system's thick. You can tell it things till you're blue in the face. It just doesn't listen."

I agreed with him and let myself out into Henrietta Street. It was still barely light, and the air was grey and muggy. A small crowd had clustered round the door of the gallery with *sekt* glasses in their hands. They were huddled together so that other people had to step out into the road to get past them. A few Scandinavians looking for a drink before curtain time stared in a puzzled sort of way. I recognized some of the faces in the crowd, mostly from advertising and publishing businesses in the area. A pair of cold brown eyes dressed in exquisitely cut linen met mine, half-recognized me and slid away again.

I spent some minutes looking at the exhibition photographs displayed in the outside window of the gallery. A printed guide taped to the glass explained that they had all been shot during the course of a recent South American coup d'état. They were a new style of photography, halfway between high art and photojournalism. One picture caught my eye. There was a tank in the foreground, part of its tracks blown off. A dead crewman slumped halfway out of the turret, a branching stream of his blood elegantly counterpointing the actual branches of a splintered tree that framed the top half of the shot.

I turned away in faint disgust. Young Proctor must have taken chances to get these shots, but they weren't newsmen's snaps taken with a motorized Nikon. They had the tasteful fluency of advertising pack shots. I didn't object to pornography, but I preferred pubic hair to smashed flesh and spent Oerlikon shells.

Inside, the gallery was stifling. The room had been divided up by rows of head-high panels with exhibits hung from them so that most of the visitors were crushed into makeshift alcoves. I recognized Don Proctor standing by the bar. His face was thin and bony, with vivid blue eyes set too close together. He had a short fringe of beard and his hair was cut pudding-basin style. He looked like a corrupt missionary of the early church. I noticed he was talking to a group of men who contrasted sharply with the general run of the clientele. They looked Junior Chamber of Commerce types. Their conservatively well-cut suits tended to have two vents in the back, and their hair curled primly over the collars of Jermyn Street shirts.

I couldn't see McVeigh or Charles Omphrey, so I accepted a glass of *sekt* from a harrassed girl wearing toy trains in her ears and edged across to the quietest part of the gallery where one of the guests was actually examining the pictures. She was a tall girl in an ethnic frock, with glowing copper hair in fat braids and big, startled eyes. She was slim and broad-shouldered, but the androgynous aspect of her stopped there. She had big breasts that swung easily from a good bone structure, and her skin glowed with health. Her feet were planted in a sturdy, at ease position, and she was tapping her glass against strong, even teeth. She turned as I came up and stared angrily through me.

"He's a bloody voyeur," she complained. "I don't care how good his technique is."

"A voyeur usually hides in a safe place to watch the action," I pointed out. "Proctor's at least got guts. Taking some of these shots must have been dangerous."

She focused on me. "What's guts got to do with it?" she demanded, conversationally, but loud. A few heads turned towards us as though we were having a lovers' quarrel.

"Men always overrate guts. Proctor just likes peering at human suffering through his expensive bloody lens."

"Annie, my love," a voice chipped in behind me. "Don't you know people never discuss the exhibits on these occasions? It's extremely bad form."

I turned. He was a thin man with a narrow, sly face and a yellow waistcoat over a narrow chest. "We've met before," he said humorously, to me, "though you probably don't remember. My name's Ben Campbell."

"I'm Annie Threlfall," the girl said.

Campbell looked at her with alarm. "You mean you've even been getting into aesthetic arguments with a total stranger? Annie, my love, you never follow the rules, do you?"

I didn't recognize him, but I decided already that I didn't like him.

The girl seemed to read part of my thoughts. "Ben's an art director at the agency which does the Global Alliance advertising," she explained. "He likes Proctor's photography. The fact that Proctor is the son of his biggest client has nothing to do with it, of course."

"While you, Annie my love, are the estranged wife of the agency account director, and you don't like Proctor's photography," Campbell said spitefully. "Which also has nothing to do with it, I suppose."

I looked round. McVeigh and a huge, shambling man I recognized as Charles Omphrey had just entered the gallery.

"Excuse me," I said. I started to squeeze past Campbell.

"Must you go?" The girl's eyes were candidly appealing. I wondered whether she fancied me or just didn't want to be left alone with Campbell. She leaned across to wave at someone, and her breasts brushed against my arm. It might have been accidental, but I didn't think so.

"There's someone I've got to talk to," I said. "Maybe we'll meet later."

McVeigh noticed me coming and changed course. Omphrey shook hands languidly when he was within range.

"What do you think of it all?" he demanded affably above the noise and chatter. His eyes were open and friendly, and there was a lot of Trinity College Dublin in his accent. "Isn't it all very like the Young Master?" People were still arriving, and we were being pushed into a corner. I could smell that the beautiful girl on my left hadn't washed in days.

McVeigh raised his voice disparagingly. "Don is a hired camera. Most of his clients are fashion magazines who pay him to take pictures of girls dressed in the skins of almost extinct wild animals. You're supposed to appreciate the technique, not the unpleasant aspects of the subject matter."

"But are you?" Omphrey asked cunningly. He dropped a heavy shoulder to resist a sudden press of people heading our way. A harassed man was trying to get past with a tray of *sekt* glasses held above his head. Omphrey deftly filched three of the glasses and handed them round. "I'd say the disparity between elegant technique and unpleasant subject matter was rather deliberate and quite typical."

The man with the tray noticed the sudden lightness of his load and glared round furiously. Omphrey met his eyes with a grave, disarming smile.

"I wonder what the old man would have made of it all," he bawled in my ear.

"What old man?" I shouted back.

"Don's grandfather. The Major. He was a professional soldier of the old school. The Proctors were always soldiers. Sir Bryan going into trade was bad enough."

"The Major couldn't have hated insurance more than Sir Bryan hates photographers," McVeigh put in, squeezing closer. The girl who used more scent than soap was pressed among the three of us, listening interestedly. A tendril of her hair was dangling in Omphrey's glass.

"The Proctors were always good haters, too," Omphrey countered cheerfully. "It's part of their military heritage. Of course, photographing war's a lot safer than waging it." He removed the tendril of hair from his glass and sucked it. The girl wrinkled her nose at him.

"We can't talk in here," McVeigh shouted impatiently. "It's impossible. Let's go."

Don Proctor was definitely the photographer of the moment. Getting out of his exhibition was even harder than getting in. When we finally emerged onto the pavement, I looked back through the window, hoping to get a glimpse of the girl with the bronze hair. The only face I recognized was Campbell's. He waved at me ironically. I stepped back and trod on a knot of Japanese ogling the outside display of pictures. They rippled apart and re-formed behind me like a shoal of cichlids on a reef.

McVeigh and Omphrey were waiting up the road where McVeigh had left his car. He was putting his topcoat inside and locking up.

"We're early," McVeigh said. "But we'll eat now. It's quieter." He set off at a brisk walk up Garrick Street.

"I thought you wanted to talk to the Young Master." Omphrey sounded discontented. He was the man who hated to leave parties and free drinks.

"We can talk to him later. The show will go on for ages, and he's taking a smaller crowd back to his studio afterwards. You won't miss anything." There was bad temper in the sneer.

We ate at Le Beaujolais where I was a member. The owner greeted me with well-rehearsed Gallic fire, and McVeigh seemed to take offence at that, too. He said nothing until we were seated at a quiet table and had ordered our aperitifs. He took out one of his expensive cigars from a curved tortoiseshell case and scowled at me over it.

"As you know, Charles was appointed by Sir Bryan to chair the committee investigating Global's losses." He lit the cigar carefully and sneered at Omphrey over the top of it. "Charles is now, of course, a worried man. Not least because his committee has failed to produce any results."

Omphrey glanced at him before turning to me. He was an equably self-confident man. If McVeigh was trying to rile him, he'd have to try harder.

"Of course I'm worried," Omphrey said calmly. "So should any man be with a grain of sense and responsibility. Our business concerns a large number of young men who all died violently in recent years. It's an alarming phenomenon, even setting aside the fact that they were Global Alliance policyholders."

He made them sound like casualties of the Battle of the Somme. Our drinks arrived at that moment, and we raised our glasses in silent respect to their memory. The girl who served us wore a flame-colored blouse kept up by small, pointed breasts that looked capable of gouging someone's eyes out. Omphrey inspected them closely until she'd gone away again.

"Violence, of course, is a feature of the age we live in," he resumed. "It comes in all forms, from political extremism to football hooliganism.

In fact, violence is a distinctive feature of all cultures at times of social crisis. People lose faith in their ability to change things peaceably, and of course, it's a literally vicious circle. The more violence seems to be the only effective instrument of self-expression, the more prone people are to exercise it. It becomes a norm of social behavior, a mode of expression to be acquired and admired by the young."

McVeigh sighed. "Charles, we didn't come to hear your vox pop philosophizing. Our objective is simple. As a company we wish to stop losing a lot of money and avoid extremely unfavorable publicity. Perhaps you could concentrate your mind a little."

"Perhaps you could open yours a little?" Omphrey's big face was so Irishly affable that it was impossible for McVeigh to take offence. "These young men lived in a real world even if you don't. It is unreasonable to expect them to behave outside a context of general influences."

He turned back to me. "We are, of course, certain that these young men did not die accidentally. The question is, how did violence happen to them, and why?"

"Morally certain," McVeigh sneered. "What use is your certitude? Will it save us one penny? What evidence have you produced so far that enables us to act?"

Omphrey ignored him. "Apart from that general worry, of course, I have a more specific one. It concerns Sir Bryan," he said quietly. "I gather you know he is ill? Perhaps you do not know how ill. It was my idea that I should chair this committee. It puts me in a position to keep a close watch on him without arousing speculation. It was also my idea that he should transfer as much of the day-to-day running of Global business as possible to Ted here. A *de facto* promotion to which, I might add, his tetchy personality seems to have expanded more than adequately."

It was high time to pour oil on troubled waters. "I've only just been put onto this investigation, but, statistical evidence apart, there's reason to think that a conspiracy of some kind must exist."

McVeigh dragged his venomous attention away from Omphrey.

"What evidence?" he demanded.

I summarized what Rose Panayioutou had told me. "I don't understand these things myself," I said, "but I gather Miss Panayioutou just doesn't believe the perfectly regular geographical distribution of deaths can be random. She also seems to think it necessary to infer some causal explanation for the timing of them."

"Does she have any idea what the cause might be?"

"That's my job, and so far, all I've got is a few hints." I turned to Omphrey. "You've been on this investigation since it started. I've just spent a couple of days visiting relatives of some of the casualties. I was wondering whether your experience tallied with mine."

Omphrey declined the offer of one of my cigarettes. He selected one of his own from a leather case, one of the exotic Russian kind. Le Beaujolais' excellent Arbroath Smokies had come and gone, and we were waiting for our main course.

"Tallied in what regard?" he asked politely.

"I get the impression that these lads must have planned their final journeys well in advance, because some of them at least ordered Ordnance Survey maps by post. By the way," I turned to McVeigh, "I assume the maps were found on their bodies. Your summary report made no mention of it."

"Didn't it?" McVeigh's face was innocent. "Ah, yes, I remember. Maps were found in most instances. I said as much in an appendix to my report. Haven't you received it?"

"No."

"My dear chap, I'll make sure you get a copy tomorrow. But I hardly imagine it's significant. We know these young men travelled to out-of-the-way places with which they were unfamiliar. Ordnance Surveys would be the obvious choice of map to obtain."

I knew why he hadn't sent the appendix report. Hearing about the arrival of maps through the post should have been one of the first results of my own investigation. McVeigh wanted a quick measure of whether I was up to my job.

He glanced at his watch. It was the kind that probably congratulated him on his birthday as well as told him the time.

"The service in this club of yours is slow," he complained.

"It's a good dining club with a reputation to keep up," I said. "They cook to order. It takes time."

The *patron* had caught my look and taken the hint. Our *entrecôtes* were arriving now. Omphrey couldn't resist testing the temperature of his plate. It was hot enough. He sucked his finger and eyed appreciatively the thin, melting slices of marrow and perfect *vigneronne* sauce that smothered his steak. We cut the shop talk until vegetables had been selected and served.

Omphrey relished his first forkful before turning regretfully back to business.

"You were wondering if my experience tallied with yours," he reminded me.

"Yes. Given the fact that your policyholders planned their trips in advance, I still get the impression they left in a hurry. Do you agree?"

Omphrey nodded. "Yes. It had occurred to me. In fact, there are several pieces of evidence to suggest that some of the lads had to cancel other important engagements at the last moment. It's one of the reasons why I find it difficult to rule out Sir Bryan's notion of a conspiracy."

"Explain that." McVeigh had decided to take an interest again.

"The apparent contradiction suggests that the young men knew their journeys were to be undertaken—but not when," Omphrey said. "It suggests they were informed of the timing at the last moment. That, in turn, implies somebody to inform."

"It suggests more," I said. "It suggests that whoever set the timing had enough clout to enforce it."

"Suppositions, suppositions," McVeigh grunted. He was wiping his lips regretfully. Even he had enjoyed his dinner. "When are we going to get some cold facts to support them? I must remind you gentlemen that time is running out. If your suppositions are right, it seems to me the urgent task is to find who is issuing instructions and how. If they were conveyed personally or by telephone, of course, there may be nothing to go on."

"They may have arrived by letter," I said. "If the sender was in a position to issue instructions, he could always order letters to be destroyed."

McVeigh shook his head. "Why take the risk? Besides, we've had a good look at any mail left behind. There's nothing anywhere that could be construed as instructions."

Nobody wanted a dessert, so I had ordered coffee and three glasses of old plum brandy from the Perigord district. When the waiter had gone, I told them about the letters from bookshops that I had come across. McVeigh wasn't interested.

"I've got a few on file, too," he said. "There's nothing remarkable about them. They're the usual sort of thing a bookshop sends out with the invoice."

"For Christ's sake, why didn't you say?" I demanded. "I want those letters if you don't mind."

McVeigh looked amused. "Certainly, if you wish. I'll send them with the appendix report. Why are you interested?"

I explained about the references to catalogue numbers in the letters I'd found.

"Your policyholders presumably didn't know they were going to die when they went on their last journeys," I said. "So what *did* they think was going to happen to them? It would help if we knew what was on their minds when they ordered the maps. The subjects of the books they enquired about may tell us. I've got an assistant on the job tracing the bookshops."

McVeigh looked interested. "It's worth looking at," he admitted.

"By the way, were there any invoices?" I asked.

"I beg your pardon?"

"You said the letters were the usual sort of thing bookshops send out with invoices. Were there any invoices?"

He thought. "We didn't come across any. I imagine they were sent back with the remittances."

I sighed. "McVeigh, you remind me of the prime minister who showed his ignorance of the working classes by suggesting they ought to give up eating overripe pheasant."

McVeigh looked irritated. "What do you mean?"

The owner of Le Beaujolais arrived to present the bill. McVeigh made no move to pay, so I signed and asked for it to be put on my account. I waited until the owner had gone.

"The lads we are investigating weren't the type to settle bills promptly and by check," I pointed out. "I also assume you have no record of receipts of any of the books they enquired about arriving after their deaths? There's something I don't understand about this bookshop business."

McVeigh was watching Omphrey struggle into his huge, fur-collared coat, making no attempt to help. "Is there anything you want me to do?"

"Yes. Apart from making sure that there are no other important bits of information you somehow overlooked, I think you ought to program Jake for a list of policyholders at risk this year."

McVeigh looked unhappy. "You want to investigate them?" he asked.

"Not if I can help it. If there really is a conspiracy, I don't want to alert the people behind it any more than you do."

"Then why the list?"

"Because it may be the only way to stop the deaths. I've got to find out what these young men thought they were up to when they took their final journeys. There may not be enough to go on, and I can't question the dead."

McVeigh still hesitated. He didn't like the idea. "I'll program the computer," he said reluctantly, "but don't make a move without consulting me first." He glanced at his watch again. "And now, if you don't mind, we've had enough idle chatter. It's time we got back to Proctor's exhibition. I've got work to do."

"You mean you'd like to get a word in edgeways?" Omphrey suggested waspishly. It was an old maid's jibe, but it seemed to put McVeigh in good humor again.

"So long as you both understand."

It had turned cold, but a knot of people still stood around outside the gallery. I could see Don Proctor's tonsure through the gloom among the group of well-dressed friends he'd been with earlier. I looked for, but didn't see, the girl called Annie.

Charles Omphrey greeted Proctor like Polonius accosting young Hamlet and introduced us.

"We've met before," Proctor said briefly. His intense blue eyes looked through me. He was wearing a heavy, open-necked peasant *blouson* with a loop in place of a buttonhole at the neck, and a suit of thin, mustard-colored cord. "You were with a merchant banker."

I didn't like that, especially since I didn't remember the occasion myself. I've worked for a lot of merchant bankers, of course. They're a natural for the kind of service I offer.

"He is working for your father at the moment," McVeigh put in smoothly.

"Really? In what capacity?" Proctor didn't look at him. His eyes were on me. I remembered McVeigh telling me he'd been involved in some shady business ventures before turning to photography. His well-dressed friends also assessed me silently.

"Mainly personnel selection," I lied, "I've looked round your exhibition. It's very good."

"It's brilliant," Proctor agreed. He made no attempt to introduce his companions. He turned slightly. "Annie, my love," he called.

A group of late leavers had come out of the gallery to the pretentious tinkling of an old brass corner-shop bell. The girl with the toy trains in her ears was locking up after them. Annie smiled when she saw me. I was relieved to see no sign of Ben Campbell, her art director friend.

"Annie, we're having a small party back at the studio. You'll come, I hope?"

Annie hesitated and glanced at me. I smiled encouragingly, and she smiled at Proctor.

"I'd love to."

"Good. We'll find space for you in one of our cars." He turned back to Omphrey, McVeigh, and me. "You're invited, too."

"So good of you," Omphrey murmured.

Proctor blinked and turned on his heels. It was as though he had pressed a shutter in his mind and fixed a memory forever.

I walked back to the Rolls with McVeigh and Omphrey. McVeigh was lost in thought and didn't speak as he drove off northwards up the Charing Cross Road.

"Don's an only child, isn't he?" I asked. Omphrey nodded somberly in the reflected neon glow of Foyles's bookshop.

"What happened to his mother?" It occurred to me that I'd never heard anyone mention any member of the family apart from Don, Sir Bryan and the Major.

There was a silence. I might have been wrong, but I thought I saw Omphrey glance at McVeigh. McVeigh, though, was engrossed in driving the big car.

"Sir Bryan married soon after the war. Lady Proctor died when Don was still a child." Omphrey sighed mournfully as though he'd just discovered that his richest patient had a terminal ailment. I was intrigued. Maybe Lady Proctor had been a patient, too.

"What happened?"

"She was American, a Quaker from one of the southern states. A beautiful and charming lady. She died in a car accident."

"Tell him the whole story, Charles." McVeigh was harsh and mocking. "He's practically one of the family now."

We were stuck in the usual crawl on the approaches to Marble Arch. Omphrey polished his nose with the back of his hand.

"Sir Bryan was an ambitious young man. It might not be fair to say his marriage was one of convenience, but it certainly did him no harm."

McVeigh laughed. "The Major had just died, and Sir Bryan was strapped for cash. The creditors were into him, and Caroline was as rich as Rockefeller. You're damned right the marriage did him no harm."

It disconcerted me to see McVeigh's urbane mask slip. It was like hearing a duchess tell a dirty joke.

"The marriage wasn't happy," Omphrey admitted. "In fact, it was probably a dead letter when Caroline entered into an unfortunate association with a young man who was about to take up some appointment in one of the then new African states. There is no doubt she would have left Sir Bryan to follow him. Fortunately or unfortunately, it never came to that. The accident intervened."

"How?"

Omphrey shrugged his big shoulders. With his coat on, there wasn't much room for me even in the back of a Rolls. "Mechanical failure of some kind on a lonely road at night," he said. "The car turned over in a ditch. Caroline and her friend died before help could reach them. It was at night and in the middle of winter, you see."

I thought of the lovers lying trapped and injured, waiting for exposure and the loss of blood to finish them off.

"Sir Bryan was desolated, of course," McVeigh chuckled caustically, "but rallied with the help of the huge fortune Caroline left him in her will. Rumor had it she was about to change the will before she died."

We were waiting in the outside lane for the lights to change so that we could turn off the Bayswater Road. I thought about what I'd just heard. Most of what I knew about Sir Bryan Proctor's life was in the public domain through the huge newspaper coverage of him. I knew he'd got a First in mathematics and a Double Blue at Oxford. Afterwards he'd had what used to be called a good, if peaceful, war as a cryptographer. He belonged, naturally, to several very select clubs. Somehow, I'd never seen him as a murderer.

Omphrey might have been reluctant to start blowing dust off skeletons in the Proctor family closet, but he'd got his second wind by now.

"Don was brought up by a succession of nannies. He got the last of them pregnant. He turned to photography after some dubious business ventures."

We had drawn up outside a house set back in a quiet mews. The whole place was brilliantly lit, and the cobbles were lined with a lot of expensive cars. Proctor's Spanish boy, dressed in a dinner suit considerably smarter than the one I sometimes wore, stood on the steps by the door greeting late arrivals.

"He seems to have done pretty well since," I commented.

"He does, indeed," McVeigh agreed in a tone of singular contempt.

A dark-haired beauty who was probably the Spanish boy's sister removed Omphrey's coat and Homburg hat. Their father gave us drinks from a tray just inside the door. We climbed a short flight of stairs into a hall that held several hundred people and still didn't look crowded. Don Proctor's idea of a select gathering wasn't modest.

The floor was on different levels, artfully lit to create strange perspectives and vistas. Illuminated alcoves were filled with lifelike dummies dressed with meticulous attention to detail in the uniforms of ancient wars and draped with tattered banners. The center of the hall was dominated by a marble equestrian statue of some general of the Peninsula campaign. I saw Proctor and his well-dressed friends grouped beside the plinth as though posed for a portrait.

McVeigh excused himself and went to talk to Proctor. Omphrey and I cradled our glasses and dipped pretzels in a sour-cream dressing with chives and cheese.

"Do you know who they are?" I asked, nodding towards the group round the plinth.

Omphrey glanced at them, brushing a pretzel crumb from his collar. "Business friends," he said briefly. "I've met a couple of them."

I sipped my drink. It was a good champagne, a very good champagne, imported from Maxim's, I'd noticed from the label. It was just the right temperature. I wondered how the old Spaniard did it with so many guests to cater for.

"I was interested in your views on violence in modern society," I said insincerely. I wanted him to talk, and Omphrey wasn't the kind who needed much encouragement.

"Were you now? Dear boy, you surprise me." There was ironic good humor in his eyes. "Somehow I assumed you shared Ted's view of me as a drunken guru to Sir Bryan Proctor."

He drained his glass and accepted another from the old Spanish waiter who happened to be passing. When he turned back, his expression was oddly pained and thoughtful.

"Dear boy, you must understand that what passes for democracy and culture these days is a sham and a fraud. As a result, we have no true morality."

I tried to look serious. "That's a bit sweeping, isn't it?"

Omphrey ignored me. "Democracy is the illusion of power conferred by an establishment upon an urban proletariat that has proved harder to control than the agricultural peasantry which preceded it. However, the concession is only an illusion. In return for the privilege of marking crosses on a ballot form every few years, common people are persuaded to continue sweating on behalf of others whose interests are certainly not their own."

He drank deeply. "Much the same can be said for what passes as popular culture among us. The state does not believe in any education other than social potty-training. Young people are culturally illiterate as a result."

"You mean those?" I was looking at a group of punk rockers in a corner of the big hall, their combined hair colors forming a human Rorschach test.

"Those," Omphrey said with contempt, "are well-born flotsam masquerading as punks. The genuine article is at least more interesting, even if it is already merging into the tawdry gallery of past fashion. Popular culture has no power of expression. It has no roots and no autonomy. A pop guitarist could no more mend his own equipment than he could fly Concorde. The music he makes profits the same leisure interests who sell him his drugs and his jeans. The young are allowed the illusion of autonomous culture because there are establishment profits to be made from it."

He stared morosely into his glass which was already empty again. There was something almost, but not quite, comic about him.

"The young are aware, of course, that they are manipulated and that there is nothing they can do about it. Violence appears increasingly as their only escape. Especially since the death of genuine morality has removed any effective brake upon it."

"Has anyone ever called you a Bolshevik and an anti-democratic Élitist?" I enquired politely.

"Lots of people," he replied happily.

"Is Sir Bryan aware of your views?"

"It's hard to know exactly how much he is aware of these days," Omphrey said more cautiously.

I took two more glasses that happened to be passing on a tray. I wanted his tongue really loose.

"You say he's very ill," I said. "How ill is very ill, Charles?"

Omphrey's eyes were already glazing slightly. He was mopping his forehead with a red handkerchief the size of a small landing strip. It was getting hot in the big room.

"He may survive until his ninety-fourth birthday, or he may be on his cosmic travels by tomorrow morning. I am not being whimsical. There is no reason why, given luck, he should not live out a normal span. Unfortunately, he has a history of illness that now puts his aging constitution more at risk from unpleasant upheavals than would be the case with most men. Events, moreover, are conspiring against him."

I drew him out further on the subject. He was now a mine of information, and I learned things about the effects of various ailments that I hadn't known before.

"All this has been very interesting, Charles," I said when he was through, "but going back to our earlier topic, I have to agree with Ted. I don't see how the decline of Western civilization accounts for the troubles Global Alliance is having."

Omphrey was now rocking on his feet. He paused, affecting thought. In fact, he was repressing wind. He prodded me in the chest with a big finger.

"To be sure, I'm not sure that I see it myself," he agreed cheerfully. His brogue was getting more pronounced with every fluid ounce. "As for McVeigh, his spiritual boundaries coincide precisely with those of the company he works for. I have never understood the baleful interior motor that propels him along life's path. I doubt whether he does himself. However, I am quite certain that we are all confronted by more than a conspiracy." He waved his arms dramatically, attracting attention. "We are confronted by a work of art. Consider the deaths of these young men. The how of their passing is a mystery, but the event itself always has elegance and precision. There is Mozart in the way our enquiries have faded eloquently into tactful silence. It is as though Global Alliance were losing a chess game with Fate. And, like all art works, it possesses a personality."

"What personality, Charles?" I listened carefully. Like Eric, though for different reasons, Omphrey sometimes had interesting insights.

He glanced round and saw McVeigh leaving the group round Don Proctor.

"Personality?" he enquired. He focused suddenly. "Why, to be sure, it has a mordantly, playful personality. Now, if you will excuse me."

He was off across the room, weaving gently like a barge among skiffs. I emptied my glass and wandered off too. Proctor had converted the building out of a terrace of three smaller houses. There were ornamental flights of stairs leading up from several directions. I tried them all.

The combined basements had been made over into a studio and

technical area with all kinds of facilities from Grant projectors to batteries of lights on hydraulic lifts. The upper floors were offices, a reception room, a kitchen, and what I took to be the living quarters of the Spanish house servants. At the very top was a single stairway leading to an elegant door. I guessed it gave access to Proctor's own apartments.

Annie was in the first floor reception area, feeding a pinball machine with old sixpences from a brass urn. When she saw me, she pulled the handle, taking no notice where the ball went, and walked straight into my arms. We kissed in a restrained sort of way. I fingered the thick braids of her hair, smelling her faint but heavy perfume.

"Are we going to have an affair?" she demanded truculently. She made it sound like a punch-up in a dark alley.

"It depends on two things."

"Meaning?"

"It depends on what you call an affair, and on whether I start one."

She nodded as though I had confirmed her worst suspicions. "I ought to warn you, my husband will kill us both if he finds out. He's an incredibly jealous man." She smoothed her dress over her thighs. "I've never given him cause to be. This will be the first time."

"I haven't started anything yet," I reminded her gently.

"You will." She sighed gustily and wrapped her arms tightly round me again. This time she opened her lips and pressed herself hard against me. I ran a hand down the curve of her back. The ridge of muscle on either side of her spine was as hard as elm.

"Will you take me home?" she demanded.

"We'll see."

We walked downstairs. The party was louder, and there was a row of glasses along the plinth where the equestrian general rattled his marble sabre. I couldn't see Omphrey or McVeigh. Presumably they had both finished inspecting Sir Bryan's investment and gone off to their clubs.

Proctor was still with his business friends. They had been joined by a man and a girl. The grouping was mannered as though they were in an unimaginatively directed classical drama. Proctor was in the middle, slightly in front of his friends, the new arrivals on either side of him.

I recognized the girl. She was Sir Bryan's frosty and untouchable secretary, Freda Harman. She was dressed in a white sheath of silk from throat to sandals. She looked like an early Christian martyr and about as erotic. The man was tall, pale, and powerful-looking in spite of his slender build. At the moment he also looked sulky.

"Who's the pretty boy?" I murmured in Annie's ear. Her fist nestled firmly in mine like a cuckoo in a finch's nest. There wasn't much doubt who I meant. Proctor's friends looked arrogantly prosperous, but they couldn't compete with the newcomer for style.

Annie took her eyes off my profile and crinkled them up. She was probably short-sighted and hated contact lenses.

"That's Horst Wohlberg."

"Who?"

She shrugged, with the reticence women generally have when talking of such matters. "He's a friend of Don's. He came to England a few years ago. I believe he's in love with Don." I didn't know another woman in the world who could have saved that bit of information until last.

"You mean they live together?" I asked.

"I believe so."

"But I thought Freda Harman was Don's girl friend."

"She is."

"Annie," I complained, "I'm confused."

"Perhaps Don is, too," she said primly. "They say he's AC/DC. Actually, I don't think he gives a damn about either of them. He just likes to have them fighting over him."

"Charming fellow."

As though on cue, a tawdry charade unfolded to illustrate Annie's point. Freda Harman had been leaning forward to place her glass on the plinth, saying something I couldn't hear. Don smiled and his friends laughed. The newcomer did neither. He moved negligently, knocking the glass from her hand. I heard it smash melodiously and saw liquid stain the whole front of her white dress.

What followed took everyone by surprise. The girl's hand flashed toward Wohlberg's face. Even faster, the edge of his hand came up to block the slap. The interception was accurate and could have broken her wrist. Proctor and his friends didn't move, but a stranger on the other side of them did. He was facing the wrong way and must have had eyes in the back of his head. He whirled and grabbed the German by the lapels of his jacket, which I could have told him is a bad move in a serious fight. Again the German moved faster, lunging his forearms upwards and outwards to break the grip. Without pause, his right hand, bunched in a half-fist, slammed into the stranger's solar plexus. It could have been dangerous if one of Proctor's friends hadn't finally moved, grabbing his arm.

The others soon got between them, laughing and calming things down. The party had grounded for a while, but nobody seemed upset. Proctor was wiping Freda Harman's dress with a handkerchief. She waited silently until he had finished, then walked off. The German shrugged off restraining hands and walked away in the other direction. Somebody started to giggle, and even Proctor smiled wintrily. The gallant stranger was still bent double.

"Lovely people," I commented, as the party got back to normal. "What does the kraut do when he's not screwing men and pouring champagne over women?"

"He's wealthy," Annie said. "I believe he works part-time for the Samaritans in Notting Hill." She rubbed her hip against mine. "That was horrible. Can we leave now?"

I wondered for a moment whether I was doing the right thing and whether I wanted to do anything at all. I've got a personal rule against intimate distractions while I'm working. I also doubted whether Annie or I had any real need for each other. I suspected I had a motive for what I was doing, and that I'd work it out if I thought hard enough. But I also knew I wasn't going to.

I unballed her fist from mine and tucked the fingers under my arm. "Let's go," I said. She followed me meekly. There was still no sign of Omphrey or McVeigh. Perhaps they hadn't left after all. Perhaps they were making book on the pinball machine upstairs.

I left Annie's flat early next morning and walked back to Covent Garden with the office workers, the admen, the experimental couturiers, and the serious people who practice obscure crafts.

Throughout the night, Annie had been sensual and tearful in turns. She had tried to abandon herself but tried too hard. Behind her failure was a lurid obsession that her husband would immediately find out about us and kill us both. With the first of many misgivings, I said I'd meet her later for lunch.

Back in the flat, I showered and made breakfast. Afterwards I called Eric. Miss Malone started to protest that he wasn't yet in but changed her tune as he came through the door.

He sounded surly and tired. "After work is the best time for finding people in," he informed me. "I've been up half the flaming night making telephone calls." He became muffled as he covered the mouthpiece to grumble at Miss Malone, who seemed to be getting off to a bad start. She always began his day with a nice pot of sweet tea the way Eric hated it. In ten years to my certain knowledge he'd never got the fact across to her. She was the determinedly self-sacrificing kind of woman who never stops to find out whether anyone wants her particular brand of self-sacrifice.

He sounded more cheerful when he uncovered his mouthpiece again. "Boss, we may have something," he said. "Apart from the ones you know about, I've found four more kids who read *The Times*. Real rough diamonds. Three of them picked it up coming home from work. The last one shared it with one of the others."

"You mean they knew each other?"

"Worked together in the factory. No connection between the deaths, though. About six months between them and a few hundred miles."

"Still, that's good, Eric. How about the letters?"

"You may have something there as well. Two letters have turned up, or so their relatives say. They're trying to find them. Another one says she remembers the kind of letter I described. She found it after her son's death but threw it away. I'll be on the road today. Some of these people aren't on the phone, see."

"Right. You do that. I may be out myself. If I'm not available when you get back, put anything you find through my letterbox. For Christ's sake, don't leave it on the stairs. Understood?"

"Right on, boss. By the way, something I forgot to tell you. Just an incident. Struck me funny, that's all. It was you talking about kids who might have known each other that put me in mind of it. One of the families I called on lived in a village about ten miles outside Nottingham. You know the sort of place. Dead as mutton because most of the youngsters have moved away to find work. Well, I got talking to one of the neighbors. Seems her son had been a mate of the lad on our books. The neighbor said our lad had been on several of these trips before, only his family hadn't twigged. Her son went on one, too. She found out and gave him a right going over. Says she never did discover what it was all about except that our boy put hers up to it. She didn't like him. Thought he was a bad influence.

"Anyway, her kid got beaten up at a disco a few weeks later. A local one for local kids, a twenty-first birthday do, like. There was no reason for the attack and everybody saw the goons who did it. They weren't local, though, and nobody saw them again. Struck me funny, that's all."

I was excited for the first time.

"Christ, Eric, do you realize this lad may be one bloke who knows what's going on and who's still alive?"

"Sorry, Boss, I knew there was a reason why it slipped my mind. He was killed last week. I sort of gate-crashed the wake. His mother was a bit sloshed. That's why she talked a lot."

"Another of our accidents?"

"No. Not like that. The kid worked at a railway yard. Got himself crushed between two trucks loaded with coal. His mother thought I was a union official sent to attend the funeral."

"Keep at it," I sighed. "Maybe we'd better make extra checks on our lads' friends."

I hung up. The phone rang again almost immediately. It was a friend of James Huddiesford. He offered me a job on Huddiesford's recommendation, but I had trouble getting him to give me his name. He spun me a tale of mundane industrial espionage. A rival firm had evolved a product suspiciously similar to the one he was working on and looked like going into production first. He wanted to know if I could do anything about it. From what he told me, the product sounded so banal that the only mystery was why half a dozen manufacturers hadn't evolved it independently.

"What will you do if I prove anything?" I asked. "Will you take them to court?"

"Good Lord, no." Huddiesford's friend sounded shocked. "Not unless the evidence is absolutely incontrovertible."

"Well, how about a little discreet fire-bombing?" I suggested silkily. "That should hold him up."

He almost gobbled in his outrage. I let him go on for a bit. I hadn't time for his assignment, but it was never going to matter anyway. He was like the odd eighty percent of my clients who can't be helped because, at bottom, they don't want to be. They just want the feeling that someone, somewhere, is on their side.

"Huddiesford suggested you might be able to find a discreet solution," he whined.

"I'm sure Mr. Huddiesford didn't say I could make discreet silk purses out of sows' ears," I countered briskly. "Tell you what, leave the problem with me for a bit. I'm busy at the moment, and I'll need time to think about it. Leave your telephone number, too. I'll be back in touch when I can."

He was still aggrieved but now grateful for the delay. He gave me his number reluctantly. I think he would have liked me to learn it by heart and burn the memory.

Annie was honest. She'd made it clear right from the beginning that her husband was jealous and that she was afraid of him. It wasn't her fault if I hadn't taken her too seriously. I thought her irrational fear was just a part of her, like her rich copper hair and her impulsive earthiness.

Later, I'd had doubts. Her fear had come to look like a barrier between us. By morning, walking towards Covent Garden, doubts had become certainties. Annie had an obsession about her husband, and the trouble with obsessions is that they isolate people from each other. That was her problem, of course. Mine was simpler. Maybe I could break down the barrier if I tried hard and long enough. But was I ready to try? As usual when I think a problem out carefully, I made a wrong decision.

I met Annie for lunch in a Knightsbridge restaurant called Freddi's. It was the kind of establishment where you bark your shins on the marinated desserts in the gloom, and I was late. Ben Campbell, her advertising friend, was with her. I should have guessed.

Annie glowed apprehensively in a kind of floating dress that expressed somebody else's taste more than her own. While we toyed over aperitifs, she talked mainly to Campbell, though she kept smiling covertly at me. Plain candles in raffia-covered Chianti bottles shed a tender light on her conspiracy.

"I hear there was a fight at Proctor's studio," Campbell said eagerly. Like a lot of overarticulate men, the idea of physical violence fascinated him.

"Not a fight," Annie corrected him. "Horst Wohlberg tipped wine over Freda Harman. Someone made a fuss, but nothing came of it."

"That poofter," Campbell grumbled, "I heard he got duffed up."

Annie looked suddenly alarmed. She grabbed for her bag below the table and bent her head.

"What's wrong?" I asked.

She straightened up cautiously. "I thought I recognized someone," she explained with a small, embarrassed grin.

The waiter arrived with a bottle of wine in a basket. Campbell performed the tasting ritual with a show of bored reluctance and admitted that the contents might just be fit for human consumption.

Annie stood up with her bag in her hand. She still looked apprehensive, but she smiled her conspiratorial smile.

"Back in a minute," she whispered, brushing provocatively against me in passing. I had the unpleasant feeling that we fellows were being left alone for a reason.

Campbell waited until she had gone through the one-way mirror into the ladies' room. "I hope you don't mind me coming along," he said. "Actually, it was Annie's idea, and this is my lunch."

I waited for the explanation.

"It's Norman," Campbell explained. "Annie thinks he's insanely jealous. She's terrified of appearing in public with you, so I'm chaperoning her."

"Thinks he's insanely jealous?" I asked dutifully. "Are you saying he's not?"

Campbell shrugged. "No way. Threlfall's a career man. He eats, sleeps and breathes advertising. If he did get to know about you, I think he'd be relieved."

He leaned back and touched his skinny lips with a napkin while a waiter served him with freshly grilled sardines.

"Norman's the type who likes living on his own. He actually prefers sending his laundry out. He can afford to. Actually," he added coyly, "I don't think he likes women very much."

"So why does Annie think he's insanely jealous?"

"Because she needs to. Norman encourages it. I think that's rather civilized of him. You'll be good for her, you know."

"I don't understand."

Campbell began to look irritated. The whole point of manly discussions is that things get understood that don't need to be said. I was being less intelligent than the script required.

"Annie and Norman are wrong for each other. Annie's a demanding woman, and Norman's indifference has been a terrific sexual put-down for her. So she left him, but she feels guilty about it. She fantasizes that he's the demanding one while she's the escapee. That's why you'll be good for her. With you, she's got something real to feel guilty about, plus a chance to regain her sexual confidence. I'd say that's progress. Wouldn't you agree?" He had a boring habit of asking rhetorical questions.

"What's the matter?" I asked. "Don't you fancy her yourself, or won't she let you get your leg over?"

Campbell recoiled as though one of his sardines had started blowing bubbles. He was still working out an answer when Annie returned, glancing nervously around her.

Lunch was not a glittering occasion. Annie's increasing nervousness began to depress her. Campbell had decided I was not one of the boys after all and ignored me. I had one espresso and Strega before excusing myself. Campbell asked politely if I really had to go, and Annie slumped further, sensing my mood. I told her I'd call her later in the afternoon.

A taxi was delivering some late lunchers in the street outside. I commandeered it and took it to the corner of Long Acre where I called in at Stanford's Map House. I bought a general map of Europe and every one of the Ordnance Survey maps of Britain. The assistant looked surprised and had to find me a carton to stow them all in. I explained that I got itchy but undecided feet in springtime.

The phone was ringing back in my flat. It was James Huddiesford's secretary. She was a well-matured West Countrywoman with vowels as comfortable and rounded as a Taunton cider barrel. Mrs. Huddiesford wasn't so stupid as to risk anyone younger and sexier in her husband's office. She was probably wise.

"Mr. Huddiesford asked me to telephone and confirm this evening's arrangements," the secretary informed me politely.

I was foxed. "What arrangements?"

"Mr. Huddiesford is a director of Chelsea Football Club. They have a UEFA Cup home semifinal against the Italian club, Juventus, this evening. I believe Mr. Huddiesford invited you and that you accepted."

It was in my mind to think up excuses, but then I thought again. I owed Huddiesford for his friend's offer of a job. My business is run on personal recommendation, and I'm not usually so surrounded by gift horses that I can afford to look any in the mouth. I had another motive, too. I knew Annie would want to see me in the evening, and I had to have time to think things through. Like most men, I can be weak-minded in these matters.

"Thanks for reminding me," I said, after she had given me the rendezvous and the place, a trendy pub-restaurant near the Stamford Bridge football ground. I hung up and called Annie on the off chance that she might be back. I was about to hang up when she answered.

"Darling," she said, nervously breathless, "I've just this minute got in. Lunch wasn't a success, was it? I'm sorry about Ben. I asked him along. Did I do wrong?"

I calmed her down. "It's no problem, Annie. Ben told me you needed a chaperone."

"Damn him. I didn't mean it like that."

"Annie, why are you afraid of your husband?" I asked it coldly and abruptly. I prepared to wait for an answer.

"Ben talks too much," she said hesitantly. "I don't think I trust him anymore."

I knew that if I asked the question again, she'd evade it again. "We won't talk about it now," I said. "I called to tell you I won't be able to see you tonight. I've got to go out. I'll call you tomorrow."

There was a long silence. "You're punishing me," she said in a small voice.

"Don't be daft, Annie. I'm not your jailer or confessor. I only punished a girl once, and that was a long time ago."

"What had she done?"

"She hadn't done anything. She just liked being punished."

There was another long silence. "You're making fun of me. Why can't you come round afterwards?"

"Because the evening's likely to go on for a bit. It's hard to say how long."

"I don't care how late it is." The dam burst suddenly. "I don't want to be punished by you. It's happened to me before, and I hate it. I've got some pride left. I want you in my bed tonight."

"You've got a lot more than pride, Annie," I told her. I told her what else she'd got, and she giggled. It was a sexy, unpracticed sound, and I thought she should practice it more often. It unhinged me. Up till that moment, I'd finally determined to break off contact and let her down as gently as I could. I'd realized I had nothing real to offer her. She was inviolate within her obsession about her husband and was going to have to find her own way out. But that earthy, innocent giggle made me forget. So I coaxed her into a better mood and promised to call if I could.

I knew I'd made a mistake the moment I hung up, but I was tired and had things to do. I sorted out my Ordnance Survey maps into numerical order, then decided I'd had enough.

Rose Panayioutou breezed in just as I started undressing. Today, she'd undergone another of her exquisite transformations. She wore a long, swinging skirt topped by a Fair-Isle jersey over a cotton blouse. She smelled of Heno de Pravia cologne, which means hay from Pravia and made me think about tumbling in haystacks.

"Your timing's fine," I said. "I was just going to bed."

Rose liked men to be witty and gallant, only she wasn't finding me witty or gallant today.

"This is London, not Aleppo," she said coldly, marching through into the kitchen. "We don't take siestas."

"I do," I said, buttoning my shirt again and following her into the kitchen. "I catnap. It's a great gift. It enables me to grab rest when I need it and stay in top intellectual form."

"From what I hear, you need it. I hear you went to Don Proctor's exhibition yesterday and spent the night with Annie Threlfall." She was fitting Rambouts coffee filters into metal containers and waiting for the kettle to boil.

"And where do you hear stories about my movements?" I asked.

Rose switched the kettle off. "All over town," she said. "If you want to keep your sex life secret, you shouldn't mix with advertising people."

I thought of Ben Campbell and swore crudely.

"Go and sit down," Rose said quietly. "I'll bring the coffee in. It's better than the stuff you make."

I'd cleared the table when she joined me. The Rambouts containers sat on two of my best Woolworth cups. The lot sat on a tray with a packet of sugar and a carton of skimmed milk.

"You should watch yourself," Rose said. "They say Norman Threlfall's a jealous and violent man."

"They say, they say," I moaned. "How should I know, and what does it matter? The advertising industry runs on reputations."

It was in my mind to tell Rose to mind her own business, but that would have been dishonest. It *was* her business. I'd been enthralled by her for a long time. We'd never talked anything but shop, and I'd never seen her naked. But I knew every nuance of her mind and her body. Compared with her, every woman I'd ever slept with was a stranger. And when I slept badly, it was her I dreamt of.

The strange thing was that I knew Rose felt the same about me and that we both knew how the other felt. That's why there'd been no hurry to bring matters to a head. Rose had waited virginally, I knew, while I put off the day. Something cantankerous in me always resists things that are Meant To Be, and there was a touch of cowardice in me, too. To me, my job is just a job, a way of scratching a living on my own terms. But for Rose, with her love and her impulsive kindness, I was an heroic knight errant. I'd never been sure how she would adjust to the compromised reality of my life.

She was looking round the room, faintly embarrassed, wanting to change the subject. She noticed the pile of Ordnance Survey maps.

"How are you getting on?" she asked.

"Eric and I are working on a few ideas. They may get us somewhere. Then, again, they may not."

I sipped the coffee. It was good coffee. "Of course, the advantage with my method is that you can refill the cup afterwards," I said.

"Do you want another? I'll get you one."

"Don't bother. Just tell me what you're doing, apart from catching up on the latest gossip." I spoke stupidly, thoughtlessly, a common fault of mine.

Rose buried her head in her art bag for a long time before handing over a fat sheaf of acetate charts. It was my day for hurting girls.

"These cover the geographical distribution of deaths in the other seven countries you're concerned with." She spoke in a muffled voice. "They have the same characteristics as the ones you've already seen. For what it's worth, there's no doubt now. The patterns are not random. There must be external factors conditioning where each death takes place."

"What factors, Rose?"

"I can only make inferences from results. There is a clear intention to produce as regularly dispersed a pattern as possible. That means, as I thought, that the distance between a policyholder's home and the place where he dies gets progressively greater as the year goes by. There are no exceptions."

"But what would be the point, Rose? To avoid suspicious concentrations?"

She shrugged. "Such an intention would be pointless. Completely regular dispersal is as statistically improbable as a pattern of concentrations."

I sighed. "I don't know what it all means, but I'll think about it. Let me know if anything else occurs to you."

She stood up, and I saw that she was crying. Her face was calm, but tears poured down it.

"That's right, you think about it. Thinking's your part of the job. If it hurts, you can always lie on top of Annie Threlfall and tell her your troubles."

She ran out, slamming the door behind her.

Huddiesford was waiting for me on a bar stool in the King's Road restaurant. I noticed right away that he'd undergone a drastic change of image. Gone was the bucolic, philosophical West Country squire. In its place was the kind of spry businessman who uses the word "keen" to describe prices in his brochures. He looked happier and fitter than when I'd last seen him.

He hadn't changed his wardrobe too obviously, though. He still wore his Country Gentlemen's Association tweeds over a moleskin shirt and was setting light to a briar pipe as I came in. We shook hands, and I picked up the matches he dropped. They were from a West Country firm who still put strips of sandpaper on the sides of their boxes and mottos on the back. This one read, "Most people spend too much time running away from something that isn't even after them."

"Can't stand London," Huddiesford boomed cheerfully. "Only come up for the football. Andy, give my pal a drink."

The barman took my order for a pint of Young's Ordinary while I took the next bar stool. The pub wasn't crowded, but then it wasn't really a pub. It had the usual incised tracery on windows and bar mirrors, and the beer engines dispensed real ale under orange-shaded lights that shone on horse brasses and polished mahogany. But the bar was only an annex to a dining room where there were scrubbed trestle tables, a charcoal grill and plenty of oak beams, some real, some not. It just avoided being the kind of place where waitresses get called serving wenches.

I thanked Huddiesford for recommending me to his friend and asked how business was going. His pipe had gone out, and he was poking it with an instrument that looked as though it had been designed by a homicidal mining engineer.

"Fine," he grunted. "I've just received planning permission to expand production and storage capacity. We're going into manufactured components for the building trade." He rubbed his hands together with a sound like vipers making love. "The building trade's coming out of recession, see? A lot of smaller suppliers have gone to the wall over the past few years."

I congratulated him and asked after Bennett, the erring marketing manager.

"John? Oh, he's fine." The voice was neutral, but the eyes twinkled in his head like stars on a frosty night. He was having trouble getting his briar to stay alight. "There's no fallout over that business."

"What's he doing?"

"He left to join Border Display Systems—officially, that is." That was the bogus company Bennett had originally set up to fleece Huddiesford, I remembered.

"It's a sound company and sells a good product," Huddiesford conceded generously. "Matter of fact, I've taken a stake in it myself and wangled a fixed-price contract to supply Fidelity over the next five years."

I grinned to myself. I bet it was a good contract. As I'd thought, Huddiesford had decided against a stand-up fight. He'd simply nailed his former marketing manager and associates tastefully to the floor and was going to gnaw their collective liver for a while.

Another waiter came, and Huddiesford ordered for us both. Steaks with bubble and squeak, treacle tart, Blue Vinney cheese, and a château-bottled claret. The standard expense-account nursery menu for which the place was famous. We left the bar and got to the restaurant by lifting the bar-flap and tripping over some barrels. It was another gimmick that went down well with the tourists.

Over dinner, Huddiesford turned the conversation to football. I didn't know much about the game, so he described for me Chelsea's rise back through the ranks of the First Division into European competition.

"It's a knock-out competition," he explained. "Previous year's performance in the League is the qualifying factor." Over a *marc de Champagne* and Cona coffee he told me about the evening's fixture.

"Juventus are a fine side. They've got nine of the national team. Still, our boys won 1–0 away from home, and away-goals count double in the event of a tie. We should be through to the Finals if we box clever, but you've got to watch these Italians on the break."

A waiter reminded us that it was near kick-off time. We had a last coffee while Huddiesford paid the bill.

The dingy, terraced streets around the Stamford Bridge ground loomed with a garish menace under the floodlighting. Crowds of youths in blue and white milled around hamburger stands, program sellers, and lines of mounted police on huge, sweating horses. They flocked and grouped like starlings waiting for a signal, aimless one moment, surging the next in a complex phalanx. A scattering of Italian supporters, mostly Soho catering staff, filed nervously by the low walls of tiny gardens.

Huddiesford and I elbowed our way to the directors' entrance. Up in the comfortable box there was a well-stocked bar and a lot of easy chairs spread out beside the sloping plate glass wall overlooking the pitch. Huddiesford ordered a half bottle of champagne for me and a large whiskey for himself. He stood laughing with some other directors while I looked out through the glass wall. The pitch was a long way down. Cigarette smoke curled like incense from the terraces. The fans' chants were like inept anthems.

A few minutes after we arrived, an immense roar signalled the arrival of the teams onto the pitch. I saw them punt white, glistening footballs among each other and practice their sprints. Under the floodlights, they were diminutive Action Men with oiled thighs and four shadows apiece. As I settled down for the kick-off, I heard Huddiesford haggling with a fellow director giving odds on the result of the game.

The first half didn't go as expected. Both teams played cautious, tactical football, and nobody strayed far from the center circle, the defenders on both sides playing precise offside traps. The crowd grew restive behind its barriers. From time to time, they let out concerted roars and fragments of hymns for no reason that I could fathom, sending dazzled pigeons soaring and falling through luminous space like scattered banknotes.

Just before half-time, there came the kind of turnabout that Huddiesford had been afraid of. A Chelsea midfield player crossed from the right, but a big defender got a strong header out of the penalty area. An Italian player picked the ball up and ran upfield, shielding it cleverly until one of his strikers was onside. He slipped the ball between two Chelsea defenders, and the striker scored with a low shot under the keeper's body. The score was 0–1, and Chelsea's away-goal advantage had been wiped out.

I finished my champagne during the interval while Huddiesford talked to his friends. He hadn't introduced me to any of them, which was a pity, because they looked like good potential business for me. It would probably have meant too many explanations for him, though. I heard them dismember Chelsea's first-half performance while a half-thought slowly formed at the back of my mind. I knew it was important, so I didn't crowd it. I leafed through the match program, studying the team picture and reading the list of past fixtures. Odd fragments of ideas came into my mind. I remembered Eric talking about the Foreign Legion and Charles Omphrey waving his arms as he described a mordantly playful personality.

The idea exploded into my consciousness. I grinned inanely to myself. It was macabre, idiotic, but I knew I had to check it right away. I jumped up and headed for the door, with mumbled thanks and apologies to James Huddiesford on my way. He gaped as I tore out of the box, scattering directors and their friends.

I heard a roar as the teams came back onto the field while I headed for the main gate. Even the policemen standing around looked surprised as I sprinted into the street. I flagged a cruising taxi that just managed to avoid knocking me down as I reached the King's Road.

Back in my flat there was a sealed manila envelope from Global House. I ripped it open and found what I'd hoped would be there. Eric had also called by. There was a smaller envelope with a Starkey Brothers' compliments slip stapled to the front.

I was still grinning inanely as I set to work. Everything was coming together at the right time. However macabre the idea, I knew it had to be right. I started by pinning Rose's charts up in order until they covered the entire cork wall. Then I got a box of felt-tipped pens, a new scratch-pad, and made a big pot of coffee. My own, not Rose's Rambouts.

By two o'clock, I knew the idea was right. The evidence was still circumstantial, but that didn't worry me. I could fill in details later. What mattered was that my answer was the only one that fitted all the facts. Sir Bryan had wanted lateral thinking, and by God he'd got it.

I double-checked and summarized my findings on a fresh sheet of paper. It was three o'clock by the time I had finished, and I was still high on elation. I broke my rules again. I made a large, last drink and washed a Mogadon down with it. I went straight to bed, taking the phone off the hook.

I woke with a thick head and a bad taste in my mouth. The room was full of the smell of last night's cigarettes.

I opened windows and curtains and poured two Disprins into the glass by my bed. The water was full of stale bubbles. I put the phone back on its cradle while I waited for the tablets to dissolve. It rang almost immediately.

"Where were you?" Annie demanded. Her tone was light, but there was anger and fear at the back of it.

"Christ, I forgot, Annie."

"Thanks a lot."

"Look, I really forgot. I was working on something important. I told you yesterday I was busy. You've just woken me up."

She hesitated. "I'm sorry," she said with an effort. "I suppose you do have to do something for a living. I never asked, did I?" There was a pause, and she went on with a rush. "As a matter of fact, I'm glad you didn't come. I think Norman has found out about us. He's watching my flat."

I sat up in bed and lit a cigarette, feeling that the last rites would be more appropriate. I needed more sleep.

"How do you know?"

"My doorbell rang twice while I was asleep. I answered on the speakaphone, but there was no one there."

"It was probably kids or drunks fooling about."

"No. I looked through the curtains the second time. I saw a green BMW driving away. I'm certain it was Norman's."

"Listen, Annie," I sighed, wanting to reassure her, "I assume your husband is not an idiot or a child. What the hell would he ring your doorbell and run away for?"

"To see who answered it," she said simply. "I was going to call you the second time, but I didn't want to disturb you."

"You mean, you didn't want me to think you were checking on me," I said lightly, thinking a change of subject might be no bad thing. "You're under too much pressure, Annie. You're chasing ghosts."

It was the standard bromide, but it seemed to work. "Perhaps you're right," she said doubtfully. "Will I see you today?"

"Tonight, Annie. I've still got a lot to do."

"Please," she said. "Sorry. I want you to be there if it happens again. I don't want to lumber you with my emotional baggage. Really I don't."

I talked her down till she was calm again. Afterwards, I hung up, showered, and drank a pint of apple juice. My stomach didn't like the malic acid, so I scrambled a plate of eggs. I've got a double saucepan for the job, a relic of the days when the Sunday supplements had something to read in them other than ads for double saucepans. Nobody scrambles better eggs than I do, probably because nobody gets so much practice.

I telephoned Rose when I'd cleared up. She sounded diffident and aloof, but I was in no mood for sensitive estrangements.

"This is urgent, Rose," I told her. "I want you here in half an hour."

"Can't you ever give decent notice?" There was a wistful venom in her voice that I chose to ignore.

"Never. I think I've got our answer. Maybe we can stop any more of these deaths. Come on, Rose, get your skates on."

Her mood changed magically. "That's marvelous. I'm in a taxi now. Do you want me to bring anything?"

"Nothing except your sweet self. Wrapped in little for preference. And that little, diaphanous."

"I'll break out the cellophane pyjamas. Please don't make any of your awful coffee. Use the Rambouts I bought you"

I rang Eric and told him to come round as well. While I waited, I tidied up and rearranged my notes. They arrived within two minutes of each other.

As usual, Rose marched in without knocking, but she didn't give me her usual sisterly kiss. Sooner or later, we were going to have to face each other for real. The idyllic, unspoken sparring was over for good. Not much had been said, but that little had been more than enough to break the spell. I knew it, and I knew Rose knew it. The morning was overcast, and an April gale was blowing up. The curtains at my French windows bellied out like the stunsails of a frigate.

"Yesterday a Sicilian," Rose complained, "today, an Eskimo." She dropped her art bag and helped close the windows. She wrinkled her nose at the state of the flat. "Do you know there's a Greek proverb about moderation in all things?"

"I haven't made coffee yet," I said hopefully, "and no coffee's better than your coffee, to coin a phrase."

I couldn't help ogling her as she walked into my kitchen, the way you couldn't help ogling Limoges porcelain in a transport cafe. This time she wore flared, exotic slacks that managed to sit tight over her hips without wrinkling. On top was a chunky sweater with a wide polo neck. I wondered whether she itched, and whether she'd let me scratch her.

Eric breezed in, his eyes alight with battle and the smell of Rose's Rambouts. The Crimson Pirate had spotted a sail on the horizon. We waited for the coffee to get half-cold as it filtered through into the cups. Afterwards, I launched into my story. I kept it short, needing to clear my own mind as much as anything else. When I finished, there was a long, appalled silence.

Eric looked at me with half-angry uncertainty. "Boss, you're pulling our legs, aren't you? I never heard anything like this in my life."

Rose's reaction was harder to define. She looked frightened and confused but didn't say anything.

"I'm not pulling your leg, Eric," I said quietly. "I know it's like nothing you ever heard before. But think about it for a while. It's the only theory that makes sense. Apart from that, it's got an eerie logic about it. It's the sort of thing that was always going to happen one day."

Rose looked up. "It's horrifying. Are you absolutely sure of your facts?"

"As sure as I can be, Rose. I want you to check the main ones for yourself." I unpinned her acetate charts from the wall. "Ignore all the chinagraph lines I've drawn except the yellow ones. The others were just first guesses. Then sort out the regions as accurately as you can. I want you to draw them out on a new sheet of acetate so that I can fit it over the ones you've already got. We've got to be absolutely certain before I make another move."

"What do you want me to do, boss?" Eric was still awed and unhappy.

I handed him a sheet of dates I had written out in longhand. "You check these. You'll need access to back numbers of *The Times.* Go to Global House if necessary. They keep voucher copies. Remember, you won't find the items we're looking for on these exact dates. They'll probably be a few days before or after. Make notes of everything you find. Get the results back to me fast, and bring all the files with you." I thought of something else. "Keep your eyes open. Note key words and phrases wherever they crop up, even if the dates don't fit."

Eric took the list gingerly, as though he thought it might contaminate him. "I won't need Global," he said slowly. "I've got a mate in Fleet Street. He'll let me work on the premises without asking questions."

One of Eric's many advantages was his immense number of friends in all kinds of unlikely places. I was relieved. I didn't want anyone at Global getting a hint before I was ready for them.

"That's even better." I looked at my watch. "I've got things to do as well. By the end of the afternoon, we should have enough for a basic confirmation. Be back here by five o'clock. That ought to be enough time if you skip lunch."

Eric stood up. He was still frowning heavily. "Sir Bryan Proctor. He's your boss, isn't he?"

"That's right. He runs the Global Alliance International group of companies and one or two other empires. Why?"

He shook his head. "I knew there was something about this job that rang a bell. Damned if I can remember what."

"Is it important?"

"Yes. I can't think of it now, but it's something you ought to know."

"Don't crowd it," I said. "It'll come." My respect for Eric's intuitions was absolute. If he thought something that he knew about Proctor was important to me, it probably was.

He waited for Rose by the flat door. She looked at me carefully as she got up.

"I wish you hadn't found what you think you've found," she said. "I wish you'd never started."

"It's too late now, Rose," I answered her gently.

She looked away and left quickly. Eric followed her.

I put Rose's fears out of my mind. Nobody had touched the coffee she'd made, so I drank mine cold while I sifted through the thin sheaf of bookshop letters I had collected from Eric and McVeigh as well as the two I had found for myself. I put them in date order and used the key map on the back of my Ordnance Surveys.

Finding answers wasn't hard. Everything was going to be simple now that I knew what to look for.

I spent the afternoon in the Jermyn Street sauna. I sweated in the steam room, gave my system a jolt in the icy pool, and warmed up again in the calidarium. Afterwards, I had a painful massage from an ex-marine who'd refound his vocation of beating up civilians for money. I finally staggered to an empty cubicle and booked a call for four hours' time.

I was awakened with a pot of tea and a plate of garibaldi biscuits. I ignored the biscuits and smoked a cigarette instead. I found a copy of *The Times* someone had left in the cubicle. There was nothing interesting in the main news. On the sports pages I read that Juventus had finally beaten Chelsea 2–0 and gone through to the Final of the UEFA Cup. I wondered whether Huddiesford had won or lost his bet.

I was back in the flat by five o'clock, but Rose and Eric were ahead of me. Rose was smoking inexpertly, probably from the spare packet I keep by my bed. Eric was eating a sandwich, Italian Joint rare beef with horseradish by the look of it, and drinking a can of Fosters. And he'd told me he didn't like lager.

"My checks confirm your conclusion on every point," Rose said briskly. She seemed to have cheered up. "Here is a key map of Britain with the divisions marked in red. Lay it over any of the other charts and you'll find the results match up. I'm working on similar key maps for the other seven countries. I'll let you have results as soon as possible. Probably tomorrow."

"Eric?"

He wiped foam from his chin and took a folded sheet from his inside pocket. He pushed it across wordlessly.

I took the sheet. There was a list of words and phrases on it with dates printed beside them. The list was nowhere near as long as I'd expected.

"I know what you're thinking," Eric said defensively. "But don't blame me. I haven't missed anything. It's just that the dates only cover three months of the year."

I swore softly. It was no good telling myself that the rest of my theory was right. If this part didn't hold up, nothing did.

"That means three-quarters of the year is missing," I said. "It's no bloody good, Eric. We'll have to start again."

Rose and Eric were silent while I went over the list once more.

"I've been thinking," Eric said. "What you told us was terrible. I couldn't believe it, but I've got to admit now that it makes sense, and everything else fits." He took another sheet of paper from his pocket and pushed it across. "You asked for a note of key phrases even when the dates didn't fit. This is what I got."

The second list was even shorter than the first. I studied it for a couple of minutes before its significance hit me. It suggested a new dimension to my theory. I was getting the germ of another idea. The second idea suggested a third. It was my week for ideas.

"Stap me vitals," I said inconsequentially. I checked my pocket telephone directory and dialed.

"Mr. Huddiesford's office." It was the comfortable secretary again.

"Is Mr. Huddiesford there?"

"He's in London, I'm afraid."

I announced myself. "The Chelsea Board are probably busy sacking each other," I told her. "What did you think of the match?"

"I only follow the rugby. Can I help you?"

"I certainly hope so. Do you know if Fidelity Fencing advertises locally?"

"Mr. Huddiesford takes eight-inch doubles, or whatever the millimeter equivalent is these days, in most Friday issues of the *Western Daily Mail*. I doubt whether they justify themselves commercially. Mr. Huddiesford only keeps them going out of local patriotism."

I guessed that the editor of the paper made Fidelity ads a condition of not blackballing Huddiesford from the local golf club.

"Do you keep voucher copies?"

"Of course."

"That's marvelous." I told her exactly what I wanted.

"I'll see what I can do," she promised.

I thanked her and hung up. I knew there was going to be trouble the moment I looked at Eric and Rose. Eric wore an expression of elaborate unconcern. He was picking his teeth with the gold cardboard corner of a cigarette packet. Rose's head was bowed, her hands clamped between her knees.

I ignored them and studied Eric's second list again. The last item read "Gustavus Adolphus meets Denfert Rochereau 9th April." The date was current. The ninth was tomorrow.

"What," Rose asked carefully, "do you intend to do about all this?"

"Plug the holes and lay it on the client as soon as I'm ready," I said promptly. I knew what was coming, and was already irritated.

"And what will your client do?"

"How the hell should I know, Rose? When someone hires you to work on Mother Hubbard's Krummy Kookies, you just do your job. Marketing decisions based on your information are none of your business."

Rose looked up at me. Her face was as stony as Chesil Beach in a storm.

"Please don't be more crass than God made you," she snapped. "I don't kid myself that the work I do ultimately matters a damn. It wouldn't matter if the home counties were flooded with cookies. This is entirely different. You are responsible for human lives."

"My client is," I corrected her.

She stood up and stamped her foot. I'd never seen it done before.

"That's not good enough," she said. "You know perfectly well what their instinct will be. They'll see the whole thing as bad publicity."

I was suddenly angry. "So what the hell do you expect me to do about it, Rose? Just pass my information over to the police and wash my hands of the matter?"

"That's exactly what I expect. They've got the proper resources, and they'll be able to stop these deaths."

"Don't be so daft," I snapped. "I'm not in business to pass the buck, and my clients don't pay me to. If they thought their problems were police matters, they wouldn't hire me in the first place. Stop trying to mother me."

We glared at each other. Even Eric looked embarrassed. On him the expression was absurd. He stood up carefully and took Rose's arm.

"Anything else you want done?" he asked. My sensitive antennae picked up hostility for the first time since I'd known him.

"Did you make copies of the lists you've given me?"

He nodded.

"I need equivalent lists for all the other countries concerned. Have you got contacts in any of them?"

"Some. I can find others."

"Fine. Get your dates from Rose's computer print-out. You know what to look for. Check local equivalents for *The Times. Die Zeit, Corriere della Sera,* papers like that. Don't tell your contacts any more than they need, and tell them you want results fast. They can bill me direct."

I turned back to Rose. "As you said yourself," I reminded her, "I'm responsible. That means responsible for doing a job in my own way. It doesn't include telling my client his business. Don't worry, though. I won't let him shelve the whole business. Now, why don't you wait until I've had a chance to lay everything on him?"

She was staring at me. There were tears in her eyes, and the pupils had enlarged enormously. I noticed a green ink smudge on the generous swell of her sweater.

"I want action taken, and you out of it," she repeated. "This is one time when I won't just fade gracefully from sight and say nothing."

She turned away. Eric shepherded her out like a stick of precious and beautiful dynamite.

I shrugged. What the hell did they expect? I was changing when the telephone rang. I dropped everything to answer it. It was Huddiesford's secretary with the information I'd hoped for. I grinned with relief. My theory was intact after all. I thanked her and rang McVeigh immediately. I caught him just as he was leaving his office.

"I want a meeting," I said.

"Already?" He sounded interested.

"I'd like it tomorrow."

I heard him chuckle. He was amused at my presumption in trying to push senior executives of large companies around. I heard the pages of his desk diary rustle.

"Sir Bryan is heavily engaged. Perhaps Monday of next week?"

"Tomorrow."

"Or else?"

"Look, McVeigh, I think I've done what you asked me to do. Action is now needed. If you don't take it, I will."

When he spoke again, there was an unpleasant chill in his voice.

"That sounds like a threat. I don't like having my arm twisted by casual labor."

"Then let's avoid the painful necessity. You can fix it."

I heard the pages of the diary rustle again.

"Sir Bryan flies back from Geneva tomorrow morning. He's engaged for lunch with representatives of one of the big clearing banks."

"Then cancel it."

"Very well." McVeigh's voice was still frosty. "Be here at twelve-thirty sharp."

The click of the receiver almost scarred my eardrum. I hung up and slumped back in my chair. I hoped Rose would be proud of me.

I had to give my name twice over the speakaphone before Annie would let me in. I climbed four flights of stairs I couldn't remember from the last time I'd been there.

She let me in shyly. She was wearing a plastic pinafore with a printed recipe for *zuppa di pesce* over a dress of some heavy material. The copper braids of her hair hung loose again. From inside the flat I could hear a record I vaguely recognized as Red somebody or other and his All Stars playing "Jeepers Creepers."

"I wasn't expecting you yet," she said. She held me tight. There was a faint hint of kümmel on her breath.

I followed her into a living room that I didn't remember either. It was a plain, bohemian kind of room with a lot of matt-polyurethaned pine and low, comfortable armchairs covered with woven fabrics in oatmeal and caramel.

Annie ran into the kitchen and came back with a glass of vodka and orange juice.

"I know you prefer champagne," she apologized, "but I forgot to get any. I was just going to start cooking."

I kissed her again, and she held me convulsively. "If we keep this up, I'll never get dinner ready," she giggled.

"Forget the cooking," I said. "I'd like to take you out. Do you mind?"

I knew it was important for her to cook for me sometime, but I didn't think this was the time. She certainly wasn't going to be able to make a sauce béarnaise if she kept jumping every time the doorbell rang.

"I suppose it can all go back in the freezer." She looked only faintly disappointed.

I made her finish her drink. "Get your pinny off," I said. "I'll book us a table."

I watched her walk back into the kitchen. Her legs were well-shaped and as solidly muscled as her back. She was a tough country girl, neither fragile nor ungainly, and the city would never suit her.

I looked round the room. The shelves were packed with books, mostly paperbacks, and there was a good sound system. On a table by the window were several photographs. I guessed that the big one in front was of her husband. He was a tall man with a thin, intolerant face. He was expensively and modishly dressed, and, like most tall men, he had no trouble looking elegant. Only his hair made him unusual. There was a lot of it, and he had it frizzed out in Afro style.

Annie came back with another glass of kümmel, the coldness of it frosting the rim. She'd changed into a simpler dress under a Welsh tweed cape. She knocked back her drink in one gulp and locked up carefully behind us, once with a Yale key, twice with a big brass one that wouldn't have looked out of place in the Lubianka.

We took a taxi to Soho Square and walked the rest of the way. I hadn't bothered to book ahead after all. At that time of day and year, I knew there would be no trouble.

They seated us in an upstairs alcove lined with smoked glass walls beside a wrought-iron staircase. There were real flowers on white molded plastic tables. It was like being in a fairy lighthouse.

Annie was radiant and neurotic in turns again, drinking a lot of cold kümmel between courses and being funny about her husband's advertising friends. But the balance was going more and more wrong as time went by. Every head that surfaced up the spiral staircase made her flinch. I knew she expected to catch sight of her husband or one of his friends at any moment.

The experiment was a failure, and it was my fault. I'd thought that getting her to deal equably and sensibly with the big world was the main priority, so I'd thrown her in the deep end by bringing her to a place where admen were as thick as fallen leaves in Vallombrosa. She was turning into a nervous wreck before my eyes. The fact that she obviously felt guilty about it only made things worse.

We skipped dessert. I ordered a last kümmel for her and a large calvados for me. We drank them while I settled the bill. By the time we left, neither of us had actually seen anyone we knew, which in itself was pretty unusual.

Annie hugged herself in a corner of the taxi and said nothing on the way back. Inside her flat, I put the "Jeepers Creepers" record on again and made coffee. As soon as I decently could, I took her to bed. That turned out to be yet another mistake. I never knew whether she'd drunk too much or not enough. Whatever it was, she couldn't unwind. Her movements were restless and deliberate, and the ridges of muscle down her backbone stayed hard and unyielding. At last, she turned over and cried herself to sleep.

I envied her female ability to find instant emotional anesthesia, but at last I slept too. I slept badly and dreamt a lot until four o'clock. Eight hours is all I can take in a day, and I'd had four of them already in the Jermyn Street sauna.

I smoked in the darkness and then got up. I didn't think Annie would want to face me in the morning, so I dressed quietly and left, locking the flat up behind me. When I came to work things out a long time afterwards, it crossed my mind that I probably hadn't made one sensible decision since the first moment I met her. My decision to leave in the middle of the night, though, was exceptional even by the idiot standards I'd set myself.

The air in the empty, predawn streets bit at my throat like an infection. There were no cruising taxis. I walked past a long line of parked cars. The end one was a green BMW, and I remembered Annie's fears. I laid my hand on the bonnet. It was warm. I'd guessed it already from the film of night moisture that had set everywhere else into a rime of frost. I looked up and down the street but saw nothing. I walked on until I found an all-night minicab office.

Back in my own flat, I showered myself awake and switched on all the lights. For once, the silence bothered me, so I tuned in to a 24-hour commercial station and kept it just soft enough to work by.

I began typing out a report for Sir Bryan Proctor, making two carbon copies for my own files. I took a break at eight-thirty to stretch my back and make coffee. By now, there was a brittle and tentative light outside. It made Inigo Jones's church look like a sarcophagus for robots.

While the coffee perked and sneered at Rose's Rambouts, I thought briefly of a quick jog around the garden but changed my mind. My aging cartilages take enough beating from the odd evening game of five-a-side football. I drank coffee instead and rang Rose at nine o'clock on the off chance that she'd be in early. I was ready to hang up when she came on the line. She sounded tired and truculent.

"Why don't you stop tom-catting around and keep decent hours?" she demanded. I didn't know how she knew where I'd spent the night, but I knew she knew. So far as I was concerned, Rose Panayioutou was West London's leading white witch.

"My hard-working forebears were of the opinion that the day began at dawn," I said lightly. "Who am I to buck the wisdom of the race? What time did you get up?"

"I haven't been to bed. I've been working."

"Rose, don't take this too much to heart," I warned her. "You'll knock yourself out."

"At least I've been *working.*"

"And don't nag. It's none of your damned business where I spend my nights. I can't stand nagging. It's a woman's equivalent of physical violence."

I let her think about that for a bit. My affair with Annie Threlfall and Sir Bryan Proctor's business had brought things to a head between us. Rose knew it too, but I hoped she was professional enough not to let it get between us and the job to be done. Our personal problems could wait.

"I'm sorry." She spoke with a kind of desolate dignity. "I've been working up the charts you wanted for the other seven countries. I've also been comparing the results on a yearly basis."

"What are they like?" I asked her gently.

"There's no doubt in my mind now. Your analysis has to be correct. Not only is the number of deaths in a particular region the same from one year to another, it's the same from one region to another as well. As a random event, that's inconceivable. The populations of the different regions vary so much for a start, you see."

"Thank you, Rose. I think that about puts the lid on things."

"It's only a detail."

"Everything's detail, Rose. The frieze on the Parthenon is made up of details."

"The frieze on the what?"

"Forget it, you Greek peasant. Can you get it all charted by midday?" I remembered too late that she'd been working all night.

"Of course. Are you presenting to the client?"

"That's right. Don't worry, love, you'll get some action."

"I know I will, tiger," she said quietly, and hung up.

I went back to preparing my report. A little later, Eric rang in.

"Boss, I've had telephone confirmation from all the countries you told me to check. The details are being telexed in now. It's what you expected. There's a newspaper in each place where there's a pattern just like the one in *The Times*."

"Fine. I'll pick the stuff up in an hour's time if you'll get it ready."

I hung up and put the final touches to my report. Rose's charts arrived in a minicab as I was filing the copies. I took a cab to the City via Starkey Brothers' offices in Holborn. Eric was out, but he'd left his telexes and a typed sheet of translations with Miss Malone in reception. I collected them. I arrived in Freda Harman's office at twelve-thirty, punctual and doom-laden as the Lutine Bell.

If Freda Harman knew I'd witnessed the depressing comedy at Don Proctor's party, she gave no sign of it. There were no scars on her immaculate face. She was a vestal geisha with an audio headset plugged into one ear. The prancing golfball on her typewriter danced a quiet accompaniment to the unwinding executive tape cassette beside her.

She noticed me and communed with the office intercom without disturbing her headset.

"Sir Bryan will see you," she said, smiling distantly as though I were a weak joke.

I walked past her into the aquarium penthouse. As always, the tinted glass registered every change in the light and transformed it. The sun was out low over the reach of river between Global House and Blackfriars Bridge. The Thames looked dangerously full and glittered like rumpled foil upstream of HMS *Belfast.* Sir Bryan Proctor was sitting at his desk, his arms on a luxurious briefcase with combination locks and a British Airways label. McVeigh stood, eager and catlike, in the center of the umber tiles, his hands rammed into his pin-striped pockets. They didn't notice me as I came in, and it sounded as though I was interrupting an argument.

"Damn it, Ted," Sir Bryan shouted, "the boy's been back weeks. I want to see him."

McVeigh seemed maliciously amused. "It would appear that your authority has limits, after all," he said. "I've talked to him several times and kept an eye on things, as you instructed. But I can't physically twist his ear and drag him into your presence. He's a grown man."

"Is he, hell." Sir Bryan saw me, broke off and stared angrily into the nearest fish pool as though the fish were in dispute with him. They probably wanted parity with the next pool in the matter of fishfood pellets. There was a sneer in McVeigh's eyes as he followed the old man's gaze. If he ever succeeded to Sir Bryan's job, I didn't rate the goldfishes' chances very highly.

"Right. You wanted this meeting and you've got it," he snapped at me breezily, turning away. "Suppose we get started?"

For once he didn't offer to shake hands, and Sir Bryan was still staring angrily into the fish pool. Social courtesies seemed to be out today. The wall connecting with Freda Harman's office had retractable aluminum brackets. I pulled them out and started stacking Rose's charts on them. If they wanted what I had to say fast and rude, they could have it that way.

"You asked me to investigate a large number of unexplained deaths," I said. "Some of them known to be cases of murder. I've assumed all of them were. That means you want an explanation for around a thousand murders, about the size of a small battle, say."

"Don't be bloody ridiculous," Sir Bryan snapped. "You can't assume any such thing." He was looking worse than when I'd seen him before. His face was grey and scabrous, and his jawline was marked by a ridge of silver bristles as though he found it hard to shave. Perhaps British Airways hadn't taken good care of him.

"Yes, I can."

It wasn't often that anyone contradicted him flatly, and he shot me a nasty look.

McVeigh seemed amused as I pressed on.

"It's a necessary inference," I said. "There's no point in my investigation unless you assume that the deaths are related, and the whole point of your findings so far is that a large number of specific relationships already exist. Therefore, I assume the cause of death is a common factor."

McVeigh remembered his manners and went to the big oak cabinet. He poured three glasses of white burgundy and handed them round.

"The obvious problem is motive," I said. "I realized early on that your policyholders travelled willingly to the places where they were found dead, but seemed concerned to hide the purpose of their journeys. I thought it might be interesting to know what their purpose was, assuming it was always the same. I considered everything, even drug orgies in the wilds where no one could see them."

"No postmortem evidence of toxic substances in the blood," Sir Bryan snapped.

"Even if you knew the reason, that wouldn't in itself explain why anyone would want to kill them," McVeigh argued reasonably.

I ignored them both. "Political murder also crossed my mind. That at least might account for an obvious lack of information and the fact the money doesn't look like an adequate motive."

McVeigh hesitated. "We found no pattern of political motive or allegiance," he said. "A lot of the victims seemed quite apolitical."

"You don't sound too sure of it."

"There were exceptions, including a few definite extremists, perhaps more than there should have been in a representative sample of young men. But we found no convincing pattern of allegiance or opinion."

I nodded, put my glass down and took up position by Rose's charts.

"There are plenty of ramifications I don't understand myself yet," I said. "The main thing, though, is that I now know who is killing your customers and how it's being done."

I had their undivided attention. Sir Bryan tore his eyes away from his fish and stared at me with cold concentration. McVeigh looked anxious and eager.

"One of my assistants charted the chronological distribution of deaths over the year," I said. "She noted a periodic regularity in them, the number of deaths always peaking in late spring and summer."

"Of course she bloody did," Sir Bryan snapped. "It's obvious. We're talking about people who got killed in the country. You wouldn't expect them to muck around the countryside in the bloody middle of winter."

"She said the periodicity was more detailed than that. There's a cumulative regularity in the build-up and tail-off which she couldn't explain and which seemed to be determined by specific factors. When I came up with the reason for the deaths, the pattern made sense."

I picked up the clear acetate sheet that Rose had drawn for me and laid it over the first chart.

"Never mind the logic for the vertical lines yet," I said. "The point is, they divide the year into spells of several months at a time. When you add up the number of deaths in each period, you get an exact geometrical progression, the totals halving as you go on, starting from the peak period of course."

Sir Bryan looked baffled and irritated. "You can get any progression you bloody like if you draw your lines in the right place," he grunted.

"Sure you can," I agreed, moving the acetate sheet on, "except that the same time divisions produce the same mathematical progressions in every year and in every country where you've been taking losses."

There was a silence. Sir Bryan rubbed his chin with the back of his hand.

"You'll check all this, Ted?"

"Certainly," McVeigh murmured, making a careful note on his pad with a slim silver pencil.

"Go on," he said.

I had removed the first lot of charts and replaced them with the other set.

"These plot the geographical distribution of deaths each year in Great Britain," I said. "My assistant is drawing up equivalent ones for the other countries." I picked up the other clear acetate sheet Rose had prepared. "Again, never mind the logic of the lines for the time being. The point is, they divide up the country into eight regions. Count up the number of deaths in each region over the whole year, and you'll find it's exactly the same. Again," I moved the sheet on, "apply the same divisions over the map for any other year, and the numbers stay the same."

McVeigh was writing fast. Sir Bryan looked apprehensive. His face was greyer. He glanced diffidently at McVeigh. "What's the odds on all this being some kind of natural coincidence, Ted?" he asked.

McVeigh looked up with a casual smile.

"About the same as some future historian being able to prove that the victims of Auschwitz died from food poisoning," he murmured.

Sir Bryan looked like a drowning man who'd clutched at a straw and seen it swim away.

McVeigh turned to me. "I think I begin to perceive the trend of your analysis," he announced quietly.

I walked to the big windows of the penthouse facing downstream. The day was getting middle-aged and a low sun was igniting the Thames.

"The regularity in these patterns is something you should have picked up. There's only one inference to draw," I said. "Your policyholders are not suffering unfortunate accidents. They're not being killed by unknown assailants." I turned to Sir Bryan with something like compassion. "They're killing each other off. It seems there exists some violent underground cult nobody's ever heard of whose members fight duels to the death at prearranged times. The survivors then fight each other, and so on. That's why there's a strict periodic progression in the number of deaths. They fight over eight regions. Fighters from the same region fight within that same region. Fighters from different regions fight on the territory of a third. That's why the geographical spread is regular and invariable. Presumably, the cult members fight for stakes, which is why the sums assured under your life policies are always exactly the same. There is no other theory that explains these facts."

There was another, apparently endless, silence in the big penthouse. McVeigh brushed cigar ash from the engraved surface of the cuff-link the size of a tomtit's egg. Sir Bryan had slipped something surreptitiously into his mouth from an enamelled cachou box. He put the box back in his pocket and stared at me.

"You're barmy," he said matter-of-factly. "I've never heard anything so insane in my life. Are you seriously suggesting that perfectly normal young men are killing each other off like knights in shining bloody armor, just for the hell of it?"

"Hardly for the hell of it," McVeigh objected suavely. "I seem to recollect you being of the opinion that Global's losses were reaching alarming proportions."

"You don't mean you take him seriously," Sir Bryan yelped.

McVeigh ignored him and turned to me. "I take it this cult you have in mind includes the young men named as beneficiaries among its members and that the policy proceeds are passed on to the winners in some way?"

"It seems logical. I haven't had time to check yet. The round of duels seems to start afresh each year, and we're not far off the beginning of the next round. My theory would certainly explain why policies are never more than a year old when the holder dies. If you put your Army of Ferrets to checking the details, they should be able to confirm that the beneficiaries never actually spent the money they got."

I went back to my chair. "There's another possibility. If beneficiaries are part of this nutty cult, there's a chance they also fight duels later on. A check through Jake should show whether any of them took out Global policies and got killed in later years."

McVeigh was covering his pad with notes. "We'll check," he said. He laid his pencil down for a moment. "Let me be sure I've understood you. Your theory postulates some kind of bizarre cult whose members fight duels to the death on a knock-out league basis. Is that right?"

I nodded.

McVeigh considered. "Well, that might account for why a conspiracy on the necessary scale has managed to remain undetected for so long. As Charlie Omphrey would no doubt point out, murderous cults seem to be characteristic of young men today, along with a certain clannish secretiveness."

"Archaic tribal rites have other features," I said. "Members usually go in for special ceremonies and badges of rank, things like that. They go in for ways to recognize their status publicly, too."

"Dear me," McVeigh observed. "You're beginning to sound like Omphrey yourself."

"On the other hand, public recognition would destroy the secrecy element unless some kind of code was used," I said. "Anyway, I went into the idea and it paid off. I found out that an unusual number of your customers took *The Times.* It wasn't so unusual as to be noticeable. On the other hand, you don't have to order a paper to read it. You don't even have to buy it."

McVeigh raised his eyebrows. "Are you telling me that results of these duels appeared on *The Times* sports pages disguised as lacrosse match reports?" he enquired.

"*The Times* carries personal announcements, some usually cryptic. I made a list of dates on which policyholders were killed and got one of my assistants to check for unusual announcements near those dates."

I picked up Eric's first list and read out the top items. "'Midlands bows to South West.' That was on the fourteenth of October. 'South East bows to Scotland.' There are ten of these in all last year," I said. I put the list down. "Each occurred very near the time when one of your policyholders from the region mentioned happened to die."

McVeigh pursed his lips and stood up. He went to the oak cabinet to refill my glass and his own. He ignored Sir Bryan's.

"Ten announcements to account for around thirty-five deaths in England last year," he remarked. "It sounds tenuous if, as I assume, the regions mentioned correspond with the geographical divisions you've drawn up." He handed me my glass. "You'd certainly have to account for why you found so few."

I put my glass down untasted. "It bothered me at first," I admitted. "But look at it this way. There are eight regions, the progression of deaths is always strictly mathematical, and you've been suffering losses of between thirty and thirty-five people a year in each country, allowing for what you called computer error."

I got up and went back to Rose's charts. "The nearest relevant multiple of eight is thirty-two. If you assume that is an actual constant number of relevant deaths, it gives us four duellists to each region. A reasonable assumption might be that those four fight each other first in regional qualifying contests, the survivor going through to represent his region."

McVeigh considered. "Reasonable, but a highly imaginative guess," he decided. "How would it answer my question?"

"Regional qualifying contests wouldn't be of interest to such a cult nationally. Only to the region itself. I've got one instance of announcements appearing in a regional newspaper. Your Army of Ferrets should be able to find others."

McVeigh made another note. "That seems feasible," he admitted. "Your hypothetical contestants fight, then, for a fifty thousand pounds stake and for some sort of recognition coded in announcements to *The Times.* Yes," he repeated, "it's feasible, if insane, as Sir Bryan points out."

Sir Bryan Proctor stirred. He'd been sunk in thought. McVeigh and I had hardly noticed him.

"Public honor. Recognition," he said calmly. "Who the hell gives a shit about those things these days?"

"Your dear father, the Major, did," McVeigh murmured caustically. "So do you. There's a caseful of his tatty medals in your desk right now."

Sir Bryan blushed, as though he'd been accused of harboring pornography. It embarrassed me before I decided that it was probably some pathological reaction related to his skin infection. As on the last occasion I'd been in the big penthouse, I found myself getting angry at McVeigh. He was an easy man to dislike, though I realized pretty well what was going on. Charles Omphrey had advised Sir Bryan to delegate the day-to-day running of Global to him. The result was that McVeigh was developing the Great Man Syndrome. I wondered why it was that top executives of big companies always have to prove their status by becoming eccentric and plain rude. I wondered whether McVeigh had got round yet to insisting on black onyx bidets in all the executive washrooms.

McVeigh turned to me again, his face open and charming. A seagull on a ledge outside screamed faintly at a parakeet on the inside.

"I'm impressed," he admitted. "Your theory is sublimely improbable, but it does seem to tally with the known facts. Thirty-two young men in eight regions fight duels of some sort for a stake of fifty thousand pounds received, and later released, by policy beneficiaries who are themselves involved in the conspiracy. The survivors fight it out in turn until there is, presumably, an overall winner. In addition, if I understand you correctly, contestants fight for overt recognition within such a cult by means of coded announcements in the press."

I said nothing and McVeigh paused. "Everything, of course, will depend on whether detailed research supports your thesis. At this stage, my main worry is that it depends purely on inference. It would be pleasant if you could produce at least one piece of hard evidence."

I shuffled my papers and picked up the small sheaf of letters the victims had received from bookshops.

"You saw fit to tell me late in the day that most of your victims had Ordnance Survey maps in their possession when their bodies were found. I accepted your view that they were travelling to out-of-the-way places and that Ordnance Surveys are the most generally available large-scale maps. But I was still puzzled. If this cult, or whatever it is, works the way I see it doing, then duellists would naturally fight on neutral territory so that neither party had a 'home' advantage. In fact, the assumption explained the even and regular distribution of deaths geographically.

"I also have verbal evidence to the effect that a lot of your victims made their travelling plans at the last moment and had to disrupt other plans to do so. That fitted, too. The scheme presumably wasn't designed to leave contestants time for a personal reconnaissance of the territory. But on both counts I couldn't understand how they had time to order and receive maps by post."

I picked up the first letter, the one I had got from Mrs. Levis at Aldershot. "I noticed first that these letters we found all made reference to other books the recipient had asked about. I had hopes that the titles would tell me something about what was on their minds at the time. Then I noticed that all the letters had typed letterheads and that the addresses had been impossible to trace."

McVeigh reflected. "If secrecy was important, it's reasonable to suppose our policyholders would purchase from small shops a long way from home," he observed. "Lots of small businesses change premises. Lots of them don't run to printed letterheads."

"I only realized yesterday that I was looking at the thing the wrong way round," I said. "These kids didn't send away for maps at all. The maps were sent to them as a way of informing them that a duel was arranged and that it would be in the territory covered by the map sent. One simple and factual check confirmed the guess. Even Ordnance Surveys cover a pretty big area, so your policyholders would have to have more detailed information where to go. The point about the references to catalogue numbers of other books in each case is that they *are* numbers."

McVeigh thought for a moment and smiled.

"Grid references," he observed.

"Right." I picked up Ordnance Survey 169. "This is the map referred to in the first letter I came across. The catalogue references are thirty-four and forty-seven. They pinpoint the exact area of Suffolk where the boy died." I read from my notes. "Other numbers pinpoint Fernworthy Forest on Dartmoor, the Changue Forest and Cannock Chase. There are others. They all check with known facts about where the recipient of the letter died."

I laid down my notes and maps. "I'm betting that every policyholder got one of these letters. The reason why only a few survive is that they would normally have been destroyed once the location had been noted. Odd letters that were left behind weren't considered important enough to be kept by relatives. That's not inference, McVeigh. That's evidence."

McVeigh used his cigar cutter with care and thought for a while.

"Very well," he said at last. "Assuming that all the detailed checks work out, I'm convinced." He turned, apparently remembering that we weren't the only ones in the room. "You agree, Sir Bryan?"

I wasn't sure he'd heard at first. He hadn't spoken for some time, and he was still staring into the bottom of his empty burgundy glass. He looked up at me at last with an expression of weary dislike.

"What you are suggesting is lunatic," he said heavily. "Our investigations have not demonstrated that all my policyholders were murdered. Postmortem investigations revealed no evidence of illicit drug-taking." He placed his glass on the desk with something like pain. "Nor has there been any suggestion that any of them were clinically insane."

McVeigh and I said nothing. We waited, McVeigh with an expression of faintly amused detachment.

"I've had a lot of respect for your talents in the past," Sir Bryan went on. "It is possible that there may be something in what you say, but I cannot accept that sane men would play ducks and drakes with their lives, still less lay bets on their own survival."

"It surprises me to hear you say so," McVeigh murmured. "Looked at objectively, our business enshrines the same principle. Our clients bet us a monthly sum they'll die before reaching a certain age. We bet them a capital sum they won't."

Sir Bryan turned wearily. "In case you hadn't noticed," he sneered with an attempt at sarcasm, "there is a slight difference. Insurance is serious business without which organized social existence would hardly be possible. We protect our clients against personal disaster. We don't bloody assassinate them."

McVeigh shrugged. "The mechanisms are the same," he repeated, "and an unfortunately large number of young men today would be indifferent to your ethical distinction. It occurs to me that if our friend's theory is correct, whoever arranged for stakes in this contest to take the form of insurance policy benefits must have had a warped but sane sense of humor."

"Dammit, Ted," Sir Bryan shouted with something of his old authority, "nobody's that cold-blooded."

"Aren't they?" McVeigh's answer was like a whiplash. "We are all of us capable of being that cold-blooded under appropriate circumstances. All of us," he repeated with a kind of feral implacability, making me remember his tale of Lady Proctor. "It seems to me you are taking an unconscionable time to accept a perfectly simple idea merely because you find it personally offensive."

It was the nearest thing to a public rebuke I had ever seen the old man suffer. He opened his mouth to reply, changed his mind and subsided into silence again. We were all silent. We had witnessed a turning point, and we all knew it. The failing head of the tribe had faced a challenge to his authority and had backed down. The primate horde of Global Alliance had a new dominant male. I found myself disliking McVeigh more than ever.

Sir Bryan made a last, halfhearted effort to recoup his position. He rounded on me, the lesser enemy. "In any event, your daft theory falls down on one simple point. You've explained nothing about who is organizing this attack on my companies. You have no idea who they are, and you've shown no conceivable reason why such an attack should be specifically directed at me."

"What did you expect to find?" McVeigh sneered. "Someone in charge like the boxing Board of Control?"

I didn't like being McVeigh's henchman, but I had no choice. "I've no idea who is organizing everything, Sir Bryan, because I've had no time to look. All I've been able to do so far is deduce some rules of this mad contest, like the fact that overt weapons seem to be forbidden and that results of duels are supposed to look like accidents, which usually seems to work. As to the fact that your companies alone are suffering, there could be a simple explanation."

McVeigh frowned. "If insurance policies work as stakes in the way you say they do, logic suggests that all major insurance companies should be affected."

I shook my head. "Not necessarily. There are lots of these duels but not many insurance companies. Spreading policy proposals around would increase the number of companies in a position to eventually realize something funny was going on. There may be another advantage to picking on one insurance group only."

McVeigh ignored the hint. He was thinking of something else.

"What happens to the survivors from these eight regions you describe? What happens to the money?"

I picked up Eric's list of newspaper announcements again.

"The next-to-last announcement I found in *The Times* read 'Scotland bows to South-West. South-West is Cromwell.' That was on 20th December. The last one was quite a bit later. It read 'Cromwell bows to Gustavus Adolphus.' I asked my assistant to make notes of key phrases that cropped up even when the dates didn't seem right."

Sir Bryan looked stunned. McVeigh's eyes danced.

"Fascinating," he breathed. "Am I to gather that this martial cult produces a national champion named after a military hero and that national champions of different countries fight each other?"

"It looks like it. Each country seems to be divided into eight regions, and you've been taking losses in eight different countries. There appear to be quarter-final, semifinal, and final rounds in each country and in Europe as a whole. The last two left in Europe at the moment seem to be Gustavus Adolphus and Denfert Rochereau," I added, consulting my notes again.

"Who," asked Sir Bryan naively, "was Denfert Rochereau?"

"A French colonel of artillery in the nineteenth century," McVeigh explained without looking at him. "He defended the town of Belfort against an entire Prussian army." He looked at me. "And what happens to the survivor of the two you mention?"

"A few of the earliest *Times* announcements my assistant picked up were dated almost a year ago. One read 'William the Silent bows to Von Runstedt. Von Runstedt is Ludi Victor.' The next one was 'Ludi Victor III bows to Ludi Victor II.' The way I understand it, there is an overall European champion each year who has the right to challenge the previous year's champion. Last year, it looks like the challenger won."

"The Ludi Victor," McVeigh breathed quietly. The sonorous Latin suited the immense penthouse and the ponderous Victoriana. "The Victor of the Game. What an extraordinarily interesting idea." He smiled suddenly. "According to my rough calculations, such an overall winner would scoop a European pot of around thirteen million pounds. Possibly twice that amount if he successfully challenged the winner from a previous year. What a most interesting idea."

He turned to Sir Bryan. "Do you still think men wouldn't lay odds on their own survival for money like that?" he enquired.

Sir Bryan shook himself and pressed a switch on the office intercom. "Miss Harman, you collect my copy of *The Times* every day. Keep an eye on the personal columns until further notice. I want to know about any references to a Ludi Victor. Yes, that's right." He spelled it out for her. "No. It has nothing to do with our senior public schools so far as I know. Just do as you're told."

He released the switch and fell back in his chair again.

McVeigh looked at me. "Where do we stand now in your hypothetical schedule?" he enquired.

I consulted my notes. "The last two survivors I mentioned from last year should be fighting about now to decide which of them is this year's Ludi Victor. I assume that, like last year, the survivor will challenge the previous year's winner. The whole process seems to take a few weeks. After that, the first of this year's preliminary qualifying rounds should begin again." I paused. "I mentioned earlier that there could be more than one advantage to having all insurance policies taken out with one company."

McVeigh and Sir Bryan looked at me.

"If all the major companies were affected, there'd be an incentive for them all to take vigorous action since none of them would be alone in their troubles. The organizers of this game may be banking on the fact that one company alone is going to be too afraid of the bad publicity to risk it."

"What are you suggesting?" McVeigh asked softly.

"I'm suggesting nothing. I just want to know what you're going to do about stopping next year's rounds. In my view, it's soon got to be a police matter if it's not already."

Sir Bryan was galvanized. He might have had a bad time with McVeigh, but he wasn't taking that kind of talk from a mere hireling.

"You mind your manners and your own business, boy," he snapped loudly. "I just pay you to find things out and keep your trap shut. Is that understood?"

"I'm sorry, Sir Bryan," I said firmly. "It's not like that, and you know it. It's in my contract that I report police business to the police. All right, so I bend the rules sometimes. But I can't let another series of thirty-two murders happen just to please you."

"You'll do what you're bloody told," he roared, "or I'll see you end up running a petrol station in Guatemala."

"Gentlemen, gentlemen." McVeigh seemed amused. "There's no need for an unseemly row." He looked to me first. "Our first priority must be to determine who is organizing this conspiracy, I think. Judging from the international ramifications and the need to recruit the large number of people who play this bizarre game, the organizing body must be considerable. There must be ways in which you can get a line on it."

"All I've got so far is a bunch of newspaper announcements," I said. "I can try to find out who placed them, but I don't expect much. They'll have covered their tracks."

"Not necessarily," McVeigh said. "Once any investigation got this far, the conspiracy was bound to be basically finished. The organizers could be relying simply on total mystification. Besides, as you said yourself, there are other steps we can take. I have already got the list you requested from Jake of new policyholders at risk. We can reexamine the proposals. Revoke their policies if necessary. The Army of Ferrets can start again on surviving policy beneficiaries from previous years. There's a lot we can do."

"You'd alarm the organizers of this game and lose your money," I pointed out. "Is that what you want? They'd go to ground and you'd find out nothing."

"My dear boy," McVeigh sighed patiently, "please make up your mind. You want drastic action, and you shall have it. Do you imagine Global can keep taking these losses indefinitely? Just leave the decision to us as to how to terminate the conspiracy, that's all."

"O.K.," I agreed reluctantly. "So long as I have your formal undertaking to inform the police before next year's rounds start if the cult's still in existence by then."

McVeigh hesitated and shrugged. "Very well, since you insist. In practice, I could hardly prevent you from doing so anyway." He looked at Sir Bryan. "Do you agree?" he demanded.

The old man looked crushed. "Calling in the police isn't a decision I could reach on my own," he mumbled. "I would have to consult with the International Holding Board."

McVeigh and I glanced at each other. We could both remember a time when the Chief Executive of Global Alliance would have altered the progress of stars in their courses without consulting the Almighty if he had felt like it.

"A board meeting is already scheduled for the near future," McVeigh reminded him. "I could bring it forward."

"Very well," Sir Bryan got up heavily and walked to the door. "Do what you damn well think best." He was greyer than ever, but he forced a genial and confident smile for me.

"Do your best, boy, but no drastic action without consulting me first, understand? Making this public could ruin Global. I'd cut off my right arm before I saw that happen." He hesitated, still anxious to reassure himself. "I know you'll sort things out, you always do. Better report in every forty-eight hours from now on."

He turned and stumbled through the door. McVeigh accompanied him. I stood by the big bronzed windows of the penthouse and stared upstream. The Thames looked like restless tufa, and HMS *Belfast* seemed to be waiting for something to happen. Eventually I stowed my presentation documents in a drawer of Sir Bryan's desk, locked it and left the office. I travelled in solitary state to the ground floor and left the desk key at reception.

I was preoccupied by a lot of things, but mostly by the vertiginous shift in power at Global House. I supposed it was the business of the old lion being hustled out of the way by an aggressive upstart, but McVeigh's brand of urbane vindictiveness had me worried. There was nothing overt about it, just a measured playing on Sir Bryan's increasing weakness. I wondered what impelled him. Somehow, a quarter of a century's subservience to the old tyrant didn't seen motive enough.

Sir Bryan's decline, though, was easy to follow. He'd been ill for some time, and now it was affecting his mind. By his standards, I'd seen him evade facts, stand aside from decision making and dodge responsibility, all within the space of an hour. It disconcerted me to see the old carnivore eat humble pie.

From the Journal of Denfert Rochereau, Ludi Victor IV

. . . Today I felt closer to death than I have ever felt in my life. There are times when one remembers the embarrassments of adolescence, those occasions when one said or committed a *bêtise* so gross that the soul cringed afterwards. It was like that today. The sense of how close I had been to death, the ease with which I could imagine the reality, made me shudder. But from distaste, not fear.

Later, naturally, there came the other sense of myself, the sense of being more than ever alive. It came as I left the combat zone at the close of the afternoon. I walked down six steep, worn steps from the hostelry at Tann past a row of chipped lead-glazed pots full of geraniums in bud. At the bottom of the steps, on my way to my rented car, my balance shifted to accommodate itself to level ground. I felt my heels attack the cobbles, the bones seeking each new position, while my toes drew inwards and down, like a squirrel grasping a nut, to propel me forward.

This sense of life is linked with the other, the sense of death, for I was feeling with my skeleton, the timeless structure of myself which will endure when the rest of me is long gone. It is a sense I have always looked for and found only in the Game. It has little to do with what my priggish father used to call self-indulgence.

When I received my map and instructions, there was no need for delay. I have my own reference library and was able to find out much about the combat zone from it. This is not, of course, to say that I sought unfair advantage. It is a simple precaution, like packing a tourniquet or a spare sweater. The zone lay to the east of Frankfurt, close to the zonal frontier with East Germany, in a wilderness called the *Spessart.*

My bag was already prepared and my car, an old Studebaker Champion, filled with petrol. I should always have liked to drive it to combats, but that is, naturally, impossible. I parked it at the airport and was able to get a seat without difficulty on an early flight to Paris. In Paris, I caught a Lufthansa flight to Frankfurt and hired a butcher's wagon, a Mercedes, to drive to Tann, where I registered at the little *gasthof* with the geraniums.

I needed no alarm call this morning. I was woken by the squealing of pigs, for the *gasthof* is a combined inn, restaurant, and slaughterhouse. I dressed and left my room, pausing briefly to view the operations taking place in the half-light of the inner courtyard below. The area was lit like a stage with lights strung from the balconies. A great sow had been stunned. An old crone was already drenching the animal with boiling water to scrub the bristles off while an old man slit the animal's throat and collected blood from which they make the excellent *boudin* of these parts.

I breakfasted on warm rolls, coffee, and fresh *charcuterie.* I ordered extra rolls to be made up for use later in the day. I do not like to eat or drink while a combat is in progress, but it is necessary. When the body is short of blood sugars, the mind wanders. I filled my canteen with a bottle of mineral water before quitting the place.

An hour after dawn, I had already completed my fast reconnaissance of the zone and assured myself that no one was there before me. It lay in a forest, itself a bulge in the zonal frontier following the banks of a small stream. There was game around, even wild boars, but it was clear from their movements that they had not been disturbed. The sun was already warm and the sky clear. Gustavus Adolphus and I were to have an excellent day for our combat.

I sat in a clearing on the side of a hill to consider tactics. This can be dangerous but useful, for it serves to concentrate the mind during the early, vulnerable stages of combat. Danger, of course stems from the fact that a consideration of possibilities may lead to shock when the actual occurs.

Below me, the forest dropped steeply. Beyond the stream, no more than a kilometer away, there was a village, a huddle of roofs with a single paved street. I consulted my map and realized that, invisible from where I sat, the zonal frontier intervened, a double line of barbed wire fencing, thickly sown with land mines. I marvelled at the absurdity of a civilization that could maintain such a barrier with nuclear terror and yet would regard me as criminal if it knew what I was in the *Spessart* for. That little village, so apparently close and inviting, was in practice less accessible to me than Lima or Macao.

I stubbed out my cigarette. It would be my last before the combat was over, or perhaps simply my last. I was nervous. I hoped passionately that the Swedish champion would prove a better opponent than the Greek in Spain.

There followed several hours in which very little happened. I quartered the zone methodically, stopping often. Once I was stalking parallel to a track where trees had been marked with symbols to guide weekend walkers, hoping that Gustavus might be rash enough to stick to such a route for the sake of speed and silence. I froze as a fawn stepped into the sunlight a few meters away from me. I knew that the doe would be nearby, keeping an eye on it. If she saw me, she would warn the fawn and Gustavus Adolphus with her honking. The reverse, of course, was also true. If she saw Gustavus, I would be warned. I waited until the fawn tripped away up the sunlit path before I resumed my sweep.

Contact came with, to me, disastrous unexpectedness. I came to a brook, the one that accounted for the bulge in the zonal frontier. There was a strip of coarse meadow beside it. I was hot and, rather than deplete my canteen, I decided to drink from the brook. I watched carefully from inside the trees for several minutes. Reassured, I lay down in the grass and dipped my face in the water. Almost immediately, hard hands clamped around my throat from behind, forcing my head under water. I fought to free myself but could not. My arms strained behind me but found nothing, and my head was immobilized by painful pressure. I had had no time to catch breath, and shock made me use up residual oxygen fast. Suffocation threatened to overwhelm me.

I acted instinctively as I have seen wrestlers do. My attacker's weight was now on my body, so I heaved my buttocks up with a mighty effort and walked my legs towards my shoulders. When I was at an acute angle, arse in the air, I rolled forward into the water. At once the hands slipped from my neck.

I thundered out of the brook, water cascading from me, and leapt around several times, my arms at full stretch. There was nothing and nobody. On all sides the forest and sky smiled in total silence. I sprinted up the meadow along a small track. I soon felt safe enough to move quietly, but I did not stop until I reached the slope from which I had seen the little village across the frontier. I was confident that I had not been followed. I was also badly frightened, freezing, and puzzled.

I always carry a small pack of spares into the combat zone. I had hidden it in a cairn of stones near the clearing. I stripped rapidly, drying myself on a small hand towel, and made a change of underwear and socks. Afterwards, I broke my rules and smoked a cigarette, knowing that the thin nylon of my camouflage top and trousers would soon dry in the sun. The last thing I needed now was stiff and inflexible joints.

As I smoked, I puzzled. Why had Gustavus Adolphus not followed me from the stream? I knew he hadn't, for at the speed I had tråvelled, there was no way he could have done so silently. For that matter, why was I still alive? I could not fathom the Swedish champion. If he was armed, why had he not used his weapon while I lay helpless with my face in the water? Alternatively, if he had felt able to rely on his strength, why had he allowed me to break his grip through such a predictable stratagem?

I decided he must be of a type I have heard spoken of with disparagement, though I have not myself encountered one in my tour of duty. It had to be that he was a prankster, a bravado expert who refined his combats by tricks to progressively demoralize his opponents. Such men are said to be unworthy of the Game. It may be so, but for myself I simply cannot see the point of such behavior. Gustavus had certainly not demoralized me, and only a fool multiplied willfully the number of occasions on which he might be killed.

I stubbed out my cigarette and moved off again. I had to regain the psychological advantage quickly, so I made for the stretch of stream where I had been ambushed.

I had my first sighting around midday. I had crossed the brook at a run, penetrated the belt of trees on the other side and crossed a narrow metalled road. The remainder of the zone lay in deep ground beyond the road.

I climbed a tall tree to view my surroundings and saw him almost immediately, or a flash of him. Two hundred meters to my left, parallel with the road, he was sprinting swiftly into a steep ravine. He was tall and thin, with a woollen cap covering his bright yellow hair. I used my monocular to verify him by his armband. I immediately climbed out of my tree and set off after him. Always, I must take the advantage. Near the end of the ravine, however, I paused and hid. There was neither sight nor sound of him.

A doubt nagged me. Gustavus had been *running* into the ravine. Why? Had he seen me? I had to assume so, for there was no other obvious reason for his haste. Did he also think I had seen him? Again, I decided to assume so. I decided also to assume that this was another trap. My reasoning was simple. His previous behavior caused me to judge him a prankster but an astute opponent. He had no cause for fear and might very well guess that my instinct would make me follow him. It was obvious, too, that the ravine into which he had run made an excellent site for an ambush.

Within the context of risk which is the whole point of the Game, only a fool takes unnecessary chances. I consulted the highly detailed map they had sent me and saw that the ravine cut into the side of a small but steep hill whose base circumference was not considerable. I backed away quietly and made a crawling detour round to the other side of the hill. Here, there was a steep precipice with ledges on which trees with roots gnarled like wrestlers' limbs struggled for purchase. While I considered the precipice, I wondered again what arms Gustavus Adolphus had prepared. For myself, I had prepared a new and untried device. After the Spanish fiasco, I was no longer happy with my well-tried slingshot. Inevitably, the violent fortunes of the Game make even the most rational man superstitious.

I began to climb. When I was halfway up, my second bad moment happened. I had paused on a ledge. Glancing up, I was in time to see Gustavus appear and begin a descent in my direction. If he had known I was there, he could not have contrived a more perfect ambuscade. I was utterly exposed and vulnerable. Slung over his shoulder was the kind of catapult called a wrist-rocket, an implacable device of tubular alloy incorporating a grip which bears down on the forearm to afford immense leverage. Propulsion is provided by surgical rubber tubing that can throw a steel ball-bearing through an inch or more of wood at considerable ranges. Endangered as I was, I found time to wonder about his weapon. Should not such devices, like Alexander the Great's bow, be proscribed? More and more it seems to me that the rules of the Game stand in need of clarification and reevaluation.

A rapid analysis told me that Gustavus had no idea of my proximity to him. Armed with such a weapon, he could have killed me without moving from the top of the precipice. By the same token, I was right in supposing that he had laid an ambush for me in the ravine, for he could have knocked me out of my tree like a roosting pheasant with his wrist-rocket. Meanwhile, he was approaching, arse first and preoccupied.

I pressed myself against the taproot of a tree exposed by erosion on my ledge. With this cover, my camouflaged clothing and naturally dark skin, I thought I was safe so long as I didn't move. I pondered various ways to turn the situation to my advantage.

Gustavus' accident happened when he was almost at the base of the precipice. He jumped the last few meters and landed awkwardly. I heard him cry out softly and collapse, clutching the base of his leg.

I reacted immediately, bounding down the precipice with no thought for my own ankles. I made a great racket doing it, but I knew I was safe, for pain absorbs the senses. I could have driven a truck towards him and he would not have heard. Unfortunately, he looked up. He hurriedly released his wrist-rocket and scrabbled for the missile which must have fallen from his grasp.

It was too late to change tactics. In any case, I could not have checked my momentum. So I took a chance and perhaps enjoyed better fortune than I deserved. I snatched up a stone and threw it. It caught him squarely on his forearm as he raised the wrist-rocket, sending it spinning away. There was no time to retrieve it. He got up and half hobbled, half ran into the belt of trees beyond the foot of the precipice.

I ran in after him, which was my first unthinking mistake. The soreness of my neck told me he was a powerful fighter at close quarters where his injury would not put him at too great a disadvantage. I think now that if I survive this year's Game, I too might let my hair grow long like Gustavus. It has the advantage of making the wearer look deceptively frail. My mistake lay in assuming that he would be on the run. I misestimated him. He might have been a prankster, but he was not a coward.

He surprised me in the first ten meters with the same trick I had used to put paid to Alexander the Great. It may even have been my own experience of the trick that caused me to register subliminally a branch of a tree bent sharply out of alignment. At all events, my reflexes and perceptions were good enough to let me duck as the branch smashed forward. Even so, I caught a glancing blow on the shoulder and was sent spinning. I ended up on my back, dazed and disorientated.

Gustavus was onto me quickly, but the undergrowth into which I had fallen impeded him even more than his damaged ankle. He seized a dead bough and whirled it above his head like a broadsword. I had enough presence of mind to roll aside as he brought it down. Even so, I was again lucky. The same brushwood and brambles that impeded him impeded my efforts to get out, but I was protected by a heavily wooded sapling that broke the force of the branch as he brought it down time after time. I remained almost miraculously unhurt, although I was continually showered with bark dust and splinters. I heard the laboured, furious keening of his breath, and I kept my eyes open as long as I dared between strokes.

At last, between strokes, I was able convulsively to roll out of the undergrowth on the other side, tearing my clothes fairly extensively in the process. Gustavus hesitated, realizing that I had regained my crucial advantage of speed and that he had no time to revert to his wrist-rocket. He threw the branch from him and ran awkwardly. I tore after him, feeling the smart of thorns and brushing bark fragments out of my eyes. I brought him down with a fine rugby tackle round the thighs, but he reacted with quicksilver speed. He was already turning onto his back before he touched ground, and the sides of his hands were chopping heavily and repeatedly down on my unprotected neck and shoulders. I immediately released him to protect myself from the heavy blows by blocking them with my forearms. I shouted with pain as one blow got through to the base of my neck. I curled up like a fetus and rolled away.

Completely enraged and with a great deal more aggression than sense, I bounded upright and hurled myself on him again in a shallow dive, intending to knock the breath out of him and then finish him off. He reacted very effectively. He was still on his back, having made no attempt to get up. When I was spread-eagled in the air, he simply whipped his good leg upright in a forward kick, catching me in the pit of the stomach.

Gustavus was the most skillfull and courageous opponent I ever met. In spite of his injury, he had bested me at every turn. But with the odds stacked so heavily against him, he was only allowed one error of judgment apart from his earlier, voluntary one of failing to kill me at the brook. He now made that error. Perhaps he was weakened. Perhaps there was no other dead branch conveniently to hand. At all events, I must have been helpless and at his mercy for at least a couple of minutes. He should have killed me then. But when I could breathe and see again, he had gone. I could hear him crashing through the undergrowth in the distance.

I stood against a tree and was violently sick, each spasm sending a terrible pain through my stomach. When the attack was over, I washed my face with water from my canteen and forced myself to think. Although the odds had been—were still—crushingly in my favor, I was lucky to be alive. I determined then that the manner of Gustavus

Adolphus' death should reflect my anger and reestablish my right to the honors of combat. There was no doubt where he was heading. He had to get a cold compress on his ankle if he was to face me again on equal terms, and the water in his canteen would be as uselessly warm as my own. He had to make for the brook on the other side of the road.

I decided not to follow him. I decided instead to get to the brook first and kill him there, just where he had threatened but stupidly declined to kill me. I was going to drown him. I backed my judgment by racing quietly towards the brook on what I hoped was a course parallel to his own.

I crossed the metalled road and paused on the other side. If my calculations were correct, I must now be slightly ahead of him again, and he should be crossing the road about a hundred and fifty meters farther down. I hid and waited to see if I was right.

It was not Gustavus' lucky day. As in all games, luck plays its part in the Game, along with skill, bravery, and intelligence. He appeared roughly where I expected, scrambled awkwardly down a bank into the road, and that is where it happened.

He had jarred his ankle again in landing. Doubled over in pain in the middle of the narrow road, he was in no position to hear a jeep which spun round the sharp bend towards him and caught him as he was straightening up. I doubt whether he even saw it, any more than the occupants of the jeep saw his camouflaged shape. There was a sickening smash. The impact shot him several meters in the air. He landed on his head and must have been dead before he stopped twitching. I noticed that it was a military jeep. The idiocy which had built the zonal frontier had claimed Gustavus before I could. Even now, the bitterness of that fact rankles.

Two national servicemen of the *Grenzpolizei,* the "Green" Frontier Police, jumped out of the jeep and stared. They were in shock, and I had to take advantage of the fact. I removed my armband and ran towards them.

"Ich habe alles gesehen," I said in my rudimentary *Hochdeutsch. "Es war eine reine Unfall. Der Mensch ist einfach in die Strasse gelaufen."*

They were clearly relieved at my assumption of authority. The country might have changed a bit in thirty years, but Germans are still happy to obey the chain of command when it clanks with the right sound.

"You, Corporal," I said to the older of the two. "Get your emergency triangles out before someone else comes round the bend and there's another accident."

He ducked his head intelligently and ran round to the back of the jeep.

"You," I said to the co-driver, a wisp of a boy with a blond moustache, "haven't you got a first aid kit?"

He went to the cab of the jeep, and I swore to myself. "Get a crowbar first," I shouted. "I'll need a splint of some kind."

Of what possible use he thought a splint might be to a man with a broken neck I don't know. Fortunately, I had assumed command and he had given up thinking. With both men out of sight, I knelt down quickly beside Gustavus Adolphus' body. I removed his key and armband and shoved them in my pocket. I also pocketed the wrist-rocket. I hoped that he had obeyed all the rules and that there was nothing else incriminating on his body.

Luckily, I really do know something of medicine and was able to stay in control of the situation for a while. By now, both boy soldiers were recovering enough to question my actions. Soon they would notice Gustavus' odd camouflage and my own ripped, damp clothing. I made my escape while they were still deferring to me, giving some excuse and promising to report as a witness to the *polizeirevier* at Tann.

I retrieved my spare pack from the glade beyond the stream, made my way to the car and drove back to Tann. From there I drove to Frankfurt and caught the next flight to Paris. I arrived in the early evening.

I gave myself an early luxurious dinner at the Coupole and booked a room at a small hotel in the rue Delambre. I called my Nîmes controller from the bar of the hotel.

"Denfert Rochereau," I announced when he came on the line. "You must congratulate me."

"I do indeed," the man with the thick *Midi* accent said warmly. "Except, of course, that you must now be known as Ludi Victor IV."

I relished the title quietly for a few moments before I explained the day's events.

"The outcome is a police matter," I concluded. "Luckily, there is no possible doubt that Gustavus' death was an accident. The only suspicious circumstance is that I failed to report to the police afterwards, but that will hardly be unusual. I do not believe the military men were in any condition to remember anything significant about me."

"The local controller will verify things," my controller assured me. "Meanwhile, you have a decision to make. Will you challenge or not?"

I knew I should wait a day or so for the euphoria to wear off before committing myself, but I had naturally, arrogantly even, made my decision long ago.

"I shall challenge," I said. "As you pointed out, it will be good to break the stranglehold of the Germans."

"It will indeed," he agreed. "I shall arrange for the issue of the necessary announcements, and I wish you the very best of luck. *Vive la France,*" he added ironically. "If I were you, I would not go to bed sober tonight."

"*Vive le Jeu,*" I responded gaily. "I do not intend to."

After the call, I wandered round the *quartier* for a while and picked up a pretty girl in the Bar Rosebud. As the quaint guide to Montparnasse that I have in my reference library puts it, the rue Delambre is "*fameuse pour ses bars et ses péripatéticiennes.*" The girl was good, and I myself performed well above average. Tomorrow, they will have to change the bolster as well as the sheets. But at two in the morning, after unsuccessfully attempting congress for the third time, the girl groaned in frustration and I grew angry. I should have liked to hurt her a little before telling her that she had the privilege of being screwed by the first French Ludi Victor. Of course I refrained. The temptation to jeopardize everything at the very culmination of the Game must always be a strong one. It is said that Ludi Victor II failed to control it. The Discipline Squads dealt with him, though he was allowed to live. He triumphed in his play-off with Ludi Victor II last year and is to be my next opponent, though he does not yet know it. Someday, when this year's game is over, I must find out more. I should like in particular to know about the higher echelons of the Game itself. I accept the need for security, but a Ludi Victor has his rights.

A taxi took me back to Covent Garden through soft, warm rain that was probably doing a terrific job for the corms and bulbs in a million City windowboxes.

My flat was stale and there was a stack of letters on the mat inside my door. The only important one was from my accountant. He wanted to see me urgently. He usually did around the end of the financial year.

I made a drink and ran a bath. While I waited, I tried to call Annie. Rather late in the day, I'd started to feel bad about leaving her asleep. There was no answer.

The rain stopped at about nine o'clock, and I was feeling empty. I wanted another drink, but I didn't want it alone. So I walked to the Brahms and Liszt where I usually see someone. Two hours later, I glided through the basement walls into Next Door. I ended up at MacReady's. I still hadn't seen anyone.

I got back past midnight and rang Annie again. There was still no answer, so I went to bed. Or, rather, the bed came to me.

The telephone woke me in the morning. It was Annie. I listened for several minutes before I caught her drift. She was nearly hysterical. She said her husband had definitely found out about us and that she'd run away to his weekend cottage near Hastings. He'd discovered where she was and was coming down in the afternoon.

I sat up and lit a cigarette. It tasted like one of the dark corners of Kensington underground station. My watch registered nearly ten o'clock.

"Annie," I said, when I managed to get a word in edgeways, "your husband is a promising young account director at a respectable advertising agency. He is not a cuckolded bedouin. He will not slit your throat from ear to ear."

The image was too vivid for her, and it was several minutes before I managed to get another word in.

"If you're really frightened," I said, "I'll come down myself. I'll be with you after lunch."

"You *can't!*" Annie screamed.

I winced and held the receiver farther away from my ear.

"Oh yes, I can. Let's have the address and telephone number."

"I won't give them to you."

"Yes, you will."

I made a note of them and carried on calming her down. When I'd managed it and hung up, I dressed and went for breakfast at The Italian Joint. I bought *The Times* on the way and read it over a small enamelled dish of scrambled eggs and bacon, capuccino, and lemon marmalade toast.

There was an announcement in the personal columns that jumped down my throat. It read "Denfert Rochereau is Ludi Victor. Ludi Victor IV salutes Ludi Victor II." Not for the first time I reflected that whoever ran the demented private army I'd unearthed had a good corps of signals. I rang Eric Starkey when I got back to the flat.

"I thought it might be you," he said, unhappily, when he came on the line. "Seen the paper, have you?"

"I've seen it. Get onto your foreign contacts again," I said. "You know how the system works now. Find out what regions of their countries these two Ludi Victors represent. Let me know as soon as you can."

Eric agreed with a sigh. I rang off and called McVeigh. He'd read the papers, too. Or, rather, Freda Harman had spotted the Ludi Victor references and brought them to Sir Bryan's attention. He didn't mention Sir Bryan's reaction.

"The announcement means that Denfert Rochereau is challenging last year's winner to a play-off," I said. "Last year's winner was a German, by the way."

"Do you know that, or are you guessing?"

"My assistant is still going through the *Times* back numbers."

"I take it the stakes will be each contestant's accumulated policy benefits?"

There was a long pause.

"We've assumed so."

"So the fellow who calls himself Ludi Victor in a few weeks' time will cop the pot for three years. That'll be around thirty-eight million pounds."

"If you can distance your actuarial brain from the financial aspect a bit," I said, "there's another side to the matter. This year's contest is definitely not over, McVeigh. It's still going on."

McVeigh sighed wearily. "You're not going to raise that canard about going to the police again, are you? I thought you were just trying to annoy Sir Bryan."

"McVeigh, sometime soon two of Global's policyholders are going to fight each other. One of them at least is going to die."

"Of his own choice," McVeigh pointed out, as though sweet reason wouldn't melt in his mouth. "More to the point, you now have a useful further way of skinning your cat."

"What bloody cat?"

"Of identifying the organizers of this ludicrous contest," McVeigh urged me gently. "Somewhere in Europe at this moment are two live, presumably traceable and informed, exponents of it. Find them, and they could lead you to the organizers."

"It's possible," I conceded.

"That's better. Now, why don't you look into it? Is there any way I can help?"

"You're darned right there is. My assistant is going through the

French and German papers now to find out which regions the contestants originally represented."

"So you weren't going to the police after all?" McVeigh said cunningly.

"Not yet. The point is, I want you to put a program through Jake in a hurry."

"What program?"

"You already have a list of policyholders at risk this year. I want a list of all those who took out policies at the beginning of last year and the year before and aren't dead yet."

McVeigh sighed. "I suppose your two candidates would have to be among them. You realize, I suppose, that it will be a very long list even if your assistant can specify the national regions? Global S.A. and G.m.b.H. are very large companies. How will you whittle your prospects down?"

"That's my problem. You just supply the list. By the way, have you brought your International Holding Board meeting forward?"

"It convenes in Brussels tomorrow morning."

"Fine. I want to know what you all decide. I'm still not promising anything, you understand."

I hung up without waiting for his answer. I intended to make an enjoyable, if minor, pleasure of needling McVeigh.

I dialled the most recent number I had for Piers Kenny. It came at the end of a list of fourteen others. He wasn't in. A girl with a world-weary smidgeon of German accent told me he wasn't back. I'd forgotten the strange hours Kenny kept. I left a message for him to ring me as soon as he got in. I said it was urgent.

I made my first ever pot of coffee using Rose's Rambouts filters and surprised myself. I drank it in the kitchen under a nude trade calendar that Huddiesford had given me. The month's picture showed a girl sitting naked in a field with a frozen daffodil tickling her privates. She would have been pretty if it hadn't been for the expression of straight-faced bad temper some photographers mistake for sensuality.

I was pouring my second cup when Piers Kenny rang.

"What do you want?" he demanded. "How did you get this number?"

He sounded brisk for a man who had probably been up all night. Even these days his voice was good enough to pass for a Sotheby auctioneer's.

"I've got a job for you," I said.

"Sorry, old son. Not interested. Try an escort agency."

"You try getting some sleep like everybody else," I retorted. "It generates energy."

"I'm an insomniac. Didn't you know?"

"I know a lot of things about you, Piers."

That silenced him.

"What's the job?" he asked cautiously.

"I'll tell you when I see you."

He thought again. "You know that Spanish bar in Swallow Street? I can be there at eleven-thirty."

"Don't be late," I warned.

I hung up. Somewhere among the papers on my low desk was a copy of the list Eric had made of *Times* newspaper announcements. He'd read once that making copies of everything was sound business practice. I found it wedged under a stale coffee cup and stuffed it into my wallet. I even found time to clear away and take the cups into the kitchen.

It was a blustering, tactless sort of day, but I risked leaving my coat at home. If the girl in Huddiesford's calendar could take the winds of March with beauty, I thought I could do the same in April. I ran into Harry's wife on the stairs and gave her another couple of pounds to clean the flat out and take delivery of any information McVeigh might send round. It was getting to be a hard job in paperwork terms.

I walked through Great Newport Street and Leicester Square on my way to Piccadilly. Kenny's Spanish bar was sandwiched between a plush Indian restaurant and an English seafood place that never seemed to do any business. He was already installed when I arrived with a cool, tulip-shaped glass and a saucer of salted peanuts. He was beautifully dressed as always and as fresh as a daisy. He ordered a manzanilla for me. I cancelled the order and asked for a Fino San Patricio.

"I really am busy," he said reproachfully. He was a slim, refined and very tough young thug, like a cultured Scipio Africanus. "I hope this job pays."

"It's small, urgent, and pays one hundred pounds," I said. "Cash on the nail. No VAT, no tax. It'll take you a few hours at most."

"Tell me."

He sipped his manzanilla with care.

"The personal columns of *The Times*. I want you to research an article on them. The stories behind the cryptic messages. The hidden romance in the lives of people who place them. That sort of thing."

Kenny inhaled a peanut.

"It's been done," he said, "about a thousand times."

Free-lance journalism was one of his more legitimate stocks-in-trade and a cover for some less legitimate ones.

"So do it again."

I took Eric's list from my wallet and handed it over.

"This is a group of announcements that actually appeared. The insertion dates are on the right. I want to know who placed them. If it was a company, I want to know the name of the individual in it."

Kenny scrutinized the list.

"One hundred pounds, you say?"

"Fifty in advance. The balance when you deliver. There's a twenty-five pound bonus if I get results by the end of the day."

He squinted briefly through the clear, pale liquid in his glass, holding it up for a second opinion against a light that hung from the mock wrought-iron well in the center of the tiled bar.

"It sounds awfully simple. Why don't you do it yourself?"

"I'm busy, Piers. I want results fast and you've got the right cover."

"Cover," he sighed. "My sensitive antennae tell me something is not nice about your job. Will there be any comeback?"

I sighed myself. He wasn't any sort of coward, but I knew he'd invent difficulties to put up the price.

"No comeback," I said. "No job could be simpler. You can even keep the information and write the thousand-and-first article on the subject. Anyway, if the tax man and your ex-wives can't find you, how the hell could anyone else?"

Kenny considered.

"You have a point. I'll do it for two hundred. Plus the bonus, of course, and a hundred down."

I had called in at my bank on the way to the bar. I counted out ten new ten-pound notes and laid them on the table.

"Always a pleasure to do business with you," he said graciously. "I'll be in touch."

He shoved the money into a side pocket, drained his glass and stood up. The devoted old Spanish waiter rushed forward to help him on with his coat.

"Adios, Luis," Kenny said shyly.

He forgot to thank me for the drink.

I called in at the Swiss Centre for a quick lunch of steak tartare made with calvados. Afterwards I walked round to the garage. Sean came over to me, wiping his hands on a bit of cotton waste and looking shiftlessly unconcerned. He was a thin man with an ironic lantern jaw and tufts of white hair curling out of his ears. He had the unusual distinction, according to him, of having served at different times in the British and Irish armies as well as the IRA. He was semiretired now, with one plastic valve in his heart and another to come.

"Look, I haven't had the time to look at her," he insisted truculently. "I took her out, though."

"What do you reckon?" I said.

He pulled the lobe of one ear judiciously.

"Could be your timing's buggered."

"Or maybe the plugs need replacing?"

"Or that," he agreed graciously. "Do you want her now?"

"Not if she's going to break down on me."

"Oh, she won't do that." He waved cotton waste in my face. "Tell you what, bring her back when you're finished. I'll see to her, I promise. I filled her up, by the way. The receipt's on the dashboard."

The total was eight pounds twenty, so I gave him a tenner. I drove the Alfa towards Westminster, wishing he'd remember to clean the grease off his hands whenever he borrowed my car. The steering wheel felt like the underbelly of a sick chameleon. At the first set of lights on the south bank, I wiped it with Kleenex soaked in lighter fuel.

I headed south through Maidstone, not because it was the shortest route, but because I liked it. The sky had cleared, and a rowdy breeze was mugging the treetops. The Garden of England was clouded with white and pink blossom, and men were restringing hop poles while a few cock pheasants took time off from foraging to promenade over the fast-drying topsoil.

I got to Annie's cottage by three o'clock. It was a pretty, two-story place of mellow red brick below and clinker-built timber above. Lime-green moss blotched the roof tiles around twin dormer windows, and yellow bursts of forsythia guarded the low oak door. Clumps of hard-pruned roses separated the cottage from apple trees that were old and strangled with mistletoe. They didn't look as though they would ever fruit again, but I guessed Norman Threlfall preferred charm to apples. There was a mud-spattered green BMW parked outside.

The tall, brooding executive with the Afro haircut I had seen in a photograph on Annie's table opened the door. He'd taken his time, and he didn't speak. He just held the door open and brooded.

I stooped to get into a small room full of dark, heavily polished oak. There was a Persian rug on a stone floor and a big stone fireplace flanked by brocade-covered highback chairs. Light came from tiny windows in deep embrasures and exploded into color over brass warming pans and bunches of forsythia in brass bowls.

Annie came down the open, polished staircase. She was wearing her peasant dress with full sleeves and a lot of embroidery on the bodice. Her bronze hair was tightly coiled again. I wanted to uncoil it and see it flood down her back. She looked bleached out, and her jaw trembled as she introduced me to her husband.

"I'll get some coffee," she said.

She almost ran into the kitchen through another small oak door. It banged open again. I could see game and fish painted on a sea of ceramic tiles above enough advanced kitchen equipment to keep Drax B power station operating all by itself.

"Greek, please," Norman called after her. "With a glass of water."

It was his first sign of life since Annie had performed the introductions. He lounged in the chair opposite me, his hands in his pockets and his feet on the fire basket.

"We'd better talk," he said morosely.

"Let's wait till Annie gets back," I suggested.

His face got narrower.

"Annie's upset as it is. Haven't you done enough?"

I lit a cigarette and laid the dead match carefully on a neat pile of kindling beside the fire basket.

"You'd better tell me what you think I've done," I said.

He avoided my eyes.

"My marriage is going through a difficult patch, but it can be saved. I want to save it. I'm not given to transports of sexual jealousy, and I don't give a shit about you. So far as I'm concerned, you're just an outsider who's turned my wife's unhappiness to his advantage."

I nodded reasonably. "Do you mind telling me something?" I asked.

His eyes flicked towards me and away again.

"Do you mind telling me how you found out about Annie and me?"

"Getting worried?" He was trying to sneer his way into real anger. He needed it to keep up the momentum of his attack.

"How did you find out about Annie and me?" I repeated.

"I got an anonymous letter. You're not so popular as you thought, my gigolo friend."

I nodded again. "That might explain it. Annie's frightened. She's scared of you, Threlfall. Has she reason to be?"

He started glaring again and finally managed to meet my eyes. He looked absurdly young and fit. He probably played squash every morning and took cold showers.

"What the hell do you mean?"

"It's obvious, isn't it?"

"She's a conventional girl, basically. I'd say there's a lot of guilt that she rationalizes as fear of me. You should feel proud of putting her in that position."

"It's possible," I conceded. "Only Annie isn't convinced, and neither am I. I don't like it when people run scared, and Annie's scared you'll harm her, Threlfall. You'd better start persuading her she's got nothing to worry about."

"I see." He smiled unexpectedly. "The best method of defence is attack, is that it? Do you know what I think? I think you're changing the subject. I simply want you out of our lives, Annie's and my life. The question is, are you going quietly, or do I get rough?"

"Meaning?"

"How would you like to start with a letter from my solicitors?"

"Enticement's a very old-fashioned charge," I said. "It's also an insult to a grown woman."

Annie had come back with a tray carrying cups, glasses of water, and a little Turkish coffee pot with a long handle. She laid them out on a table between our chairs.

"Does anyone want sandwiches?" she asked nervously. "I can make some."

Threlfall stood up and she flinched.

"Our friend," he said loudly, "is of the opinion that we should have a talk and that you should be present."

Annie straightened up. The sleeve of her floating dress caught the handle of the Turkish coffee pot and tipped it neatly onto the floor. In the silence that followed, Threlfall placed a foot carefully in the path of steaming coffee edging its way towards the Persian rug.

Annie fled back into the kitchen. She came back with a bucket and squeegee mop and started to clean up the mess.

"I can't," she said. The bronze braids of her hair hid her face. "It may be the civilized thing, but I'm not civilized enough." She looked up. There was hurt, sadness, and anger in her eyes. "You two sort it out. You're both so damned good at that kind of thing."

She disappeared back into the kitchen. I heard feet on wood. I guessed there was a second staircase leading to the upper rooms.

Threlfall turned, his hands in his pockets again.

"A ploy to avoid your discussion *à trois,*" he said triumphantly. "Annie always ducks real issues."

He turned back the edge of the Persian carpet just in case. He looked suddenly genial.

"There's no sense in snarling at each other. You can't win, you know. Annie will drop you like a hot potato now. I hope you're enough of a gentleman not to pester her."

He glanced through the window, then at his watch.

"Do you shoot?" he enquired.

I sighed, remembering Huddiesford's vermin safari.

"I have done."

"Let's get some fresh air."

He took a pair of 12-bores from a rack by the door and handed one to me. I looked at it. It was a sidelock ejector by Roberts. I knew the firm. They lived just down the road from me in Covent Garden. It was a very good, very expensive gun. Threlfall rummaged in a drawer and came out with a box of Ely Number 6 Super Game cartridges. He shoved a handful in his Barbour coat. I put some in my jacket pocket.

We strolled through the rose bushes and fruit trees into a neighboring piece of pasture. An old Labrador with rheumy eyes had joined us from somewhere. The sky had cleared like young wine except for the lees of mist in a few hollows.

Threlfall paused by a ditch choked with twigs and brambles. He lifted a flat stone. There was a sudden terrified squeaking. I couldn't see the trap because his leg was in the way. His heel came down firmly, and I heard the crunch as a tiny skull splintered.

"Annie claims you're pathologically jealous," I said as we crossed the pasture. "That friend of hers, Ben Campbell, maintains you just play at being jealous because Annie expects it of you. What's the truth of it all, Threlfall?"

He was scanning the field ahead. There was a covert, thick with rhododendron bushes below the gaunt ribs of its branch canopy. On the topmost branch of the tallest tree, swaying in the breeze, a crow watched us.

"Truth?" he queried. He was watching the crow. "Perhaps Ben's right. Annie needs to think I'm jealous. Perhaps I indulge her. She's a child in many ways. One indulges children."

We were nearing the copse and the crow flapped lazily away without haste or conviction. I stopped.

"Threlfall, you're a bastard. If you really want to keep your marriage in one piece, you can get Annie back any time you want, you know that. All you have to do is tell her you want her. Why don't you do it—or let her go?"

"Birds have got tiny brains," he remarked, "and they can't count. Walk on a bit. It'll think we've gone."

I climbed the field and looked back. Concealed by the copse, Threlfall had entered the trees. The crow was sailing confidently back to its perch. I saw it crumple in the air before I heard the thump of his 12-bore.

He came out with the crow in his free hand. I watched him walk towards me as a second crow climbed the ridge between us, saw him and turned on a track parallel with the one I had taken.

The books say you should never aim a shotgun like a rifle, but Threlfall did. I realized that a straggling thornbush concealed me from the crow. Threlfall held his fire as the bird wheeled. In a second, I would be in line with his muzzles.

I ducked round the thornbush and snapped off a quick shot. A scatter of feathers drifted down and the crow looked as though it had run into a wall. I heard the thud as it hit ground, but I wasn't looking. Threlfall was aiming somewhere near my head, and I had my second barrel pointed at his stomach. A nasty accident was on the cards. The British Field Sports Society would have hated us. Threlfall watched me carefully and lowered his gun. He broke it, hefted it over his arm and pocketed the unused cartridge.

"What was your question?" he said mildly.

"Never mind."

I broke my own gun. We walked back companionably, like two field marshals discussing a truce. Threlfall was thoughtful when we reached the fruit trees around the cottage garden.

"I shall drive back to London when I've changed," he said. "I've a dinner engagement this evening. I'll think over what you've said."

"That's marvellous."

He shrugged.

"What did you expect? I've told you, I want Annie back, and I'll get you out of her hair any way I can. But the actual decision has to be hers."

He lied in his teeth, and he knew I knew it. There was no way he was going to let Annie make a real decision, ever.

"You could start by telling her you want her back," I repeated. "Your problem begins and ends with the fact that she doesn't believe you want her."

His eyes slid past mine. There was something like embarrassment in them.

"Whose side are you on?" he asked.

"Annie's side."

"You think that gives us a common interest?"

"You and I have no common interests, Threlfall. The only person's side you're on is your own. And you're the only one on it."

We were in the cottage now, and the downstairs room was still empty. The glow of brass and old wood had retreated into a quiet dusk. Threlfall switched on a pretty array of oil lamps converted for electricity and fiddled with a concealed rheostat. Then he set a match to the kindling in the fire basket. The air was soon sharp with the smell of oak and apple billets. Incongruous suggestions of roasted chestnuts and mulled cider came to my mind. There was something elegiac and autumnal in the air, the wrong end of the year. It probably had something to do with the emotional atmosphere.

Threlfall was squat on his hunkers, staring into the blaze. When he spoke, it was in a hushed voice, as though Annie might be listening from the ancient, polished staircase.

"I'm not a philosopher," he explained, "but I believe everybody lives basically alone. I believe they do what they do for their own reasons ultimately, and that the only way you can get along with anyone is by sharing enough reasons. I've no time for blandishments or rhetoric. It just confuses things."

It was a strange confession for an advertising man, but I didn't comment.

"How about threats and fear?" I repeated. "Do you have time for those?" Even I spoke quietly.

He stared at me with exasperation.

"I've told you, Annie has nothing to fear from me. She *is* frightened, I'll give you that, but it's a reflection of guilt, that's all. It is also, by the way, the reason why I am leaving now. I'm willing to prove what I say if it'll help get rid of you." He smiled unexpectedly. "So make hay while you can, my friend."

He went upstairs. There was silence while the last of the daylight went. He came back carrying a pigskin grip and slipped on a light brown topcoat.

"I'm not a hypocrite, so I won't shake hands. We'll meet again in any event. You'll do me a favor, though, by cleaning the guns before you leave. The stuff's in the drawer."

He went through the low front door. I heard the BMW start up and idle for a while. Then the engine revved and he was gone. There was more silence. I made myself a stiff drink from ye olde oak cocktail bar and dialled Eric in London.

"How did you get on?" I asked.

"Piece of cake. I've pinned down the regions you want. They're Hessen in Germany and the Bordeaux part of France." He sounded tired but cheerful.

"That's good. Now listen. There'll be quite a few candidates, and the client's providing a search list. The next step will be to sort out the possibles. Can you do that?"

"You bet."

"Fine. The list will be sent round to my flat just as soon as you phone my client with the exact geographical definition of the regions. You'd better get over and pick it up. Start work this evening if you can."

"Will do." Eric sounded grim and determined. I realized again how much he hated the killing and the very idea of the game we had uncovered.

"What do you want me to do when the short lists are ready?"

"I'll be back in London tomorrow morning. We'll go through them and decide."

"O.K. There's something else. You remember I told you the Proctor name rang a bell? Well, it all came back to me. It was funny sort of business. It happened years ago, but I think you ought to know about it."

I thought for a moment. "Not now, Eric. Tell me tomorrow," I said.

I rang off. Long afterwards, when I came to look back on that conversation, the only excuse I could think of was that I was preoccupied with the problem of what to do about Annie Threlfall.

The cottage was silent except for the muted hiss and tumble of the open fire. I adjusted the rheostat behind the door and topped up my glass at the bar. I climbed the worn oak staircase. The steps looked as old as the *Book of Kells,* but there wasn't a squeak anywhere. Threlfall would have resurrected a medieval craftsman if there had been.

Annie was in the master bedroom under the eaves, curled like a fetus on an intricately carved four-poster bed with oatmeal colored sheets and silk hangings. For a moment, the thought flashed through my mind that she was dead and that Threlfall had killed her. Then I heard her slow, quiet breathing. She wasn't the first woman I had known who could hibernate at the first touch of an emotional winter.

I sat in a high-backed chair and drank while I watched. She was unmoving for about five minutes. Then her eyes opened. She looked puzzled. Then she smiled.

"Where's Norman?"

"He's got an important prior engagement in town."

"Norman's entire life is an important prior engagement," she said simply.

She sat up and stared round in the half-light from the door, the oatmeal sheet drifting down off her naked shoulders.

"What are you doing out there? Come into bed and get warm."

"Not now. We're going to dinner. Get dressed."

She got up and stood directly in front of me, her breasts brushing rhythmically across my face. A dusting of talcum powder was caught in the hair between her thighs.

"Don't change the subject," I said.

I waited downstairs until she was ready. We drove into Hastings and had dinner at a tiny restaurant where the seafood cocktail came with a sauce made of fine sand, ketchup, and preserved horseradish. Annie giggled as the proprietor dashed out of his kitchen between courses to knock off a few bars on an electric organ. She was vividly gay and intent on getting us both drunk. If she thought of Norman at all, she hid it well. It wasn't much like the last time I had taken her to dinner.

We drove straight back to the cottage afterwards. Annie ran upstairs, throwing off her clothes as she went. I came after, picking them up and hoping she wouldn't break a leg before she got to the four-poster bed. She wasn't drunk. Neither of us was. But it had been a good try.

We made love under the dangerous low eaves. Annie was everywhere and insatiable. She fell asleep at last, and I lay quietly in the darkness, listening to the new growth of an apple tree tapping against the dormer window while a barn owl screeched in the yard outside like a demented grand duke.

Annie's mood had changed by the next morning. She was somber and preoccupied as she scrambled eggs and made coffee. We ate in the kitchen. I asked her if she was coming back to London with me. She shook her head.

"I want to be alone for a while. I'll stay here."

She wasn't the kind of girl to want to be alone for very long. I guessed that marriage to Norman Threlfall had given her that problem among others, but I let it go.

"How will you get back?" I asked.

She smiled slightly. "Norman's got a tame minicab company. Someone'll collect me and get me to the station. There's a good service to London."

When I left, she kissed me chastely as though she were packing me off to school. She had gone back inside before I got to the car.

It was a fine morning with a luminous layer of mist spreading from hundreds of dew ponds scattered over the downs. I thought the sun would burn the last of it off by the time I got to London, but I was wrong. Crawling round the South Circular, the mist had become a fog condensing on power lines and the eyebrows of passers-by.

I left the Alfa in the garage with a reminder to Sean to get working on it this time. I walked round to my flat.

I knew something was wrong before I got there. Harry was on the doorstep with his wife. Apart from the fact that he rarely put his head outside the house except to go drinking, he never talked to his wife.

He saw me and came limping down the street.

"You've been done over," he announced. "They've made a bleeding mess of everything!"

I put my grip down. Harry's wife followed him down the pavement.

"When was this?" I asked.

"Last night. Around seven o'clock."

"We didn't know where to reach you." Mrs. Harry pushed him aside. She blinked with a mixture of compassion and nervousness.

"Shut up, woman," Harry growled.

"Shut up yourself."

Harry was thunderstruck. I'd never heard her answer him back before. I doubted whether he had. She turned to me.

"That friend of yours was here. Eric whatever-his-name. They beat him up terrible."

I shoved my hands into my pockets and looked up and down Henrietta Street. If Mrs. Harry hadn't been so Catholic, I would have sworn. I felt shabby and disreputable.

"How bad is he?" I asked.

"Pretty bad. He's in hospital."

"Hey, you can't bugger off." Harry sounded aggrieved, as though I were breaking the rules. "The coppers have been poking round, asking questions. You're supposed to get in touch with them right away."

He teased a paper out of an inside pocket with his one good hand. There was a name on it plus some careful directions showing me how to get to Bow Street police station. I folded the paper and put it in my pocket.

"Where is he?" I asked Mrs. Harry.

"St. George's Hospital. On the South Bank."

I gave my grip to Harry, told him to keep it in his flat and tidy mine up as best as he could. I found a cruising taxi on the corner of Long Acre.

The hospital rambled for hundreds of yards beside the Thames. The casualty department was vast. I located Eric eventually. They'd put him in a small room by himself overlooking the river.

His brother Olly was sitting in the dead-end corridor on a chair made of metal tubes and scarred yellow laminate. Marian and two of the kids were huddled on a bench under a window. I recognized José, the elder boy who had just won a university scholarship, and the daughter, Enid. Marian was a thin, beautiful woman with a broad, pale forehead and a mass of raven hair. Eric had brought her back with him from Malta when he was in the army. Unlike a lot of Mediterranean women, she hadn't lost her looks early and run to fat.

Olly walked to meet me, and we talked in low voices.

"How is he?" I asked.

"Broken collar-bone and two fractured ribs. A lot of contusions. Maybe some internal damage. They put the boot in."

Olly had the clipped style of a man used to making reports. He was a slightly older, more compact, and tougher version of his brother. He'd been a professional soldier, a paratrooper, only he'd stayed in the service longer. He specialized in the rougher side of the family business, which wasn't the one I was interested in. Usually.

"Who were they? Any idea?"

He shook his head.

"Three big kids, with West Country accents."

"All of them?"

"That's right. An out-of-town lot. They probably came up specially for the occasion. Didn't take any trouble to avoid identification. Funny, you'd think they'd have records. It looked like a practiced operation."

"Tell me about it."

"Eric went round to your flat round six-thirty last night. He was there when the bastards walked in. Someone must have left your front door open. They turned the place over, but it doesn't look like they took anything." He paused. "They carved you up good and proper. You seen it?"

"Not yet."

Olly shrugged inside his shapeless Donegal tweed topcoat.

"You won't like it. They didn't leave much in one piece if they could smash it. One of them took his drawers down and crapped over your carpet. They smeared that around a bit. Your janitor heard the racket and called the police, but they went before anyone got there."

I walked to the window. Marian looked up and smiled weakly. The kids looked awed but apathetic.

"Eric's sorry," she said. "There was nothing he could do."

Her voice still had a trace of accent and a staccato lilt.

I felt tired and disreputable again.

"I'm the one who's sorry," I said. "Eric was working for me. How's he taking things?"

"He spent a comfortable night," she quoted. "He's awake now. The nurses are cleaning him up and the doctor's with him."

"In himself, I mean."

She sucked her full lips between her teeth.

"It's like he's depressed. I don't know."

"Eric's always been a romantic," Olly interrupted. His hand was on his nephew's shoulder. "He hasn't been in a barney for years. He probably thought it was all still straight-lefts and take-that-you-rat stuff."

"Today, he is like a man who has looked for the Holy Grail and found it made of plastic. "Marian's voice was sorrowful. Her turn of phrase surprised me.

A doctor came through the door from Eric's room. He read the question on her face. "Your husband is comfortable, Mrs. Starkey," he reassured her.

Outside, the fog had cleared and the Thames was in flood. A pile of flotsam whirled past. One day, I thought, the river would burst its banks and St. George's Hospital would be an island in a big lake.

"His blood pressure's low," he added. He'd been wondering whether he could divulge privileged information. "It's shock."

"He's not so young," Marian said sadly.

"He's aged ten years in a night," Olly put in. "Can we see him?"

"Two of you can. For a few minutes."

Marian looked at Olly.

"You go in. Me and the kids can wait."

Frowning, the doctor trudged off down the corridor. His stethoscope was about to fall out of a torn pocket in his starched and tatty white coat. He either didn't notice or didn't care.

Olly and I went inside. I didn't pay much attention to the room with its crisp cold linen and stark utility furniture. It was just another hospital room.

Eric was propped up on several pillows. His thick hands cradling each other on the white sheet were blue and restless. His face had collapsed, and his thinning hair had been combed across his forehead. I hadn't noticed how grey it was before. He had the frail, condemned look people have when you see them in hospital.

His face turned as we came in. The resigned humiliation in his eyes was a pain to me.

"Sorry, boss," he said. Even his voice was low and heavy. "I couldn't stop them."

I sat on the edge of the bed. Olly took the only chair in the room. There was a turban of bandage round Eric's head, and the top of his chest was strapped underneath his faded blue pyjama top.

"Don't you start," I growled. "There wasn't supposed to be any rough stuff on this job. Why the hell did you put up a fight? It wasn't that important."

"It was," Eric whispered. "You know how I feel about this business. It's terrible." A smile flickered momentarily in his eyes. "Anyway, I didn't put up a fight. They just piled into me. They were making a point."

"You mean I was supposed to be on the receiving end?"

I was getting quietly and savagely angry. I'd hoped Eric might think the attack had nothing to do with the Global business, but I respected his judgment. I couldn't stomach the idea of anyone taking stick on my behalf.

Eric looked at me with a trace of anxiety.

"Don't worry about it, boss. They didn't take anything much. At least, I don't think so."

"I'm not worried about it." My voice was harsher than I'd intended. I made an effort to sound easier. "There wouldn't have been much to take. I left the main presentation with my client."

I had a sudden thought. "What about the lists you went round to collect?"

"Olly's got those. They found them in my briefcase, but I fooled them. I had some books with stamps in the case as well. I told them the lists were names of French and German dealers I correspond with."

"You did well."

A brief, hurt smile showed on his face.

"Not so well as that. They ripped my books to pieces and tore up the stamps."

They probably weren't penny blacks, but stamps were sacred to Eric. His voice had weakened in the few minutes we had been there. Olly, who hadn't said a word, got up. He nodded towards the door and patted his brother on the shoulder.

"Don't worry, old son. You take it easy. We'll get on with the job until you're back in circulation."

Eric's eyes had closed. Olly and I left quietly.

Marian and the kids looked up as we came out. I didn't think they'd moved while we'd been away. Olly smiled at Marian reassuringly.

"You wait. Eric's getting some kip." He glared with mock ferocity at the kids. "You two, mind you look after your mother."

I said good-bye to them all, and we left them huddled at the end of the corridor like refugees at a reception center.

We took the lift to the ground floor. Olly didn't speak until we were at a table in the grubby hospital cafeteria, drinking lukewarm cups of instant coffee on a stained surface that rocked when I stirred. He gripped the chromium sugar dispenser and looked as though he would have liked to break its neck.

"Give me the story," he said simply. "No funny business, mind. Starkey Brothers took this job on. We'll see it through. Besides, I'd like to find out who duffed my brother up."

He hadn't let himself get out of shape since his paratrooper days. The sloppy Donegal didn't hide his big shoulders as he hunched over the table, elbows apart. He looked solid and hard. It occurred to me that the yobs with West Country accents were in for a rough time if Olly ever caught up with them.

"I'll buy that," I answered. "Only you've got to promise me you'll get back-up. Marian and the kids are short of cover now."

"Don't worry about it. Just give me the story." Olly took some folded sheets of paper out of his inside pocket.

"These are the lists Eric went round to your flat to collect. What makes them important?"

I explained. He listened without comment, making notes in a small leather notebook. At the end, he turned McVeigh's lists round so that he could read them.

"Craziest business I ever heard of," he commented. "Can't say I'm surprised, though. It's the way things are going. So somewhere in these lists are the names of two dopes who are shortly going to beat each other's brains out in a spirit of fun?"

"That's the way we read it."

I turned the lists round again.

"The main thing is, I've got to find out who's organizing everything. Those names are the best lead I've got."

"It's a long list."

I shook my head.

"Eric's already crossed most of them off. Those are the ones who live in the wrong places. There are a few dozen names left."

"How are you going to whittle them down?"

"I've thought of a way. It's not a great one, but it may do. Eric's been using your contacts in France and Germany. Have they got enough talent for some field work?"

"It could be arranged."

"I want as many blokes as your contacts can lay on. The story is that they work for a PR company promoting the opening of a new Club Mediterranée in Yugoslavia. They're to go round to the men on these lists and explain that they've been selected at random by the local radio station to spend a couple of days free at the club, with tickets for two and everything laid on, as a promotional gimmick. You follow me?"

Olly nodded. "Opening day coincides with the time your two candidates are supposed to be fighting, I suppose?"

"That's it. Your contacts can rule out anyone who accepts the invitation with alacrity."

I thought of the carefree thugs who had beaten up Eric and not even bothered to try and hide their identities.

"They can also rule out anyone who says he'll have to think about it. The boys we're after are fanatics. They'll probably turn your offer down flat, without explanation."

"Good enough." Olly closed his notebook. "Anything else?"

"One thing. Tell your contacts I want Polaroid shots of all subjects. Tell them to say they're needed for PR purposes. I want those shots."

Olly pocketed the lists and his notebook. We left the cafeteria and made for the main hospital entrance. A taxi was drawing up outside. Three women were getting out. Two were crying and the third was paying. The driver looked bored.

"You look after yourself," Olly warned. "You're out of shape. You haven't been down to the gym in a long time."

We got into the taxi and I gave the driver directions. Olly didn't speak again until we had crossed Waterloo Bridge on our way towards Starkey Brothers' Holborn offices. He stirred as though he were waking from deep thought.

"Eric was lucid early this morning," he said. "He mentioned something he said you wanted to know. About your client. He told me to tell you that Sir Bryan Proctor was the subject of Starkey Brothers' first ever investigation. That was before my time."

I was interested. "A big target for a first case," I said.

Olly shrugged. "Sir Bryan can't have been so big himself in those days. It was a long time ago. It seems his wife was killed in a car smash. Someone thought it wasn't an accident. Starkey Brothers were supposed to prove it."

"Did they?"

Olly shook his head. "Eric remembers that a hydraulic brake line had been deliberately yanked apart on the car but there was no proof of who did it."

I remembered Charles Omphrey's implied conviction that Sir Bryan Proctor had murdered his wife for her money.

"Who hired Eric?" I asked.

"Dunno. It'll be on file somewhere. Eric files everything. You want me to find out?"

"Please."

I thought in some obscure way that the answer was going to be important.

"Please," I repeated. "Put an extra bloke onto it if necessary."

The taxi drew up and Olly got out.

"Don't worry Eric again until he's feeling better," I warned.

"I won't."

He looked morose and dangerous as he stamped up the shabby stairway leading to Starkey Brothers' offices.

Harry had left the door of the flat open to get rid of the smell. It wasn't important. There was nothing to attract even the Henrietta Street derelicts.

I walked through the rooms, propping open the remains of the glass windows leading onto the balcony with the smashed legs of the low pine table I used to work on. The draft would help. Everything breakable had been broken. Shards of crockery mixed with pages of books torn from their bindings had been ground into slashed carpets and window drapes. Shit had been smeared up the walls and someone had made good use of a cobalt-blue paint spray. As well as some rough notes I had left on the low table, there had been filed copies of my report to Sir Bryan in a drawer. They were all gone, but I'd never had any real doubts about what the raid had been about, anyway.

The bedroom was the same. The telephone was lying by the wall behind the bed. Its base was smashed, but it still worked. I dialled Global House. Freda Harman listened in polite silence.

"Sir Bryan cannot possibly see you." She sounded amused, concerned and appalled, all at the same time. "His schedule is quite full."

"Tell him I'll be round at about two o'clock," I repeated. "Tell him I've got to talk to the police anyway. It'll be no trouble to talk to them twice."

I hung up, took a last look round the flat and left. I met Rose on the stairs, hearing her light, fast steps reverberating round the stairwell before I saw her. Her face was strained like a child's having a bad dream. We met on the first floor landing where the windows reached down to the green tiles. She was framed by an aureole of sunlight shining through the fringes of her hair.

"I've just heard about Eric," she said. Her eyes were only vaguely comprehending. "Is he badly hurt?"

"He'll survive," I said. "He'll get over it."

Her face didn't change. I wondered whether she'd heard me. "It could have been you," she said.

"It could have been. But it wasn't. Eric was here instead. He was unlucky."

"It could have been you."

"Don't let it knock you out of your stride, Rose. You were right. Maybe I should have gone to the police right away."

Outside in the street, a tall van drew up silently. Its broad black roof appeared unaccountably on the other side of the landing windows like another floor. Then I couldn't see it anymore. Rose's hands were on my shoulders. Our kiss seemed to cover an immense space and time. It was a kiss beyond sex, almost beyond love. When she drew away, the space between us failed to separate anything.

"I love you," she said.

"I love you, Rose."

"You'll forget all this? You'll go to the police?"

"Not yet."

"Why not?"

"Because they've hurt Eric. It's personal now."

"Aren't we personal?"

"Yes. But we'll still be personal when it's over."

She shook her head sadly.

"I love, you Rose," I repeated. "I've loved you for a hell of a long time. Only I've never wanted to recognize it."

"Why not?"

"Two reasons. One was that I was happy just loving you. There was no need to hurry."

"You were that sure?"

"It's why I never worried about you. It's why I knew you were never really jealous."

"That woman," she said flatly.

I said nothing. She breathed once, deeply.

"What was the other reason?"

"You wanted too much of me, Rose. You didn't just love me. You loved the caped crusader you thought I was. I was Sir Galahad, your John Wayne, your Cyrano with the big red nose. I've never been any of that. I'm just a fellow with an odd job."

She stared at me. It nearly unnerved me. The stare probed deep. It was the stare of a microbiologist mapping the outline of a black death bacillus.

"I don't want anything except you," she said, finally. "All I want now is that you go to the police and get out of this dangerous business so that I can love you without interruptions."

I loved her more than ever then, and with a tenderness I didn't know I had. But I was bitter too.

"That's the trouble, Rose. Now, for the first time, you want just me. Only now, also for the first time, maybe I am just a little finger of Sir Galahad. I don't have many unbreakable rules, but the berks who beat up Eric have just broken a cardinal one. I can't drop everything and run away from it all. Not now."

The space that hadn't been between us was there once more. It was a gulf. I looked at her as though for the first time. Hers was the nerve-wracking beauty of a triple goddess, and the air seemed suddenly full of dangerous quarter moons and horses' hooves.

"You don't love me, so you won't let me love you. Love frightens you. You don't love anybody, not even yourself. You don't want to be dragged down into life. You just fidget, wanting no real part of anything. All you want is that whore of Norman Threlfall's."

There was only one way to stop her, so I took it. I had a lot to do just then. If I fought with her, it would be a battle royal. And one she might win.

"And what you want, Rose," I said very deliberately, "is a nice slum curate with a university boxing blue and a big heart."

She slapped me then, hard. I heard her footsteps clatter down the stairwell. I looked through the long windows as the tall lorry pulled away from the curb, knowing this was one of those occasions when you see things so clearly that you won't ever take the risk of remembering them properly. Rose was right in her way. Probably I would never let anyone love me. Maybe I only ever wanted to involve myself in other people's lives in small ways and on terms of my own making. Maybe McVeigh was right as well. Maybe other people needed to use me because I used them and gave them no chance to give more.

I tried to hoard the moment anyway, like a girl hurrying to retrieve a broken string of beads before they all disappeared down a drain. I was still looking out of the window, seeing the brown paint flaking off the facade of an old fruit warehouse turned trendy bookstore. On a scrap of pavement, a male pigeon courted a drab female who pecked and took no notice of him at all. His stiff wings trailed in the dust, and his throat puffed out like a coloratura's bosom. On second thoughts, though, he wasn't taking any notice of her either. He was just a mad matador caping an imaginary Miura round the arena of his mind.

I saw Rose Panayioutou cross the road, her head bowed and the wind pounding at her artwork bag. Her bare legs flashed like knives in the weak sunlight.

It was the last time I saw her.

I walked to the big, florid police station opposite the Opera House. Nobody seemed interested when I got there. I waited ten minutes on a hard bench before a tired, soft-spoken CID man came to escort me to an interview room.

It was a shiny cell with plain wood furniture and mimeographed messages pinned to the walls. The CID man had drip-dry eyes. The rubber ribbing on the elastic waistband of his trousers had worn, and one shirttail was making a break for it.

We sat round a table and talked. It was mostly questions and answers. He covered sheets of foolscap with a meticulousness which implied that note taking was the key to detection.

At the end, he went to the door and bawled for coffee. A woman I couldn't see shouted back, and he became suddenly deferential. While we waited for the coffee to arrive, he tilted back in his chair and went through his notes, holding them away from him.

"I'd like to wrap this up," he said. "It was a serious attack. Covent

Garden is getting to be very fashionable. We can't have nasty men ruining its reputation."

I was glad he seemed more concerned by the attack on Eric than the damage to my flat.

"There's not a lot to go on," he said. "Forensic's not likely to come up with much. Still, there's four out-of-town geezers with faces your friend might recognize when he's better, being a trained observer and all that."

The thought collapsed beneath the weight of coffee cups. It was instant coffee, heavily sugared.

"You may not get far by questioning ticket collectors at Paddington," I said unhelpfully. "Among other things, the letters S.T.F.C. were sprayed over my walls in letters about two feet high."

He didn't catch on.

"Swindon Town Football Club. They had an away game at Fulham last night. There must have been several thousand of their supporters milling about the West End."

He declined to be depressed.

"Still, it's a start. We can get in touch with the club secretary. Your friend can look at some pictures when he's better. Maybe in time for Swindon's next home game."

"There is also the fact that neither Mr. Starkey nor myself are Fulham supporters," I said.

He nodded, not particularly surprised. Perhaps he was cleverer than he looked.

"I take your point. There's no obvious motive for an attack, and a football crowd's lovely cover for a couple of paid hooligans. That, of course, would argue some more subtle motive." He looked at me speculatively and tapped his teaspoon against his teeth. "About your line of business. You been making any personal enemies?"

"I have no reason to believe the attack had anything to do with my job," I said with as much finality as I could muster.

"At the moment, what job would that be?"

He sensed our relationship was becoming the proper one of inquisitor and heretic. The modulation seemed to please him.

"I'm afraid it's confidential."

"Perhaps I could be the judge of that?"

The platitude fell to earth like a comedian's trousers.

"I'm engaged in a private investigation for Sir Bryan Proctor of Global Alliance Assurance. Your superiors would have to clear the matter with him before I could say anything."

It was like stealing. The financial empires of the City of London lay only a mile or so away through the legal jungle of Lincoln's Inn Fields. The CID man knew too well that tycoons like Sir Bryan Proctor tended to be on first name terms with senior police officers and rented the ears of junior civil servants.

"Oh, well, we could go into that later," he sighed.

We talked a while longer, then I left. I walked back through Floral Street as far as Inigo Jones's restaurant and turned up the narrow, cobbled street towards the Lamb & Flag. The pub was crowded with lunchtime office workers, but I managed to get a plate of crackers and cheese with a pint of Directors' bitter. I even found a backless chair under the partition with the built-in snuffbox.

Saul and Gerry were later than usual. They came in as I was finishing up, so I bought three more pints. They were regulars of the pub and the *quartier.* If you didn't find them at one place, you found them at another. Saul was a carpenter and both were jobbing builders. They weren't wearing overalls—a good sign.

They listened, sympathetic but unsurprised, while I told them my troubles.

"It's an Act of God," Gerry remarked obscurely.

As I'd hoped, they had no work on at the moment.

"I want the whole place redecorated and refurnished," I said, "as near the original as possible. I didn't have time to get used to it the way it was."

They looked pleased. They were happy boys, often stoned on one substance or another. They were also minor artists, but not creative ones. They liked a simple brief.

"All the original stuff's ruined," I said. "Take what you like and junk the rest. Don't watch the expense. Somebody else will be paying."

That pleased them more, although I knew they wouldn't rip me off. I'd already decided that the cost was going to appear as an extra on Sir Bryan Proctor's bill.

We drank another round for which Saul paid. I told them the keys to the flat would be with Harry, the janitor, and that they could start as soon as they liked. I also told them to ask him for an envelope in which I would be leaving a cash float to cover ongoing expenses. Afterwards, I walked to the embankment to catch the underground to the City. Taxis would be hard to find, and I didn't want to keep Sir Bryan waiting.

I went up to Freda Harman's office. She gave me the impression I had ruined her lunch hour. Her ice-blue eyes snapped at me like Jack Russell puppies.

"I've been trying to reach you." She made it sound as though I had been trying to avoid her. "You've wasted your time. Sir Bryan cannot see you."

I sighed. The day already felt as though it had gone on too long.

"Perhaps I didn't make myself clear," I said. "I intend to see Sir Bryan. You get on that office thing and tell him so. Remind him I've just had an interview with the police. If he won't see me, I guarantee to go straight back and give them another."

She bridled but looked uncertain.

I ignored her and sat by the window while she called. I helped myself to a cigarette from a crystal box big enough to house the mortal remains of a Kremlin commissar and kept an eye on the river traffic.

Exactly ten minutes later, Sir Bryan's penthouse door opened and a crowd of ex-public school boys tumbled out. I could tell by the way they laughed. Sir Bryan laughed with them all the way to the lift. When they were gone, he looked at me and his face shut like a gate. He went wordlessly back into his sanctum, leaving the door ajar.

I stubbed my cigarette out and followed him. The room was full of whiskey smell, even though the air conditioning was humming at full strength. McVeigh sat in his usual chair, elegant as always and amused.

"I don't like my schedule being bulldozed," Sir Bryan said deliberately. "You'd better have a very good reason."

"Once in a while won't do any harm," I answered him.

He bridled, and McVeigh looked more amused. They waited, knowing something was on my mind. I told them about the break-in and the attack on Eric Starkey. Sir Bryan had the grace to look disconcerted.

"I'm sorry to hear this," he said formally. "It's unfortunate, but what the hell do you expect me to do about it?"

"There's nothing anyone can do about it," I said. "The point is, there's been a leak."

"You don't know the attack had anything to do with this job," he sneered. "There must be lots of people who don't like you."

"It won't wash. Apart from the coincidence of timing, two copies of the report I made to you are gone."

"Do I infer that you hold me responsible in some way?"

"You infer right. But that's not the point either. The point is, I can't function when people other than my employer know what I'm being paid to do. As of now, you can consider me off your payroll. You'll get a properly itemized bill as soon as I can put one together."

He ran a hand over the clipped stubble on his chin again. This time the sneer cost no effort at all.

"One whiff of grapeshot and you're through, is that it? Really, I expected better."

"You don't get the point. Somebody opened his mouth. It doesn't matter who. The effect is the same. I'm no use to you now. Without confidentiality, I might as well advertise my services in the *Financial Times* and *Wall Street Journal.*"

He bounced to his feet and made for the door.

"Send in your bloody bill, then," he snarled. "Only don't expect to work for me again."

He slammed the door after him.

There were a few moments' quiet. McVeigh laughed softly. He went over to the drinks cupboard and opened a half-bottle of champagne. He took a jug of fresh orange juice from the tiny refrigerator, half filled two glasses and poured champagne over it. He handed me a glass.

"Now what," he asked, "was that about?"

"Didn't I make it clear?"

"You made it very clear. It's obvious you want the gaffer to think you're taking yourself off the job. I don't believe it for a moment. I know you. You're a lurcher after a hare when you're working. You don't just give up."

"You flatter me." I took a long, cold pull from my glass. "But you're right. I want Sir Bryan and anybody else interested to think I've turned my job in. We don't want the play-off cancelled at the last moment. It's our only lead."

McVeigh nodded. "But I don't follow you entirely. You can't suspect Sir Bryan of breaching your confidence. He's obsessively discreet. You heard him. He'd cut off his right arm before he'd harm his company."

"Whereas you," I said brightly, "wouldn't cut off your right toenails if it didn't suit your book."

"Must you be so bloody impertinent?" McVeigh sighed. He stoppered the champagne bottle with a bronzed metal closing device. "You haven't answered my question."

"I don't know the source of the leak. I'm sure there's been one, that's all. I've known the Starkey brothers and Miss Panayioutou for years. I trust them completely. It doesn't prove anything, but I'm more inclined to suspect a leak here. The point is," I added cunningly, "two's company and three's a crowd."

"I beg your pardon?"

"I mean, I'm not interested in the source of the leak so long as there's not another one. Only you and I will know the score from now on. If there's any more trouble, I'll know who to blame."

"I see."

McVeigh smiled easily and hesitated, which made me certain he was about to shoot a line.

"Of course, apart from the people directly involved, there is one way a hint could have got out."

"Tell me," I invited him.

"It seems reasonable to suppose that a leak occurred about the time you made your original presentation in this office. The kind of attack you describe would presumably take a day or so to set up."

"So?"

McVeigh looked uncomfortable.

"One piece of information left this office during the course of your presentation. Sir Bryan asked Miss Harman to check *The Times*' column for announcements."

"Good heavens. Are you suggesting that Miss Twinset and Pearls is behind it?"

"Of course not. Be serious. Miss Harman is completely loyal. She's been with Sir Bryan for years. But she does have a private life. In fact, she's been Don Proctor's lover for years."

"Now there's a thought," I said. "Are you saying the young master could be the source of the leak?"

McVeigh was definitely uncomfortable. Perhaps my attitude bothered him. "Don has run some shady businesses in the past. He is also," he searched for the right words, "a voyeur of violence."

The phrase rang a bell. I located the echo. Someone had used it the night of Don's exhibition. The night I met Annie.

"Don loathes his father," McVeigh reminded me.

"Does he now? Is there a reason?" I only asked it because I could see McVeigh was looking for an excuse to tell me.

"He is afraid of him. He also believes Sir Bryan killed the late Lady Proctor."

"Ah," I murmured. "The famous car accident."

McVeigh grinned cynically. "Charles Omphrey reminded me. He was the first person I thought of when you said there had been a leak. He's an incorrigible gossip."

"Except that he wasn't present when I made my presentation. Did he, by the way?"

"Did who what?"

"Did Sir Bryan kill his wife?"

McVeigh shrugged.

"It's possible. Caroline died a long time ago, before I joined the Company. Conceivably Sir Bryan drove her to it—do forgive the pun. He may even have fractured the brake lines on her car before it crashed. The point is, Don holds his father responsible."

I finished my glass. "It's an interesting suggestion," I said. "I'll look into it."

"You agree then?"

"I told you, I'm not concerned about the source of the leak so long as it doesn't happen again." I smiled. "Besides, it was inevitable. The nearer we get to answers, the more certain it is we'll come up against people in the know."

McVeigh took my glass and ferried it to the bar.

"In that case I'm surprised you didn't think of it for yourself."

"I'd thought of it. I just wondered whether you had. No more for me, thanks."

He put his glass down. There was real anger in his face. "You really are a very exasperating person," he said quietly. "Why should you wonder that?"

"I wanted to see how you would introduce the subject."

"Don't try to make a fool of me, sonny," he said softly.

I got up to leave.

"Where are you going? I'd like to know what you have in mind."

"First off," I said, "I'll be getting my flat put to rights—at your expense."

"You get automatic personal insurance while you work for us," McVeigh snapped. "Damage to property is your affair."

"Don't worry. The place and contents were insured with Global anyway. You might put in a good word for me, though. I don't like quibbles when I make claims."

I crossed to the door. "I'll be moving into a room at the Tower Hotel. But only you and I will know that. I want things to stay that way. I'll register under the name of Willcox to be on the safe side. Sorry about the melodrama."

"Do you need help?"

"The play-off takes place sometime soon. I'll be trying to find the exact date and place. Since the attack on Eric Starkey, I've decided to attend the event personally, only I may not have time to make my own arrangements."

"I'll arrange everything," McVeigh said. "Just let me know the details when you have them."

"I'd also like a talk with you and Charles Omphrey tomorrow. I thought we might have dinner at the hotel."

"Why?" He looked suspiciously at me.

"Sir Bryan's meeting with the International Holding Board will be over by then. I want to know what's decided."

"You're still considering your threat?"

I thought of Rose on the stairs to my flat. I saw her crossing Henrietta Street, the wind in her hair and her art bag banging against her legs.

"I'm considering it," I said. "I'll also be lodging a written report with my bank with instructions to forward it to the police if anything happens to me."

McVeigh was silent. When he spoke, his tone was veiled, neutral. "We'd better discuss that tomorrow. Why do you want Omphrey to be present?"

"Sir Bryan thinks I've taken myself off his job. Omphrey is chairman of the monitoring committee set up to oversee the investigation. From now on, I want to keep things very regular."

McVeigh shrugged and finished his drink. He called the motor pool for a car to take me back to the Garden. I was overwhelmed, hoping this wasn't the kind of last minute consideration executioners show to their victims.

I waited in the mock classic portico of Global House, sheltering from the sudden rain, for my car to arrive. While I waited, I thought about McVeigh steering me in the direction of Don Proctor. I wondered what he was keeping from me and why. The possibility of a leak through Freda Harman had been obvious, but Don was still the son of Global's chief executive. I didn't think McVeigh would have gone out on such a long limb unless he was sure of his ground.

As the car drew up and I got in, I found myself thinking of something else. I thought of a broken brake line on a car in which Lady Proctor had been killed a quarter of a century ago. Olly Starkey had been that specific about the cause of the accident, only he was a trained investigator and his firm had worked on the case. McVeigh, according to himself, wasn't even working for Global at the time. I wondered how he knew that sort of detail.

By mid afternoon, rain was slanting down onto the pavements with enough force to bounce off and soak socks.

My flat was now an orderly shambles. I could tell Saul and Gerry were around by the husky aroma of dope above the stink of disinfectant. The remains of my furniture and fittings were piled in the center of the main room. Around them, a start had been made on preparing the surfaces of walls and woodwork.

I walked through into the bedroom. The smell wasn't so bad there because the windows had been left open. The rain had turned into a storm, and my soaked curtains moved in a rising wind. Lightning flickered on broken glass and a pool of rainwater below the windowsill.

The kitchen was empty, too. Saul and Gerry weren't around. They must have gone across the road for the tea and cinnamon toast they liked before the serious drinking of the evening. A clap of thunder made me jump as I went back to the bedroom, and I half fell over a pile of black rubbish sacks. It was like listening to *Götterdämmerung* in a bus shelter. I picked up the phone and dialled. Piers Kenny's socially acceptable drawl still sounded as though he had just got up.

"What kept you?" he enquired politely.

"Have you got my information?" I knew I sounded sharper than I meant.

"Of course. Do you want it now?"

"Read it out." I eased my notebook from my pocket and held my pen ready.

"The announcements you were interested in were all placed on behalf of one or other of five smallish companies. Here are the names."

I wasn't bothering with notes yet, I just listened.

"Did you get the names of the individuals who placed the ads?"

"Be patient," Piers urged me civilly. "I know phone charges have gone up."

I doodled a giant gun barrel with too much perspective while I listened to him. I added petals and turned the gun barrel into a sunflower.

"On reflection, I decided against your daft scheme of pretending to research a free-lance article," Piers said. "For a start, hardheaded businessmen would tell me to piss off. I told them I was on the staff of Times Newspapers instead, doing a survey on small-ad usership. So much more compelling. Businessmen love surveys."

"Get on with it, Piers."

"By all means. A few of the names proved difficult to extract, but I persevered. I'm getting to the point. By the way, when do I see the balance of my fee?"

"How would you like a knuckle sandwich delivered electronically?" I asked.

Piers began to read out a string of names. I slowed him down several times and got the lot.

"Does that fit your bill?" he enquired.

"It fits nicely," I said. "Thank you very much, Piers. I'll post you your check tonight."

He was still whining about cash payment when I hung up. I sat down on a rung of Saul's stepladder and considered my list.

The second name on the list was Don Proctor's. In one way I wasn't surprised; in another, I was. The biggest fools, like Huddiesford's marketing director, sometimes devise schemes of piercing subtlety, yet the cleverest make stupid mistakes. There had always been a chance someone might crack *The Times*'s code. Why in hell's name would Don Proctor place an ad personally? Come to that, it wasn't bright to arrange a raid on my flat so soon after I had reported to his old man.

I pushed the list into my pocket. The other names didn't mean a thing to me, but I thought I probably knew the faces. I remembered the Junior Chamber of Commerce types around Proctor at his exhibition opening. They must have thought it all a laugh. *Le tout* Covent Garden admiring Proctor's images of violence while they plotted real violence in their heads.

I looked for my green canvas hold-all and found it slashed to ribbons on the pile of rubbish in the other room. I started filling one of the black plastic rubbish sacks instead with the few things I needed and which were still in one piece. The management of the Tower Hotel would think it strange, but I could always tie the bag on a stick and say I was a future Lord Mayor of London.

Saul and Gerry let themselves in as I was leaving. Gerry gave me his special, slow, warm smile that all women, and some men, took for a come-on. Often rightly in both cases. Saul was setting light to one of his strange, homemade reefers.

"I've left money in an envelope downstairs," I said. "Do you need anything else?"

"Do not disturb yourself," Gerry murmured. "We have bought paint on credit at Bolloms in Long Acre. All will be well." He'd once had walk-on parts at the Abbey Theatre in Dublin.

We talked a while longer. Sometimes it's a relief to talk to uncomplicated people, people who know in their hearts that it's a delusion to think life anything other than a simple primrose path to a simple destruction.

I took a taxi to the Tower Hotel. I registered under the name of Willcox. They gave me a room on the tenth floor overlooking the tastefully converted Ivory Wharf where convicts once took ship for Australia. These days, it was thronged with status symbols of the international sailing set. Craft of all kinds from five-ton sloops to ocean-going racers lined the quays below me like toys in a bathtub.

I went back downstairs to reception. I bought a new green hold-all at the hotel shop, some shaving tackle, underwear, and sent Piers the balance of his money in a plain envelope. The girl at the counter only imagined she knew why I didn't want to send the money in Tower Hotel stationery. Her eyes flirted with me.

Back in my room I took a bath—I like the clinical feel of good hotel bathrooms—and got the number of Don Proctor's studio from directory enquiries. I sat comfortably in the hotel's white terry robe while I made the call.

A girl answered. She took her time. Her voice was diffident, well-bred and bored.

"My name's Willcox," I said. "I'm an art director at KKB—Kellerman, Knapp and Broadstreet. Is Don in?"

"I'm afraid not." She sounded like a depressed flute. "Can I take a message?"

I was relieved. So far as I remembered, Proctor had only once heard my voice, but there'd been a risk.

"That's a pity," I said. "It's urgent. I've arranged a shoot for an important client tomorrow, and my photographer's gone down with a tummy bug. I was hoping Don could fill in at short notice. There's no time to put the shoot off. Copy dates, you know the sort of thing."

"Oh, dear," she moaned, "I really couldn't say."

"How's he fixed tomorrow?"

"He was due to shoot some fashion stuff for a magazine, only the model's gone down with a tummy bug, too. It must be going round."

"So he's free, then? Do you think you could pencil me in? I'll call later to confirm the booking and arrange details."

She sounded more depressed at the idea, but I won her round before I hung up. So far, so good. I had three calls to make. That had been the first. One strike, two to go. I got the number of the Samaritans in Notting Hill and dialed. I changed my tone, speaking slowly and carefully, like a man trying to stay sane under panic. It wasn't hard.

"Yes, Mr. Willcox?" This girl sounded tougher and more practical.

"Look, I know it sounds ridiculous, but I'm in terrible shape. I'm not sure I can cope. Actually," I went on with a rush, "I got out of Coney Hill Hospital in Gloucester a few days ago. I'm feeling suicidal."

"Yes, Mr. Willcox. Would you like to talk to one of our counselors?"

I paused.

"Mr. Willcox?" The girl spoke sharply.

"Actually, I'd prefer to come round and talk personally. I came once before and saw a man called Horst Wohlberg. Is he there?"

"Horst is away, but we've got other counselors. I'm sure one of them will be able to help."

"I want to talk to Horst," I persisted, letting despair seep into my voice. "When will he be back?"

"At nine tomorrow. He should be available until about noon."

"Thank God." My relief was genuine. Two strikes out of three. "I'll leave it until tomorrow, then. I've got a few 10mg Diazepams left. They should let me get some sleep."

We talked for a while longer. I had to reassure her that I was only going to get a good night's sleep, not a permanent one. Fortunately she knew you can't do yourself much harm with Diazepams, even in quantity.

I rang off, ordered a large vodka with orange juice from the bar, and made my third call. I kept my fingers crossed. If this didn't come off, I could still arrange something, but it would be harder.

Ben Campbell came on the line after his secretary had intercepted me. He was a Creative Group Head at KKB, whatever that meant. It evidently rated him a nubile coffee-maker. He sounded surprised to hear my voice.

"How's everything?" he asked. "How's Annie?"

"Still at that cottage in Hastings," I said noncommittally. "How are you fixed tomorrow?"

"Work-wise?" He sounded anxious. He probably thought I wanted him to do a favor, like send his mother some flowers.

"Work-wise," I agreed.

"Bloody shambles. I was supposed to be shooting some stuff for a car ad, only the client buggered around so much I've had to cancel. He's changed his mind again and I don't know whether my photographer's still available. If he isn't, it'll cost a fortune in cancellation fees."

They say you've got a one-in-sixty-four-thousand chance of being dealt a full house in poker. I now knew what it felt like.

"That's great," I said.

"Beg pardon?"

"How would you like to earn yourself a hundred and fifty quid? Discreetly, of course."

"I'd like it," he said cautiously. "What do I have to do?"

"I'll tell you when I see you. I'm coming round now. Is that O.K.?"

"I suppose so. But make it fast. I've got a lot of arranging to do for tomorrow."

"Don't do anything until I get there."

"You mean your business has to do with advertising?"

"What hasn't?"

I dressed quickly and went back down to hotel reception. On my way out, I stopped at the gift shop and sent a bunch of flowers with a card to St. George's Hospital. I didn't know how Eric felt about flowers, but the shop didn't sell stamp albums.

I hailed a taxi. The afternoon storm had ground to a temporary halt, but Oxford Street was jammed because a drainage conduit had given up under the strain. There was a mess of vehicles with flashing lights holding everything up.

The rain started again and was coming down heavily when I paid the taxi off outside KKB. I had to shake myself like a dog as I took the lift to the Creative Department floor, even though I'd had the fare ready and only one pavement to cross.

Campbell's secretary was in an outside office. She had ginger hair streaked with emerald green. Campbell's own office was a white room with French windows leading onto a balcony overlooking a formal Belgravian square with gardens. He probably used it to harangue the mobs when he had a great creative idea. There was a lot of harsh light, some big plastic armchairs in brilliant crimson, and a couple of Habitat molded knickknack holders on the wall. Mini-proofs of his latest work were mounted on pinboard.

Campbell came in with a plastic container of coffee. He waved it at me. "Do you want one?"

I shook my head and sank into an armchair. He was wearing a green suit that caved in over his pigeon chest. His lank, brushed-back hair gleamed under the harsh light. It was getting dark outside, and the cloud cover was still emptying itself over the square. The whiplash of lightning on green and crimson made my head swim.

"I've been talking to my account director," Campbell said. He sipped. "You know, I think I may have pressed the oxtail soup button by mistake."

"What did you decide?"

"The client wants to go ahead. The original photographer's still available, as it happens, but I haven't confirmed the booking, I've stalled everything as you suggested. What's the deal?" He looked at me with the eyes of an intelligent stoat.

"Is it a location job?" I asked.

"In an English spring?" He gestured through the windows to the melodrama in the skies. "No way. I've hired a disused aircraft hangar in Essex. That's why it would have cost a packet to cancel."

I listened to the clatter of typewriters above the rattle of thunder. "One hundred and fifty quid says your original photographer's not still available after all. You've decided to use Don Proctor in his place. He is available."

"Proctor?" Campbell grinned with surprise. "Are you his agent?"

"No questions," I reminded him.

Campbell took his coffee to the window and thought for a moment.

"He's not got much experience in advertising. I don't think I've even seen his portfolio."

"I'm not an expert," I said. "I just happen to have a hundred and fifty quid to burn. Speaking as an amateur, though, I'd say he'd make an interesting choice. He's got flair. He's good at action photography. Choosing him might be construed as an act of bold imagination."

Campbell was quiet. When he turned round, he looked intrigued.

"You could have a point," he said mildly. "My client likes style. The product's a new car, and he's keen to impress the trade. As you say, Proctor's got chic, and he's unknown. With proper art direction, he might do very well. I think I like the idea. You say he's available?"

"I called him an hour ago. I said I was an art director here. You can sort out the misunderstanding over names. Why don't you confirm the booking now?"

Campbell nodded with sudden decision and picked up the middle of three telephones standing on a white melamine table balanced on chromium-plated steel hoops. I listened until he'd finished and hung up.

"Well, that's arranged," he smiled. "Maybe I should have thought of him myself."

I got up. "Where's the best place to get a taxi?"

"You wouldn't stand a chance in this weather and at this time of day. I'll get Daisy to arrange a minicab."

He disappeared into the outer office.

"It'll be here in a few minutes," he said when he came back. "You're lucky. A hundred and fifty pounds, you mentioned."

"It's yours tomorrow when you get back from the shoot. I never carry more than loose change. Too dangerous. There's one more thing. Proctor's got a combined rep and assistant. She works in the studio. I want her with you for at least part of the time tomorrow. Offhand, I'd say the best thing would be to wait till you get to wherever you're going, then think of some piece of equipment you need urgently, something you know Proctor won't have brought. The girl can bring it by car."

Campbell looked at me carefully. "You are a mysterious bloke, aren't you? I wonder what you're up to. O.K., I know, no questions."

The telephone rang. He attended to it and told me my cab was ready.

I thanked him. I said I'd be round in the morning before Proctor arrived. "Will you have time to brief him properly?" I asked.

"I've arranged to do it tonight. It's a complex job. He'll need time to work out the lighting."

"That should be good for a dinner at The Gay Hussar," I agreed.

Since KKB was paying, I took the minicab to the City via Holborn and stopped off at Starkey Brothers. Olly was in his office, morose and worried. I asked after Eric.

"No change," he grumbled. "Blood pressure's still very low. The doctors don't like it."

I changed the subject. "How are you getting on in France and Germany?"

"I've got our locals at work. They're going through your list. It should be ready tomorrow night, maybe the next morning. There's a lot of names."

I carried on trying to cheer him up. Ten minutes later, I took the minicab on to the Tower Hotel. Back in my room, I had a light dinner and spent the rest of the evening writing up a report of the Global business to deposit with my bank. When I finished at eleven o'clock, I ordered a drink and turned on the TV. I caught the last minutes of the UEFA Cup Final Eurovision recording in which Juventus, Chelsea's conquerers in the previous round, were routed by three clear goals. The weather looked as foul in Paris as it did in London.

I booked an alarm call before I went to bed. It had been a long day and I didn't want any mistakes. My mind wandered to Rose Panayioutou even before I fell asleep, my already dreaming hands wandering over her long, faintly olive body.

I got to KKB in good time, but not good enough. Campbell's door was shut, and I could hear voices and see shadows moving against the corrugated glass dividing wall. There was a row of aluminum coathooks outside the door. One of them had a dark cape with an astrakhan collar on it. I didn't think it would be Campbell's. Below the coat, on the floor, was a photographer's reinforced metal case. Inside, I knew, there would be lenses, light meters, and the rest of the professional's paraphernalia deployed in shaped sockets of tough foam. I thought I saw a way of turning the situation to my advantage.

I went through the pockets in the coat quickly. I found a bunch of keys with a BMW tag. There were more than car keys on it.

I took the bunch with me back down in the lift and telephoned Campbell's office from the reception area. I asked how long it would be before he and Proctor left. If talking to me in Proctor's presence bothered him, he concealed it well.

"Just as soon as you stop taking up my time," he snapped. Campbell working was a more abrasive personality than Campbell listening to an offer. For all I knew, he might even be a good art director.

"Fine. When you leave, don't hang about. Go straight off—in your car."

"Christ, proper martinet, aren't you?"

"I'm paying you a hundred and fifty quid for damned little," I reminded him. "Just do as you're told."

I hung up and left the reception area via the fire exit. I went down the ramp to the underground car park converted out of what must have been kitchens and servants' quarters originally.

There was a green BMW beside the space marked with Campbell's name. Campbell's Audi was also green. Green seemed to be the advertising color of the year. In case Proctor was a careful man, I unlocked the BMW and left his keys in the ignition. I shut the door again and went to sit on an oil drum in the space concealed by the curving ramp.

A few minutes later, Campbell and Proctor came down the ramp. Campbell was talking fast. I heard him hustle Proctor into the Audi. The door slammed and they were away. The tires squealed briefly as they took the curve of the ramp.

I gave them ten minutes in case Proctor discovered he'd forgotten something, then emerged from under the ramp. I slipped his keys out of the BMW's ignition and left the building. I waved down a cab at the corner of Grosvenor Square and took it to Notting Hill. I found a tatty cafe near the studio and settled down with a bacon sandwich and a large mug of sweet tea with a scum of tea-dust on its surface. Outside, over the head of the resigned-looking Cypriot who ran the cafe, I could see a knot of out-of-work school-leavers planning a vandalization project.

Nothing happened for thirty-five minutes. Yesterday's storm had blown itself out, but it was still a drab day with a lot of low-flying cloud. I watched a polystyrene coffee cup chasing itself in the stiff breeze.

I could see the entrance to Proctor's mews. The main door was just in sight. It opened. Proctor's girl Friday, the one I'd christened the Depressed Flute, came out and threw herself lethargically into a blue Mini Cooper. She was carrying something swathed in a piece of material. I hoped it was the vital piece of equipment Campbell was supposed to need. The Mini drove off towards the Bayswater Road. I waited another ten minutes, just in case.

Nothing happened, so I paid the resigned Cypriot, strolled across into the mews and let myself quietly into Proctor's studio, with his own keys, just like that. I listened, but there wasn't a sound. By now, the Depressed Flute ought to be jammed in the West End, Wohlberg bringing aid and comfort to jaded losers, and Proctor well into his second roll of film, at least. Silence ticked like a clock, and the marble general sneered from his plinth in the big hall.

I started at the top of the building where the private apartments were. If I'd expected heady signs of perversion, I was disappointed. Apart from a bathroom that wouldn't have looked out of place in Herculaneum, there was nothing unusual. Just two small bedrooms and a small study with good pictures and a wall covered with books. No sign of sin, unless you included the slate-grey silk bed linen in one of the rooms. The other bedroom, by contrast, was Spartan. It had an iron bed, a utility wardrobe, an open washstand and a plain wooden crucifix. Obscure instinct told me this was Wohlberg's room.

I found nothing, so I moved down to the half-landing. An hour later, I was down in the basement, sweating. Like do-it-yourself carpentry jobs, searching a house always takes a hell of a lot longer than you think. I was hoping the Depressed Flute wouldn't hurry home. I hoped the traffic was as thick as cassoulet.

I found what I had been looking for in the last place I looked, of course. The basement was plain and functional, built to the entire ground plan of the house, with white painted brick walls and overhead strip lighting. I had already searched the racks and cupboards filled with supplies, the Grant projector, and the piled boxes of film stock. I was sitting on one of the boxes, looking at the run-of-the-mill files I had pulled from a battery of cabinets bolted to the wall, when I noticed that the filing drawers were only half as long as the cabinet itself.

I reached inside. At the back of the top row, two more drawers had been concealed. It was as simple as that. Like hiding a needle in a pincushion. I was relieved and very happy. Bearing in mind the scope of the Game and the logistical problems it implied, I'd been certain there had to be records somewhere, and near to the Game's nerve center at that. I'd banked on finding them somewhere in Proctor's rambling mews headquarters. I emptied the contents of the first concealed drawer onto a trestle table and started to go through them.

It was packed with cardboard folders, each with a name, a code and a date stamped on the front. They were in two groups. A small group of rust-colored ones in front and a larger group of buff ones behind. I riffled quickly through them. These were Game records, all right.

The first group all had the letters COMB stencilled across the top. A quick examination showed me that these were dossiers of combatants for the coming year. The second group all had RES stencilled across them and, in about half the cases, GAUGEHOLDER as well. I guessed these comprised inactive personnel waiting to take their turn in the Game, including those appointed to be life insurance policy beneficiaries. I hefted the whole lot in both arms and got my first real feel of the Game's scope. There must have been more than a hundred of the files, and these were just the ones for Britain in the coming year.

I examined a few of them in detail. They were all made up the same way. There was a capsule biography of the subject, together with a separate page of competence assessment notes and a photostat copy of an original Global life insurance policy proposal. In the case of the rust-colored Combatant files, there was another large sheet divided by ruled lines. The date of an opening qualifying combat had been marked in in each case. In the space beside it was a number which I guessed referred to an Ordnance Survey map with grid references. Another number opposite the "v" for versus referred to the personal file code of the opponent. Spaces had been left for details of later combats to be filled in. There was also a third code number that meant nothing to me.

I turned my attention to the second drawer. The first item in it was a thick leather folder like a plush restaurant menu. It was embossed in gold on the front with the number 1/64 and the words THE GAME. Inside the front cover was a longhand declaration like the one in the front of a passport. It set out, briefly and nobly, the Game's nature and objectives, some of which I'd already guessed for myself. I also guessed that this was the first of sixty-four similar folders held in eight regions of the eight countries where the Game was played. The declaration was signed by eight names over an imposing address near Brussels and dated four and a half years previously. The first signature was Don Proctor's.

The remaining pages were all made of thick vellum, and there weren't many of them. The first ones set out the Game's rules and method of operation. Again, I had guessed some of the rules for myself, such as the fact that all combats were to the death and that no overt weapons such as guns or knives were to be used. There was no provision for umpires or referees, though there was some official called an Arbiter who intervened under special circumstances.

One chilling subsection covered action to be taken in the event that both combatants were killed, or neither of them able to finish the other off. The victor was supposed to report to his Regional Controller by a certain time on the day of combat. If no report came in, the Regional Controller was instructed to order the local Controller to send in something called a Discipline Squad and sort things out. There was a proviso that when both combatants were badly maimed, the Squad was to finish both of them off, the technical winner of the combat being decided by lottery at National or Supreme Council level.

The organization was surprisingly hierarchical. At least, it surprised me. There were eight Regional Controllers in each country who made up a National Council, the president of it being also a delegate to the European Supreme Council of Eight that met at least once every year at the aristocratic-sounding address near Brussels. Each rank of officials was responsible for the organization of the Game up to his own level, while

National Councils were jointly responsible for the appointment of officials like Discipline Squads and lower ranks like the Gaugeholders. It seemed that Discipline Squads were made up of combatants who'd had to pull out of their own Games at some point through injury or illness. I decided that whoever devised the Game's jargon had had a nice line in poetic fancy.

After all the neo-militaristic rigmarole of the opening pages, the final section of the folder came as a macabre surprise, but at least it explained the third set of numerical codes on personal dossiers I'd been unable to work out earlier. It seemed the whole hierarchy of the Game from Regional Controller upwards was actually obliged to bet on the outcome of combats. There was a complicated series of rules and a system of fixing odds that would have done credit to Ladbroke's. There was even the outline of an ingenious system for transferring winnings tax-free from one country to another.

I closed the folder and put it down. There was another folder behind it, a simple blue cardboard one labelled CURRENT BUSINESS. The top sheet in it was photocopied and blank. From the column headings I gathered that this was the form on which betting odds and stakes were entered up. The next sheet came as a very nasty surprise. It was headed MINUTES OF AN EXTRAORDINARY MEETING OF NATIONAL COUNCIL ONE and dated a few days previously. If I'd been inclined to treat everything I'd seen so far as some kind of lurid academic joke, this sheet brought it all home to me in an unpleasantly personal way. There was a head-and-shoulders photograph of me stapled to the right hand corner. I had no idea where it had been taken, but it looked recent. The minutes recorded a decision to discipline me "in the First Degree" for unauthorized intervention in the Game, by a Discipline Squad to be convened by South-West Regional Controller. A subheaded section also recorded a decision to convene an extraordinary meeting of the European Supreme Council of Eight in Brussels on May 2nd to discuss a new communications procedure. A pencilled addendum at the foot of the page noted that the attempt on me had failed and that another was being arranged.

The final sheet in the folder contained the information I had wanted to find more than anything else. It was headed LUDI VICTOR II CONTRA

LUDI VICTOR IV. There were no photographs, and the coded numbers in the notes were unlike the ones I had found earlier. I swore to myself. I guessed that since the combatants weren't English, the different systems referred to biographical files in other countries. There was a lot of other useful information, though. It included references to April 16, to Arizona, and to Rand McNally 6.8.B1.

I closed the folder. The only other object in the second drawer was a bulging box file full of what looked like draft arrangements for the coming year's combats. I flipped through it all quickly, closed the file and checked my watch. I ran upstairs to the smaller of Proctor's studios and borrowed the simplest camera I could find. I set it up with a portable studio light in the basement, slipping the night-chain on the front door of the mews studio first.

I loaded the camera with film from one of the basement boxes and shot off several rolls, starting with the current business file. Afterwards, I dismantled the equipment, put everything back where I'd found it and prepared to leave.

In the Depressed Flute's office by the main door was an Economist desk diary. I flipped through it to 2nd May. The whole space was crossed out and the words "Château de la Broderie 6.45 BA186" pencilled in. I called McVeigh's office on the Depressed Flute's telephone. His secretary took the call. I told her to make my air tickets out to Phoenix, Arizona, for 15th April.

It was raining again when I finally locked the studio door behind me and left. It was still raining when I found a taxi in the Bayswater Road. The driver hadn't wanted to pick up a half-drowned fare, so I made him wait outside KKB while I ran down the ramp and replaced Proctor's keys in the BMW's ignition. He wouldn't be the first driver who could have sworn he'd had them in his pocket all the time.

I took the taxi to a shop near Charing Cross where I dropped off the rolls of film I had shot in Proctor's studio. I got a promise that the negatives with two sheets of contact prints would be sent the same day by special messenger to the Tower Hotel. I paid in advance. I stopped into another frowsty shop nearby, the kind Eric knew all about, where they sold old stamps. I bought a small magnifying glass.

The taxi finally dropped me at the Tower Hotel. I had lunch in the downstairs restaurant before going up to my room. I telephoned instructions for my evening dinner party, then called my flat. Gerry took the call and listened patiently.

"It's coming along fine," he said consolingly. "I'm waiting for the second coat to dry before we lay carpets. Saul is arranging delivery of furniture. You won't see much change out of the money you left us, but I believe you'll like the effect. You should be able to move back the day after tomorrow. Will that satisfy?"

"It satisfies fine, but I probably won't be here. You'd better leave keys to the new locks with Olly Starkey, a friend of mine. Harry, the janitor, will give you his address. Have there been any calls?"

"Several. One sounds nice. She keeps calling."

"Has she got a name?"

"Unfortunately, not. A man called Threlfall also called. He sounded strained. He says the matter's urgent."

He gave me a long number, and I made a note of it on sepia-colored Tower Hotel stationery. I remembered the menacing pencilled jotting promising further "disciplinary" action on Proctor's Current Business file.

"Have a good time," I said, "but watch out who you open the door to. We don't want any more accidents."

Gerry smiled down the phone. "Lightning never strikes twice, and all that."

"Who said anything about lightning?" I wasn't really worried. Saul and Gerry were both keen students of the martial arts. They could look after themselves.

I hung up, lit a cigarette, and placed a call to Ottawa. I waited ten minutes for the connection. When I got it, I had to wait again while the conference center paged Norman Threlfall. I glanced at time ticking away on the electric clock set into the headboard of my bed. I also watched three kids throwing stones at a plastic bottle moored by the current in a backwater of St. Katherine's Dock. It was raining so heavily I could hardly see where Thames-water stopped and the air above began. The kids didn't seem to mind.

Threlfall was brusque and nervous when he came on the line.

"I've been informed that my wife tried to commit suicide last night," he said. "She's in a clinic near Hastings."

I caught myself swearing as I copied down the address. I made him repeat it.

"The attempt was not serious," he went on. "An amateurish piece of wrist-slashing, I gather. The standard plea for attention. Naturally, I'll return to England as soon as I can, but that won't be until tomorrow."

"Why me, Threlfall?" I asked. I was genuinely interested.

"Because Annie has no family. Nor any close friends. Listen, lover boy. Look on this as a golden opportunity to prove you're more than just a good-time lay." He rang off just as his voice rose to a pitch of well-bred savagery. It was the first genuine emotion I'd heard from him.

I left the hotel and took a taxi to Henrietta Street. Sean was pottering in his garage, a portable radio in one hand and a wad of cotton waste in the other. He put both down when he saw me.

"Your timing's off, is it?" he enquired. He loved to parody his own Irish accent. "There's nothing wrong with your timing. It's your blessed air filter."

"It can't be," I said. "I had the car officially serviced a few weeks ago."

"Can't it now?" Belligerence was part of the blarney. He reached into a waste bin and waved something in my face. "Then you wuz robbed. Just you look at this."

"Not now, Sean. I'm in a hurry. Is the car fit to drive?" I reached for the door handle.

"Not so fast. I've put a new filter in. I don't want you telling me later it wasn't necessary."

He reached through the open window and released the bonnet catch. "Let me show you what a new. . . ."

He'd opened the bonnet. He was holding it up with one hand, staring inside, his thin face faintly puzzled.

"Mother of God," he remarked, conversationally.

I moved round towards him. A big lump of what looked like putty was stuck at the rear of the engine housing. A metal tube projected from it and wires disappeared through into the body of the car.

There was a long silence while I thought of Proctor's memorandum recording a decision to make a second attempt at disciplining me. Say what you like, these boys were nothing if not fast.

"You're always bragging about having served in the IRA, Sean," I remarked in as normal a tone of voice as I could manage. "Don't tell me you've never seen a car bomb?"

I stared at the putty substance. I knew the principle of plastic explosive just well enough to know it was harmless without its detonator. I also knew myself well enough to know that if I waited, my nerve would go. I blocked out thought, reached under the bonnet and pulled the metal tubes free with a quick jerk.

"Sweet Jesus and Mary," Sean breathed. "Are you trying to kill us both?"

"There's no danger." I borrowed some pliers from a loop in his overalls and snipped the wires from the tube. I pocketed the detonator and threw the lump of explosive on the back seat of the car.

Sean stared as though I were changing sex in front of his eyes.

"I'm calling the police," he said. He backed away, his eyes on my face.

"Fifty quid says you won't, Sean," I said. "I haven't got time to answer a lot of questions. Besides, with your reputation, they'd think you were responsible. They'd jug you before you could say Guinness."

His eyes slid away, and he wiped his hands on the cotton waste. "Bastard," he muttered mechanically. "I found the bloody thing, didn't I?"

"Fifty quid, Sean." I peeled the notes out of my wallet and held them out. He reached slowly.

"I don't want the police involved," I insisted, quietly. "Besides, I know who did it. No tales, mind." I was hanging onto the edges of the notes. "To the police or anyone else."

He took the money. "If you say so. Only do me a favor. Get someone else to service your car—find another garage to park it in."

I got into the Alfa without answering and drove off. Sean was still shaking his head when I glanced back, fingering his nice crisp banknotes. He'd forgotten to charge me for the air filter.

I buried the plastic explosive and detonators at the bottom of an earth ramp off a newly repaired section of the M21 near Maidstone. The ground was freshly turned, and the winter storms weren't over yet. Heavy rains would soon come and wash fresh topsoil over them. For the time being the sky had cleared and a douce South-Westerly had set in. Light mist was coiling off the fields as I headed south for Hastings.

I drove to Threlfall's cottage. It nestled peacefully in its hollow. Apple blossom buds flirted with the wind. I half expected ducks to cluster round the low green door and maids with milk pails and mob caps to appear.

The lady who ran the post office in the village directed me to the clinic. It wasn't far. It turned out to be a rambling collection of one-story buildings made of red brick for the first four feet, with painted clinker-built timber above. The grounds were neat, and there were a lot of rosebushes pruned to within an inch or so of the topsoil. An old man with a trowel and a box of bedding plants knelt on a sack by the main door as though he were saying vespers.

I spoke to the receptionist inside and waited in a cold anteroom. Time passed, and a doctor arrived. I seemed to have been hearing her heels punctuate the emptiness of long corridors for minutes. She was in her early forties, with shining black hair over the shoulders of a white coat and nails half as long again as the top joints of her fingers.

She was hard to talk to, but I persevered. For some reason she was cool and watchful. Perhaps she was always like that. I had the impression that failed suicides were no more new to her than drug addicts and alcoholics. It was that sort of clinic.

"I'm a friend," I explained. "Mr. Threlfall called me. He's on a business trip in Canada and can't get back until tomorrow. I said I'd take a look at the situation for him. May I see Mrs. Threlfall?"

The doctor hadn't given me her name. She tapped her long nails on the double-glazing of the windows. Her legs were unexpectedly good. I tried again.

"Was the suicide attempt serious?"

"Any suicide attempt is serious." The reply was a casual put-down.

"I mean, was Mrs. Threlfall in danger?"

"She slashed her wrists," she said, dryly. "Her wounds were in no way cosmetic. But she's as strong as a horse. She was more at risk from infection than loss of blood."

"How did she get here?"

"She telephoned us when she realized that the attempt wasn't going to work. She was angry as much as anything. Self-dislike is always a factor in depression. A suicide bid, a failed one, won't have improved her opinion of herself." It was her longest speech so far.

"May I see her?"

She looked me in the eyes for the first time, still with cool, hostile appraisal. I didn't think she accepted my account of myself as a friend standing in for a missing husband. Perhaps Annie had said something. There was a hint of the feminine crusader in her manner, as though she thought Annie was yet another victim of male aggression. Weren't we all, I thought.

"I'll take you to her room, but don't stay long. Mrs. Threlfall is on a course of drugs. You'll find her drowsy. She's supposed to be. You mustn't excite or upset her."

She walked me through corridors with more twists and turns than the maze at Knossos. We parted company at an end door. She walked off without saying good-bye. I hoped I'd be able to find my way out again.

Annie was in a dim corner room with windows on two sides shaded by vertical strip blinds. She was lying quietly, her heavily bandaged wrists posed ponderously on the bed coverings. Her gorgeous braided hair spilled over the pillow. It was the only real color in the room. There was a vase of pale flowers on a table beside the bed with a card from Ben Campbell. I wondered when he'd sniffed out the news. He'd said nothing earlier in the day.

I sat on the edge of the bed. Annie was awake, staring at the ceiling.

"How are you, Annie?" I asked her in my friendliest tone.

There was no change in her expression. She lifted her wrists and looked at them with distaste.

"I've been stupid," she said, matter-of-factly.

I held her arms above the bandages. She didn't resist.

"Why, Annie?"

She pulled her arms away. I let her go rather than hurt her. She turned her head aside. Not a muscle moved, but tears flooded helplessly over the starched pillow.

"Norman and I are finished. I thought we were finished months ago. I was wrong."

"When he came down to the cottage, it was because somebody sent him an anonymous note," I said, quietly. "Did you send it, Annie?"

She nodded. The tears were soaking into the pillow. She made no move to dry them. She looked utterly defeated.

"I couldn't take the tension anymore. I had to know whether Norman knew about you and me. I wanted to make him jealous so that he would realize he loved me after all. But he never loved me. He never has."

Her body shook. I wondered whether to ring for the lady doctor and half got up. Annie stopped me.

"I've used you. I've used Norman," she wept. "Only it doesn't feel like that. I feel like the one who's been used. I feel raped. Even the doctors use me. I don't want their bloody pills and injections."

"They can't take away the pain, Annie," I said. "All they can do is stave it off until you're in better shape. After that, you're on your own. You couldn't escape if you wanted to."

"I don't want to escape," she half screamed.

I listened. There wasn't a sound from the corridor. Outside, the old gardener swore as he tried to start his Flymo for the first time that year. If he'd heard anything, he wasn't letting on.

"Norman will be here tomorrow," I said. I didn't know whether it was a threat or a consolation.

Annie breathed noisily to steady herself. She wiped her eyes with a corner of the pillowcase.

"I don't want him here. I'm getting out."

"Where will you go?"

"Back to London. I'm going to start divorce proceedings." She was suddenly calm and matter-of-fact. "I've got to start somewhere."

"Do you need help?"

"No. And please don't pretend to worry about me. I don't want your damned pity. Get out."

I went quietly.

I drove back to London feeling moody and restless. I was worried about Annie. At the same time, I was relieved. Since that last meeting with Rose, I knew Annie and I weren't just finished. We'd never really started. We'd each been using the other. I was even glad about her anger. It's a strong emotion. It helps keep morale up when you're lonely, and Annie was lonely. I accused myself of getting involved with her in order to dodge the issue with Rose. Then I tried to sweeten the pill by reminding myself that I'd never intended things that way, as though it made any difference, and that I'd only pushed Annie a little farther along a route she was determined to travel anyway.

Back at the hotel I left the car in the most conspicuous and best lit part of the underground car park I could find. If anyone wanted to sabotage me again, there was no need to make it easy. I walked round the perimeter of the hotel. It was coming on to rain yet again. Fine rain, the kind that dampens rather than soaks. While I made wet footprints in the carpet by the lift, my mind ran on the idea of sabotage. Don Proctor had had my car sabotaged. Years ago someone had sabotaged Lady Proctor's car. Maybe I was getting morbidly suspicious.

There was a parcel on the table in my room. Still suspicious, I handled it gingerly. It was just a parcel containing the developed film and contact prints I had ordered earlier. I examined one set of prints with the help of the magnifying glass I had bought. I was never going to do Proctor out of a job as a photographer, but they were adequate.

I sat down then and finished my longhand report of everything that had happened since I'd started this job. It wasn't so full as the official report I'd made for Sir Bryan, but it would do to replace the copies stolen from my files. I put one set of the prints and the magnifying glass in my new hold-all. I put the report and the second set of prints inside a large envelope. Finally, I wrote out two copies of my bill to Global Alliance. I put one of those in the envelope as well. I sealed the envelope and addressed it to my bank. I also made out a check to Ben Campbell. Then I went downstairs for a drink.

When I got back, the circular table was laid for dinner. Napery and silver made the room glow like a TV commercial. There were crockery and chafing dishes on the sideboard. Two bottles of Sancerre were cooling themselves in a bucket; a couple of bottles of claret warmed themselves discreetly in a pool of light from the standard lamp.

McVeigh and Omphrey were on time. McVeigh was still taking off his coat when I handed him the copy of my bill I had sealed in Tower Hotel stationery. He opened it and looked faintly apprehensive.

I reassured him. "Your secretary's probably told you I'm off to Arizona tomorrow," I said. "It could turn out to be a dangerous visit. I'd hate my estate not to know you owe it money. I'm lodging a copy of it with a written report at my bank."

Omphrey looked at McVeigh enquiringly.

"All in good time, Charles." McVeigh finished peeling off his overcoat and took an envelope from its side pocket. He was smiling.

"I've something for you, as well. Tickets, currency, and travelers checks. You catch a TWA midday flight to Chicago tomorrow. You connect there for an internal flight to Phoenix, Arizona, arriving at about six o'clock local time. Are your visa and international driving licence in order?"

I reassured him and put the envelope in my hold-all while a waiter served us aperitifs. Omphrey looked wracked because nobody had told him what was going on. He consoled himself by walking to the window and telling us in a loud voice how much one of the boats in the dock below reminded him of the ketch he kept moored at Kinsale.

Dinner was good, the atmosphere somewhere between a wake and a discreet celebration, as though some rich but unloved relative had died. McVeigh was in brilliant and witty form, making it tacitly clear that he wanted no shop talk until the meal was over. Even Omphrey melted, forgetting his impatience in the glow of fine food, wine of a proper age, and good conversation. Afterwards, with port and cigars on the table and the waiters gone, McVeigh brought the evening abruptly back to earth.

"I've gone over your findings very thoroughly," he announced, "and made further checks of my own. My findings confirm your hypothesis on every point. Even Sir Bryan now reluctantly concedes that you have made your case. I have already, by the way, given Charles a resumé of the matter."

Omphrey's glass was already half-empty, so I refilled it. I was interested in his reaction.

"You'll gather I had some trouble convincing Sir Bryan, at least," I grinned. "What do you think of it all?"

He surprised me. "Yours is the only explanation that fits all the facts," he said simply. "More to the point, the facts cry out for an explanation of the kind you offer. There is a reasoned inevitability about it. So much so, that in retrospect, the real mystery is why we didn't arrive at the same conclusion ourselves a long time ago."

"Obvious?" There was a restrained, gleeful malevolence in McVeigh's manner. "I should have thought a cult combining the less desirable features of the Mafia and the Boy Scout movement was hardly obvious. It may be the correct conclusion, but I should have thought it took an eccentric imagination like our friend's to arrive at it."

Omphrey looked at me. "There is a mawkish myth still held even by serious historians that society advances steadily and travels progressively away from its animal and tribal origins. The assumption is not true. The most brilliant civilizations depend on the most primitive of instincts, and at times of rapid social decay, old archetypes of feeling and behavior re-assert themselves. Your Game represents a classic reversion to tribal principles. Because they sense a threat to their existence, the young men engaged in it reaffirm the old primate instinct of male bonding with the old carefully judged attempt to combine heroic aggression with docile submission to an ethos of group cooperation. They do so with the usual symbolic paraphernalia of emblems, badges of rank, trials of courage, secret rituals, and the like. Fundamentally, it's a healthy instinct."

McVeigh grinned sardonically. "You, a doctor, approving of pathological violence?" he said. "You missed your vocation, Charles. You should have been one of these sanctimonious hooligans yourself."

Omphrey flushed. "The retribalization process has been pretty common throughout this century," he answered curtly. "The Major's generation did it on nationalistic lines and started World War One. You and Sir Bryan's generation did it on ideological lines and invented Auschwitz and the annihilation of Dresden. The young men in this Game are at least less lethally sanctimonious than that. They acknowledge that their Game is a game, and they don't kill millions of innocent bystanders."

McVeigh grinned delightedly. He was in a mood to needle anyone. He glanced at his watch and regretfully changed the subject.

"What's the progress since our last meeting?" he asked me.

I sipped my brandy. It was a grand old Armagnac *hors d'age.* It tasted of cavalry boots with a hint of grave-dirt. There was a muffled, mechanical bellow from the Thames outside. From where I sat I could just see the superstructure of a small steamer gingerly negotiating the raised spans of Tower Bridge by the light of brilliant lamps.

"There've been developments," I agreed. I told them about Piers Kenny's researches and my own discovery in Don Proctor's flat. I made no mention of the negatives and contact prints in my hold-all. As I went on, the impish malevolence on McVeigh's face became more marked, while lines of worry deepened around Omphrey's eyes.

"I haven't really been brilliant," I said deprecatingly. "Once you've noted the careful organization of the Game, it stands to reason there had to be detailed records and files somewhere. Young Donald was obviously the mastermind. The records were unlikely to be far away from him, so his studio was the obvious place to look. I've left everything exactly as I found it, so I don't expect him to realize he's been rumbled."

"This will kill Sir Bryan," Omphrey said quietly. "We've got to keep it from him."

"We can't," McVeigh sighed. "Our friend requires a final solution, otherwise he goes to the police and we can't stop him. I've protected the old man from the demands of his job as much as I can, but I can't hide something like this."

"You're sure Donald's the actual ringleader?" Omphrey asked pathetically.

"It was always obvious," I said. "I tried to slip the idea to Sir Bryan that the conspiracy wasn't directed against Global at all, but I didn't convince him or anyone else. The Game is a deliberate and lethal parody of Global's own business. Whoever put it together has obviously got all the old man's flair for organization and admin. And whoever wants to hurt him that badly had to be pretty close to him."

Omphrey sagged. "What are you going to do?" he asked quietly.

"I can still leave Sir Bryan out of things for a while," I said. "I've got one important job left to do first."

I explained about the combat between Ludi Victors in Arizona.

"I'm attending it personally," I said, making no mention of Eric and my private reasons. "There are a few more answers I want before we confront young Don. Besides, the only reliable way to stop the Game is to break it up on the ground. The two Ludi Victors are the only active players left before the next Game starts."

I turned to McVeigh. "What happened at your Holding Board meeting?"

McVeigh shrugged. "More or less what you'd expect. No action has been decided upon for the time being. They were impressed by your analysis but not convinced."

"How much more evidence do they bloody want?" I asked, irritated. "If you give them my latest findings, you'll have to let Sir Bryan know about Don."

"Holding Boards aren't necessarily logical," McVeigh said primly. "They can equivocate and run scared like everybody else. We'll decide the next step when you return from Arizona."

He grinned, and I was puzzled again. I sensed that, deep down, he found the situation exquisitely funny.

"More to the point, what do *you* intend to do when you get back from Arizona?" he asked.

"For what it's worth, I don't think action against Don need necessarily be taken for its own sake. I'm attending the combat because the last two contestants will be slugging it out. I intend to make sure no Ludi Victor ever gets the chance to issue a challenge again. What you do about Don is your business."

It was an honest opinion I'd arrived at during the saying of it, and, even as I said it, I knew I didn't mean it. There was no way I intended Proctor to get off lightly after the attack on Eric. Perhaps I was beginning to feel the stirrings of respectful pity for Sir Bryan. Everything seemed to be closing in on him.

McVeigh was still silent. The expression on his face was remote and ambiguous. I reminded myself that he was nobody's fool. He knew how I felt about the attack on Eric, and he couldn't have helped noticing how I'd left that part of the story out of my account to Charles Omphrey.

Omphrey looked sick. "You're going to stop these men any way you can, aren't you? Don't you think you ought to tell us what exactly you expect us to condone?"

I eased an inch of ash from my cigar. "The idea," I explained, "is for nobody to get killed. I intend to try and convince two so-called Ludi Victors that the Game is literally up and that there is no point in anyone trying to keep it alive. That way, young Proctor remains your pigeon, and you avoid the kind of publicity that could sink Global Alliance without trace." I turned to McVeigh. "The attempt, by the way, is going to cost you another five thousand pounds."

McVeigh stared, the raillery tinged with contempt now.

"Those, I take it, are your terms for getting a crack at a forty million pound jackpot?"

"I hadn't thought about it," I said honestly.

"The hell you hadn't. Global's books are straight. If nobody goes to the police and your attempt at peaceful persuasion succeeds, the money will be lying around looking for someone to keep it warm. Officially it won't exist."

"Those are my terms," I said. "There's a big risk. I'm asking a fair price."

Omphrey gaped from one to the other of us.

McVeigh nodded. "Very well. I accept. I can authorize a further payment to you of five thousand pounds."

"Then you'd better authorize it now. There's paper on the table under the window."

He didn't move. "Payment, of course, will also depend on a successful outcome to your trip." He hadn't forgotten about the written account I'd said I would lodge with my bank.

I shook my head. "No conditions."

"And if something goes wrong?"

"The report gets sent to the police."

"So if you fail in Arizona, we lose a whole business?"

I shrugged. "One way or another, this Game's got to stop. I can't rely on you or your fellow directors to do the necessary. You understand that. I'm offering you a straight deal. You give me the chance to get you all off the hook—at the possible expense of my life—or I go to the police now."

It was a stand-off. McVeigh guessed how badly I wanted to go to Arizona, but he couldn't be sure. Like all big gamblers, he had much to win but most to lose.

He got up from the table and sat by the window. While he wrote, I sat on my bed and put a call through to Olly Starkey. I found him at the Nightingale Lane house on the second try. Left to himself, Omphrey drained his glass and refilled it. He looked as though he would have liked to swig the decanter from the neck. One of Eric's kids took the call. When Olly came on the line I asked him about Eric. He sounded depressed and anxious.

"Still no good." There was a burst of TV sound behind him and I heard a woman's worried voice, presumably Marian's.

"I don't want to talk about it," Olly said. "I've got your pictures and information. The last lot's just come in. What do I do with it?"

"I'm catching a plane at Heathrow tomorrow morning," I said. "Can you meet me in the bar of Terminal Three departure lounge at ten-thirty?"

"Will do." He hung up. I had the uneasy feeling he wanted his line kept free for more important calls.

When I got up, I found McVeigh had ordered a bottle of champagne. The waiter was pouring it into tall, fluted glasses.

"A small celebration with The Widow is called for," McVeigh announced with mock solemnity. He handed me my glass and a folded sheet of paper.

"To the success of all our ventures."

I sipped and read the paper. It and the champagne were satisfactory. We were finishing our first glasses when a call came through from reception. McVeigh's car had arrived and was waiting on the forecourt. We finished the bottle and I walked them to the lift.

The door of the next room was open. Clouds of cigar smoke rolled out as we passed, pushed on by small gales of laughter. As the lift door closed on Omphrey and McVeigh, I finally pinned down McVeigh's strange mood. His mock solemnity was being subverted from within by eruptions from some deep, subterranean well of dangerous, anarchic laughter.

I surfaced at dawn like a U-boat in the middle of a convoy. Early light filtered through clouds like badly hung curtains and reflected off the gunmetal Thames water above Tower Bridge and HMS *Belfast.*

I showered and packed while I waited for breakfast in my room. Afterwards, I settled my bill and inspected the car carefully. There was nothing sticking to the engine, and the brakes were working. I drove to Covent Garden through streets empty except for delivery vans, winos, and yesterday's dead newsprint.

My flat smelled of fresh wood-shavings and incense left burning in a bowl. It was like entering a temple to Metropolitan Krishna. I had had to wake Harry up for my keys to get in. Saul or Gerry had fitted an impressive Chubb lock to the door. I wandered round the rooms, switching on all the lights. By sympathy or design, the boys had carried out my instructions to the letter. The place looked the same as it had before the raid, only newer. I half expected to find my pencilled memoranda pinned back in place on the cork wall. I wasn't sure whether I liked the effect or not.

I checked my new green hold-all, making sure McVeigh's letter was in its envelope. I readdressed it to my bank after inserting a covering note and slipped it in my other packet. There wasn't much else to pack. I would have to buy new clothes in America.

I locked up, walked to Leicester Square tube station, and caught a Piccadilly line tube to Heathrow. I took the *Guardian, Private Eye,* and a few other bleary travellers for company.

I walked the moving pavement to Terminal Three. Olly was waiting for me in the bar. I registered what was wrong before my brain coped with the knowledge. He looked somber and out of place in a black suit and tie. He got up when he saw me.

"I'm sorry," he said, as though I were the victim. "Eric died early this morning."

We sat down. The bar was closed. Olly had a glass of milk and a pack of cafeteria biscuits. I must have gaped at him.

"Why?" I asked stupidly. "He's as strong as a bull. His injuries weren't that bad."

It was probably the most tactless speech of my life. Olly didn't seem to notice.

"Shock and depression," he explained. "Whatever the postmortem says. His blood pressure never stopped falling. Let's not talk about it."

I glanced round. Somewhere in the building I thought there was an Interflora shop. "I'd like to send flowers," I said mechanically, "and a telegram."

"I've done both for you. I knew you wouldn't have time."

I shook my head. "God, I'm sorry, Olly."

"Let's not talk about it." He took a manila envelope from the pocket of his topcoat.

"How's Marian coping?"

"Badly. But she's got the kids to look after her. Don't worry about it. We're a close bunch. We look after our own."

I remembered the big, rambling house in Nightingale Lane from the last time I had visited it, years before, packed with people, furniture, trinkets, and lumber, all gleefully orchestrated by Eric.

"How's she off for money?"

"Don't worry. Eric carried good insurance, so there's no problem. It's with one of the Global companies. Eric would have seen the funny side of that."

It was true. Eric had loved practical jokes, especially when they were played on him.

"Somebody will be paying more than insurance when I come back from this trip," I said.

"That's right. You keep thinking along those lines. I want to see the bastards nailed who hired those kids."

He emptied the contents of the envelope on the table. "Your prospects are narrowed down to five. Two from the Bordeaux district, three from Hessen in Germany. I can't guarantee anything, but the faces you want should be in there."

I looked at the photographs on the table, hardly seeing them because shock knocks out portions of the mind. I eventually registered that they were glossy 12 × 8 prints, mostly in medium to long shot against backgrounds of apartment houses and city buildings. I had the impression that Olly's investigators had not wanted to get too close to their subjects. They had been very discreet. They weren't good pictures, but they would have to do. Stapled to each photograph was a précis of information about the subject.

I slipped the prints in my bag and pushed my packet across the table towards Olly.

"What's this?"

"It's a full account of my work for Global Alliance. There's also an extra contract inside from Global for five thousand pounds payable whether or not I get back from Arizona. They're to go to my bank, if I don't get back." I stopped him by holding up a hand.

"No questions. I don't think there'll be trouble, but I'm not taking chances. If something should go wrong, the five thousand pounds is payable to Eric, so it will go to his estate. That's specified in the contract."

Olly nodded.

I tried to smile. "That's apart from my main fee, of course, which would be paid direct to my bank. You'd have to haggle with them for your share.

"Anyway," I said, "you won't have to worry about anything until I get back. You can do me a favor, though, and post this." It was my check to Ben Campbell.

Olly took the packet and letter unwillingly. "You'd better check in now," he said. "It's early, but I've got things to do, and there's talk of a lightning strike by ground controllers."

He walked me to where a painted board said NO VISITORS BEYOND THIS POINT. I wanted to tell him again how sorry I was. But I couldn't think of any words, and there wasn't much point.

"I'll be away a few days at most," I said. "I'll keep in touch."

"Fine, I'll pick you up when you get back. The funeral will be over then and things will have settled down. Just take care."

A transatlantic businessman hustled by while the announcement system sprayed something unintelligible over the concourse. Olly waited until he could be heard again.

"You wanted to know who hired Starkey Brothers when we did that first job on Sir Bryan Proctor," he said. "I asked Eric when I saw him last night. He was cheerful and lucid then. He remembered. I've even found the original of our final report."

He handed me a folder, and I took it wordlessly. We shook hands, and I walked through passport control into the departure lounge. I had plenty of time, so I ordered a large vodka and orange juice and found myself a seat near the bar in case I needed another drink. I read the report thoroughly several times.

I considered the information in it and found I wasn't surprised. I remembered McVeigh lecturing me on the way back to London from James Huddiesford's West Country manse. He'd said my professional independence was a delusion. He'd warned me I would always be manipulated. Of course he was right. Deep down I'd always known it. Maybe I've found it convenient to forget, though, and need a hard reminder from time to time.

Even bluff old Huddiesford had manipulated me in his own way. He couldn't have known in advance the results of my researches into his bent supplier of tape and slide booths, but it couldn't have suited him better if he'd arranged the thing personally. When I'd first met him, I'd seen immediately that he was bored with his leisurely country squire routine and his drunken wife. He'd been pining for an excuse to roll his sleeves up and get stuck in the mud again—breaking men, launching enterprises, and coming home pissed at midnight. I'd just given him the excuse he needed.

But the Global Alliance trick was a lot more blatant. I was realizing that I had been consciously and expertly manipulated from beginning to end, if this was anything like the end. I probed the feeling over my vodka and orange juice, liking the drink more and more and the feeling less and less.

I found in myself a sneaking sympathy for the dumb kids who played the Game according to the rules of Don Proctor and his friends. But I wasn't feeling exactly philosophical, and I knew I was going to be more than a little revengeful if and when I got back from Arizona.

I finished my drink and ordered another. The electronic board said there was going to be a slight delay over flight departure time, and I'd arrived early to start with. The bar was going to be busy.

A male steward with compassionate eyes took us through life jacket and oxygen mask drill while TWA's Jumbo took off late from Heathrow, crossed the coast near Manchester, and flew over a corner of northern Ireland. Neat fields and loughs reflected the un without the blink of an outrage or an explosion. Nothing looks outrageous from 37,000 feet. As D.H. Lawrence said in the days when planes had struts and spars, an air traveller is like a boiled sweet wrapped in cellophane. There's no contact with the world.

The Jumbo left a fringe of surf beating against the last Irish outcrops before setting off on a wide parabola over the North Atlantic. The flight was packed, the air under-conditioned, and the in-flight movie had broken down. I ordered a large drink and toyed with lunch when it came round. It was *boeuf bourguignon* spiked with granules of rice like fine volcanic shingle.

I tried to work. I went over my papers and studied Olly's photographs with my magnifying glass until I could have recognized my subjects on a smoggy night at fifty paces.

The plane made a landfall two hundred miles north of Goose Bay. The pilot told us so over the PA system after giving us the latest American football scores. We flew on over Labrador and the empty quarter of Northern Ontario. It was mid afternoon, local time, when we landed at Chicago. I adjusted my watch.

I had an hour to wait for the connecting flight to Phoenix. O'Hare looked pretty much the same as Heathrow except that the taxis were bigger. I walked through to the transit lounge for a drink and found an automat dispensing Rand McNally maps instead. I fed it two quarters and selected the button for Arizona and New Mexico.

During the southwest stage of the flight, we chased a declining sun across the euclidian swathe of middle America where flatlands darkened among rumped ridges of mountains. I ordered a whiskey sour from a freckled stewardess and studied my map. I got my notes out again and studied those, too, smoking steadily from a pack of Tareytons.

My respect for Proctor's staff-work increased. I pinpointed the map reference from his files and compared its general location on the Rand McNally map with a blown-up inset of it in the top right-hand corner. I had to hand it to the boy. If you wanted an impressive venue for a meeting of Ludi Victors, you could do worse than the Grand Canyon.

The combat zone lay halfway along a road on the southern rim, not far from a Navajo reservation. Proctor's note carried the simple word "Grandview," and I found it on the map inset. It was a tourist viewing point. For a moment, I wondered about the choice after all. The Canyon was one of the wonders of the world. Millions of tourists visited it every year. They could be a danger and a distraction to Von Runstedt and Denfert Rochereau. Then a glance at the scale of the map changed my mind. Apart from the fact that we were outside the main tourist season, the area was so huge that the Red Army could have got lost in it without even trying. There might still be problems like park rangers to contend with, but if I was right in my estimate of Proctor, their presence would appeal to the planners, lending the spice of uncertainty to the combat.

I put my work away and thought about Von Runstedt and Denfert Rochereau, the German and French champions. I needed to know more about them as well as the actual ground conditions, but there was nothing to do until I got out of my cellophane wrap. So I ordered another whiskey sour and smoked a last Tareyton until the warning lights came on. It had been a long and boring flight, but at least I'd hardly thought about Eric lying dead in the basement of St. George's Hospital.

Phoenix was a stopping-off point on the plane's route to Los Angeles. We had been losing height over the plains of Utah, and there was still just a little light left as we dropped down over Arizona's lush Valley of the Sun. Palms and rivers of neon formed a backdrop to the airport. I left the terminal building on a courtesy bus to the Hertz office where they rented me a Ford LTD not more than thirty feet long. I felt I could have done with something less conspicuous, but a glance at the other vehicles in the lot showed me I would be just one of the guys.

I locked my hold-all in the trunk and consulted the courtesy map in the car's glove compartment. All I had to do was follow Interstate Highway 17 northwards to Flagstaff. After that, I had a choice. I could continue on Highway 89 towards Lake Powell, branching left at Cameron onto Highway 64 to meet the Grand Canyon. Or I could take Highway 180 direct from Flagstaff to Grand Canyon Village through the Coconino National Forest. There were no towns on the second route, so the journey would be discreet. Highway 89, on the other hand, would probably be busier and, thus, more anonymous. The two routes joined the Canyon's southern rim road at points about twenty-five miles apart.

I decided to leave second-guessing Denfert Rochereau's and Von Runstedt's plans until next morning and spend the night at Flagstaff where the routes diverged. I started the LTD up, turned west on the Maricopa Freeway and pushed the car along. Daylight disappeared completely as Phoenix petered out into the desert and Camelback Mountain came up on my right. There was already a good moon, silhouetting tall saguaro cacti still studded with lemon, wax-textured flowers and leaves. According to a note on my courtesy map, the saguaro was the home of Arizona's national bird, the shy and speckled cactus wren that builds up to five nests among the spines to confuse its enemies. Bearing in mind what happened to my flat, I thought I could learn something from the cactus wren.

An hour or more later, cacti and desert gave way imperceptibly to rolling plateaux of chaparral and high mountains beyond. Near the turn-off to Oak Creek Canyon, still some way short of Flagstaff, I passed a sign telling me I had climbed from around 1,000 to 7,000 feet in 140 miles. The air was sharp when I got to Flagstaff, and a glitter of frost shone on the sidewalks along the storefronts.

I picked a motel between Interstate 17 and the Santa Fe railroad tracks. With luck, the locomotives would wake me if hotel reception didn't.

I took a room about the size of a squash court beside a heated swimming pool. I showered and had a quick dinner of New York strip steak and salad smothered with Roquefort dressing washed down with a pint of Almaden red from California. From the twilit bar, an innocent succubus of a boy with glasses from the nearby university sang an ironic song to the accompaniment of his own guitar. The song described something nasty the Americans did to the Royal Navy during the War of Independence. It annoyed me, not because I'm a patriot, but because it meant someone had been snooping through the motel register. It's a problem in small towns.

By the time I had finished dinner, it was six o'clock in the morning in London and I was ready for sleep. I called Olly's office from the motel room and left my address and telephone number on his automatic recording machine. I was asleep instantly.

The eve of combat. That was the thought in my mind when I woke up. I guessed it was also the thought in the minds of Denfert Rochereau and Von Runstedt.

I opened the curtains of my glass-walled room leading to the patio outside, its concrete surround, and the swimming pool. The sun was brilliant and the air so clear I could pick out individual twigs of mountain trees on the other side of the railroad tracks. Steam writhed dramatically from the surface of the pool, and mountain light bounced with cheerful ferocity off the frost-filigreed grass.

I closed the curtains before turning on the TV and shower. On Channel 8, a squad of newsmen were firing pointed questions at the President about a new energy crisis. I was having an energy crisis of my own, so I switched to Channel 5 and watched cartoons instead.

I breakfasted on waffles with blueberry syrup and thin rashers of fragile bacon with eggs and hashed brown potatoes. At that moment, I couldn't be sure where my next meal was coming from. Remembering the sly minstrel from the night before, I would have preferred to eat in my room, but I needed to question the waitress.

She was a pretty stereotype with ash blonde hair and a retroussé nose, dressed in what looked like the uniform miniskirt. She turned out to be another freshman from Northern Arizona University working her way through college.

I began by telling her how eager I was to explore the real American wilderness now that cheap Laker flights made it all simple. She reassured me that the southern rim of the Canyon was accessible year round and that there were entry points at both ends of the rim road. It would cost me two dollars to use them, but there wouldn't be many other visitors. The winter season of the Arizona Snow Bowl was over, and the main tourist rush had yet to get started.

I asked her about temperatures and weather conditions. She shrugged and pointed through the insulated glass wall of the dining room towards steam coming off the heated outside pool. There didn't seem to be much of an energy crisis in Flagstaff. She told me that night temperatures dropped below freezing and there could still be snow. But the days were fine and should hit the mid sixties around noon. She added that if I needed anything special, she knew a good store selling hunting equipment and groceries a few blocks north. It turned out her illiterate boyfriend, a pure Navajo, was the son of the owner. According to her, William could find and track a deer up to a quarter of a mile away by smell alone. She sounded proud of that. She was a liberated girl.

I thanked her, left a large tip, and went outside to the LTD. I switched on the heater and ventilator to clear the screen.. While the car warmed up, I went back to my room and packed. Afterwards, I changed some travelers checks at reception and paid my bill.

I drove the few blocks north, drawing up a shopping list in my mind. I found the store on a sharp bend where a bridge crossed the highway near the center of the town. It was the only bend for a hundred miles in either direction.

There was one assistant in the shop and no other customers. I picked out a heavy canvas hunting jacket with a blanket lining, high leather boots, a soft hat of the kind Navajos wore, a powerful flashlight, and a coil of nylon climbing rope. I added a compass, a thermos flask, waterproof matches, a water canteen, and a pair of 8 × 50 Bushnell binoculars. I had already packed a camera to keep up my tourist persona.

There was a locked case of handguns near the cash desk. I put on my best home counties accent and asked the girl nervously about wildlife in the mountains. She was a dumpy, wise-eyed Navajo with broad black braids and exquisite silver and turquoise jewelry at her wrists and throat. She was probably William's sister. Her eyes despised me, but she sensed another sale.

"You never know," she grinned. "Maybe a mountain lion gets up and bites you on the butt. It don't pay to take no chances."

I nodded nervously again and pointed to a 9mm Browning automatic. I asked her about permits.

She shrugged. "Ain't no problem. You file a permit application with the police department. They check state records and clear you. Shouldn't take more'n two, three days."

"I can't wait that long," I objected. "I'll only be around a few days anyway," I allowed myself to push the other pile of gear reluctantly to one side. "I suppose I could forget the whole trip."

The girl pouted and waited. She knew I hadn't finished.

"Tell you what." I let an expression of low cunning come over my face. "I don't plan to use the gun, and I'll be back before the end of the week. If I gave you a good deal on the resale, do you think you could forget the permit business?"

She affected to consider the proposition, inspecting me carefully. "This is a class establishment," she said finally. "Ain't too much call for a used handgun. That Browning costs two-fifty. I sure couldn't take it back for more than a hundred and fifty."

"A hundred dollars for a few days rental?" I protested. "I probably won't even use the damned thing."

She waved a generous hand. "Tell you what. It's a risk and the cops would land on me real hard if they found out. You give me three hundred now, and I'll give you a receipted bill for two-fifty. You get the two-fifty back when you bring the gun back. That way, I cover myself in case you're just a bum looking for a cheap weapon, and you drop fifty for having a gun without a licence. Seeing you're a friend of that white girl at the motel," she added more generously still, "I'll throw in a box of shells."

I grumbled and gave in. I paid for the lot in cash and didn't get an unwieldy heap of change from a thousand dollars. I didn't need to be told that there was one price for Navajos and another for out-of-state tourists with nervous dispositions.

Back in the LTD, I studied the courtesy map with care and finally tossed a coin. I found I had picked Highway 180 through the Coconino National Forest.

I found the turn-off and left Flagstaff, skirting the Snow Bowl. I was alone on the road. The morning was brilliant, the route lined with forests of piñon and ponderosa pines broken by trembling copses of aspen. Volcanic, snowcapped mountains were a theatrical backdrop. Strange, soft saucers of white cloud hung over them, and the sun struck a million mirror images from shards of frost by the roadside. The temperature was still rising, and snow that had fallen overnight was pouring rather than melting off the lower slopes.

The forest thinned, and with it the oozy aromatic sap smell that the LTD's air vents washed over me, giving way to scrubland and Utah juniper. I passed two trucks, a handful of cars and a couple of gimcrack trading posts displaying turquoise trinkets and beaded belts made in Hong Kong. I arrived at Grand Canyon Village around midday.

The village was just another trading post with a snack bar and nobody around. In fact, the only non-motorized life I had seen since Flagstaff had been two black, scavenging crows and a tatty cowboy waiting patiently for me to pass so that he could cross the highway. He had hunched unmoving, his hands clasped in prayer over the horn of his saddle.

I found an old Navajo with a face like a leather cushion in the cafeteria. A sign above him said the place specialized in tacos and burritos. I ate an omelette washed down with Coors beer and drove on to the barrier on the southern rim road. I paid my two dollars toll and was told to have a good day by a bored ranger wearing an official *bola* tie with a clasp of turquoise in worked silver and a starched shirt that divided him up into impeccable squares.

I drove straight to Grandview Point, parked, and got my first good look at the Canyon. Just looking kept me quiet for a time. I sat on a low stone wall over a sheer drop and smoked a Tareyton. The Canyon at that point was a mere six miles from rim to rim. Dark schist, pink granite, and immense flat-topped mesas bloomed through an afternoon light that made distance itself look rose and violet. The total silence of an immense volume of space merely ignored the piping of unseen birds and the crunch of gravel as I walked around. There was nobody else in sight.

I locked the car and began a reconnaissance of the combat zone. It was shaped like a blunted wedge, perhaps half a mile wide at its thick end, the sides being formed by the southern rim road and the edge of the Canyon itself. It was covered for the most part with juniper, piñon, and ponderosa. There wasn't much in the way of secondary growth beneath them, but there were plenty of boulder outcrops poking up through the forest floor and some steep, small gulleys, generally running at right angles to the Canyon. It was difficult terrain and would make a good test of two men's abilities who between them had already killed nearly twenty times over on a variety of different grounds.

I went back to the car and drove the rest of the way to Desert View Point at the other end of the rim road. There was another snack bar, a souvenir shop, a small museum, and a ranger station. I ordered a malted milk in the bar and examined some cases of stuffed exhibits showing the fauna of the Canyon. There were eagles and great owls as well as rattlesnakes, scorpions, and furry, poisonous spiders.

Finally, I drove back to Grand Canyon Village. The sun was already well down the sky, stealthily changing the colors of the rocks. Soon the light would be gone in the sudden way of mountains and deserts. I decided Von Runstedt and Denfert Rochereau should have landed at Phoenix now and be on their way north. But there were other possibilities. They might have flown to Las Vegas and be pushing on by road. I wished I had had more time to study the possibilities, but I was certain that neither of them would have had time for an in-depth reconnaissance like mine. The system wasn't designed to allow it. Still, I made a note to keep a careful watch on the occasional road traffic.

I drove back to my original entry point and explained matters to the forest ranger. I said I had left an important filter I needed for a sunset shot back in the village.

"Better hurry it up," he warned. "In an hour's time it'll be too dark to shoot a thing."

I restarted the engine. "Do you keep a note of cars coming in and out?" I said. "Or do I have to buy another ticket?"

"No way. Most of the year there's too much traffic. Don't worry about it. The ticket you've got is good for the day."

"That's fine. I'm expecting some friends to meet me here. I thought they might have arrived already."

He shook his head. "Nobody's come through since you did. I guess it's too cold."

"Right. I'll be back soon. If my friends don't turn up, I'll probably drive out through Desert View Point. Thanks a lot."

"You bet."

There was a grocery store attached to the Grand Canyon Village trading post and restaurant. I really did buy some 35mm color film as well as some vacuum-packed strips of dried beef like South African biltong, a bag of biscuits, a six-pack of Coors beer, and a bottle of Jack Daniels. I filled my canteen with water, got the thermos flask filled with coffee, and bought a Navajo blanket. The blanket alone cost almost two hundred dollars, and it was the cheapest they had. I reminded myself not to lose it. It would look fine on the newly decorated wall opposite my cork memorandum board.

I waved to the ranger as I reentered the national park and drove straight to Grandview Point. Two hundred yards past it, there was a closed dirt track I'd noticed earlier leading towards the Canyon. It was inside the combat zone and set off from the road by a pole slung over free-standing crosspieces. I got out, sniffing a sharp frost. The road was empty. I lifted the pole, drove inside, and put the pole back. I parked round the first bend of the track, under a giant alligator juniper and out of sight from the road. I switched off the engine. Silence sang above the ticking of hot metal.

I unpacked my grip on the hood of the LTD and changed my city clothes for the jeans and wilderness gear I had bought in Flagstaff. I pulled on the high boots, tested my flashlight and slung it from a loop on my hunting jacket. As an afterthought, I filled the magazine of the Browning, checked the action, and shoved the gun into the top of my jeans. It dug into my left hip.

I took a can of Coors, followed the dirt track to the rim of the Canyon and watched the last of the daylight leave the sky. I saw cold moonlight replace it, wiping out slim bands of orange and lilac along a horizon of mesas and the flushed vapor trail of yet another 747 carrying pleasure-seekers to Vegas where the neon at night is brighter than the sun by day. I sensed rather than saw the sheer drop below my feet.

I smoked a Tareyton and drank Coors until it was completely dark and the night already full of animal rustlings, slitherings, and foragings. I heard the rush of air as an owl swooped somewhere nearby. A small animal squealed once.

I walked back to the car, avoiding the deeper patches of moon-shadow. I knew the Canyon rim was too high and the weather too cold for the scorpions and sidewinders of the Painted Desert and the valley floor, but I was glad of my boots anyway. In nature, man is one of the few creatures to be a raptor by day and a sleeper by night.

Back in the LTD, I turned the heater up and listened to plangent Bacharach beamed from a radio in Albuquerque. I ate strips of dried beef, drank Jack Daniels, and began to put flesh on the bones of my provisional strategy.

I could only close the Game down for good if I stopped the combat between Ludi Victors in such a way that they themselves broke up its organization on the ground. It would be dangerous. Both men were experienced killers and committed Game players. On the other hand, I had had time for a thorough reconnaissance, and I was armed. They, of course, wouldn't be. Not, at least, with obvious weapons.

What could I do when I found them? I could threaten them with charges of multiple murder and fraud. I could even threaten to nail them for the attempted murder of each other. On the other hand, there was an unpleasant possibility that they wouldn't be impressed. If they had any intelligence, they would realize that most of my evidence was inference rather than fact, that I couldn't actually prove much, and that my employers would have taken official action already if they had been prepared to stand the publicity.

Not to put too fine a point on it, all I really had to bargain with would be Don Proctor's files and my own eyewitness evidence of their combat. But what if they thought it wasn't too late to destroy the files, and me with them? I was suddenly fond of the Browning. I dug it out of my jeans, checked the action again and wished I had had a chance to test-fire it.

On balance, I thought my main effort should be towards convincing both men that the Global Alliance companies would prefer to cut their losses and keep matters quiet—so long as the Game was wound up—but were prepared to go to the police if it wasn't. The deal sounded like a poker game for uncomfortably high stakes. I wondered what cards the morning would show.

On that thought, I ate a handful of biscuits and washed them down with some more Jack Daniels. I put a sweater on beneath my hunting jacket and arranged myself comfortably on the broad back seat of the LTD. I locked the doors from the inside and kept the Browning handy beneath the Navajo blanket which I spread over myself. I had no worries about waking up. The hard, brilliant light of a mountain dawn would see to that.

I woke well after sunrise and swore quietly about jet lag. I got out of the car quickly, scanned the surrounding area, and did a short series of exercises to ease the cold out of my bones. I splashed a handful of water from the canteen in my face and dried myself on the Navajo blanket. Afterwards, I sat on the hood of the LTD, sipping lukewarm coffee and eating more strips of dried beef. It would have been wiser not to smoke, but I smoked. William the Navajo might have been able to track a deer by scent alone up to a quarter of a mile, but I didn't think Von Runstedt or Denfert Rochereau would be in that class.

I checked my equipment, locked the car, and walked quietly along the edge of the dirt track towards the rim road. There was no sound. Keeping inside the line of trees parallel to the road, I edged my way to the Grandview Point turn-off.

I swore again when I got there. In the gravel turning-circle at the end of the viewing area, its fender against the low retaining wall, was a beige Pontiac. There was nobody in it. I used the Bushnells to scan the area thoroughly. I saw nothing and nobody. I concentrated on the car itself and studied the rental company sign stuck on a side window.

I lowered the glasses. The Pontiac hadn't been there the night before, and it was too early for tourists. A forest ranger would be using a pickup or his own car, not a rented one.

Still inside the trees, I edged my way down to the canyon rim. On the other side of the retaining wall, just before the big drop, was a narrow, packed earth track made by construction workers and daring kids. I negotiated it quietly, out of sight below the rim. Once round the other side of the viewing area, I made my way back to the road. I was in the trees again. When I got there, I still hadn't seen or heard anybody.

I thought things over. I was certain the Pontiac's presence meant that either Von Runstedt or Denfert Rochereau was in the zone already. Possibly both of them. The fact that I hadn't seen a second car didn't mean it wasn't around. I was angry again for oversleeping. But it was still early, so whichever Ludi Victor had arrived in the Pontiac was probably making his own reconnaissance. I wondered what he would make of the LTD when he came across it. I hoped it would confuse him. On the other hand, both he and I might still be awaiting the arrival of the second Ludi Victor. Neither of us could be sure.

I was still working things out when I heard the other car travelling fast from the direction of Grand Canyon Village. The air was so still, I heard the sound for such a long time, that when the car hurtled past, I was taken by surprise. It slackened speed momentarily opposite the gravel track to Grandview Point, then accelerated towards Desert View Point. No more than a few minutes later, before the sound had died completely, I heard it coming back.

It passed me at high speed again, a bronze Malibu with white trim, but this time I got a look at the driver's face. It was big and almost round, with a tight shock of thinning black hair. The owner looked well over six feet and built to scale. Dark glasses shaded his high forehead and eyes, but I easily recognized from Olly's photographs the man called Von Runstedt, undefeated Ludi Victor for the last two years.

Seconds after the Malibu had pounced round the bend, its tires howled. There was a crash of branches, the slam of a door, and a brief scrabbling of stones. Then silence again. So that was that. Von Runstedt had gone to ground. His entry hadn't been subtle, but at least I knew where he was. So, presumably, did Denfert Rochereau, who'd obviously arrived first in the beige Pontiac.

I listened for a few minutes, heard nothing, and consulted the rough sketch I had drawn during my previous day's reconnaissance. Grandview Point was in the center of the wedge-shaped zone. Von Runstedt was somewhere in cover at the thick western end. The whole area, I knew, was bisected down its length by a gully that started near me. I could just see its shallow lip, but I knew it got steeper and stonier as it ran westwards, parallel with the Canyon on the outer edge of the zone.

From what I had seen already, I thought the German was hardly the type to wait quietly in ambush. I guessed he would make his way eastwards towards me, Grandview Point, and the center. That gave him two options. He could cross the dangerously exposed gully but advance afterwards with his left flank covered by the Canyon's rim, or he could advance more quietly through the thicker belt of trees on this side of the gully—towards me.

I stayed where I was. Twenty minutes later, a couple of undisturbed birds in the trees up ahead told me I was staying in vain. Von Runstedt must have chosen the bolder option. I should have guessed it. It meant he was headed for Grandview Point on the other side of the gully. I decided it might not be too late to head him off.

I glanced at my sketch again, shoved it in my pocket and moved directly towards the viewing area, skirting the shallow end of the gully. When I could see the viewing area through the trees, I angled left towards the Canyon rim. The sun was higher now and the birds weren't singing anymore. There was utter silence.

When I got to the rim, I checked. As I'd hoped, the track I'd negotiated earlier continued westwards. I climbed down onto it and began to edge my way along. From time to time, I raised my head and scanned the trees. The ledge kept me conveniently out of sight. On the other hand, it was vulnerable and dangerously narrow. Once I dislodged a small boulder. I never heard it hit ground.

I had travelled about twenty yards when I came to the first bend. I edged round it and stopped. A few yards on, the track had been gouged out by a small landslip and overlaid by a sharply-angled slope of loose shale. Above the slope, a horseshoe-shaped depression had been left among a jumble of boulders, its open side towards the Canyon. Von Runstedt sat peaceably on a boulder, his back towards me. He was working quietly and methodically, scanning the rim ahead of him often. I was sharply suspicious for a moment, for this was an experienced fighter, but he clearly had no idea of the ledge's existence, so it didn't occur to him to look behind.

He wore a hunting jacket and high boots like mine, but he was bigger even than I'd thought. His shoulders and upper arms were massive. His skin looked the kind that would redden painfully in the mountain sun. On one of his sleeves he wore the wide, embroidered yellow band I had read about in Proctor's files.

He was sitting forward, legs apart, working on a stone about a couple of pounds in weight. He was tying thin nylon rope to it. Two more stones, similarly tied, lay beside him on the boulder. In each case, the loose ends of rope were several feet long.

As I watched, he picked up the three ends and began to knot them together. Every expert has his favorite way of doing things. I guessed every player of the Game had a favorite weapon he could improvise on the spot and use in ways that might make the result look like an accident.

Von Runstedt was improvising a form of the *bolas,* the device used by South American gauchos to bring down steers on the run. Whirled hard and accurately, the centrifugal force of the stones would wrap the ropes tightly round a victim's legs, bringing it crashing down. If the device worked on cattle, it would work on men.

The follow-up wasn't hard to guess. He was a big, heavy man. With an opponent immobilized, it would be simple to apply pressure to the carotid artery. The unconscious body could then be dropped out of a tree—or into a canyon.

Von Runstedt didn't look round until he heard the action of the Browning. He turned slowly, his eyes moving from my face to the gun, then to my sleeve where there was no armband.

"Who are you?" he asked quietly, politely. "What do you want?"

I climbed cautiously along the edge of the shale until I was in the horseshoe depression with him.

"What do you want?" he repeated. His voice was unexpectedly high for such a big body, with a thread of Germanized American accent in it. His huge right hand rested lightly on the *bolas.*

"Leave it alone," I said, more sharply than I'd meant. I leaned against the rim of the boulder depression and scanned it quickly. I didn't want Denfert Rochereau joining us just yet.

"I have nothing of value," Von Runstedt sneered, "apart from some travelers checks. If I give them to you, will you leave me alone?"

"Just lean forward and keep your hands on your knees."

He did it slowly, faintly puzzled but unafraid. I was an obstacle to be got round and disposed of once he had found out who I was and what I wanted. He was a man with an obsession, and I reminded myself to be very careful.

"You are Von Runstedt," I said, "Ludi Victor of the Game for the last two years. You are here to fight Denfert Rochereau, current Ludi Victor. I myself am not of the Game. I am here to stop you. It is no longer a secret, you understand. You have no choice."

His face registered shock, irritation, and finally amusement. The transitions took time, but less than I'd thought. Maybe every player since the Game started had subconsciously prepared himself for this moment.

"You are here to stop the Game," he echoed dryly. "You are, then, a policeman?"

"No. I represent privately the insurance companies you and your friends have been swindling. My employers have the evidence they need to get you all jailed in any country of Europe. In those countries where there is no death penalty, that is. But they would prefer a discreet solution."

Von Runstedt thought for a while and nodded solemnly, humoring me. "And what would their solution be?"

"For the Game to be abandoned permanently, here and now, starting with you and Denfert Rochereau. If you agree, no further action need be taken. This is, naturally, in everybody's interest."

The sun was hot on my face, although the other side of me was still cold. I could feel sweat running from my armpits under the heavy jacket. Von Runstedt scanned my face absently for a long time.

"The arrogance of men like your employers never fails to amaze me," he remarked eventually. "Do you have any idea how many men are involved in the Game?" He spoke simply, as though explaining things to a child. "Apart from the Ludi Victor, two hundred and fifty members engage in combat every year. Hundreds who are not combatants take other roles. And hundreds more simply wait to be awarded a role of any kind. Do your employers really believe that stopping such an enterprise can be as simple as throwing a switch on a toy train?"

"It doesn't matter how big your Game is," I said patiently. "Society is always bigger. If you don't cooperate, your members will wind up in society's jails. It's as simple as that."

He shrugged. "We will not argue. It is difficult in any case to reason with a man holding a gun. Technology makes communication so difficult. What exactly do you wish me to do?"

I uncoiled the nylon rope I had tied round my waist and tossed it at his feet.

"You start by tying that round your ankles. Make a good knot, then wind the rope onto one wrist. I'll take it from there."

He looked down at the rope but made no effort to pick it up. "What is the point of this charade?" he asked irritably.

"I intend to immobilize you while I look for Denfert Rochereau," I said. "It makes sense to put my proposition to you jointly."

"Why do you not simply ask me for my *parole d'honneur?*"

"Don't be daft."

He looked at me bleakly. "I can assure you the word of a Ludi Victor is likely to be a great deal more reliable than that of some minor functionary in a commercial enterprise. But perhaps you cannot be expected to understand that."

"As you said, we won't argue."

"Very well." He smiled again, frankly amused. "I was careless. I was impressed by the Canyon and failed to check it for possible approaches. I am fortunate that Denfert Rochereau did not use it instead of you. You may not be so lucky in your attempt to coerce him, by the way. But let us assume you survive the attempt and that both Denfert Rochereau and myself agree to your terms. What then?"

"You get out of here and take the first plane back to Europe. I shall be placing an advertisement in all the major European papers. It will read 'Ludi Victor versus Ludi Victor postponed indefinitely. The Game is finished.'"

"And if players simply ignore your pronouncement?" he asked dryly. "What if the Game refuses to die at your command?"

"That's not your business. All you have to do is stay out of things. As I promised, there will be no consequences."

He shook his head, mock patience and pity on his face. "But you see, it is my business. The Game is subject to strict discipline. There are special squads for the purpose. Men have tried before to break the rules. Denfert Rochereau and myself are contracted to this contest. If we complied with your request, we should not live long. The Discipline Squads would see to that. It would be an absurd and undignified way to lose our titles, wouldn't you agree?"

I was now uncomfortably hot and my patience was fraying. My nerve too. In spite of the artfully concealed hollow, Denfert Rochereau should have found us by now. I kept scanning the boulder rim without taking my eyes off Von Runstedt for longer than I had to. I was feeling dangerously exposed.

"Get it into your head," I snapped, "that by the time my employers have finished, there won't be a Game left to discipline, let alone anyone to do the disciplining. The Game is over, as of now."

The patient good humor vanished from Von Runstedt's eyes.

"And you get it into your head, little friend, that the Game will never be over. It is a way of life for too many people. Until society itself is changed, only the Game confers dignity and freedom."

"Dignity and freedom," I sneered back. "Big words for embezzlement and murder by juvenile delinquents."

"Yes, dignity and freedom." His face set hard. "Do you and your employers not also play games? You make bets on other people's lives and possessions. You stack the odds in your favor and grow fat on the profits. And do not tell me all this is innocent because nobody is hurt by it. All over the world, lives are destroyed and corrupted by the weapons and manufactured goods in which insurance companies invest."

He controlled himself again. "But I do not have to justify myself to you. Those who take part in the Game do so voluntarily. They prefer to risk death rather than merely survive, trapped in prisons of exploitation you call democracy, socialism, capitalism, and all the other isms. The very existence of the Game gives them a freedom they would not otherwise have. In the society you represent, they can only be losers."

I had had enough. I stood up.

"Fine. You want freedom and choice, Von Runstedt. You've got it. Start tying that rope."

He glared at me. "And if I refuse?"

"You get the choice of being shot in the leg." I spoke brutally and shifted my point of aim.

"I do not think you would, little friend," he said softly. "You are, after all, only a minor mercenary. Violence is a big thing for such a little person. It is not what you are paid for."

I thought of Eric. They were probably converting him into cinders right now.

"Try me," I said quietly.

Von Runstedt hesitated for the first time. "Denfert Rochereau will hear you. He will come looking."

"Fine. It will save me having to look for him."

He bent forward slowly and picked up the rope. He started knotting it round his ankles. His eyes didn't leave mine.

"If it is of interest, little friend, the Game is not of indefinite duration. It has a five-year span, and the coming year will see an ultimate Ludi Victor. When that happens, the accumulated gauge will be directed to revolutionary purposes, mainly the purchase of arms and equipment. I intend to be ultimate Ludi Victor. When I am, I shall assume authority and commence the support of subversion and protest in many countries. Movements of the kind in your country are now high on my list."

He spoke deliberately, flatly. "But I do not know why I trouble to say this. Your employers, at least, are men. You merely exist on the fringe of life, doing society's dirty work for a few stinking pfennigs. You are nothing."

I fell for the oldest trick in the book, probably because it was the oldest and most effective. His eyes had been on me, and I was watching them rather than his hands. I didn't even see the shower of sand and rubble he threw.

There was nothing I could do about the pain of temporary blinding. I fired at a half-blur of movement before the gun was knocked out of my hand. Then his huge weight was on me, wrestling me to the ground.

With the breath knocked out of me and one arm pinioned between us, I fought to claw my free hand into his eyes. It got me nowhere. He fumbled for my throat. I had a split-second vision of the huge hands that could make easy work of the nerve centers in my neck, and I thought of the immense drop of the Canyon.

He found my throat. As he shifted to get a better purchase, I heaved desperately. My knee had two inches to travel into his groin. I used both of them. As he reared upwards in pain, I rolled convulsively out from under him and drove an elbow into his stomach. I staggered to my feet, clawing at my eyes, but he was on me again in a flash.

This time the huge arms pinioned mine as we crashed sideways. The boulder on which he had been sitting was in our way, and my ribs took the weight and momentum of both of us. I had time for one brief scream before my head slammed into the shale.

I must have passed out for a moment, because when I opened my eyes, I could see again. Von Runstedt was on his feet.

"You must forgive a little *ruse de guerre,*" he said gently. "At least you tried."

He reached out to take my ankles and I knew he was going to throw me over the rim. There was nothing I could do about it. Apart from the pain in my ribs, I could hardly breathe. My lungs refused to stretch against my rib cage, and one ankle was trapped at an angle between two boulders.

Suddenly he was moving, yet not moving. His bewilderment made him delay fractionally, fatally. To him, it must have seemed as though the entire universe had begun to slide past. In fact, the unstable shale slope was on the move, rustling softly towards the brink of the Canyon. When he realized what was happening and threw himself flat, it was almost too late. The trembling shale had stopped, but his legs up to the thighs were over the edge.

I clamped my teeth and reached out for my rope, jerking my twisted ankle brutally out of its trap.

"Don't even move," I said. My tongue felt as big as a dead rat. What came out was more a distorted whistle than a voice.

I crawled painfully round the boulder. When I'd taken the rope right round, I made a firm knot with fingers that kept fumbling.

Von Runstedt's voice was quiet and puzzled. "You realize that I shall still kill you if you succeed?" he whispered.

"Shut up. Even your voice could start another slide."

I tested the knot and began to coil the rope. I rolled over painfully and prepared to throw him the loose end.

He spoke again, comically solemn. "I have perhaps dishonored you. You would have made a worthy opponent." He had taken the yellow armband off and was slowly, gingerly, slipping a key on a chain from round his neck. He hefted them in one hand.

"I do not wish to sacrifice myself unnecessarily, but the cardinal priority is to protect the emblems of the Game. In case you fail, these belong to Denfert Rochereau. He will find you, and you will answer to him."

He threw them up the slope. The tiny movement was enough. The shale rustled briefly and he was gone.

Before I passed out again, I had a recollection of the printed guide I had read at the Desert View ranger station. It explained that a drop of a thousand feet in height is equivalent to three hundred miles of distance from the equator, which explained why the climate of the Canyon rim was like that of Canada, while the climate of the Colorado River winding through the bottom of it was more like that of New Mexico.

As my world faded into a humming, sepia-patterned emptiness of endlessly forming and re-forming geometrical shapes, I had a vision of Von Runstedt turning stiffly and silently through Canyon space, falling all the way from Canada to New Mexico.

The lowest branch of an alligator juniper trembled several feet above my head. Two birds squabbled and made up on it continuously. I stared at them, puzzled. Judging by the position of the sun in my eyes, it was around noon. Then the pain came back.

When the nausea ended, I raised my head cautiously. The man standing in front of me was Denfert Rochereau. He was as easily recognizable as Von Runstedt had been. He was posed in an attitude of unconscious elegance, his legs apart, his weight on one slim hip. He was about my height, with broad shoulders and a mop of tight, golden curls. But unlike Von Runstedt or me, he made no concession to camouflage. He wore beautifully cut brushed denim and soft moccasins. His face was sensitive and narrow. He was a pretty boy. I noticed immediately that he was wearing a yellow band on his right sleeve. I wondered if he was a southpaw.

He was reading with attention, juggling Von Runstedt's key and ribbon with his free hand. He was also frowning. He looked up, saw me with my eyes open and walked over.

"You are not badly injured," he said in quietly modulated, almost accent-free English. "You have probably broken two ribs. There is bruising and laceration on your scalp. Perhaps you also have concussion. What happened?"

I shifted carefully. "I'm a geologist," I said. "On vacation. Some guy jumped me when I was out walking. He would have killed me, I think, only he slipped on some loose rocks and fell over the edge of the Canyon. I guess he was crazy." I gestured toward the key and the armband. "He threw those at me before he went over the edge and called me Don something. Can you get me to a hospital?"

Denfert Rochereau frowned with absent concentration.

"You are lying. I have examined the contents of your pockets." He gestured toward a small heap of my belongings. My passport and Olly's glossy 12 × 8 prints were on top. "You are neither a geologist nor an

American. Also, you appear to have been looking for Von Runstedt and myself. You will now tell me who you really are and what really happened."

I closed my eyes and leaned back against the juniper. I was in no condition to argue, and I had no choice. I told the story the way I had told it to Von Runstedt and ended by giving him the same option.

"Don't let the fact that I'm helpless now fool you," I warned him. "The situation's the same, and there's nothing you can do about it. If you've got any sense, you'll keep your winnings and clear out while the going's good."

Denfert Rochereau had listened with polite attention, nodding abstractedly as though really thinking of something else.

"I have often thought that communications were a major weakness in our organization," he observed. "The system is too public. Obviously it must now be changed. The Supreme Council is compromised. Its members will regrettably have to accept whatever repression the *technocrates* impose."

I felt exhaustion and frustration augment the hammering in my skull.

"For God's sake, don't you start," I said. "Can't you accept a simple situation either?"

Denfert Rochereau stared at me earnestly. "The Game will go on," he said. He picked up the Browning and examined it with distaste. "It was the sound of a shot which led me to you. Did you kill Von Runstedt with this?"

I shook my head very slowly. "I used the threat of it to keep him quiet while I explained things. Afterwards, the fool jumped me and I didn't get a chance to use it properly. Don't worry about your precious reputation in the Game. He won't be found with embarrassing pieces of lead in him."

Denfert Rochereau considered for a moment, then nodded. "You are only a mercenary of the *technocrates*. I see no reason why you should lie about this. It is as well."

He moved so fast that at first I didn't register what he had done. He hurled the Browning clear over the trees to the right of me. There was no sound to tell me it had hit ground. Although I couldn't see the

Canyon from where I lay, I still felt its tremendous presence. It altered the sound of our voices and made everything solid seem brittle and provisional.

I had an insight then into how Denfert Rochereau had become Ludi Victor. He wasn't big and powerful like Von Runstedt, but he was neat, lithe, and blindingly fast in his movements, like a rugby wing three-quarter.

"The Game is now at a grave disadvantage," he resumed, "but that can be overcome. The first problem is to deal with you."

He studied me with some concern. I didn't think his concern had much to do with humanitarian considerations.

"You are an interloper, and you are responsible for the death of the greatest combatant in the history of the Game. I myself am not a functionary of the Discipline Squads, but perhaps this is not the time to be ruled by distinctions in rank."

I thought as fast as my banged-up brain would allow. I was helpless, but there had to be some way of dealing with this moral imbecile. He was a different proposition altogether from Von Runstedt. The big German had had some kind of ideological beef against society. What made Denfert Rochereau tick? There was an urgent need to find out.

I reviewed what he had said so far. For all his elegant prettiness, there was a lot of old-fashioned hauteur in his manner. He was aware of distinctions in rank, and there was aristocratic contempt in his voice when he talked about what he called *technocrates.* He spoke about the Game in a hectoring, didactic sort of way and seemed the type to want to take command and initiate things. If he'd been English, I would have put him down as a half-baked public school fascist. I sounded him out.

"While you're making up your mind," I said humbly, "would you mind answering a few questions? There are still some things I don't understand about the Game. I'd like to know the answers, even if it is too late."

Denfert Rochereau nodded with ponderously tolerant approval. "Your professionalism does you credit. If you were of the Game, I would call it integrity. It is in extreme circumstances that men's characters are proved. That, of course, is the whole point of the Game." He glanced at his watch, a heavy, expensive-looking one whose reflective surfaces had been overpainted matt green. "A few moments may be spared. What is it you want to know?"

"For a start, how do men like you come to get involved in this Game in the first place?"

Denfert Rochereau considered my question, as though trying to remember.

"Every Game player is also a recruiter. Prospective entrants are sounded out carefully by word of mouth. It is a measure of the Game's appeal and the loyalties it generates that there have been very few breaches of security. The Discipline Squads take care of the few, of course. I myself was recruited by an old school friend who worked for Dassault. Regrettably, he fell in the French National Quarter Finals last year. I myself defeated him. He was lucky. It is not often a combatant has the privilege of dying at the hands of a friend."

Even as I pondered his eerily lethal morality, I noted the word "fell." More and more, the language of the Game sounded like a badly translated medieval saga.

"I know about the life insurance policy stakes," I said. "But how exactly is money passed on?"

"In the early stages, policy benefits are credited to the victors and form part of the Game's contingency fighting fund. From National Quarter Final rounds onwards, the accrued gauge is converted into gold plaques worth ten thousand dollars each and stored in bank safe deposit boxes provided by the National Council in suitable places." He grinned. "Since our object is to subvert society's systems, we naturally avail ourselves of those systems when appropriate. At the present time, my total gauge, which now must include that of Von Runstedt if the Supreme Council agrees, is worth considerably more than the accumulated value of the insurance policy benefits due to increases in the value of gold. It has long been assumed that such things would happen as the Game reached its culmination and the time came for collective action."

"What kind of action?" I enquired feebly. I was in a lot of pain again, and I forced myself to concentrate. I wanted answers anyway, and I was still probing for a chink in his armor. "What's the ultimate point of your damned Game?"

"The Game is an end in itself," he said simply. "There is no ideological common factor among players except a general commitment to the destruction of contemporary societies, capitalist, communist, or middle-of-the-road."

"How do you value it personally?"

"As a training ground. Combatants may die, but, through their heroic example, thousands of other young men learn the value of trained courage, disciplined submission to common objectives, and the need for sound organization. The Game is the military service of modern revolution."

I raised myself on one elbow and ignored the shattering pain.

"And what of National Council members and the Supreme Council? What do they get out of it, Denfert Rochereau? How much do you know about them?"

He shrugged. "Above the ranks of novices, combatants, Discipline Squads, and so on, I am not competent to speak. For obvious reasons, higher identities and information are revealed only on a need-to-know basis. In general, the role of the Supreme Council is to ensure the proper running of the Game as a means of promoting revolutionary morale. They have no personal stake in its operations."

I laughed, completely genuinely, in his face, and the tears that ran down my face were only partly caused by pain. I'd looked for a chink in his armor and found a chasm as big as the canyon itself.

"Your information doesn't extend very far, Denfert Rochereau," I gasped. "As the last surviving member of the Game, you owe it to yourself to learn a little more than that. The Council members who run your little Game aren't revolutionaries of any kind at all. On the contrary, they're vicious little fat cats, well-born thugs to the stumps of their grimy fingernails. They're the nastiest specimens of the kind of society you say you want to overthrow. I should know. I've met a few. They want a revolution the way you want a *légion d'honneur.*"

Denfert Rochereau frowned with irritation at his watch again.

"I believe you are trying to postpone the conclusion of this discussion. I gave you permission to speak, but I do not intend to listen to slander. Beware how you insult men of honor."

"You don't have to take my word for it, you pompous idiot," I shouted at him. "Before I came out here, I had a look at the records kept by the guy who runs your Supreme Council. I took photographs of them. They're on the back seat of my car. Go and look at them. They're an education."

He still looked self-assured, but I could see his confidence had taken a tiny dent. I fought hard to keep the balance right. If I didn't dent it enough, he might not go and look. If I dented it too much, he could still kill me out of hand.

"Your slander makes no sense," he sneered fastidiously. "If the Supreme Council were as you say, what possible reason could its members have to damage their own class interests by supporting their enemies?"

"Maybe they're not very hot on Marxist dialectic at Eton," I sneered back. "Maybe they don't see you as the dangerous enemies you think you are. The reason's simple, Denfert Rochereau. They're bored little rich boys. The kind of gamblers who'd lay bets on which of two raindrops would beat the other to the bottom of the window. Your lot just makes a pleasant change from backing the horses at Epsom and Chantilly. They get a kick out of arranging for you to kill each other off, and they make bets on the outcome of combats. Big bets. Have a look in the back of my car, Denfert Rochereau. Maybe you'll find out how much your own Controller's made out of you so far."

He had just lit a cigarette. He stood up abruptly and flicked it towards me. His expression was ugly and dangerous.

"Yours is the Ford on the other side of Grandview Point? I shall check your claim as a matter of courtesy. When I have established that you are lying, it will be a pleasure to kill you. I do not think you will manage to move very far, but by all means feel free to try while I am away. I prefer hunting to butchery." He turned on his heel and walked off. I reached painfully for his cigarette and drew hard on it.

"Maybe they've a better reason still," I shouted after him. "Maybe it makes sense to encourage you tatty fighting cocks. The Game keeps you out of serious mischief and persuades the real troublemakers to bump each other off. Sort of natural selection. Maybe you gladiators are just too dumb to hear the senators farting all round the arena."

He couldn't have heard me. The forest was silent as I passed out again. When I came round, the sun was farther down the sky and I was unexpectedly comfortable. I'd been straightened out and given my own Navajo blanket for a pillow. The top half of my chest had been expertly strapped. It took me a few seconds to realize that I had won my reprieve.

I lifted my head and saw Denfert Rochereau repacking a small canvas medicine chest. He smiled slightly when he saw me looking at him. Whatever else there was to be said about him, he had a good temperament for a fighter.

"I trained in medicine for a while," he explained. "I always bring some equipment with me as a precaution against the weakening effect of wounds."

He was burying a disposable syringe in the loose sand at his feet. I realized then why I was feeling so breezy, and I was suddenly, horribly, alarmed.

"What have you shot into me?" I demanded. I had an irrational fear that he had decided to dispose of me after all while I was asleep. But a moment later, I knew I was wrong. Clandestine murder would be alien to the ethos of the Game.

"Do not disturb yourself. It is only Fortrol, a nonaddictive substitute for morphine." He stood up. He was still rapt and assured, but now there was an unfamiliar restraint in his manner. I realized that he was embarrassed. He was like some minor sprig of French nobility who'd just learned that his family title was only a Napoleonic creation.

"It would seem you have been telling the truth. I have examined your evidence. There is no doubt that those in charge of the Game are utterly unworthy. I see no way in which your evidence could have been contrived. In any case, it is inconceivable that you should have anticipated your present situation."

I watched him carefully. "You agree to close the Game down, then?" I asked.

He smiled slightly. "It will no doubt exasperate you to hear me say so, but the Game will go on. The treason of those now in charge invalidates nothing. The Game can and will be reformed. I myself shall act as Arbiter and Discipline Squad. There may be a delay before the coming year's combats can begin. That is all."

I heard myself starting to giggle. "There are eight Council members in each of eight countries," I reminded him. "You'll need a heavy machine gun to get through that lot, Denfert Rochereau. And you'd better make sure of all of them. You don't think your Supreme Council was ever going to let the ultimate Ludi Victor get away with all that loot that's been building up, do you?"

He considered the point, lapidary and polite as ever. "It is only the head of the hydra that must be destroyed now, the Supreme Council. National Council members can be purged later by their successors whom I shall appoint."

He picked up a paper from my pile of belongings. "I see you have noted that there is to be an emergency session of the Supreme Council in Belgium shortly. That is convenient. All the members will be present. It should not be difficult to effect a mass solution. Perhaps the Game can recommence sooner than expected."

I was feeling brave, or maybe it was the effect of the Fortrol coursing through my overworked blood. "And what about me, Denfert Rochereau?" I asked. "You wouldn't have dressed my wounds if you had decided to kill me on the spot."

His eyes slid away. He was bashful again.

"I have decided to postpone both the time and the manner of your death. It remains the case that you are a mercenary and that, through your unauthorized intervention, Ludi Victor Von Runstedt is now dead, even if, as you say, you killed him in fair fight. Also, I have not earned these." He weighed Von Runstedt's key and armband in one hand, then shoved them into his pocket. "However, your intervention has also exposed a dangerous scandal. On that score, you deserve better of the Game than summary execution."

He stared emptily ahead like a young Apollo pronouncing sentence.

"You are a usurper of the Game's highest accolade, but I have decided that even a usurper should be deposed by the true successor in fair fight, not stabbed in a corner. I am leaving now. I shall inform the police of your whereabouts and give you ample time to recover from your wounds. I do not think you bear me any personal ill will. Besides, I shall be hard to find if you tell the so-called authorities your story. Later, when I have disciplined the desecrators of the Game, you and I will fight a combat according to the rules. I shall inform you of the time and place, and I shall arrive with the keys and armbands of Von Runstedt and myself. If I fall, it will be your task to begin the Game again. Do not imagine that you can shirk either the combat or your responsibility."

He shifted my belongings nearer to me, removing all my contact prints and notes, and walked off without a backward glance. This time I didn't call after him. I was floating several feet off the ground and I could hear the small talk of angels. I was drifting effortlessly towards sleepyland, aware only that the electric-blue birds in the alligator juniper over my head were gone. I thought they must be out looking for leaves to cover me with. Denfert Rochereau's Fortrol might be chemically nonaddictive; psychologically, it was something else. I felt I could say good-bye to all the world's joys and cares and live on Fortrol forever and a day.

Consciousness was like a bad singer slipping in and out of key. Sometimes I was on the point of coming round, then I was gone again. Once I was aware of voices and hands lifting me. Later, I felt the cold touch of ambulance linen.

I woke in a hospital room. There was a turban of bandage round my head, and my ribs were a battleground between my need for oxygen and my need not to use my lungs. I was strapped from armpit to diaphragm.

Hospital rooms look the same in any country. I could hear traffic outside. It was daytime and a nurse was grinning at me through the porthole in the door. I grinned back and she came in.

"How are you doing?" She had a furry voice and flat, Navajo features. She made me more comfortable, handling me with the deft proficiency of a meat porter.

"Tremendous. Where am I? When can I see a doctor?" My voice quavered unexpectedly like a dear old man's.

"You're in the Flagstaff Community Hospital."

Seeing a doctor wasn't difficult. One had just come into the room while she was taking my vital readings. He was a casting director's dream. Tall, young, and saintly in a crisp green smock with three-quarter length sleeves and probably nothing on underneath. His forearms were aseptically bare except for a gold Rolex which I almost didn't see against his tan and body hair.

He introduced himself, and I asked for the damage report.

"Concussion. We've taken X-rays and you'll be O.K. Let the nurse know if you get sick or start having dizzy spells." His voice was softly modulated and considerate, not unlike Denfert Rochereau's except for the accent.

"How about my ribs and ankle?"

"Two ribs cracked, and the tissue between them is messed up. You may have some discomfort for a while. A ligament in your left ankle is torn. I've put you in plaster up to the knee to make sure it mends properly."

I leaned back against the pillows. "How long do I have to stay here?"

His eyes evaded me. "That's hard to say. I'd like to keep you under observation for a few days." His voice became more diffident. "Do you have medical insurance in this state?"

"I haven't got medical insurance in any state. I'll pay cash."

"Fine. The nurse will bring you the paperwork." He now sounded constrained to the point of hernia. "By the way, you have a visitor. I guess you can see him now."

I was surprised. I still hadn't really started thinking. I considered Denfert Rochereau, but knew it couldn't be he.

"A Lieutenant Pendry of the Flagstaff Police Department. He's been waiting for you to wake up."

"How long have I been here?"

"Going on twenty-four hours. Whoever shot you full of dope wasn't wise, in my opinion."

He went out without more comment. I heard voices in the corridor. A thin man with sunken cheeks came in. His eyes were permanently embedded in a mesh of those fine wrinkles men get when they don't habitually wear sunglasses in a climate like that of Arizona. He wore a lightweight suit of conservative cut and carried a hat which he turned over and over in his hands. He looked like a civil servant. His bedside manner was awkward but standard. He leaned across to shake hands. Rather than disturb my freshly made bed, I used my left hand, feeling like a freemason.

"How're you doing?" he asked, with the kind of studied American informality that's easy to mistake for real informality. He sat down on a hard-backed chair. The hat immediately tried to slide off his thin knees, and he wasn't sure what to do with it.

"Fine," I answered cautiously. "What does the Flagstaff Police Department want with me? I'm not dead."

He smiled. "I can see that. You feel up to telling me what happened?" Over a pale mauve shirt with an open weave like linen, like every other male in the state, he wore a leather and turquoise *bola* tie. He adjusted the tie and leaned forward.

I tried to look as though I was remembering. "I'm an Englishman on vacation," I said. "I've only been in the country a couple of days. I was exploring the south rim of the Canyon when someone attacked me. I believe that was yesterday."

"Any idea who did it?"

"No."

"Can you describe your attacker?"

I creased my face up and gave a fairly accurate description of Von Runstedt. Since the German was dead, there was no reason not to. Besides, if there was the remotest chance of his body being found in recognizable condition, my description ought to tally.

Lieutenant Pendry listened with attention. He wasn't taking notes.

"Where exactly was this?" he asked politely.

"I don't know for certain. I'd been walking for hours without paying too much attention to where I was going. It was on the rim of the Canyon, somewhere not far from Grandview Point."

He got up and walked to the window, ran a finger along the ledge and inspected the finger.

"What happened after the guy attacked you?"

"I haven't the faintest idea. I got knocked out when we fell on some rocks. I woke up here."

"You didn't wake up before that?"

I fingered the turban of bandage round my head. "If I did, I don't remember," I said ruefully.

"Sure." He sat down again, picked up his hat and put it back on the bed. He looked faintly hostile.

"Damned if I can follow this," he complained.

"Why not? I mean, I don't follow it myself, but I don't suppose muggers are that uncommon in Arizona."

"Sure, we have hotheads. That's not what I meant. I guess the guy who attacked you wasn't after something in your possession. If you'd been carrying anything of particular value, you'd have asked about it."

I decided to pay more attention. Pendry was nobody's fool.

I assumed, hoped badly, that Denfert Rochereau had removed all the Game documents and photographs. "I've just woken up," I pointed out. "You haven't given me time to ask after anything. No, I wasn't carrying anything particularly valuable."

He nodded. "The rented LTD we found was yours?"

"That's right," I agreed.

"It's at headquarters now. So are your personal effects. I'll have them brought to you here. So far as I can see, robbery wasn't a motive. Passport, clothes, that kind of stuff, it's all there. Travelers checks and cash are in your pockets. What does that leave?"

I eased a Tareyton out of the pack beside my bed. Pendry lit it for me. He didn't smoke himself.

"A grievance of some kind, maybe. Except that you've only been in the state a couple of days. You know anybody here? You been tickling some guy's wife?"

I grinned faintly. "I don't know anybody here," I admitted.

"So what's the motive?" he repeated. He began to prowl the tiny room. "And that's not all I don't understand. The way we found you, you were strapped up and shot full of dope. Also, you must have been carried quite a way."

"Why do you think so?"

"You said you banged your head on some rocks near the Canyon rim. There ain't no rocks where you were found. No sign of a struggle either. You were fifty yards from the rim. Besides, the doctor says you must have lost a lot of blood through that split on your head. We only found a couple of drops. Cosmetic stuff."

"Maybe the fellow was a maniac," I suggested helpfully.

Pendry looked sour. "Sure. That would explain why he beat you up, then dressed your injuries. It might explain, too, why he drove all the way to Phoenix and called us from the airport to tell us where to find you."

"He did that?"

"Somebody did."

He couldn't resist it any longer. He got up, took a clean handkerchief from his pocket and wiped the dust from the sill under the window. He put the handkerchief away, took out a photograph and threw it on the bed in front of me.

"Seen this guy before?"

It was a head-and-shoulders shot of Von Runstedt, probably a dupe from his passport photograph.

"It's the fellow who attacked me," I said truthfully and without hesitation.

"That's what I figured. He rented a Malibu sedan in Phoenix. We found it parked near your Ford."

"Then he must have got back to Phoenix some other way."

Pendry looked at me coldly.

"You can do better than that." His voice was now definitely hostile. "In this state, if you don't travel by car, you don't travel. There's no sense in thinking the guy who cleaned you up and telephoned us was the same guy who attacked you. There must have been two guys. Question, what happened to the guy in the Malibu, your attacker?"

I shook my head and barely lived to regret it. Pendry was making me uncomfortable. Maybe it was because I was in bed and couldn't maneuver.

"Why ask me?" I complained. "I'm only the bloody victim."

Pendry pointed a bony finger at me. "I don't buy that necessarily. The guy in this picture is a citizen of the German Federal Republic. He flew into the States yesterday. Like you, he's a European. Like you, he was only in the country a few hours when the attack happened. The guy who called from the airport had a European accent. A different one, maybe French or Italian. Maybe he'd only been in the country a few hours as well. You know what I think? I think these guys followed you from Europe. Maybe together, maybe not. Maybe you all arrived together. Maybe you know more than you're telling me."

I closed my eyes. "I'm damned certain nobody followed me," I said. "Nobody had reason to. I've told you all I know, and you're giving me a headache."

Pendry got up and retrieved his hat. "Doesn't matter a lot," he said briefly. "I've talked to your doctor. You'll be here for a while. I guess there are things I could be doing right now. Maybe I'll start by finding out where the guy with the Malibu has got to. Maybe he's in the Canyon, hey? Maybe you or the guy who patched you up pushed him there." He smiled. "Don't go away."

When he'd gone, the nurse came back, took some more readings and pursed her lips. She fed me some more tablets.

I did a lot of sleeping in the next few days. The pain in my ribs slowly became a continual, raging itch, and I was kept sedated to stop me moving around too much.

Lieutenant Pendry called in from time to time. He was polite and studiedly informal again, the way he had been when we first met. He didn't seem to be getting anywhere, and I couldn't work up any real interest in the progress of his enquiries. I felt depressed. Maybe it was the delayed effect of Eric's death. Or maybe I just didn't like being drugged and kept in bed.

On the fourth day, I woke fresh and bright in the afternoon. I decided it was time to go home. I told the photogenic doctor, who didn't seem to approve. We argued, and he finally agreed that if I promised to take things easy and see a physician as soon as I got home, I might just survive the flight.

After he'd gone, I demanded a telephone. I made a booking for a midday flight out of Phoenix the next day and arranged a charter from Flagstaff airport to get me there. Then I called Olly's office in Holborn. It was around midnight in London. I left a message on his answering machine. I gave him my flight number and asked him to collect me from Heathrow. I also left a message to inform McVeigh that I was on my way back.

Lieutenant Pendry arrived soon after I made the call. My doctor had been on the hotline. Pendry wasn't happy with my plans either. But he'd turned up nothing and there was no reason to hold me.

He turned his hat in his hands and put it on the foot of my bed. He had a new suit on but the same *bola* tie. He talked for a while in a philosophical way, without rancor. The Canyon was vast, and he hadn't found Von Runstedt's body. I wasn't surprised.

"I guess there's nothing to stop you going," he admitted. "Do something for me, though. When you get outside my jurisdiction, I surely would appreciate it if you'd write me and tell what the hell's been going on."

I was smoking a Tareyton and wishing I had a whiskey sour. I hadn't had a drink in the best part of a week.

"If I ever find out, I'll let you know," I promised.

He smiled forgivingly. "The kraut who attacked you lived on his own in the Sachsenhausen district of Frankfurt," he said. "I got that on the wire this morning. Nothing's known about him except that he was a laborer for the city sanitation department. Would you believe it? Some of you Europeans have more money than a U.S. bank president these days. Maybe you should give us Marshall Aid."

"How about the other fellow, the one who telephoned you, if it was another fellow?"

Pendry shrugged. "A big opera company on tour started a two-day visit to Phoenix about the time you guys arrived. The tour companies rented out lots of cars to Europeans. Tell you what, I'll call by tomorrow morning. Help you get your stuff to the airport and check the car in with the rental company. I guess it's the least I can do."

When he'd gone, I had a long sleep to prepare myself for the trip. He arrived early the next day. I was still eating breakfast, but I was glad to see him. I preferred his company to that of the suave doctor.

When I had packed, he drove me to the airport while another cop drove the LTD along behind us. I checked the car in and walked to the hangar where the charter company operated. I was predictably rocky on my feet. Pendry accompanied me, carrying my bag. The other cop stayed with the police car. The duty pilot hadn't returned from taking a party of geologists on a guided air tour of Meteor Crater, so Pendry and I sat in a tiny lounge decorated with old flying prints above a wooden propeller and drank beer from the manager's personal refrigerator.

"You sure you can make it?" Pendry looked out the window to where a wind-sock was being blown back almost rigid. He was full of sudden solicitude.

"I'll manage. I'll send you a postcard from London."

A tall, stooped figure with a clipboard entered the office from the connecting hangar. I guessed he was my pilot.

Pendry drank up and accompanied me to the plane.

"I enjoyed last week," he confessed above the howl of an executive jet preparing for take-off. "Made a change from keeping angel dust off the campus and liquor off the reservation. Too bad we never found out what really happened.

"Tell you what we did find, though," he added. I stopped suddenly. "We found the place where you were jumped. There was dried blood on some rocks. It checked with your group. Pity we didn't find it earlier."

"Why?" I asked.

"Been a few minor landslides in the area recently. One of them near the place where you were attacked shifted a few thousand tons of Arizona into the Canyon. There just could be a body or something underneath the rubble, but you try getting permission to move bulldozers in and desecrate a national monument just to follow up a hunch."

"I don't suppose there's anything there," I consoled him. The pilot looked at his watch as Pendry swung my grip into a rear seat.

"Maybe not," Pendry said. He helped me up the awkward step into the Cessna 182 and slammed the door after me as the pilot started his engine.

"The professors tell me the Canyon's in a state of geological change," he yelled above the roar. A thin fringe of sun-bleached hair blew in the slipstream, and the wrinkles round his eyes deepened. "In a million years, the whole area will be eroded down so the Colorado River will be flowing through a nice flat plain. Me, I'll believe it when I see it. Take it easy now."

The Cessna was cramped and cold. We flew south past Oak Creek Canyon and the artists' resort of Sedona with its tiny airstrip, perched like an eyrie atop a steep mesa. The landscape crowded us with caramel-colored cliffs. Thermals buffetted us among the flat tops until we were over Interstate 17 again, eight lanes of concrete running straight as a die for Phoenix.

Crossing the suburbs of Phoenix, we jinked past sheer cliffs again, this time gold skyscraper cliffs of insurance buildings, and landed among an armada of executive jets. My pilot was a kind man. He carried my grip and found a cab to take me to the international terminal on the other side of the airport.

The flight back to Europe was the earlier flight in reverse, with the same dogleg via Chicago. I slept for most of the time and woke to a breakfast of bacon and eggs as the plane crossed the coast on a bright, gutsy morning and began a slow descent beyond Birmingham.

At seven o'clock GMT, I carried my grip carefully through the "Nothing to Declare" line at Heathrow. Olly Starkey was waiting at the arrivals barrier. He looked pinched and grim. His expression didn't improve when he saw the cast on my leg and the way I was carrying myself.

"What happened?" he demanded. He almost tore the grip out of my hand. It wasn't exactly a welcome.

"A bit of trouble. Nothing to worry about. Just don't make me laugh."

It was then that he realized my body was damaged as well as my leg.

"Had any breakfast yet?"

I had the impression that he would have liked to pick a fight there and then if I'd been in better shape. There was a suppressed, uncertain anger in him.

"Yes. Why?"

"Come and have some more. I want to talk to you."

He stamped off towards the restaurant. I followed more slowly. We sat as far away as we could from the only other customers, a foursome of businessmen being served by an intellectual-looking Indian. Olly ordered a mixed grill for one and two pots of coffee. I lit a Tareyton.

"How did the funeral go?" I asked.

"It's over. Marian and the kids are fine. Everything's fine." He pulled a folded newspaper from his pocket and pushed it across the table. "You'd better read that."

It was the morning's *Daily Express.* A headline across five columns screamed LONDON LOVE TRIO SLAIN. I read the story carefully. Early the previous evening, Don Proctor, Freda Harman, and Horst Wohlberg had been shot dead in Proctor's Notting Hill studio. Their bodies had been found by Dr. Theodore McVeigh, a friend of the family. The reporter had done his homework. He'd even got the make of a gun, a heavy-caliber Smith & Wesson that had belonged to Don's grandfather. The story stank of equivocations. The headline was left unexplained, but there were hints of Don's sexual ambivalence and a subtle suggestion that Wohlberg had shot the others before killing himself, with jealousy as the motive. I read the story again and handed the paper back.

"They were the bastards who set up Eric's death, weren't they?" Olly was staring at me in sullen anger, but there was a hint of pleading in his manner.

"Yes," I said tiredly.

"Why didn't you tell me?"

"Because they didn't intend Eric's death, and because they weren't the only ones involved. I didn't want you going off at half-cock. How did you find out?"

"Mr. McVeigh told me. He rang me. He said you'd been in touch, and he told me about Proctor. I thought Proctor might make a run for it before you got back. I offered to keep an eye on the mews."

"That was good of you, Olly. Did McVeigh offer you money for the job?"

"Yes, he did. You got any objections? So far as I'm concerned, it's Eric's money. God knows he's earned whatever he can get out of you bastards."

I knew now why he was angry. He felt let down, but he was also uneasy, a feeling calculated to make him madder than anything. He was worried about taking another fee without consulting me first. He was also worried about whether he'd done anything stupid. He had, but I saw no point in telling him.

"O.K., what happened?"

He was still glowering. "I kept an eye on Proctor's place. Two other blokes from the office took turns with me. Early last night I was on duty when the kraut, Wohlberg, turned up in a bloody great Rolls. He was driving like a maniac. He left the engine running, ran inside, and banged the door so hard it swung open again. Nothing happened for a few minutes except a lot of effing and shouting. Then there were about four or five shots together, grouped pretty close. I was still getting out of the car when there was another shot, a single one."

"Anybody take any notice?"

"You know what it's like around there. You could blow up a bloody gasworks and no one would take any notice."

"What did you do?"

Olly was calming down, but he was still nervous. This was a report for my inspection.

"I went inside the studio. They were all there, lying on the floor round that bloody great statue."

"I know it."

He took a gulp of coffee and poured himself another cupful from a pot that looked as though it had been thrown off a cliff before being sandblasted.

"I didn't call the police. I kept my gloves on and called Mr. McVeigh on the office reception phone. He told me not to touch anything and to get out fast. He said he'd take care of everything."

Mr. McVeigh again. I might have guessed. Olly was a tough ex-Army pro, but faced with any sort of dilemma, he'd always turn to the officer class for guidance.

"Did Mr. McVeigh say why you should get out and let him take over?"

"He didn't want the shootings tied in with the business you're investigating. He said he could just turn up and sort of discover things without questions being asked. The police know me. They'd want to know why I was keeping an eye on the mews in the first place."

I shrugged. "That makes sense. Anything else?"

"He wants you round at his office now. I told him I was picking you up from the airport. He wants a full report so that you can all agree on a story before the police put two and two together."

I finished my coffee and got up. "Let's go, then," I said. I reached for my wallet and remembered I hadn't got much U.K. currency on me. "You pay the bill."

Olly almost knocked the Indian waiter over in his hurry to do as he was told. There was a different sort of anxiety on his face now.

"Did I do right?" he asked when the waiter had gone to change a fiver.

"You did well."

He examined me carefully. "Are you badly hurt?" he demanded.

"Two cracked ribs. They're mending. The ankle's all right. The cast makes it look theatrical, that's all. I'll tell you the story sometime."

He collected his change and shepherded me out of the restaurant through a raised corridor leading to the car park.

"You needn't go to Global right away if you're not feeling up to it," he said. "That lot can wait."

The turnaround was complete. Now he was protecting me from a cruel world.

"I'd rather get it over with," I said. "I'll drop my bag off at the flat. You can take me on to Global from there."

He held the door open while I got carefully into the car. It was an old, immaculate Railton, and Olly felt about it the way Eric had felt about his stamp collection. We left the airport on the motorway approach road. Olly filtered onto the M4 between a line of juggernauts speeding towards London at well over the legal limit. The Railton's suspension was good, but my ribs still felt as though they were being worked over by a sleepy litter of wild kittens.

I made myself as comfortable as I could. Olly drove very fast and competently. He carved up an assertive Jensen in the lane-closure leading to the inevitable roadworks. The Jensen bottled out after one look at his face. We didn't speak until the last stretch of motorway before the roundabout at Chiswick, then I relented.

"The boys who killed Eric were members of the underground cult I told you about," I said. "They'd been organized by someone responsible to Proctor. Proctor was in charge of everything anyway. He ordered the attack on the flat."

Olly brooded. "I've been thinking about it," he said. "The way I felt when Eric died, I could have killed those bastards with my bare hands. But it's like a shunt on the motorway. Your first instinct is to take it out on the nearest other driver. After a time, though, you realize he was just some poor bugger like Eric in the wrong place at the wrong time."

I knew he didn't really think that, but I said nothing. Back in

Henrietta Street, Olly carried my bag up while I had a look round. The place still smelt of paint and raw woodwork. There was a colorful arrangement of dried grasses and flowers beside the reglazed windows leading to my balcony. Several scribbled notes from Rose lay on a low table. Looking round, I could see more of her touches. They blended in warmly with Saul and Gerry's decor. The phone rang as I was leaving. I ignored it and followed Olly down the stairs. He drove me on to the City where late office arrivals and victims of trains on lines with iced-up points were still making their way to work. The late cold snap, which had been the other main news item on the *Daily Express* front page, hadn't killed off all the flowers in window boxes. Headlines about the Proctor shootings screamed from curbside news placards.

Olly and I said good-bye on the steps of Global House. He was still uneasy. He wanted me to give the interview a miss and rest at the big house in Nightingale Lane for a few days until I was stronger. I told him not to worry. I said I would be in touch soon and tell him the whole story one day.

Nothing much was happening in the main foyer, but there was genteel hysteria in the air. Men in sports jackets and shirts with rumpled collars hung around, some carrying camera equipment. There were several commissioners standing by the lifts. One stared hard at me while I explained who I was. He kept staring while he telephoned. Afterwards he ushered me into a lift, still without speaking.

I got out at the penthouse outer office. For a brief moment I wondered about Freda Harman's absence. She'd always been an easy girl to overlook. I guessed that after the immediate staff had clubbed together for a wreath, they'd soon forget even her name. Her replacement was a temp with circumflex eyebrows and the inevitable Cheltenham accent. I stated my business. She checked my name on a list, consulted the office intercom, and told me to go in.

The big penthouse looked the same as ever. Bronze sunlight filtered through tinted glass, and the absurd white birds outfaced the fish in the pools. The center of the room looked like a campaign manager's office on election night. Glasses, plastic coffee cups, and overflowing ashtrays lay around everywhere. A lot of people had been in and out. At the moment, there were just Sir Bryan, Charles Omphrey, and McVeigh.

Sir Bryan looked terrible. His distinguished silver hair was ruffled. There was ash on the sleeve of his formal coat, and his face was the same color as the superstructure of HMS *Belfast.* Omphrey kept a close watch on him as he looked at me with an expression of blank, stony despair. As usual, McVeigh didn't turn round. As usual, he stared upstream, his hands rammed in his striped trouser pockets.

"What the hell do you want?" Sir Bryan's voice was as hoarse as a fairground barker's. At that moment he was a man who badly needed an enemy on whom to focus his pain. I had the impression I'd been elected.

McVeigh still didn't turn round. "I asked him to call in," he said tersely over his shoulder. "We misled you, Sir Bryan. It became necessary to pretend to you some time ago that our investigation into the insurance losses was temporarily at an end. In fact, it continued—on my authority. I'm afraid you must now hear the report."

"For God's sake, no." Omphrey was on his feet, embarrassed and furious.

McVeigh turned. He waited in icy silence for the big Irishman to subside.

"In case it had escaped anybody's attention," he said quietly, "there is an important connection between that investigation and the events of last night. The connection will not escape the attention of the police for long. It is necessary to put Sir Bryan in the picture immediately so that we can agree on a strategy to defuse the situation."

Sir Bryan moved his head with terrible slowness. "Connection?" he demanded. "What connection? What's going on?"

I eased myself carefully into a chair. Nobody seemed to be noticing my war wounds. They weren't important.

"I don't see the police making a connection immediately or at all," I said to McVeigh.

"What the bloody hell's going on?" Sir Bryan repeated loudly. There were unhealthy patches of color in his cheeks. "Everybody now knows my son was a degenerate and a fairy. What else is there to know?"

Omphrey stared down unhappily at the penthouse tiles, his hands squeezed between his knees. McVeigh chose a cigar critically.

"Our friend will no doubt be submitting another of his carefully documented reports in due course," he said. "For the moment, the gist which you need to be aware of is this. The underground cult he unearthed actually existed. Still does, in fact. Donald was not just involved in it, he was the brains and prime mover behind it. There is a regrettably large quantity of evidence in his studio which the police are now examining. It proves all these things incontrovertibly. The question is, what defensive action is open to us as a company?"

"Is this true?"

I nodded, unable to speak. There was another silence.

"Why?" Sir Bryan whispered, an agonized appeal in his eyes. "Why did he do it?"

I was suddenly angry. "How the hell should I know? Kids of all kinds turned on to this Game. It gave them something they couldn't get any other way. The bastards who organized it, including your son, just enjoyed bucking the system and biting the hands that fed them. Don't ask me why."

McVeigh inspected the ash on his cigar severely. "Putting it bluntly, it's as well that Don hasn't survived to come to trial. Defence council would have had a field day suggesting extenuating circumstances. You were a remote and forbidding parent. The boy was always terrified of you and never forgave you his mother's death, for which, of course, he blamed you. He believed you killed her to further your business interests, so he tried to get back at you through your business interests. Personally, I think he succeeded rather well. The Proctor name will be a national joke in very bad taste for some time to come. Very possibly he has also ruined this company."

Omphrey looked as though he would have liked to say something mitigating. He glanced from Sir Bryan to McVeigh and shut his mouth again. Sir Bryan looked utterly defeated, but when he spoke again, it was in his normal, almost casual tone. He looked only at me.

"I realize that if these thoughts didn't occur of themselves, Ted would be the first to suggest them. I've great confidence in you, boy, so I accept what you say. But I refute this bastard's implications. The Proctors are a dynasty. We always have been. We don't need to live in each other's emotional pockets. It's enough that we're men of our family."

It was a strangely formal speech. His hands crawled along the arms of his chair and seemed to clutch for support. He began to talk to himself.

"I was always at odds with my father, and I feared him. But I respected him, too. He was his own man. After his death, I set myself to build up the family's means again and provide another Proctor who was also free to fear and hate me if he wanted." He glanced round the penthouse. "All this is a contribution to a long and possibly boring history." He blinked and seemed to come to himself. "Or was."

He got up slowly and painfully. "I think," he grunted, with a last attempt at casual indifference, "we could all use a drink."

What followed was like a scene out of a Greek tragedy. He swayed as he passed McVeigh, not deigning to look at him. He swayed again as he crossed to the oak drinks cabinet. Then he fell, smashing his head against the side of the big oak desk. We all watched, rooted to the spot.

As he hit ground, Omphrey and I jumped forward. Omphrey was shouting. It took me several seconds to take in what he was saying. He wanted me to call the London Clinic and get a bed prepared in Intensive Care. There was also a small, private ambulance kept ready in the executive parking bay. He was giving me instructions to have it sent round to the main entrance.

McVeigh's voice lashed softly across the room as I ran to the door.

"Have the ambulance sent round to the executive car-park lift. Get the attendants up here. Make the calls yourself, Omphrey, and kick that silly bitch out of the office. I don't want reporters climbing through my windows."

I hobbled painfully to the executive lift while Omphrey did as he was told. When the ambulance attendants arrived, I led them into the penthouse. Omphrey hadn't moved Sir Bryan. There was a big pool of blood under the old man's head. He was heavy, and the corner of the desk must have split his skull open. I held the doors of the lift ajar while the attendants stretchered him inside. The main office doors were rattling, probably because Omphrey had hustled the Cheltenham girl out in tears and locked them behind her. He opened them when the lift had gone and I was making my way back into the penthouse. I could hear his voice, urbane and panic-stricken, making hushed, vague explanations.

McVeigh hadn't moved since the moment Sir Bryan fell. He stood with his feet apart in the center of the floor, smoking coolly. There was a rapt, vulpine look on his face that I recognized. It was the face of Denfert Rochereau towering over me under the alligator junipers of the Grand Canyon. In the outer office, I could hear Omphrey trying to answer several telephones at once.

He slammed the last one down and came into the penthouse, shutting the door behind him. He was sweating furiously.

McVeigh spoke again. "In case there are any questions, neither of you will ever refer publicly to what has been discussed in this office. Is that clear?" His voice was crisply different. He had taken command.

Omphrey found some blood on his hand that he hadn't noticed. He scrubbed at it with a silk handkerchief.

"Doctor, what are your patient's chances?"

"I can't say, just yet," Omphrey mumbled. "I couldn't make a proper examination. I'm leaving for the clinic now. If you'll excuse me, I'll call Dr. Tyler."

"You can do better than that, you old fool. You're his doctor, such as you are. Surely you can offer some prognosis."

Omphrey bridled furiously. "Sir Bryan is very poorly," he said with as much dignity as he could muster. "It is impossible to judge what additional effect the blow to his head may have caused."

"Will he live?"

"Obviously, we hope so. It's impossible to tell at this stage."

"Will he work again?"

Omphrey hesitated. "No." He rarely gave short answers and the solecism embarrassed him. "If you've finished," he added sarcastically, "I would like to attend to my patient."

"You may go," McVeigh said with grim, sunny humor.

Omphrey was quiet until he got to the door. "Your callousness and indifference appall me," he declared violently. "I hold you partly responsible for what has happened. I shall report to the full board accordingly."

"I said you may go."

McVeigh waited until the door had shut. He strolled across to the cabinet where the drinks were kept and opened the lower cupboard. There was a pile of Irish linen inside. He took out a tablecloth and unfolded it. He went to the pool of blood by the desk where Sir Bryan had lain, flipped open the cloth and watched it settle. Almost immediately the dark blood began to show through. He stood back, his head to one side.

"Do you know," he said softly, "I had the distinct impression Sir Bryan thought I had engineered that little scene." He walked to the big bronze windows and stared upstream, his hands rammed in his pockets again, his face frozen with a venom tinged with sadness.

"You warned me a long time ago I should expect to be manipulated on this job," I said.

McVeigh laughed. "Yes, I thought you'd remember that. As a matter of fact, I hardly manipulated anything. I did worry that you weren't making the connection between Don and the Game fast enough, so I pointed you discreetly in the right direction. I should have known better. You hadn't missed the significance of the Harman girl."

He crossed to the cabinet and poured himself a single malt. "It made no difference, though. You're a good little retriever. You unearthed your facts and reached conclusions in your own way. Sooner or later you could have come trotting up and laid them at Sir Bryan's feet. It's what you're for. The shock, coming after Don's death, would have killed him eventually."

He settled himself comfortably at Sir Bryan's desk, picked up the Meissen jar of fishfood and casually threw it in the waste bin. I heard it smash.

"We might as well get used to the facts. Sir Bryan may or may not die. He is certainly finished so far as this organization is concerned. I willed that outcome passionately. I have done for years. The joke is that I didn't have to engineer anything. You are doubtless shocked, but you have nothing to complain of. I simply knew about the Game and Don's involvement in it long before anyone else."

"How long had you known, McVeigh?"

"For fourteen months. Don got high one night on alcohol and funny pills. He told the story to Freda Harman. He probably didn't remember doing so the next day. She, poor bitch, came running to me. She was terrified. She thought he was in danger."

"She certainly went to the right man." I spoke without irony. I was tiring and the pain on the right of my chest was coming back hard. But I knew McVeigh wanted to talk, and I needed to be at my best. I wasn't feeling it by a mile.

"Freda Harman gave you the ammunition you needed to destroy Sir Bryan," I said. "But you didn't do anything about it yourself. What is it with you, McVeigh? Are you afraid of getting dirt under your fingernails, or are you just a coward?"

McVeigh flicked ash at the fish and smiled. "I understand your feelings. There's no need to try and rile me. Obviously I couldn't use the information myself. Sir Bryan knew I hated him. I took care that he should. I even had to remind him of it from time to time. He was a man who disliked close associates and he got bored easily. He needed the stimulus of my hatred. But my hatred provoked an equal hatred that armored him against me. Hatred is a great armorer of the soul, you know."

His insistence on the past tense was getting through to me. I was beginning to take it in that the head of the great Global empire was no longer with us.

"Fortunately, you appeared on the scene. I knew I could rely on you. You really are good at your job, my dear fellow. But it was Sir Bryan's idea to hire you in the first place. I find that droll."

I went to the bar for a drink. I didn't want to dull the edge of my concentration, but I needed the stimulant.

"It might have made a difference if Eric Starkey had told me earlier about the first assignment he ever undertook," I said.

"The investigation into Caroline's death? I doubt it. When did you learn about that, by the way?"

"Just before I left for America."

McVeigh nodded. "I guessed you would recruit the Starkey Brothers. There was always a chance that one of them would tell you, but I thought the risk worth taking. Tell me, did it really make any difference when you did find out?"

"No," I admitted. I was admitting too much. He had more of the initiative than I liked.

He nodded. "You and I had a long conversation in my car right at the start of this investigation. All you remember is my warning that you would be manipulated. That is a pity. You should have remembered something else. I remarked that you could have been a very good businessman in your own right if you had only learned to school your sentimental tendencies."

He spread himself comfortably in Sir Bryan's chair and stretched his legs.

"You have a delusion about being a seeker after objective truth. That's childish. The soul of a rabbit is of no concern to the dog that hunts and kills it. The dog simply exercises the talents God gave it. It's the same with you. You pretend an interest in the people you work with because you're a lonely man. But you're a hunter pure and simple. You trample anybody underfoot if they get in your way. Sir Bryan understood that and respected it. It made you efficient and reliable. That's why he could accept the truth of Don's involvement in the Game coming from you—but not from me. You killed Sir Bryan. He was a dead man the moment you walked through that door this morning."

I was looking for an opening. I needed something to puncture his complacency. It was like being lectured by Denfert Rochereau under the junipers of the Canyon all over again.

"Tell me about Eric's first investigation," I said. "What really happened to Lady Proctor?"

McVeigh inspected the bottom of his glass for a long moment.

"Yes, I'd like to tell you about that. I've never told anyone before. I'd like just once, to see if someone can understand."

He got up, walked to the bronze windows and rammed his hands into his pockets.

"Stephen was my brother," he said calmly. "During the last months of his life he had a disastrous romance with Caroline. It was all very farcical and pathetic. Caroline was unhappy in her marriage. Stephen was an impulsive idealist. They fell catastrophically in love. The trouble was, they were both so young and guileless that a much less acute man than Sir Bryan wouldn't have been deceived for five minutes."

He paused. "I hadn't seen much of Stephen for a couple of years, but we had always been close. He was a year younger than I, and he always turned to me when he was in trouble. He was in trouble then, all right. He was in agony. I arranged for him and Caroline to go away to Africa for a while. I doubt whether that would have solved anything in the long run, though. Stephen was unbelievably upright. Wild horses couldn't have torn him away from Caroline. At the same time, he could never forgive himself for what he was doing to her and Sir Bryan.

"In the event," McVeigh added, turning round, "it made no difference. Sir Bryan simply killed them."

"So you decided on a long-term plan of revenge," I suggested quietly, not wanting to interrupt his mood.

"My mother and I hired Starkey Brothers to investigate Stephen's death. We were satisfied Sir Bryan was responsible, but nothing could be proved. A short while afterwards, my mother died and her annuity with her. I was without money or prospects. So I went baldly out for my present position as Sir Bryan's right-hand man. I knew my value, and I understood something of his character."

He looked at me then, and I saw him clearly for the first time. There was an immense, half-forgotten sadness in his eyes like the terminal moraine of a long-melted glacier.

"You see, I didn't just want an eye for an eye. I wanted both eyes and everything Proctor ever valued. Because he destroyed the only people I ever valued. And I was prepared to be patient."

"And now you've got everything," I said. My ribs were on fire. "Almost."

"You mean Sir Bryan's position with Global?" McVeigh smiled faintly. "I don't expect any problems there."

"You're not exactly loved and admired by your fellow directors," I said. "They may not care to see you move into his shoes."

"If I were you, I wouldn't speculate about matters you don't understand. People in the financial services industry overestimate their own value. You hear a lot about the importance of Britain's invisible earnings because the City's PR is good. In fact, the country couldn't survive twelve days on them. Besides, financial services depend on a strong and stable currency. The strong currencies are all in the Common

Market now. Global's real power has long shifted towards our European partners. Most of my work is with them."

"And you think they'll regard you as Sir Bryan's natural successor?"

"I'm sure they will. You see, I have another card up my sleeve. In one respect only I engineered the outcome of this morning's little drama. There is one matter you failed to clarify that has been of enormous benefit to me."

I was piqued in spite of myself, but I kept quiet.

"If you had thoroughly researched the Game's progress over the years, you would have learned that the first Ludi Victor was a German who chose not to defend his title. If you had done your homework on Horst Wohlberg, you would have discovered that he was a German of considerable means but no background, who simply appeared in Don Proctor's life three years ago. You might then have put two and two together."

I was rattled. "You mean Wohlberg was the first Ludi Victor?"

"That's right. It was one of the things Don told Miss Harman when he was high, and the main reason why she was so terrified. As an elementary precaution, I instituted my own enquiries into that dangerous young maniac. He had an interesting background. His mother's husband was one of the thousands of German soldiers who went missing on the Russian front but weren't declared officially dead until years after the war was over. Horst was born half in and half out of wedlock. He was brought up in a religious institution that appears to have done little to curb his violent and manic-depressive instincts. He was initiated into the Game while he was an apprentice at a factory owned by one of the German Regional Directors. That year, of course, he became the first ever Ludi Victor.

"It seems he only just made it. After his final combat, he was fished out of the River Meuse by a bargeman, more dead than alive. He was also instrumental in determining the final shape of the Game. You see, Don didn't actually invent the Game. He merely came across it as a minor daredevil cult and saw its possibilities. Wohlberg tracked him down out of hero worship when he became Ludi Victor. Don was flattered and intrigued. He took the monster in and made him his lover.

It was Wohlberg who introduced the revolutionary element into the Game and became Don's Chief of Staff."

"And he's been running the Game ever since?"

"Except for the gambling element, yes. That was Don's dangerous secret, because it was completely contrary to the spirit of the Game as Wohlberg saw it. Keeping that side of the operation hidden was probably the major attraction of the Game for Don over the last three years. All the Proctors were extraordinarily similar in character, you know. None of them could resist the *frisson* of living on a powder keg. The old Major insisted on staying in the most restless part of India when it was clear that the Raj had outstayed its welcome. Sir Bryan needed me to supply a stimulus of danger. And Don just couldn't resist exploiting Wohlberg's gullibility."

McVeigh stubbed out the remnant of his cigar.

"Wohlberg was always dangerous. He was a Ludi Victor and a practiced killer. He was also in love with Don and wildly jealous of Freda Harman. When he finally learned the truth about the gambling aspect of the Game and the real motives of its organizers, he was never going to stop at just slapping Don's wrist. He was a powder keg I was able to detonate any time I wanted."

I got up and walked round the penthouse to give my ribs some relief, carefully avoiding the stained cloth near the big desk.

"You haven't explained how all this is supposed to help you step into Sir Bryan's shoes," I said politely.

"You don't understand? It's quite simple. Before I revealed the truth to Wohlberg, I hired your friend Oliver Starkey to keep an eye on the mews. He phoned me when the explosion occurred, as I knew he would. I was able to get into the building and remove the incriminating documents before I called in the police. In a moment, I shall be telephoning all the chief executives of Global companies to break the sad news. I shall tell them exactly what has occurred and assure them that I have destroyed the documents. It is possible, of course, that they may not altogether believe me. As well as recognizing my outstanding qualifications, they may feel obliged to offer me Sir Bryan's job in order to ensure my reticence."

I felt angry and beaten. I didn't enjoy losing. I enjoyed McVeigh winning even less. Walking around was now getting to be more painful again than sitting down, so I sat down.

"Just don't give me that crap about not manipulating anybody, McVeigh," I said. "You used me. You used Oliver Starkey. If you hadn't used his brother, he might still be alive."

McVeigh sighed. "My dear chap, how you do go on about these things. Don't you realize that civilized life depends upon people using each other to their mutual advantage? In your case, you were clearly warned, but it would have made no difference in any event. I didn't hire you, and you were always going to complete your assignment with or without my help. It is hardly my fault if a squad of goons attacked your apartment and found your friend Eric there instead of you. As for his brother, he was burying Eric while you were in America. He needed something to take his mind off his sorrows, and he was not averse to milking a little more money from Global on his own account. I merely obliged him in our mutual interest."

I knew then why Olly had been angry and unsure of himself. He'd been obscurely aware of betraying me and of being used by McVeigh. A simple and upright man had had the rare experience of losing a little self-respect.

McVeigh stood up. "Please don't be misled by my frankness, by the way, or imagine that you can take advantage of it. This chat is quite off the record. Global's books are in order. The documents and your report are, as I say, no longer available. The remaining minor members of the Game have every reason to maintain a low profile if there should be any sort of official investigation. To put it bluntly, you have no shred of evidence to support what would always be an inherently fantastic allegation."

"And Jake, I suppose, has been re-programed to lose his memory," I said bitterly.

"Just so. Was it Lord Acton who said there were lies, damned lies, and statistics?"

He walked to the door.

"Now I must make my calls. Don't feel bitter, my dear fellow. Apart from the satisfaction of having done a good job, you've been generously treated. There's a check on the desk outside for your full fee, including the agreed bonus and a sum to cover the expenses of yourself and your assistants. If I am not mistaken, there may be more." He smiled patronizingly. "If I understand your account of events in America correctly, the surviving Ludi Victor has stormed off, swearing to purge the Augean stables of their pollution. I imagine he will want to square his account with you later. Look on the bright side. If you are forced to fight a combat with him, you could yet become the possessor of an extremely large and untaxable fortune with no official existence."

The weariness in my mind and body was like those last moments in the Canyon all over again. Then, too, I had been helpless, listening to a dangerous man, looking for an opening. Only this time there was a difference. I had nothing left to win. On the other hand, I didn't have to look for an opening, either. It stared me in the face. For Eric's sake at least, I intended to use it. I remembered McVeigh's need to tell me about his brother's death. It hadn't just been that he'd wanted to get a long-buried pain out of his mind. He'd wanted to tell it to me in particular. He'd needed me to verify his emotional calculations. Even for McVeigh, however much he sneered, the telling of objective truth had talismanic value, like touching wood. I let his hand get as far as the door handle.

"Eric Starkey was another man who was good at his job but lousy at business," I said loudly. "In fact, he was lousy at business precisely because he was good at his job."

McVeigh turned in the doorway, a frown of absent irritation on his face. He was already composing the substance of his telephone calls in his mind. Or maybe he didn't like being reminded of Eric.

"You see, he was a great investigator because he actually liked and respected people, even some of the nasty ones he investigated," I said. "That's why, when he made his reports, he didn't always tell the whole story if he thought some facts were useless and could hurt. The report he gave you a quarter of a century ago was only part of the story. His brother gave me a folder with the whole of it inside before I went to America. It's time you heard it, McVeigh."

His eyes focused on me, puzzled, and he glanced at his watch again. "Get on with it," he said briefly.

"Your guileless brother and Lady Proctor didn't just stumble into an innocent romance during the last weeks of their lives. They'd been having it off long before Caroline ever married. Your incredibly upright brother seems to have approved of the arrangement. He liked his sex without responsibility, and marriage gave him a stabilizing hold over Caroline. Caroline liked it too. She fancied gutless Stephen, but she respected money, or the power to make it, a lot more. She knew which side of her bread was buttered. You might say Sir Bryan was a cuckold even before he married. But the funny thing is, he knew about their affair and approved the arrangement. In fact, it was one of the reasons why he married her."

McVeigh looked faintly disturbed. "You're lying," he said. "You make no sense."

"I've got the report, McVeigh. I'll give it to you if you like. The explanation's simple. Sir Bryan came back from India to restore the family fortunes and father a child to continue the Proctor dynasty. Marrying a rich woman was the obvious way to kill two birds with one stone. Only there was a problem. Omphrey told me about it when he got drunk at Don's exhibition party. He revealed a carefully kept detail from Sir Bryan's medical records. The old man contracted TB while he was in India. They removed a kidney and most of his gonads. He was sterile, McVeigh. So he needed a rich bitch who could present him with an heir outside wedlock. He didn't fancy the idea of adoption. It didn't fit the romantic dynasty concept. So the charming Caroline fitted his bill admirably."

"You're lying," McVeigh said again softly. "Starkey cannot possibly have known such things."

I walked painfully to the bronze windows and rested my backside carefully on a ledge. It wasn't quite sitting, and it wasn't quite standing.

"Did you ever visit Mallins?" I asked.

"Sir Bryan's Dorset place? Never. It's a pointless piece of seventeenth-century masonry. I never knew why he bothered to buy it."

"That shows how little you really knew about him. Mallins was always the Proctor family seat until the Major sold it while he was in India to pay off gambling debts. Sir Bryan's first self-appointed task when he came back to England was to buy the place again. While he was supervising the restoration work, he met a girl and they fell in love. She's dead now, but I won't give you her name. It's still a big one in Dorset. She was wild and headstrong, a hunting addict and a drinker. Sir Bryan would have liked to marry her, only he didn't. She loved him too much to get pregnant by somebody else. Anyway, her family wasn't rich. So Sir Bryan put his proposal to Caroline instead."

My head was beginning to swim a little. I lit a cigarette to make it swim more pleasantly.

"Eric met the woman when he went to Mallins and got the story in his usual inimitable way. He said she was still a hell of a woman. When Sir Bryan left her, she got wilder still and busted up half of the respectable marriages in Dorset. She was killed in a hunting accident just a few months after Eric spoke to her. She jumped a hedge, only there was a deep gravel pit on the other side. They found the horse and her both with broken necks. She'd never married."

The cigarette wasn't working, so I made myself another drink. I didn't hurry. I knew I had McVeigh's undivided interest.

"Eric was naturally puzzled," I said. "If Sir Bryan knew what he was getting into when he married Caroline and approved the arrangement, why did he knock her and Stephen off a few years after he got the heir he wanted? Eric wasn't sure, but he made a good guess."

I'd made myself a very strong drink. I sat down to get the best out of it.

"He found some learned medical books that didn't strike him as quite in Brother Stephen's line in his flat. There was also some correspondence with a private clinic in London. Eric went to London and managed to get a look at the records. Stephen had been having blood samples analyzed. You know what I think, McVeigh? I think your delightfully upright brother realized that keeping the truth of Don's paternity a secret was very important to Sir Bryan indeed. I think Stephen and Caroline rashly tried to put the bite on him, and that he had them killed for that reason. You see, Eric was sure by then that Sir Bryan had murdered them. And you know what? I don't think I blame him.

"Stephen conned you into trying to arrange an escape for himself and Caroline when he realized the danger they were in. Stephen conned everybody. And you're wrong about something else. Sir Bryan never hated you. I doubt whether he ever thought much about you at all. He was a hard man, but not small and vicious. I think he let you get where you are now and failed to set the record straight because he wanted to make amends without shattering your illusions."

McVeigh stood with his hand still on the door handle, staring vaguely upstream. I waited a moment before delivering the final thrust. For Eric's sake, I wanted it to count.

"You realize, too," I said, "that your theories about the Proctor character are bullshit. Don was never exactly like Sir Bryan and the Major. He couldn't have been. He was never a Proctor. The runt whose death you arranged last night was a little McVeigh, your only beloved brother's only beloved son. If you'd had the wit to realize that a long time ago, you could have made a satisfactory deal with Sir Bryan and saved all of us, including Eric Starkey, a lot of trouble."

The door closed softly.

"How does it feel to be a posthumous fucking uncle, McVeigh?" I roared after him.

I don't think he heard me. It made no difference anyway. I thought that any real feeling he had ever had for his brother, any real hatred of Sir Bryan, even, had died long ago. What survived was a reflex twitching galvanically inside the iron carapace of his obsession. That, I considered, was probably the point of all obsessions. They make possible the semblance of life inside things long since dead. Trying to read the minds of men like McVeigh is like trying to decipher inscriptions on old tombstones in country churchyards. It made him invulnerable.

I walked painfully to the big bronze windows, dodging the blood-stained linen on the floor again. The sun was high and the sky was brilliant. Past the archery slits of Tower Bridge, HMS *Belfast* lay rooted to the floor of the Thames, her big guns manacled forever to her sides.

That last meeting with McVeigh was some weeks ago. When I left Global House, I went straight back to my flat. I wrote out checks for

Rose Panayioutou and Olly, enclosing an edited version of recent events for Olly. I wasn't in the mood to meet him and answer a lot of questions. Afterwards, I came down here to rest up and give my body a chance to mend properly. Luckily, I'm a fast healer.

It's a small cottage, dilapidated but sound, in the east of Kent, not far from the sea. I rent out my few acres of grazing to a local farmer. In return, he keeps an eye on the place when I'm not around and lets me shoot over his farm. His two hundred acres of chalky soil, coverts, and hedgerows support a surprising amount of game, and sometimes we go out together with guns and ferrets. Not this trip, though. My ribs wouldn't stand the recoil of a 12-bore yet.

The cottage is set back from the road by a dirt lane lined with damson trees covered with small, dusty fruit in autumn. But at this time of year, the fields are full of young cereals and the lane clucks with foraging fowls. It's been a good end to spring. Two weeks of sun have bleached the lane so that my feet scuff up small clouds of dust on my way back from the pub. My farmer friend likes it. He says it's the weather when the ears are setting on his wheat that counts, not the weather at harvest-time. I wouldn't know.

Soon after I got here, a long letter arrived from Rose, sent on by Harry the janitor. It was passionate and rambling. She loves me and wants me under any and all circumstances, with no conditions. I know how she feels. I dream of her almost every night, of her long olive body and huge, urgent eyes. But will I act on it? Maybe McVeigh is right. Maybe I'm a callous bastard who goes after what he wants without regard for anyone. A human lurcher with a taste for Bach. If I'm still around when this is over, I'll see Rose. We'll find out. Experience is what makes us. Maybe I've been having an overdose of the wrong sort of experience.

A few days later, I read a report in *The Times* about a fire-bombing at the Château de la Broderie outside Brussels. The article lamented the fact that eight of Europe's brightest and best young business brains had met untimely deaths. Arson was suspected, and an unnamed young Frenchman had been found hanging in a wood on the estate. The detail of the hanging puzzled me.

On the same day, the obituary columns carried a piece on the death of Sir Bryan Proctor. His brain had died. The writer paid tribute to a brilliant and forceful man who, after his wife's tragic death, had spent a lonely but exemplary life rebuilding the fortunes of his old Dorset family until illness and his son's death, a second tragedy, felled him. He was a late exemplar of a visionary and talented breed now, alas, one member rarer than before. It was all very moving. The writer was McVeigh.

Further on, in the business section of the paper, I read that Dr. Theodore McVeigh had been appointed Chief Executive of Global Alliance and Chairman of Global Alliance International. The accompanying article stressed his lifelong devotion to Sir Bryan and the company as well as his brilliant actuarial brain. There were hints of dynamic changes to come in the great insurance conglomerate.

All I've done since I've been here is slop around, soak up the sun, and set down this account. Once or twice, I've been out at dawn with a silenced .22 for rabbits. Rabbits go well with pigeon in a pudding, and the .22 has no recoil to speak of.

I got into a routine as soon as I arrived. Every morning I walk down to the village, putting up the odd pair of partridges from their dust baths in the corners of fields. I call in at the combined post office and general store to buy supplies, check my mail, and read the Vicar's *Times* before it's delivered to him. I study whatever there is on the warm wall outside, smelling the year's first gillyflowers.

Early this morning, I went out after rabbits and came back with my sneakers covered in a rich paste of seeds and dew. I'd taken a doe and a stoat, its jaws still clamped in the back of her neck. I'd seen him stalk and pounce, nailing him at around fifty yards. It's strange how a stoat will single out a victim and pursue it so single-mindedly that other rabbits nearby will graze on unconcernedly, knowing they are safe.

Afterwards, I walked to the village as usual. There was a letter with a Paris postmark waiting for me. I read the Vicar's *Times* first. The announcement in the personal columns jumped out at me. LUDI VICTOR SALUTES USURPER. The date given was tomorrow's. The letter was brief and unsigned, conveying the writer's distinguished sentiments and informing me that we would meet on my own ground. There was no need, he said, to provide stakes other than my person. There was even a veiled hint that he had taken his Regional Controller to Brussels and that it was the latter's body that had been found hanging in a wood near the Château de la Broderie. I wondered how Denfert Rochereau had persuaded him to make the trip and act as convenient scapegoat. There was no need to wonder how he had got hold of my address. Global's cocky computer would have been glad to oblige. McVeigh wouldn't consider me important enough to get vindictive about, even if he'd had cause. On the other hand, the death of one or other of us, Denfert Rochereau or me, was useful extra insurance, and insurance is McVeigh's business.

I went back to the cottage and considered the options yet again, knowing I had long ago made up my mind.

I'd never told McVeigh about my photographed copies of the documents I'd found in Don Proctor's studio. I could still take them to the police and tell them my story. But even if they believed me, what good would that do? They might put a temporary guard on me, but Denfert Rochereau was in no hurry. He could wait. The only difference would be the next time he'd come after me as a Discipline Squad, giving me no chance. In tomorrow's duel, at least, I have a chance.

Alternatively, I could hunt Denfert Rochereau down myself on the basis that the best method of defence is attack. But am I really capable of killing, or at least maiming, in cold blood? I realize now that I am enmeshed in Denfert Rochereau's Game on his terms whether I like it or not.

So I made my decision. I began by burning the photographed documents in the cottage's kitchen grate. It is mid-morning now, and the doe lies on the draining board, her candid hazel eyes with big black lines radiating from the pupils staring back at me. Beyond her, through the kitchen window, I can see the only piece of high ground commanding the cottage. It's a wooded knoll that would make a fine spot for a sniper with a deer rifle and telescopic sights. But Denfert Rochereau won't be using one because it's against regulations. So neither will I. We are both that kind of punctilious oaf. McVeigh and Von Runstedt were right about one thing. Players in this Game determine their own ends.

Suddenly, and for no reason, I find myself more cheerful than I have been in a long time. Looking through the kitchen window, I can see the clear, acid-green foliage of young trees and soft puffs of high cloud drifting in over the downs. The pain in my ribs has dwindled to an occasional itch, and outside the sun will be hot on my forearms.

It occurs to me that I am actually looking forward to Denfert Rochereau's combat, like a castaway spotting a stripper on a raft. I love more than ever this cottage and the warm covert in the valley where woodcock return every year. I defy him to take all this away from me.

After lunch, I shall go over my few acres with a notebook and cover every centimeter of ground. Denfert Rochereau will be fitter than I am and have the advantage of surprise. On the other hand, I am at least as strong and cunning as he is, as experienced in combat, and I know my territory. It should be an even match.

After the reconnaissance, I shall put my rabbit and pigeon pudding on. Summer rabbit hasn't the flavor of winter rabbit that's been feeding on tree bark, but the pudding will taste fine anyway. I may even have time for half an hour with Bach's *Goldberg Variations* on the Steinway upright before ending up at the pub in the village for a few late pints. Why not? There's no hurry, and tomorrow looks like another fine day.